RETURN TO THE CANADIAN WEST

WHERE TRUST LIES

JANETTE OKE
WITH LAUREL OKE LOGAN

KENNEBEC LARGE PRINT

A part of Gale, Cengage Learning

GALE
CENGAGE Learning·

Farmington Hills, Mich • San Francisco • New York • Waterville, Maine
Meriden, Conn • Mason, Ohio • Chicago

GALE
CENGAGE Learning®

LIBRARY OF CONGRESS CATALOGING-IN-PUBLICATION DATA

Oke, Janette, 1935–
    Where trust lies / by Janette Oke with Laurel Oke Logan. — Large print edition.
        pages cm. — (Kennebec Large Print superior collection) (Return to the Canadian west)
    ISBN 978-1-4104-7531-2 (softcover) — ISBN 1-4104-7531-X (softcover)
    1. Women pioneers—Fiction. 2. Canada, Western—Fiction. 3. Large type books. I. Logan, Laurel Oke. II. Title.
    PR9199.3.O38W545 2015b
    813'.54—dc23   2014048967

Published in 2015 by arrangement with Bethany House Publishers, a division of Baker Publishing Group

Printed in the United States of America
1 2 3 4 5   19 18 17 16 15

LIST OF CHARACTERS

The Thatcher Family

Beth — Elizabeth Thatcher

Mother — Priscilla Thatcher

Father — William Thatcher

Julie — Beth's sister, four years younger

Margret Bryce — Beth's married sister, two years older

John Bryce — Margret's husband

JW Bryce — Margret's toddler son, Beth's nephew

The Montclair Family

Charles Montclair — Father's business partner and family friend

Edith Montclair — Edward's mother and Mother's closest friend

Edward Montclair — Beth's childhood friend and would-be suitor

Victoria Montclair — Edward's teenage sister

Others

Jarrick "Jack" Thornton — Beth's romantic interest from *Where Courage Calls*

Emma — the Thatchers' maid

Miss Lucille Bernard — JW's nanny

Lise — the Montclairs' maid

Monsieur Emile Laurent — French guide and friend of Father's

Penny, Jannis, and Nick — friends from aboard ship

CHAPTER 1

Beth gripped the velvety rose petal and gingerly tugged until it released from its place in the still-fragrant bloom. *What a shame! If only I had a way to preserve the whole bouquet.* But during much of the trip she had occupied herself with considering her homecoming scene at the Toronto station, and this solution seemed best. If she descended from the train carrying a box of fading long-stemmed roses, Mother would instantly be on alert to the fact that there was much more to tell about Beth's year of teaching in Coal Valley than she had previously disclosed. A flood of questions and assumptions would ensue, many more than Beth was prepared to answer. And she could think of no better way to conceal Jarrick's farewell gift — while still secretly treasuring it.

With a sigh she freed another of the wine-colored petals and gently tucked it with the others in the white handkerchief on her lap. She of course knew she needn't collect them all, but it was painful to face discarding even the smallest, most tightly curled petal. She drew the lace hanky with its delightful essence close to her face and breathed in deeply . . . remembering.

She could still see Jarrick back at the Lethbridge station, touching his pocket holding Beth's Toronto address and telephone number. Tall and broad-shouldered, his copper hair glinted blond where the sun's rays shone on it, trim mustache over a smile that also held sadness at her departure. The daydream of soon receiving his first letter, maybe even hearing his voice at the other end of the telephone, made her face grow warm. *If only there's a reason to return to the West. If only news arrives soon inviting me to another year of teaching in Coal Valley this fall . . .*

Beth glanced out the window of her compartment as the train slowed for the Toronto station. She knotted the corners of the handkerchief and tucked the sweet-smelling little bundle safely away in her handbag. Next she quickly unwrapped from around the remaining rose stems a second handkerchief, repeatedly moistened during the journey to keep the flowers fresh. She rinsed and wrung it out in the sink basin in her compartment and tucked it away in a corner of her carpetbag. Her pulse was racing as the train whistle sounded and the station came into view. With a last nostalgic glance at the barren stems in their florist box, Beth picked up her carpetbag and followed the porter, who carried two more bags for her down the narrow hallway.

Squeezing past other passengers, she descended the oversized steps and arrived on firm pavement. Despite her anticipation, Beth felt exhausted. *No more trains!* she thought with a sigh. *At least for the next few months. It's so good to be home. Why does travel consume so much energy — even when I mostly sit?*

She scanned the station around her to locate her porter again. What she noticed first, though, was her father, his arm waving above the crowd.

But it was Julie's voice she heard. "Bethie! We're over here!" Beth chuckled to see her younger sister's head bobbing intermittently into view. She pushed through the mass of travelers and into the arms of her family.

"You're home, darling. Oh, welcome home!" A tangle of arms encircled her, along with laughter and excited greetings.

Beth finally managed, "I can't tell you how

good it is to see all of you! There simply are no words —"

"We've been *so* anxious for you to be home," her mother put in quickly, patting Beth's face with a white-gloved hand. "You look well. Are you well, Beth? But you seem thinner. Have you been eating?" Her mother leaned back to survey Beth, who was dressed in the same travel suit she had worn when she left Toronto last year.

"I'm fine, Mother — never better. Truly."

Julie pressed closer, grasping Beth's arm. "There's so much to tell you! Just wait till you hear! It's simply glorious." Julie's eyes danced with delight.

Immediately the girl was shushed and nudged aside by Mother. "Now, Julie, all in good time. All in good time." Turning back, her mother quickly said, "Here, darling, let Julie take your bag." Something in Mother's tone caught Beth's attention, but by then Julie had quickly grasped the carpetbag, and Beth was wrapped in her father's long, warm hug.

All speaking at once, they took her other bags from the porter, Father paid him, and the joyful family headed for the street. Her trunks from the baggage car would be delivered in due time, the porter had said.

They tucked themselves into Father's

Rolls-Royce, and he nodded to the driver. Beth stared out at the long lines of traffic on familiar, nicely paved roads crowded mostly with rowdy little roadsters, delivery trucks, and periodically a sleek expensive touring car — all swerving at random to dodge an oncoming streetcar or daring pedestrian. *What a contrast to Coal Valley!* she marveled silently. *I must have forgotten. . . .*

At last, they left downtown, rolled through a residential area under a canopy of trees, and stopped on the circle of brick pavers in front of the lovely place Beth had called home most of her life. She drew in a satisfied breath as her mother and sister climbed out ahead of her, Julie giggling and Mother pushing her forward with familiar admonitions. Beth was grateful to find that all was as she had left it ten months earlier. Her eyes lifted to the façade of the three-story stone English-manor-style dwelling. *It seems far larger than I remember,* she noted as she stepped out of the car.

As if on cue, Margret and her husband appeared in the open doorway. Beth ran up the front steps and into the embrace of her older sister, and on to John's as well. But her gaze soon was searching beyond them. Margret, wearing a knowing smile, placed a hand on Beth's arm and nodded toward the wide parlor doorway. Beth's hand flew to her mouth. A sturdy little figure with chubby legs was moving away from them as fast as he could. *My beloved JW!*

"Margret, he's gotten so big! Oh, he's grown up." A mixture of joy and sadness filled Beth's eyes with tears. Wiping them quickly away, she hurried toward her precious little nephew and tried to scoop him up in her arms.

But he twisted and wriggled free, taking refuge behind his father's legs. *He doesn't remember me!* The realization struck like a cold wind from the Rockies. Margret slipped an arm around Beth with a small chuckle. "Just give him a little while — he'll soon be following you everywhere until you're begging for respite."

Beth smiled, but she still mourned silently, then was further jarred with another realization. *I don't really know him anymore, either.*

"He's such fun for us, Beth," Margret was saying. "You'll see. We even taught him how to say 'Auntie Beth' — though it still sounds more like 'Annie Bet,' I'm afraid."

"He's even *talking*?"

"Yes, more every day, it seems! He's well ahead of others his age." Margret paused and gave a little laugh. "At least, we think so."

Julie had crept up behind JW, and the almost-two-year-old giggled when he saw her. "And you say Annie Bet just as perfectly as you say Annie Doolie, don't you, little man?" Her tickling fingers sent the toddler squealing up the hallway with Julie chasing behind.

Margret gave Beth's waist a gentle squeeze and led her into the dining room, explaining that lunch was waiting. "We want to hear all about your life out west, Beth. Mother shared most of your letters, but I'm sure there's much more to tell."

Beth pictured the flower petals safe in her bag. *More than you know, Margret dearest. More than you know.*

Beth opened her eyes cautiously, looking around the once-familiar bedroom. It had felt strange to wake up with her arms over the blankets rather than tucked deep beneath as she was used to in response to Coal Valley's chilly nights and Miss Molly's woodstove-heated home. She remembered the feel of the thick carpeting last night as she had made her way to the large, inviting bathroom. And that long soak in the huge tub was absolutely delightful — a stark contrast to the iron tub near Miss Molly's kitchen that needed to be filled by hand from the stove.

But any opportunity to quietly reorient herself was interrupted by a quick knock, the door opening, Julie's sparkling face and "Time to get up, lazy bones!" greeting her. Beth couldn't help but laugh.

"Come on, breakfast is laid out, and your trunks are here." Julie pulled her into a sitting position and urged her to hurry before darting out as quickly as she had arrived.

Beth dressed and joined the rest of the family downstairs. She certainly was no longer accustomed to having the breakfast items on the sideboard being quietly refilled by a servant while the family ate and chatted around the table. But mostly they all had mercy on Beth, letting her eat and drink her tea without bombarding her with too many more questions.

After the meal, and once her luggage had been carried up to her bedroom, Mother insisted on helping Beth unpack and organize her things. Margret came along and dropped into the window seat, while Julie scurried between the trunks, peeking and poking and commenting on whatever caught her fancy. Beth, her mother, and their maid, Emma, pulled items out to store away.

Wouldn't Miss Molly be astonished if she could see all this commotion just to unpack?

"Oh my!" Mother sounded genuinely alarmed. "What on earth is this?" She held up a simple calico blouse.

Beth took the garment from Mother's hands and tucked it back into the trunk with the other modest clothing, explaining quickly, "It's what I wore for teaching. I had items like this sewn for me. This made it so much easier for the students to relate to me." She was aware of a defensive tone in her voice and tried to produce an easy smile.

The very idea seemed to leave her mother speechless. She was lifting out similar skirts and shirtwaists, her eyes wide with dismay. She held several of the garments up and turned first to Margret, then to Julie.

But Margret only said, "How gracious of you, Beth, to think of helping them feel at ease. No wonder your teaching was successful."

Julie laughed brightly. "Don't worry, Mother. From my visit I found she was well-suited to the area. But Bethie," she coaxed — and for a moment Beth appreciated her deft change of subject — "you really haven't told us *everything* about your adventures. Isn't there anything else — *anyone else* — we should know about?"

15

Beth shot a sideways frown at Julie, then answered evenly, "No, I think I've been quite thorough about it all. And from last night's dinner discussions and our breakfast conversation, I'm sure you've all heard a sufficient account, at least for now."

Julie leaned into the trunk, near enough to whisper in Beth's ear, "Liar!" Her sister's short visit to Coal Valley had given her the edge over others in the household. Julie knew about Jarrick — had met him. And there was no way to predict what the girl might dare say next. Beth was relieved to see her sister sidle away toward the dresser with a brush and a box of hairpins.

But Julie wasn't finished with her little game. Before Mother could question her about her evocative comment, Julie declared, "That's all right, Bethie." And with a teasing shrug, she added in a mock haughty tone, "It seems I'm the only woman among us anxious to hear *all* of the truth laid out *fully.*"

This time it was Mother who frowned, directing her words to Julie but obviously meant for all. "I will wait for an appropriate time for further discussions . . ." Mother's voice drifted away.

"But we can talk about *our* secret now?" Julie insisted, leaning in closer.

16

Beth closed the trunk lid and straightened. "All right, what's going on?"

Mother sighed, gave an almost imperceptible nod, and with a squeal of delight Julie burst out, "Don't put your trunks away just yet, sister darling. You're going to need them!"

Mother dismissed Emma with a wave of her hand and motioned for Beth to take a seat beside her on the bed. Beth's heart raced. *What on earth . . . ?*

"As you know, we have wanted for several years to do some traveling. But with Father's business requiring so much of it, we've not been able to do so. He has, however, agreed that now you all are of sufficient maturity that we would be able to go on our own. We have arranged for a cruise to see some of the large cities and other sights along the St. Lawrence and also along the eastern coast of Canada and the United States."

Margret was nodding with an affirming smile. Mother hurried on, "Ships are not at all the cumbersome, unsuitable transports they once were — now very modern and comfortable, equipped with every convenience. I've heard they even hold indoor swimming pools, if you can imagine. Many of our friends have found a cruise to be an excellent way to travel."

"New York City!" Julie burst out. "Just think of it!"

Beth felt her heart pounding and swallowed hard. "And when are you — when is the planned departure?"

A moment of silence hung awkwardly around them. The other three exchanged glances, then turned back to Beth. Mother finally said slowly, "The plan is that we — all of us — will leave for Quebec City this coming Monday. In fact, we've agreed to travel with Mrs. Montclair and her daughter Victoria. We've been planning this for several weeks now." Her mother's voice had grown more confident with each phrase.

Beth studied her hands, avoiding the eyes fixed on her. *They're waiting for an answer. Expecting enthusiasm. My agreement.* Yet she suspected that if she said much immediately she would disappoint them all. "I've just come home, Mother." Beth swallowed again. "I had thought . . . I'd looked forward to . . ." Beth looked around at their expressions. She struggled for the right response. "I'll need to consider it." Another pause. "I certainly do need a bit of time to think it over."

All the anticipation had instantly dissipated. Margret stood and slipped away with a pat on Beth's arm, Julie quickly followed, and Mother last of all. She hesitated at the door. "We were so excited to tell you, Beth. Particularly Julie. I wish you had . . ." She stopped and sighed. "Your response is rather unexpected since you've often begged to travel. I hadn't thought there would be any doubt of your agreement." She shook her head. "And I don't know where you might stay, what you will do, if you do not join us. Father will be gone also. The house will be as good as empty. Please *do* consider carefully, darling. We've missed you dreadfully all this time. It hasn't been the same with you gone. And I don't think I could bear to leave you behind." Mother's last statement followed her into the hall.

Beth gazed down at her partially unpacked trunks and refused to give in to tears. But as she reached trembling hands to continue the task, her heart felt heavy in her chest.

"Would you have time for a walk with me?" Her smile for her father felt a bit tremulous as she looked at him from the door of his study.

He set aside the book he was reading. "Of course, my dear." He stood and slipped into his jacket, then followed her out.

Wrapping her shawl around her shoulders against the unusually cool June evening,

Beth descended the broad steps with Father and surveyed the possibilities. The driveway, though long, was not suitable, so she turned instead toward the expansive lawn. Beth expected that at least a circle or two of the property would be necessary to express all her thoughts and feelings.

With a chuckle Father fell into step beside her. "I don't suppose these shoes have ever been on the grass before." Beth stopped to look down at his hand-sewn calfskins. She had become quite used to walking outside whenever she wanted to think. Father took her arm, though, and they moved forward together. "My dear," he said with a laugh, "I'm not as fussy as all that! It's just that I've never walked the grounds before. It simply never occurred to me. Could it be I've become one of those dreadful snobs?" His eyes grew large as he feigned fear at the thought.

Beth laughed despite her emotions. "Never, Father. Not you."

For some time there was silence as she gathered her thoughts. They crossed the lawn to a long row of French lilac bushes shielding the property from the street. Several large clusters of fading flowers still clung to the branches, emitting a familiarly pungent fragrance Beth had always loved.

She breathed in deeply, then turned to her father. "I'm not sure I want to go," she whispered.

"Mother mentioned that to me."

Beth looked away for a moment, shaking her head and wincing. "What else did she say?"

"That's not important right now." They walked on a little farther, stood for a while before some large purple irises.

Shaking her head, Beth exclaimed, "I just got home! I can't even explain how wonderful that feels. I haven't even finished unpacking yet!" The next sound she made could have been a sob or a chuckle.

"I see." Father tucked his hand under her arm. "Would it have made a difference if you'd had a week or two before departure?"

"I don't know." She sighed. "Maybe — but probably not."

"What is it, then, that's bothering you about this little venture?"

Beth turned to begin walking again, Father beside her. "Well," Beth admitted, "primarily, I'm worried that I'll get a letter asking me to teach again. And if they don't hear back from me quickly, they might fill the position with someone else."

"So you think the trip might put in jeopardy the possibility of a return to your school out west?"

"Yes, it could."

"I see. It sounds as if you've decided to take the position if it's offered?"

Beth whispered her answer, lifting her eyes to meet his gaze. "I have, Father. I love it there."

She watched as sadness flickered across his eyes, and she turned her head. He gave no reply. Another long silence passed as they continued their circle of the grounds, Beth wrestling with conflicting thoughts. She finally asked, "Can mail be forwarded to wherever we are?"

"Yes, that would be a rather simple matter."

"And we'd receive it whenever we arrived in port?"

"That's typically what happens when I travel. Do you recall how many letters you've written to me over the years? And I've received every single one." He paused and then said, "I can't promise there wouldn't be a delay. But then again, sending a telegram is always an option. In addition, we could instruct Jacob here to open any letter addressed to you that seems to be from the school board and telegraph the news to the ship when it comes."

The thought ignited a faint hope. "That

would be very helpful."

"You might *enjoy* the trip, Beth. Have you yet considered that possibility?"

She felt herself softening. "Where will *you* be, Father? Why aren't you coming?"

"Ah, yes, well . . . I shall be in South America. Mr. Montclair and I have acquired some new contacts there that need immediate attention. We may even hire an aeroplane once we're in-country to visit the factories where the goods are produced. Who would have ever dreamed of such a thing? I may very well *fly.*" He held out his arms in mock wings and winked at Beth.

His dramatics made Beth laugh again. They had reached the tidy rows of fruit trees far to the back. A few still wore their late-spring blossoms. Father reached up for one to tuck in Beth's hair.

He added more seriously, "The economy around us is booming once more after so many difficult years, and perhaps we shall see it grow as never before. And though I'm not as convinced as some who are throwing caution to the wind, I do believe in a steady expansion of our business endeavors — striking while the iron is hot, so to speak." He paused thoughtfully. "I have always *enjoyed* travel, Beth, which is why I suppose I'm well-suited to this business. But I do regret my many absences from home. I've been gone too frequently as you've all been growing up. However, that is the harsh reality of life. I'm afraid there is a cost to *any* achievement, and often a decision to strike out in one direction means being forced to release what we leave behind, including those we regard with fondest affections."

Beth knew by the look in his eye and the way his voice was tightening that he was not really talking about his business any longer.

"I would like to keep you close with us always, my dear," he said quietly. "But I could never begrudge you the privilege of making up your own mind and choosing your own road. In fact," he said with a playful smile, "last year there was a rather easy path in front of you. You could have settled down with young Edward Montclair with the blessings of both sets of parents, and lived quite comfortably, I'm sure."

"Oh, Father," she interrupted, blushing at his teasing words. "You know he could be a friend only."

"Actually," he said, turning serious once again, "I rather doubt Edward will stay for long in the West. But you have chosen otherwise. Perhaps there is a little of me in you after all." He took her arm, and they continued on. "You bear enough resemblance that your mother will certainly blame me for your nomadic propensities far away from us. I've no doubt that you've already encountered hardships and gone without much to which you were accustomed, but it seems to have suited you well. In fact, you seem all the stronger for it. I'm very proud of you, Beth."

She leaned her head against his chest and slipped her arms around his waist. "Thank you, Father dear. It means more than I can say that you understand."

She could heard him chuckle again, deep inside his chest. "Then again, sometimes choosing to strike out on one's own takes one closer to *new* friends and special people."

A gasp caught in Beth's throat, and she buried her face in his suit jacket. *Julie! What has she been telling out of turn?*

But as they moved on, he said, "I received the most unusual telephone call two nights ago — on the evening before you came home. It was from a man, someone I've never met. Imagine that!" He chuckled, not with humor so much as significance. "I think this man is someone I will need to meet. Someone I would very much like to get to know. At any rate, he asked to speak with *you,* my dear."

Breathless, Beth asked, "What . . . what did you say?"

"I told him that you had not yet returned to Toronto, but that he could telephone again this evening to determine if you had interest in receiving his call."

"Father!"

"I was *very* cordial, Beth. I introduced myself, asked him how he knew you. We had a little chat, the two of us. It was very . . . enlightening." Though his words were lighthearted, he had turned his head and was studying her face carefully.

Beth, heart beating fast, tried not to imagine any details of what they had discussed. "Are you going to tell Mother about him? I'm afraid she'll make a fuss. Are you — ?"

"No, dear. I shall not tell your mother. But before he calls tonight, I believe it would be wise for you to do so."

Beth gulped and nodded.

CHAPTER 2

"Mother, do you have a moment?"

When Beth had gathered her courage enough to take her father's suggestion, Mother was seated at her writing desk in the sunroom. *She's probably assuming I've come to discuss the cruise. Oh, heavenly Father, please help me find the right words. Please help Mother to understand.* Beth's prayer helped calm her. "Could we sit on the sofa? I think we'd be much more comfortable there."

With a sigh, Mother rose and repositioned herself on the embroidered silk settee facing the tall windows overlooking the back garden. Beth took a seat beside her, hands fidgeting nervously on her lap. She said the first words that came to her. "I expect someone to telephone me tonight."

"Who, darling?" The eyes surrounded with only tiny wrinkles sparkled with surprise and pleasure. She obviously was assuming this was one of Beth's Toronto friends . . . maybe an eligible male.

"Someone I met in Coal Valley," Beth rushed on. She watched as Mother's eyebrows knit together. There was no retreating now. "It's — it will be from a man."

Mother cleared her throat, blinked, and managed, "Go on."

"His name is Jack Thornton, but I call him Jarrick, his given name. I suppose at first it was just to tease him . . . but he's not nearly ordinary enough to be a 'Jack.' " Mother did not seem to be impressed. "He's an officer of the Royal Canadian Mounted Police."

"You met him through Edward?" The question sounded quite pointed.

"No. He was working in our area. We met . . ." Beth's mind searched for a moment, struggling to recall exactly when she had first seen Jarrick. "We were introduced by the local pastor. On the first Sunday I attended church. The two of them came to where I boarded as guests of Miss Molly — for Sunday dinner." She hoped this first meeting would set an appropriate scene in Mother's mind.

"And you've been keeping company ever since?"

Beth shook her head quickly. "Oh, no, we haven't truly been keeping company at all.

He's never even called on me. Not really. We've only had interactions through — through everyday life. I've seen him at community events, worked alongside him sometimes. Julie met him too when she was in town." Beth knew she was sounding rushed and nervous. She stopped for a breath, thought back over the day the three of them had explored the countryside around Coal Valley, she and Jarrick and Julie. *He was so gracious with his time, thoughtful and charming,* she remembered. But she couldn't express such thoughts aloud to Mother. Instead, she added weakly, "Surely I've mentioned him in my letters."

"I don't recall the name."

That's quite possibly true. In her efforts to shield Mother from some of the more alarming adventures, she probably had omitted all but oblique references to Jarrick. "Well, he's a nice man, Mother, a little older than me — almost thirty, I think. But I don't know when his birthday is." *What else should — can — I say?*

"He's from a good family in Manitoba; his father is a pastor there. He has one sister and some brothers. I don't know much more than that about his family." It seemed a painfully inadequate summary, one which would not suit Mother's now-piqued interest at all.

"How long has he been an officer?"

"I don't know. We didn't discuss it."

"Does he intend to remain in that area or will he be moving around — as Wynn and your auntie Elizabeth did? Edith Montclair has said that Edward will settle in Calgary, has just announced his engagement to a woman named Kate Duncan. They plan to wed soon." The words were forceful, seeming to increase in volume as they rebounded off the painted floor tiles and echoed back accusingly from every corner of the high-ceilinged room.

Beth's answer was quiet. "I'm pleased for Edward. And I don't really know where Jarrick's job will take him. We haven't . . . discussed it."

"Hmmm. I see."

Beth thought about his parting words spoken only a week before — that she had the qualities he wanted in a wife, that if God were to bring her back, he hoped she would consider giving her permission for him to call. "He did . . . we did express our interest in . . . in getting to know each other better. We talked of not losing touch while I'm home over the summer." Though the words were true, such euphemisms shaded the truth just a little. Beth knew her bond with

Jarrick was much stronger than she was admitting.

She watched her mother's mind work its way through the information. "So that is why you do not wish to travel. You want to be here to receive his telephone calls?"

"It's not only that. I've just come home, Mother. I . . ." It occurred to Beth as she began to argue that it would be best not to confuse the two issues. She changed direction. "At any rate, Mother, I plan to accept the call from Jarrick tonight. I hope that doesn't distress you. He's already spoken to Father about it. I'm not sure how or when it might be possible for you to meet, but I do hope that can be arranged. I think you'd approve of him. I think you'd *like* him. He's such a . . . such a *gentleman.*" She felt the description was wholly inadequate, but maybe one that would impress her mother. Her gaze dropped to her fidgeting hands as she continued. "He's kind, and articulate, and good with children, and thoughtful. And I've watched how hard he works to keep people safe — to protect us all. He truly cares about his job —"

"I see."

Beth almost asked, *Were you never in love, Mother?* but caught herself at such an audacious, maybe even disrespectful, question.

31

Her thoughts continued, though, in response to her own query. *Is that what I'm feeling — this thrill at the very thought of him? Am I in love with him?* Somehow identifying that label made Beth both uncomfortable and elated.

At that moment they heard the tinkling of the dinner bell. They rose together, and Mother linked an arm through Beth's. "I shall endeavor to keep an open mind about all this, my dear. I do hope you'll not be hasty or rash in your own judgments. There is no need to hurry such a relationship along."

You wouldn't say that if it were Edward we were discussing! But Beth remained silent and allowed herself to be led away to supper.

No reference was made during their pleasant evening meal to anything Beth had discussed with her parents. Father was quiet, as was typical, making a comment from time to time, but largely allowing John and the women around the table to manage their own conversations as their plates were filled by Emma. She supposed both Mother and Father were pleased they were all together again at last. And were it not for the impatient flutters in her stomach, Beth would have thoroughly enjoyed the meal.

After dessert, they rose together and retreated to the parlor. Margret took up a bib she had been stitching, Julie continued with her sketch of Father — the outline of face and shoulders had begun to take shape — while the rest settled in with books. Beth didn't even pretend to turn the pages of hers.

"Father," Julie complained, "you must stop shifting in your chair! I can't sketch properly if you're going to keep moving."

"I'm sorry, my dear. I seem to be somewhat distracted tonight."

Beth's eyes involuntarily turned toward his office door. *At any moment we might be interrupted by the telephone. The rest will expect Father to close the door as usual before answering. Will he do so tonight? Will he expect me to follow? Maybe he'll actually receive another call instead, forcing the operator to tell Jarrick the line is busy and to try again later. . . .* And on and on, Beth's what-ifs whirled through her mind. She forced herself to settle back and actually begin reading.

When the telephone did ring, Beth jumped, and Julie giggled, wondering aloud if her poor sister hadn't heard a telephone for a while. Father stood calmly and went into his office, shutting the door. Only Mother cast a knowing glance at Beth.

After a moment, Father reappeared. "Beth, would you come please?"

All eyes watched her move through the room, which suddenly seemed much larger. Father motioned toward the handset on the desk beside its base and quickly exited, closing the door behind him.

Beth sank into his leather office chair, leaned forward, and rested her elbows on the massive desk. She cleared her throat and positioned the handset next to her ear. "Hello?"

"Hello, Beth. It's Jarrick. It's so good to finally hear your voice."

She laughed a little. In reality only a short time had passed, yet she felt the same way. "Yours too, Jarrick. It feels so long since I left — almost as if I dreamed it all. It's the strangest sensation to be home again."

"How was your trip?" It seemed like an awkward question, too formal for the enthusiasm she was feeling.

Working to steady her voice, she answered, "It went rather well. No difficulties, though it was every bit as long as the first time." An attempt at a little joke, but he made no indication he caught it. "I was just as anxious to see it come to an end," she finished a bit lamely.

"And your family — how are they doing?"

"Oh, very good. Everyone is fine." She smiled and repositioned herself at the desk. "Umm, I hear you spoke with my father." The comment moved the conversation beyond small talk. She waited breathlessly for his answer.

"I did," he admitted. "I knew before I placed the call that I likely would be speaking to him. I doubted you would be the one to answer the telephone. So at least I was ready for the questions — I'd prepared my answers as best I could. I do wish I hadn't called before you arrived, though. That was quite embarrassing! And disappointing."

"I hope he wasn't too hard on you. My father can be rather protective of his girls."

"Not at all, not at all, Beth. He was surprisingly calm, courteous, and matter-of-fact. I'm sure he hadn't anticipated my call. But he stepped up to the occasion." He laughed a little nervously. "I would expect that by now he's telephoned Edward. Since he's the only person — other than you — who knows both your father and me. I would expect him to look into my credentials, so to speak."

Beth hadn't thought of that possibility. *It does sound like what Father might do. What would Edward have had to share about Jarrick? At least he's one of the few aware of our interest in each other. Perhaps he would be inclined toward being gracious and kind. Surely there was no reason for him to say anything else. But would Father have reached Edward on such short notice?*

Jarrick was saying, "Have you heard that Edward is already engaged?"

"I did. My mother mentioned it today. I knew it was his intention to ask Kate soon. Have you met her?"

"Only once. She seemed quite nice — rather shy but a sweet young lady. They say one should marry an opposite, so they should be well matched."

"Um-hmm," Beth agreed, unable to keep herself from wondering if she and Jarrick also were opposites.

He sighed and said quickly, "I'm afraid we won't have long to talk, Beth. I'm at the station in Lethbridge. I was able to borrow an office here, but I doubt I'll be allowed privacy for much longer. I did want to tell you how much I've missed you. To . . . to express again how much I'd like to keep in touch with you over the summer. I haven't heard anything more about the teaching position here in the fall, but —"

"Jarrick," she interrupted, "I'm sorry, but

I do have something I must tell you." She didn't wait for a response. "My mother and sisters are planning to leave for Quebec City this Monday," she hurried on, "and the ship will depart on Wednesday afternoon. You see, they've planned a cruise. They want me to go along."

"How nice for you, Beth. I'm sure it would be a wonderful experience." He paused. "You'd be back in time for school in the fall?"

"Yes, it won't be a long cruise. Just six weeks. Julie would have very much preferred a world expedition — as if she can immediately catch up on all the traveling she's wanted to do for years. Father vetoed that idea. Still, the travel and distance will make it much more difficult for us to — to communicate. I doubt I could receive calls on board the ship."

"We could still write?"

"Yes, but letters will be slower. I'd receive them when I arrived in the next port." She waited for any indication of his reaction, fingering the braid-covered cord dangling from the receiver, then lowered her voice. "I haven't decided yet. I haven't committed to going along."

"Oh, you must!" His insistence was surprising. "It's such a good opportunity for you. I'm sure you'll have a wonderful time with your mother and sisters — and you deserve a good, relaxing vacation. No one knows that more than I do."

"You're very kind, but . . ."

"No, you *should* go, Beth. You really must." He seemed to be searching for the proper words. "It might be the last time that you can travel with them. I mean, well . . ." He hesitated. "I don't know if I can be so bold, but since I've already introduced myself to your father, and it might be some time before we speak again by telephone, it seems necessary." He cleared his throat, and Beth pressed closer to the handset, squeezing her eyes tight to conjure up an image of Jarrick's face.

His words came slowly. "I wanted to leave no doubt with him that my intentions toward you could be trusted. Though, of course, any future plans would require that we grow to know one another better — and it all would include much prayer as well as counsel from those who know us. But I wanted your father to know that my ultimate intention is . . . well, it's marriage." Another pause, and while sounding flustered, he persisted. "I assured him that although my employment as an officer will undoubtedly be a strong influence on the future, it also provides me with an adequate and steady income so that I'm able to support a family. I've been careful with money, have already been saving."

He hesitated again, then amended his words suddenly as if an afterthought. "That is, I didn't say it only for your father's benefit. I want you to know this too, that I believe I can care for you — or I wouldn't be pursuing this relationship at all. I doubt I'll ever provide for you at the level of your family's standard, of course. But I believe we could have . . . have a comfortable life together." He was rushing his words but clearly was hoping for her to respond. "I hope I haven't spoken too boldly, too quickly."

Beth could hear herself drawing in a slow breath. *He'll have heard it too.* She finally whispered, "I didn't realize you had laid it out quite so plainly to Father."

"I felt it was necessary. I wanted to be — to be honest and forthright. Particularly since the possibilities for meeting are in the distant future."

For a moment the only sound was the crackling over the telephone line.

"Please don't let that trouble you, Beth. It was meant to give you assurance. Maybe I've said too much or been too outspoken.

I'm afraid I do that sometimes. And I've probably been aware of my feelings — been interested in a relationship with you — for longer than you might have known. If it hadn't been for Edward's ungrounded claim, I wouldn't have waited until you were ready to leave Coal Valley before revealing any of this to you."

Beth's mind was spinning with more questions than she could quickly address. *How did Father respond to such a declaration? What did he say to Jarrick?* Her mind worked back through Jarrick's words, struggling to process all the implications. She wondered if she dared allow herself to anticipate a future . . . with Jarrick. *Things are moving too quickly. I haven't been offered the job yet. What if it's given to someone else?* It was all rather overwhelming, even frightening.

"Beth?"

"May I . . . could we take one step at a time, please?" She pushed away from the desk and sat back in the chair.

"Of course, of course, Beth."

"I'm very fond of you, Jarrick. And I admire your character. I'm honored by your words, and I do appreciate your candor. I do. But I can't say that I know just yet if it's the right thing for me and for you. I need time to hear what God is saying. I want to be very careful with something so important. I need to pray, wait for an answer, one that goes beyond my feelings. Is that fair? Please don't be upset."

"Of course," he agreed, yet the energy had drained from his voice. "It will be difficult in your absence, but I can be patient — even if it's not what I do well." She heard him try for a chuckle and could sense his struggle to regain some confidence.

"I know the summer will be an obstacle. But it won't last long, not really. It will provide time to pray about the future, to consider all the implications. But, God willing, I truly would like to be back in the West with you again soon."

"Are you sure?" Jarrick asked.

"I'm sorry — what do you mean?"

This time his playful tone was easy to detect. "It must be a very different world for you there. Dressed to the nines in fine clothes, eating elegant meals, going to fancy places. And now a cruise as well — living the life of the wealthy aristocrat. Nothing like Coal Valley! We don't have nearly as much to offer, I guess."

"Nonsense." Her answer sounded rather coquettish. She didn't know whether to be dismayed or glad but continued anyway. "There *are* other considerations, Jarrick."

"Such as?"

"You're rather good company. Do you suppose that if I come back, you might take me to that same lovely restaurant for dinner — on an evening when I'm not worried about a sick little boy?"

"It's agreed," he said, sounding relieved. "*When* you come back, I'll plan to take you there."

CHAPTER 3

When a shopping trip was announced over breakfast, Beth cringed inwardly. Shopping with Mother was difficult. Shopping with Margret and Mother was taxing. But shopping with Julie and Margret and Mother would be nearly unbearable. She steeled herself to endure the day.

"And we have barely a week to get everything we will need," Mother was saying. "Let's finish up quickly here and be on our way."

Last night's telephone call had not been mentioned — at least not yet. Father's questioning expression was all Beth had encountered when he had returned to his office afterward to find her curled up in his office chair, the receiver already resting in its cradle. She had smiled up at him and nodded. The questions raised during her conversation with Jarrick had already turned to tears, still visible. Father, of course, had understood about happy tears.

"And your plans for summer?"

She had merely nodded again.

"I shall inform the ladies." And he'd left her beside the silent phone, her thoughts swirling with joyful anticipation of Jarrick's letters.

Beth was not aware of exactly what information Father had relayed to the others upon his return to the parlor. However, she was certain about one instruction he had given — neither of her sisters was to pester Beth with questions at this time about her telephone call. It was the only possible reason for Julie's utter silence on the matter. And as for Mother, just to have learned that Beth had agreed to travel with them seemed to have been enough that she also held her tongue.

While waiting for her sisters and mother to assemble for their shopping excursion, Beth pulled on white gloves, which Mother insisted were still necessary. Beth caught herself thinking once again, *Why on earth does a trip for clothing require one to be dressed to the nines?* Although she knew how Mother felt about keeping up appearances, it remained an odd bit of irony, particularly after life in Coal Valley, where a roof over one's head and food on the table were far more important than the latest fashions.

Four women with feathered hats and ample handbags crowded into the back seat of Father's spacious car, chattering about all the particulars of their travel needs. Julie recommended they seek out breezy skirts and billowy white blouses — perhaps even something in the sailor style so in vogue. Long gowns for lavish dining, sensible shoes for sightseeing, and hats of every shape to protect from the sun were also on the lists. And, at Julie's further insistence, bathing suits for the pool and for the beach. Beth wondered if she would ever dare wear such scanty clothing in public. However, to her surprise, Mother seemed perfectly agreeable so long as they were appropriately modest. She even declared that she would purchase one for herself. "After all," Mother explained, "I'm not a prude. And I have every intention of enjoying our adventure to its fullest."

Beth was quite certain she caught their driver's discreet smile in his small mirror. In fact, Beth was equally amused. Mother was one of the most modest women she knew. Mother still wore a corset, though most women her age and all of those younger had long ago discarded the unpleasant undergarment. When pressed on the subject, she claimed to be so accustomed to wearing it, she would feel brazen and unprotected without it. Her daughters merely smiled behind their hands. Mother was still slender and petite without such apparel.

Stepping out onto Toronto's busiest shopping street, Beth clutched at her hat in the breeze. She looked around with some bewilderment at all the activity, moving quickly to avoid being run over by a lad on a bicycle, a leather messenger bag across his shoulder. She followed the little group into the first shop. Mother was already searching out a salesperson to help them.

"Mrs. Thatcher," called a young woman, hurrying over to greet them and take their jackets. "So pleased to see you here with your daughters. With what might I help you today?"

Mother glided ahead, listing off items needed. Beth sighed. Then she felt Margret's arm slip through hers. Leaning close, she whispered, "Heavenly Father, please give my sweet sister the courage to endure all her blessings!" It was said with an encouraging smile, but the intent was clear.

"I'm being dreadful, aren't I?" Beth admitted.

"Not at all. Perhaps just wishing for some

other moment and place than this." Margret patted Beth's hand. "Do remember, though, that we'd like to have you *here* with us today. We love you, darling, though it may be shown at times in strange and inconvenient ways."

"Oh, Margret," Beth laughed self-consciously as the pair moved to catch up with the others.

Late afternoon found them returning with a car full of parcels, having spent what Beth finally decided had been a lovely day together in the city. The larger boxes would be delivered to the house in the morning. Smaller parcels were placed on the dining table while Margret hurried off to the nursery to check on JW. Father could only shake his head in mock distress as Julie and Mother showed him their treasures arrayed on the dining room table. Beth noticed his true pleasure was in seeing his family so animated and happy.

After dinner, he reminded them, there would be guests. Father had arranged for a traveling companion, deeming it appropriate for these cherished women to have the kind of assistance this gentleman could provide. He would conduct their travels, but more importantly, he would keep them safe and make certain all their needs were met. The Montclairs would join them for the meeting with Monsieur Emile Laurent, who arrived at precisely seven in the evening.

"Emile, so good to see you after so many months," Father welcomed him in a friendly manner. *"Ça va?"*

"I am well, my friend. *Et toi?*"

"Very well. Very well indeed."

Father directed him toward the others in the parlor. "Please, I'd like to present my family." He gestured toward each as he spoke. "Emile Laurent, this is my lovely wife, Priscilla Thatcher. Our eldest daughter, Mrs. Margret Bryce, and her husband, John. Middle daughter, Elizabeth Thatcher — known as Beth — and our youngest, Julie Thatcher."

"I'm so pleased to meet you all," he answered with almost no trace of an accent and a gracious bow toward Mother.

He was older than Father, tall with a lean frame and receding hairline, gray-white waves of still-thick hair combed back. Beth guessed, looking beyond the weathered wrinkles and into the bright blue eyes of the distinguished man, that he had once been rather dashing. It was impossible to know for sure, but Beth sized him up quickly as

48

someone she would likely find agreeable.

The Montclair family arrived before the Thatchers had even seated themselves again. Mrs. Montclair burst into the parlor first, her fan busy keeping her cool. "Priscilla, thank you ever so much for hosting our little bon voyage event tonight. I'm simply overcome with excitement about our upcoming tour. Only four more days! How will we ever be ready in time? Oh, and look! It's Elizabeth — back with us from the western wilds. Did you have a nice time, dear?" But she was already sweeping over to Monsieur Laurent. "And this must be the brave gentleman who has agreed to escort us." She held out a hand, palm down, and the gentleman stepped forward and bowed low over it, murmuring graciously. She drew small glasses from her round face, folded them importantly, and smiled all around.

"Emile, may I present Mrs. Charles Montclair," Father quickly introduced them. "And Edith, this is Monsieur Laurent."

Mrs. Montclair drew back a step. "You are French?"

"I assure you, madame, that I am *Canadian*. And I have spoken both French and English since I was a child."

Father rushed to intervene. "Emile will be an invaluable help, Edith. He has traveled

49

extensively along the St. Lawrence, much of which is in Quebec." He continued, "Also through the maritime provinces. He is familiar too with the places you'll travel in the United States. Indeed, he served for some time as one of Canada's ambassadors before the Great War. We would be hard-pressed to find a place in the world where Emile has not visited."

Mrs. Montclair nodded, looking mollified, and took a seat on the sofa next to Mother, though not for a moment ceasing her flow of comments. Mr. Montclair, Father's business partner and longtime friend, quietly found a seat. Beth wondered if this husband had found it the better part of wisdom to let others enlighten the woman during the awkward encounter.

Mrs. Montclair perched her glasses on her nose once more and peered at Monsieur Laurent. "Now, please tell me how you say your name, sir. I've never been able to pronounce all these French names correctly."

Father leaned forward, but their guide answered quickly, "Eh-meel Loe-rah, Madame Montclair," he said with a smile and just a bit of French flair when pronouncing her name.

"Spell it, please," she insisted, not picking

up on his clever little touché.

"E-m-i-l-e L-a-u-r-e-n-t."

"Well, isn't that just like the French!" She chuckled and shook her head. "You're pronouncing only half the letters!"

Mother had heard quite enough. "Monsieur, would you care for some tea — or coffee? We'll be serving dessert shortly."

Mrs. Montclair's glasses were hastily removed once more, folded, and tucked away. "Priscilla always serves the best teas, *Mr. Lorant.* You really must try some."

He nodded to both women. "Thank you, Mrs. Thatcher. I would enjoy a cup of coffee, please." He seated himself again, poised and unruffled.

Mother addressed each of the others by turn. "Edith? Charles? Victoria?" Only then did Beth notice Victoria Montclair. Edward's younger sister had entered behind her parents and slipped quietly into a seat near the piano. She was holding a music book from the stand nearby. Beth tried to smile warmly in her direction but could not catch the girl's eye.

Once Mother began overseeing the tea service, all conversation was directed to the delicacies on her dessert tray and the quality of her teas and coffees. Beth took a seat near Victoria.

"How old are you now, Victoria?" she began. "If I remember correctly, you've just had a birthday."

Not raising her eyes from the book of music, the girl said flatly, "Yes, I'm sixteen."

"That's nice!" Beth congratulated. "I remember when I was sixteen. There were so many exciting things I was able to do that I hadn't been allowed to before — concerts in the city with Father, and staying up late at Mother's parties. How did you celebrate your birthday?"

Victoria turned the page before responding. "This cruise" was all she said.

Beth cleared her throat. "Very nice. A special celebration. Well, happy birthday, even if I am a little late." After a few sips of tea and a bite of a scone, she tried again. "Are you excited about the trip, Victoria?"

The girl shrugged, rising from her chair and taking a seat on the piano bench. "Mother says I'll enjoy myself, but I'm not so sure."

"I wasn't certain at first about going," Beth said with a nod. "But I do think it will be a nice break from ordinary days — and a lovely way to travel together."

For a few moments, the girl simulated playing the chords of the song she had been examining in the piano book. Her long fingers skillfully danced over the keys without making a sound. "Perhaps it will be nice — so long as I don't get seasick."

Beth hadn't considered that possibility. "Well, we won't be out in open sea for some time, not until we've left the St. Lawrence."

Finally Victoria turned to face Beth, declaring plaintively, "There are plenty of storms on Lake Ontario, and on the St. Lawrence too. Ships go down all the time, Elizabeth."

Beth tried to smile. "I'm sure we'll be fine, dear." *I suppose that sounded just like what Mother would say,* she thought ruefully. Beth lapsed into silence, the reticent teenager still "playing" through the piece in utter silence.

The conversations elsewhere seemed to have divided into two groups, the women gathered around Mrs. Montclair at the sofa, with Father, John, Mr. Montclair, and Monsieur Laurent on the other side of the room. Beth smiled at such an odd collection of traveling companions. *It might even have potential for a bit of friction,* she mused, gazing at Victoria's mother dominating the female conversation. She couldn't help but feel sorry for the lone man among the travelers.

She noticed the men begin pulling their chairs over toward the sofa, and Father announced, "We'd like to spend a little time discussing some of the more functional aspects of the trip. Is this an opportune moment, ladies? Beth and Victoria, would you please join us?" Beth set her cup and plate aside and waited for Victoria.

"Of course," answered Mrs. Montclair. "Why, we were just —"

"Wonderful, Edith. Thank you very much for allowing us to interrupt your conversation. Now, just to review the itinerary," he continued quickly, looking at a sheet of paper in his hand, "your train departs Monday morning at eight thirty. You'll change trains in Montreal, and then you're off again to Quebec City. Each of these is an express train, so you won't be stopping frequently but will still arrive rather late. You'll spend two nights at Le Château Frontenac — a lovely place, and one of Canada's hotels built by the railroad. I've stayed there twice, and it was splendid. Tuesday will be sightseeing in the Old Town. Wednesday morning your cruise begins from the harbor there. You'll want to be on board just after breakfast." He looked around at the group, nodded, then hurried on.

"Now, on board we've booked three suites with two bedrooms in each, situated as closely together as possible. You should all be very comfortable. For the Thatcher suites, Priscilla, Beth, and Julie will share the first. Margret and JW will be across the hall, with the nanny and Emma in the second room."

Beth hadn't heard that Emma would be going too and was pleased. Their domestic was only a few years older than she was, and they had become friends, though her mother wasn't sure that was quite proper. Beth hoped Emma would have at least some time free to enjoy the sights, but she likely would be washing and ironing and keeping up with their many belongings for most of the trip.

Father was saying, "The Montclairs also have a suite together — as I understand it, mother and daughter sharing one room and their lady's maid in the other. Emile has chosen a room on a lower floor —"

"So nice for you, Priscilla!" Mrs. Montclair interjected. "You have a room to yourself. I would have done so, but Victoria refuses to share with anyone but me. She could have been so comfortable with Lise, but she simply wouldn't hear of it!" While the words were said a bit proudly, Beth could see Victoria was put off by the comment.

"As I was saying," Father persisted, "that should cover the room assignments. There will be several stops at hotels along the way. Emile's primary concern is your safety." He looked once again around the circle, and Beth thought his gaze lingered a bit longer on Julie, who still needed particular attention because of her tendency toward risk taking. "He will see to it that all luggage is loaded and transported to the appropriate places. He will also accompany you whenever you're touring and will handle all matters pertaining to payments required. Those will be his main roles, but he's willing to help out in whatever capacity along the way." Monsieur Laurent nodded his agreement. Then Father added gravely, "I'm certain no one will take advantage of his kindness." Father kept his eyes on the paper, and Beth avoided looking at Mrs. Montclair.

Beth's head filled with all the details of the trip, the places she had longed to see for many years — Prince Edward Island, the setting for *Anne of Green Gables,* one of her favorite childhood books; Nova Scotia, with its beautiful lighthouses set atop rocky escarpments; the Bay of Fundy, with its extraordinary tides. Watching Julie's face, Beth knew that for her, the cruise was merely incidental until they arrived in New York City.

After the meeting with Monsieur Laurent and the Montclairs, the furor in their home only seemed to heighten. Another day of shopping, then a long day of packing and repacking to get everything stowed into a reasonable number of trunks and cases. Beth found herself on several occasions repeating Margret's prayer — for courage to endure all these blessings.

In her dressing gown, Beth crept down the long stairs and into Father's study. She had awakened early and begun thinking about what books she should include for the journey. Perusing Father's extensive collection, she spent some time accumulating a tall, tidy stack on the corner of his desk.

"What's this? I thought I heard a burglar," Father quipped. "Beth, what on earth are you doing up so early?"

She laughed and hurried across the room for a good-morning hug. "I couldn't sleep any longer. There's so much commotion with all the packing, and I don't feel I've had nearly enough time to plan what I *really* need."

Father shook his head. "You're not taking *all* of those, are you? You won't have time to leave your room and see anything!"

"Oh, no, I just can't decide. What would *you* suggest, Father?"

He followed her to the desk and scanned the titles. "It appears we have a bit of a theme here, eh?"

Beth quickly explained, "I thought perhaps some stories about travel would suit."

"Ah, yes, a good idea. That might just serve you well. Would you consider *Don Quixote*?" He pointed toward its place on his bookshelf.

"I attempted that once, and it was a little too much. Of course, I was younger then."

"Give it a few more years, my dear. When I've grown old enough to reach my 'jousting at windmills' age, you'll find you have more ways to relate to the story."

"Oh, Father! You'll never be like that."

He moved several of the books, one at a time. "You might try *Huckleberry Finn,* or *Heart of Darkness, The Odyssey* — have you read them already? Yes, I suppose you have." As he contemplated each volume, Beth could see him growing more pensive. At last he placed a book with a blue cover in her hands. "It's a funny thing about travel narratives, Beth. I think you'll find it's often the sort of journey which the protagonist doesn't desire to take that ends up telling the greatest story. The kind that has the most to teach us." He smiled a bit wistfully. "I wish I could have arranged things to come with you all on this voyage."

Beth reached out to touch his arm. "I know, Father. I especially will miss you. I've just gotten back —" But she could say no more.

He smiled and nodded his understanding. He looked as if he were going to depart, then paused. "If you'll allow me, Beth dear, please don't forget that the summer will be all too short. And perhaps you'll be leaving us again. I wish you would — that is, I *suggest* that you use your days wisely." His expression deepened, graying brows drawing together in contemplation of the words. "I realize Mother can be — what shall we say? — difficult at times, but only if you misunderstand how she thinks. Could you spend some time, some effort, in getting to know her better, dear? Stepping away from the shadow of the image you've come to accept as your mother? She's a remarkable woman, really. Pay attention to her many gifts. I know that you can grow to appreciate her — the manner in which she loves, her unwavering faith — if you just try."

Beth dropped her gaze. *Have my frustra-*

tions been so obvious? "Of course, Father. I'll do my best."

CHAPTER 4

Monday morning, bright and clear, turned out to be an excellent day to launch their adventure. Most of the luggage had been sent on ahead to the train station, but now the family loaded the last bags into Father's car and a taxicab — both would be necessary to convey them all.

"When do you suppose your ship will pass ours, Father?" Julie asked with a twinkle in her eyes.

"Well, Julie," he answered thoughtfully, "Mr. Montclair and I will board our train on Friday, but our ship won't depart Quebec City until Saturday afternoon. I suppose the ship will pass yours sometime the day after you're done watching whales in Saguenay Fjord."

Julie held his arm. "Won't that be exciting? But we'll miss you so much, Father. It's a shame you have to go on another trip. Have you ever been to Caracas before?"

"No, dear," he chuckled. "I've never been to anyplace in South America before. We won't be watching whales or seeing many of the sights."

She hurried on, "But you said you'll meet us in Florida, won't you? On your return trip?"

Father placed Julie's bag in the trunk of the automobile, slammed the top down, and turned back to her. "Yes, we plan to meet you in Florida. That is, we'll do our very best. But much could happen between now and then. So I'm grateful to know you'll be in the hands of Providence in the meantime . . . and our good friend Emile." He pulled Julie close and motioned for the others to join them. "I'd like to pray together before you leave."

He drew Mother to him with his free arm, and John and Margret with JW stood near. With a warm smile, Beth reached out to link arms with Emma. Only the nanny, Miss Lucille Bernard, stood alone, though Beth motioned her into the circle too. Father led in a short prayer, expressing his gratitude that God would have His hand on all these loved ones while absent from one another. Murmured amens followed Father's.

With kisses and hurried words of farewell, the travelers were bundled into the waiting

62

automobiles. Beth cast a glance back toward Father as he stood next to John, both waving. Her throat felt tight, and she wished to the core of her being that she could have spent more time with him. *But even if I wasn't leaving, Father will be gone anyway,* she reminded herself.

Beth found herself in front of the first oversized step of their waiting train — it had been only last Tuesday when she'd arrived at this same station. At least this would only be a one-day trip on the rails. Best of all, she would not be alone. In fact, Julie, who had grand ideas of documenting each stage of the journey with her new Brownie camera, had already enlisted the aid of a bellman to take a picture of the Thatcher women and JW in their traveling compartment — "for posterity."

In their small compartment, Beth settled beside Mother and across from her sisters, waiting for the train's departure. JW, thrilled at everything he was observing, climbed and wriggled from one lap to another, exploring all around the tiny room with the curiosity found in someone almost two. Emma and JW's nanny were in their own compartment.

Beth pulled an illustrated children's book from Margret's bag. "Here, darling," she called to JW. "Come sit with Auntie. I'll read to you."

His arms reached out to Beth, and she cuddled him in her lap, opening the book. There was time to read only a little from each page before the small boy was busy turning to the next. But what she had wanted most was an excuse to hold him — and give Margret some rest.

Julie leaned over. "Margret, I'm surprised the nanny permitted you to have him for the morning," she teased. "She hardly lets him out of her sight."

Margret allowed herself a weak smile, but Mother quickly put in, "Lucille Bernard is a well-educated, well-respected professional nanny. We are lucky to have her. I only wish I had found someone half as good as her when I was raising you girls."

Julie caught Beth's eye before affecting an innocent reply. "Why, Mother? Didn't we all turn out as well as you'd hoped?"

Mother waved away Julie's nonsense. "She employs the latest and best practices of child rearing. You would do well to co-operate with her, Margret. Who knows how many important people she's had a hand in raising."

Julie suggested, "Henry the Eighth, per-haps."

"Julie Camille Thatcher, that's quite enough."

Beth returned her attention to the child on her lap and read a little more in a dramatic tone, pointing at pictures of ducks to keep JW interested.

"Duckies, Annie Bet. Duckies."

Margret sighed. Sitting directly across from Beth, the frustration written across her sister's face was obvious. "She wants him with her at ten o'clock sharp. She's insisted that he's going to take his nap as usual."

"As well he should, Margret."

"But, Mother, he's going to have such a difficult time napping on the train. And she won't rock him to sleep — the most she'll do is pat his back. I'm afraid he just won't fall asleep today without even a crib, just on the settee beside her. Don't you think that I could — just this once?"

Mother reached across and patted Margret's knee. "Darling, she knows what she's about. Just let her do her job."

Margret shot a miserable glance toward Beth. And in one small moment, Beth construed that the two had been struggling for quite some time. She tightened her arms around JW and determined to provide whatever support and encouragement she could to Margret.

Beth heard the signals of the train's departure and waited for the blast of steam she knew would follow. When it hissed past the window and the cabin lurched forward, JW scurried across onto Margret's lap. In no time he had settled in for the ride, seated comfortably with his mother and sipping water from a little engraved silver cup. Beth noticed that his eyes did look sleepy, yet he seemed perfectly content nestled in right where he was.

As the miles rattled past, Beth too settled into the pleasure of chatting with her sisters and mother. There was much she needed to catch up on, and she was delighted to hear that Julie's paintings had been given a wall at a local art gallery — three of her still lifes had already sold, and also that Margret's husband, John, a stockbroker with a well-known firm, had recently been promoted.

Margret sounded rather astounded at how successful John had quickly become in the booming investment market. "Sometimes he tells me what our stocks are worth and I can hardly believe it! It seems so unreal." She added with amusement, "I almost chuckle when I hear him speak about stocks with Father. The two see things very differently."

"Dear old Father," Julie laughed. "You should hear them, Bethie. John keeps insisting that Father should invest more — that he wouldn't have to work nearly as hard if he were making the great gains to be had through investments. But poor Father can't seem to understand the modern era."

"Julie! That is quite enough," said their mother. "I won't stand for one word of criticism of your Father."

"I'm sorry, Mother." But the gleam in Julie's eyes spoke a different sentiment.

Beth listened to discussion of their shared circle of friendships and the social events she had missed. It was pleasant and satisfying simply to be with her mother and sisters again.

Then Julie exploded the calm. "I was just thinking, Beth, now that Father can't hear us . . ." She scooted forward and cast an eye about for support. "Shouldn't we be discussing what we'd all like most to hear?" Margret nodded encouragingly, and Beth winced as Julie said, "Tell us all about your Mountie, big sister."

Beth's eyes moved sideways to Mother next to her. She found no suggestion of an escape. "Well, I . . . I'm not sure what to tell."

"Everything," Julie said with a grin.

"Oh, goodness." *Where to begin?* "I met him one Sunday after church. He wasn't stationed in Coal Valley, but that was one of the communities for which he was responsible. So his work brought him frequently to our area. I got to know him rather well in the months I was there."

"What was he doing?" Margret asked, shifting JW to another position and offering him a new toy, which was immediately flung to the floor. Unflustered, Margret added, "I've always wondered what they — the Mounties — actually *do.*"

Beth confessed, "I don't really know that much. He came and went — and seemed to know everyone. He said once that there wasn't much of a jail at his post, but I'm sure he was involved with law keeping somehow. And I know there was some detective work toward the end of my year, though what he did at other times, I can't really say."

This seemed only to intrigue Margret further. "What *kind* of detective work?"

Beth would need to tread cautiously. It would never do to go into detail concerning Davie Grant and his bootlegging misdeeds, or how little Wilton Coolidge had unwittingly imbibed some of the noxious drink and been rushed to the hospital many miles away. It was perhaps best that they not hear that Beth had stumbled upon Mr. Grant when she was alone in the woods and been threatened if she didn't leave his town at the end of the school year. She would never forget the look of hatred and anger on his face when at last the Mounties led him away in handcuffs, never to return to their little community.

As matter-of-factly as she could manage, she answered, "Jarrick was working to catch a particular criminal. Actually, Edward was also called in to help. I was told he's quite a natural at such work."

Mother nodded at the familiar name.

"What kind of criminal, Beth?" Margret almost whispered.

"Nothing dastardly and dreadful — a moonshiner who operated from our area." *It's nearly a lie to phrase it so carelessly.* She wished she'd had more time to plan her wording.

"I knew it!" Mother cut in. "I *knew* that saloon where you taught school was just a front for drinking. I should have sent your father to bring you home the minute I heard it was to be your classroom."

Well, this has quickly spiraled out of control. "I'm fine, Mother. The man was apprehended. And I never saw a trace of alcohol at the pool hall. I did not see anyone breaking prohibition laws. The whole point of the story is that Jarrick and the other officers involved sought out and put to an end the criminal activity."

"Yes, by the grace of God you've come back to us —"

"Precisely," Beth agreed, reaching for Mother's hand and giving it a squeeze. "By the grace of God, under whose protection I was not for a moment in jeopardy." She sat back and hurried on to another tack, addressing Margret. "Jarrick traveled frequently. He was in and out of Lethbridge, often making deliveries in our area when he returned. He was a great friend of our local pastor — if you could call him local, since he moved from community to community every week. The two of them once shared living quarters in Calgary. So I think sometimes, especially on Sundays, Jarrick came to see Philip — that is, Pastor Davidson."

"Hmmm." Mother was not willing to give ground about her issues with the location of the classroom.

"Go on," Margret coaxed. "How did you discover you were interested in each other?"

The question caused Beth to cast another sideways glance at Mother. But she determined to answer Margret despite Mother's uneasiness. Beth's mind quickly sorted through what she might say. *Should Edward's role be mentioned? Would it be gossip? But what's left if those details are skipped — the lost luggage, return of the violin, his misleading comments to Jarrick? On the other hand, if all this is omitted, will there be a story left to tell?*

"Well, for a long time Jarrick believed I was already spoken for — that I was already committed to someone else."

Margret's eyes were as large as teacups. "He did? To whom?" Even Julie had not heard this part of the story. She leaned forward, motioning for Beth to continue.

"I'd prefer not to go further with that," Beth was quick to add. "Suffice it to say that Jarrick was respecting what he understood to be the case. And it wasn't until —"

Julie jolted upright in her seat. "Edward! It was Edward! Unless you mean Philip, but Jarrick knew him far too well for that. It would simply have to be our Edward. There's no one else." Julie drew in a sharp breath. She whispered loudly, "Edward told Jarrick he had already spoken for you? Isn't that *rich!*"

Beth's heart was pounding, and she knew her face was flushed with embarrassment. Her gaze dropped to the floor, then shifted toward Mother. *Did Mother too assume that Edward had offered marriage? More than that, had Father shared with Mother his telephone conversation with Jarrick? Was she already aware that he had officially begun courting me?*

The only response from Mother came with a careful nod. "Do go on, Beth." It was impossible to decipher the guarded expression Beth saw on Mother's face.

Clearing her throat, Beth continued, "It wasn't until Jarrick learned that I was *not* attached that he chose to express his feelings. It was, in fact, not until he was driving me to the train station on my way home." Beth chose to defer at least a portion of her secret for the time being. "The only other thing I'll tell you about him is that I've observed his conduct for almost a year, and I think he's a perfectly pleasing man. That he's just the sort of person . . . well, I could see myself marrying. I'm praying fervently for wisdom, for clear direction from God . . . one step at a time." It was a rather sensible summary of something very personal — of emotions that ran deep.

"Well," Mother said, seeming pleased, relieved, "there's not much to it, then."

Clearly, Father had not shared Jarrick's courtship request.

"Not much?" Julie exclaimed. "You should have seen the way he looked at her! And how handsome he is — most especially when dressed in his uniform!"

Beth took a breath, drew the knotted handkerchief and its shrinking mound of fragrant rose petals from her handbag, and carefully opened it. "These are from him," she said softly. "I found a box of long-stemmed roses in my cabin after I boarded the train. Somehow he was able to make arrangements for them to be waiting there for me."

Margret whispered in awe, "How romantic!"

A firm knock sounded through the compartment. Julie opened the door to Miss Lucille Bernard, her narrow face and thin lips pressed together as she announced, "Mrs. Bryce, it is now nine fifty-five."

Margret rose unsteadily to pass her already sleeping son to the nanny.

The gray-haired woman frowned. "How long has he been asleep?"

"I'm not certain. We were . . . talking."

"Humph. This does not bode well for a happy day."

Miss Bernard turned away and disappeared without another word. Margret dropped back down onto her seat.

"It's for the best, Margret," Mother assured her. "You'll see. He'll be all the better for it in the end."

Watching Margret's crestfallen face, Beth tucked the rose petals away, wishing she'd had a chance to share more of their significance. She suggested quietly, "It's almost time for morning tea. Should we find the Montclairs and see if they would like to join us in the dining car?"

CHAPTER 5

"How on earth is one to drink tea while this train is clattering along?" Julie grumbled as she wiped at her mouth, making Margret giggle.

"With a firm grip on one's cup and a napkin in hand," advised Beth, joining her sisters in their levity. Only Victoria, who shared their table, remained withdrawn and distracted — staring out the window as she munched on finger sandwiches.

Beth searched for a topic of conversation that might capture the interest of their young companion. "I wondered, Victoria, did you bring along your violin? I had given some thought to bringing mine, but decided against it — with the humidity and all."

The girl's eyes met Beth's. "Oh, yes, I did — but only my old one. I couldn't have come at all if I wasn't allowed at least to bring that!"

"I understand how you feel, dear. I'm

afraid I'll miss playing mine a great deal. It's relaxing and . . . well, heartening, somehow."

"It feels like being home to me, even when I'm not."

Here, at last, were sentiments from Victoria that Beth could share. "I've had such difficulty carving out practice times. But I'm sure *you've* been very faithful."

"Oh, yes." The girl nodded vigorously. "Mother complains that I practice too much. But it isn't really practice to me, it's *playing*. And I love to play. Why should it matter that there's no one to listen?"

Margret smiled warmly. "Well, we'd love to hear you play sometime, Victoria. That would be very nice."

"If you like." The young girl shrugged and returned to gazing out the window. But suddenly she looked at Beth. "Elizabeth, you can play *my* violin whenever you want. I'd like to share it with you."

"Thank you. That's very kind. I would appreciate that so much."

And just as suddenly Victoria looked away again.

Julie lifted her brows in dramatic response, shifting her eyes from Beth to Margret about the odd youth. Beth spent a quiet moment regarding Victoria. She was such a study in disparity. The girl was indisputably attractive — dark curls down around her shoulders without any adornment. Her delicate features, perfect complexion, and striking coloration set her apart. And yet she seemed entirely unaware of her appearance.

Yet even this natural appeal was worn carelessly by Victoria, giving not a nod toward the common social graces. She could be found sitting cross-legged in a corner at many a social gathering — the skirt of a lovely new dress selected by her mother bunched up and crushed beneath her. When Beth had observed her at the Montclairs' home, Victoria was usually sprawled out on a rug next to a dog seldom away from her side.

In addition, Victoria might complain of some need to her mother, and Mrs. Montclair would stop all else in order to attend to her daughter. It had been so for as long as Beth had known the family. Mother considered the child to be spoiled and difficult. Margret often stood up for her, expressing that there was "more than meets the eye." However, they all had been rather surprised that she had not grown out of her peculiarities as she'd reached her teen years. At any rate, the offer of Victoria's cherished violin — so freely extended and without selfish thought — had given Beth pause to reconsider what she knew about Edward's young sister. *Perhaps it is possible to understand Victoria better. To be an influence. To encourage her interactions with the group.*

"Hello? Beth? Are you still with us?"

"I'm sorry, Julie, I'm afraid I was thinking . . ." She shook her head briefly and picked up with the conversation.

"I'm going back to the cabins," Margret finally announced, placing her napkin on her empty plate. "Perhaps my little J-bird is awake now. I'd like to walk around with him for a little while. Would you care to come?"

"Of course," Beth and Julie answered in unison. Even Victoria rose to join them.

They made their way through the cars until they reached their assigned rooms. Margret knocked softly on the cabin door where JW had napped.

Beth looked at her empty hands and touched Julie's shoulder. "I'm going back to the dining car. I think I've left my handbag."

"You should hurry, Bethie dear. You never know who might claim it — such a . . . an interesting old bag." It obviously was not a compliment, merely Julie's way of poking fun at her less fashionable sister.

Hurrying back again, Beth approached the

dining car, pausing just inside the doorway. Even from here she could see nothing left on their table — all had been cleared away.

"Miss," a voice called. The man was holding up the familiar bag. "Is this what you're looking for?"

"Oh, thank you. I'm afraid I left it behind."

The smiling waiter bowed slightly. "You're very welcome, miss. Have a nice day."

Mother and Mrs. Montclair were just rising from their places. Beth decided to wait for them. She ducked out of the way into a short hall off to one side, allowing two diners just arriving to pass. She could hear Mother and Mrs. Montclair as they approached.

"I've told you, Priscilla, you've been far too lax in attending to Beth. Mark my words, she'll end up wed to someone far beneath her station, raising umpteen kids, and poor as church mice."

Beth pressed herself deeper into the corner, frozen in shock while they passed. They paused just outside the doorway. Only the back of Mother's dress and her carefully pinned hair remained in view.

"I'm afraid you're right, Edith" came her mother's hushed voice. "But I'm not certain what to do. She can be so headstrong and

79

uncooperative. I've said as much to her, but she does not listen. And now here's a man we know nothing about, who turns out to have designs on her. I'm beside myself with worry. Is it the money he wants? Is it William's influence? We have no way of knowing. And I'm all too aware that Beth's idealized view of the world will hinder her from making a rational decision."

"Well, it's a shame she wouldn't accept my Edward. Goodness knows, he tried. He could have attempted no more."

Beth could see Mother's head shaking with her dismay. "Yes, I have always tried to help her see Edward's good qualities, but I'm afraid she doesn't value my opinion — on anything. After all, her aunt Elizabeth married a Mountie too, and what a treacherous, nomadic existence that produced. I do *not* want that life for my fragile daughter! She was not made for such trials — her health is not up to it."

Beth could feel her hands clenching and unclenching at her sides. She closed her eyes and willed the women not to look in her direction before continuing, their conversation growing fainter.

"As soon as we arrive in Quebec, dear," Mrs. Montclair was saying, "I'll call my Edward and ask him for any information he can share with us. I'm certain he'll cast some light on the situation."

"Thank you, Edith. I'd consider that a great kindness . . ." And the two moved beyond Beth's range of hearing.

The exchange was a crushing blow to Beth. She had not realized how poorly Mother still regarded her decision-making ability or her physical stamina. *If you'd only seen me, Mother. If you'd only allow yourself to believe what you read in my letters. I managed just fine — for almost a year. I don't need to be mollycoddled. I'm not a child.*

Beth tried a brave face when she arrived at their shared seating compartment, but she could not bring herself to join Margret, Julie, and Victoria as they wandered through the train and entertained the toddler. It appeared that Mother had gone into Mrs. Montclair's compartment to continue their chat. Beth withdrew to their now-empty cabin, heartsick and pacing for some time before rustling through her bag for a book to read. She finally chose the novel Father had recommended. She was determined to put her attention to reading rather than crying.

"Father dear," she whispered to the empty seat beside her, wishing he were there, "you're right. I don't understand Mother.

This doesn't feel like love. And I'm afraid I'm not off to a very good start at keeping my promise to you."

The fact that Beth declined lunch surprised no one. She had always been a light eater, and traveling usually seemed to heighten her lack of interest. The train groaned to a stop in the Montreal terminal, and Beth dragged herself along with the others, keeping her head low and trying not to look as downcast as she felt. On the second train, she curled up on the seat by the exterior wall, head resting on a sweater she had rolled up into the corner, and went to sleep. No one seemed to notice the mood that had overcome her.

"What are you reading so ferociously?" Margret's query cut into Beth's solitude. Margret was preparing for bed in their shared room after JW had fallen asleep across the hall with the nanny. The group had arrived in the darkness at the looming Château Frontenac, of which Father had spoken so admiringly. Its shadowy silhouette had towered above them as they entered, but Beth was entirely indifferent, keeping to herself and avoiding any eye contact that might elicit questions. Now that they had settled into their rooms, Beth had retreated once again behind her book.

"It's *Redburn* — by Melville," she answered.

"I don't recall that title. What else was it Melville wrote? I'm certain I should know."

Beth sighed. "*Moby-Dick.*"

"Oh, yes, I read that. It was very long. I'm not sure I understood it all," Margret continued, pulling the pins from her hair and shaking it out. "What's this book about?"

"A young man going off to sea. His family lost their fortune. But he doesn't know anything about sailing, so it's very hard for him."

Margret turned away and laughed. "Well, I hope there isn't a shipwreck, darling. I don't suppose that would bode well for us at all."

Beth gave no response.

As Margret slipped beneath her duvet and turned off the small Tiffany lamp on her nightstand, she said with a yawn, "Don't stay up too late, Beth. We'll be sightseeing tomorrow."

"I napped today. I'll be fine."

It was well past midnight before Beth closed the blue cover, feeling as if she had just spent some time with Father, just the two of them sharing the story. She hurried into her nightgown and slid carefully into bed. However, in the darkness and quiet, the dam of pent-up tears began to flow unchecked. *Why is it so difficult to earn Mother's approval? Why is she always so disparaging of me? Am I truly headstrong and uncooperative? Do I truly have an idealized view of the world, making it impossible to make rational decisions? What am I misunderstanding about our relationship? Will there never be peace and trust between Mother and me?* And on and on went her silent questions in the darkness.

Beth began the next day with her Bible, hoping to improve her attitude. She determined that she could not begrudge Mother her concerns about a man she didn't know, or her need to confide in a friend. She would honor her, even though she had felt very hurt by the meager appraisal she felt her abilities and judgment had been given.

Beth chose the simplest of her new dresses and slipped on the sensible new walking shoes. Let Julie complain about Beth's attire being far from stylish — at least she would be comfortable. While repacking her handbag for the day, she withdrew the packet of rose petals and placed it in a corner of her suitcase where it wouldn't get crushed. Unable to abandon the keepsake entirely, she withdrew one withered petal and wrapped it in her handkerchief. Somehow she felt as if Jarrick were along for the day, at least in spirit.

She hurried down the hall to the Montclairs' hotel room, where the others were gathering.

"Do hurry, Edith," she heard her mother urging as she opened the door. "He says we're to leave in ten minutes. And I'm afraid he'll go without —"

"Oh, no, he will not, Priscilla. A man in our employ will *not* make such demands of me. I simply won't have it." The woman sat in front of the vanity, trying on her hat at various angles.

"It's just that he's made all the arrangements, Edith. It seems prudent for us to oblige —"

"Nonsense! This is my *vacation.* I have waited patiently for years for it. And I will not surrender its control to a stranger — and a Frenchman at that."

Beth didn't know whether to step into the chaos or not. Margret, JW in her arms, and Julie were waiting just inside the door. Victoria was curled up in a chair, seemingly indifferent to all the hullabaloo.

Mother coaxed, "But, Edith, the breakfast

he's arranged for us — he's found a patio with a lovely view of the St. Lawrence. Wouldn't you like that?"

Mrs. Montclair turned around. "*Mr. Lorant* may as well know from the start that I shan't let him bully me. I shall be ready when I am good and ready."

Mother, looking a bit pale, walked toward the door, advising softly, "Girls, would you please go to the lobby to meet Monsieur Laurent? If we're not down by the time he needs to leave, you are free to go without us. I shall try to hurry Edith along. However, if it comes to that, please ask him to leave the address at the front desk, and we'll follow in a taxi."

Julie spun on her heel and marched down the hall. Margret cast a glance toward Victoria, who seemed to abandon her mother in favor of the promise of breakfast, and followed them. The last they heard was a frustrated, "Now, where did I leave my glasses?"

Monsieur Laurent allowed very little further waiting time before shaking his head and leading them out without the two matriarchs. He conducted them expertly through the hotel's maze of wide, elegant hallways until he reached a broad set of doors. Stepping out into the bright sunshine, Beth was amazed to find herself in a different world from what she had glimpsed through the darkness last night. She followed their guide across a wide, paved walkway and up to a long railing. Looking beyond, Beth was awed to see a sudden drop over a sheer cliff and a magnificent view of the lower city and the river. Gazing from one side to the other, Beth became lost in the spectacular vista.

With a dramatic gesture, their guide drew their attention to what lay behind them. *"Regardez vous."*

Far above loomed the sprawling, imposing structure of Le Château Frontenac. The brick-and-limestone edifice with its neat rows of windows soared floor upon floor, angled here and there in surprising corners and turrets. The walls stretched up to the steep gabled rooflines and the central tower thrust into the blue sky. It was truly magnificent — perhaps the most beautiful building Beth had ever seen.

"It's marvelous!" Margret gasped. Julie was busy snapping pictures with her camera, and Monsieur Laurent was happy to take several of their group with the hotel as a backdrop.

"Oh, won't Father love to see these photographs!" Julie enthused.

"Are you ready to see more of our city? *Oui?* Then follow me," Monsieur Laurent instructed. "It is a lovely day. We shall walk to a favorite patisserie for our breakfast. It's not too far, and I believe you will all enjoy the stroll."

The way was rather long but always downhill, so it was indeed a pleasant walk — even for Margret, who was carrying JW, though Beth cheerfully shared the task halfway there. Weaving in and out along the narrow lanes and broad intersections, past lovely gardens, they were soon enclosed by stone walls and crowding shops, Julie continuing to point the camera at everything that caught her eye.

Their guide encouraged them on. "Let's keep moving, ladies. Yes, we'll be there shortly."

"But, Julie, you won't be in any of the photos," Margret pointed out. "Do you want me to take the next one?"

Julie laughed. "You're right, darling. I'd like to prove that I came too!"

"There'll be plenty of time," Beth cajoled with a little more firmness than the patient man. "Do hurry, Julie. We don't want to fall behind."

"Monsieur," Beth called to him, "I feel as if I've somehow stepped out into Europe this morning, or at least as I've imagined Europe. Quebec City is so much . . . well, much more 'foreign' than I had expected."

He responded with a charming smile and a slight bow, pride in his eyes over his city of birth. "Yes, I understand what you mean, mademoiselle. It is a very old city, founded in 1608 and the heart of *la Nouvelle-France*. Much of the Old World is still to be enjoyed here."

And soon, just as promised, they found themselves seated on a crowded patio overlooking the river. The delicious pastries were indeed worth the walk, they agreed, including JW, who had signs of his treat across his cheeks.

"Mrs. Bryce," Monsieur Laurent said to Margret, "I am finished eating. Allow me to hold the little one so you may enjoy your breakfast." He reached for JW as he spoke, and the small boy eagerly held out his arms.

"I'm afraid he's covered in crumbs, monsieur," Margret demurred.

"Oh, that is no trouble at all. I've held many a baby in my day." Leaning back in his chair, he bounced JW on his knees, all the while performing a singsong verse in French. His face moved through a range of exaggerated expressions, causing the toddler to giggle in delight.

Julie remarked, "You must have children, monsieur."

A fleeting shadow crossed the man's face before he could say quietly, "Yes, two sons. But we lost them both in the war."

"I'm so very sorry," Margret replied.

"Merci."

Beth felt her heart constrict at his loss and would like to have known more, but Mother and Mrs. Montclair arrived by taxi just then.

"Welcome to you both. I trust you are enjoying a pleasant morning."

"Good morning, monsieur." Mother's smile looked a bit forced. "I'm confident that it will improve."

"We have a car coming to pick us up in ten minutes," the man said cordially. "We shall have a look around before lunch — and then shopping in the afternoon. Does that suit you all quite well?"

"Ten minutes," Mrs. Montclair repeated. "One can hardly eat in such a short time!"

"Oui, madame." His smile never faded.

Delighted at his approach with Mrs. Montclair, Beth smiled at him warmly. "Here, monsieur. Let me take JW so that you can gather your things." But the boy turned away from Beth's hands and tucked himself up against the guide.

"I believe, Miss Thatcher, that he's made

up his mind," he said with a laugh.

Beth's heart sank. Her nephew had chosen a stranger over an auntie. She hoped this wasn't a sign of things to come.

CHAPTER 6

Sightseeing turned out to be a rather constant battle between Mrs. Montclair and Monsieur Laurent. She would notice a small shop or kiosk nearby, but their guide would move them along, insisting that shopping would take place in the afternoon. Periodically, Mrs. Montclair would simply ignore his instructions and disappear, turning up later with another bag in her hands, seeming pleased with herself for having outwitted Monsieur Laurent.

When they returned to the hotel for lunch, Beth fell across her bed, fatigued from walking and the constant interruptions of Edward's mother and Julie's camera. The new shoes would likely be comfortable once broken in, but today they had left little blisters on the backs of her heels. She wished for a short nap rather than another meal, but rose with a sigh, switched shoes, and followed the others to one of the hotel's fine dining rooms.

After lunch, they climbed into taxis for a large shopping area with row upon row of quaint shops and street vendors — a much better site than the morning's tourist places. Again, with merely a twinkle in his eye, Monsieur Laurent directed them to the best values. Mrs. Montclair looked less smug as she realized here was a far better selection of merchandise at lower prices than her morning purchases.

Monsieur Laurent waited close at hand, helping to barter for the best value and answer their many questions, particularly interpreting the French signage and currency. Out on the street, Beth was caught by a display of paintings that captured not only the look of the enchanting French city but also something of its mood and character.

"How much?" She pointed to a favorite and tried her best to pronounce, *"C'est combien?"* Unfortunately, she had not considered that she would not understand the rapid answer given in response. Monsieur smiled and repeated the price in English.

It's a suitable amount. Actually, rather inexpensive — though the painting will be bulky to pack. Beth paused to weigh the idea carefully. *Perhaps, though, a painting is bet-*

ter for teaching the children about this city than a photograph that's small and only black-and-white. It would give a beautiful, more accurate impression of Quebec.

"Oui," she said as she looked into her handbag for the amount. But Monsieur Laurent was already holding out the correct bills to the artist as he murmured to Beth, "Your father instructed me to handle all the financial transactions during the trip."

The painter folded brown paper around the purchase and smiled broadly. "Enjoy, mademoiselle." Monsieur reached for the package.

Beth paused, looking once more at the art display. *Instead of knickknacks and baubles, a painting would accurately convey to my class these other areas of Canada.* Immediately Beth broke into a smile. *And Julie could do the paintings!*

"Monsieur, ask him, please — does he have any blank canvases?"

"Miss Thatcher? You want them blank — you mean, unpainted?"

"Yes, so my sister can paint scenes on our journey."

Eyebrows raised, Monsieur Laurent posed the question to the startled artist. They discussed the unusual request for several minutes before it appeared they had arrived at a price.

"It's not a very good arrangement, miss. He's charging a considerable amount for having already prepared the canvases."

"It's all right. Please tell him my sister will paint for me along the way."

"I did so, Miss Thatcher. But he'll still go home and tell his friends about the silly tourist who preferred to buy his paintings blank."

Beth blushed as Monsieur Laurent added more coins to the ones in the man's hand. He grinned, giving an exaggerated shrug.

"Bethie, did you see this bag?" Julie called. "Isn't it exquisite?"

"It's very nice. Don't you have one about that size?"

"Yes, darling, but it's a different color. They're *completely* different. Don't you think this would go nicely with my green-and-white plissé blouse?"

"Really, Julie, I don't know why you bother asking me. You would certainly know better than I." This was met with a bright laugh.

"You're right of course, sister dear. I guess I'm just making conversation." Julie grinned. "What did you buy? A painting?"

"Several, actually. Monsieur is having them delivered. But . . . well, they're not painted yet."

Julie's eyebrows drew together.

"I want you to do them . . . along the way. So I can show my students how eastern Canada looks and teach them about other parts of our country."

Julie shrugged and turned back to the handbag. "I guess I'll have time. What else will there be to do at sea?"

But Beth's attention was drawn to someone behind them. "Don't look directly, Julie," she whispered, "but have you noticed that young man who keeps looking in our direction? No, don't look at him!"

Nervous laughter erupted from both of them, and Julie quickly slipped behind a display of broad-brimmed hats, her face a mixture of amusement and alarm. "Is he still looking? Did he walk away?" she said, her giggles uncomfortably loud.

Beth put a hand to Julie's mouth. "Yes, he's coming this way. He's looking right at us." Julie's eyes grew large, and she peered around a hat.

"Bonjour," called the stranger as he approached. "Do you speak English?" he asked boldly. "Will you help me, please? I could really use a woman's opinion. And you look as if you might know a thing or two about scarves."

"You're English?" Julie wondered.

"I'm American." Then shifting his bags into one hand, he extended the other toward Beth. "My name's Nick — Nick Petrakis. And I promised my mama that I'd bring her back a new scarf, but I have *no idea* what constitutes a good one versus a second-rate one. Can you help a fellow out?"

Beth took the offered hand with a nod. "Of course."

Julie's hand was already out. "Hi, Nick. I'm Julie, and this is my sister Beth."

"Well, aren't you both just a pair of beauties." The flattery made Beth recoil, yet it had the opposite effect on her sister.

"I'd be happy to give you a hand." Julie slid past Beth, eyelashes batting. "If I do say so myself, I believe I have quite an eye for fashion. I merely need to know the color of your mother's eyes?"

"Come again?"

Beth was uncomfortable with the flirtatious way they were interacting. Nick leaned closer, one hand resting above Julie's head on the hat rack. "What does her eye color have to do with a scarf?"

"Everything," Julie insisted, tipping her face in a coy manner.

"Well then, her eyes are brown. Dark

brown like mine." He leaned closer still. "Does that help, Julie?"

She suddenly spun toward the table holding a mound of scarves. "Well, I like this one. Or no, this is better. The red in it will go nicely with her brown eyes . . . the yellow trim will complement them too." She began rummaging further into the pile.

Nick turned his attention to Beth. "You see, I'm leaving by ship tomorrow, so I have to finish my shopping today."

Beth took an awkward step back. "We . . . we leave then too."

"You don't say. Tell me you're not sailing on the *Royal Phoenix,* are you? Wouldn't that be a strange coincidence?" He seemed to stand uncomfortably close.

"I don't know the ship's name." Beth found it difficult to meet his gaze.

"Then I can only hope," he said with a grin and a wink from those brown eyes.

He joined Julie, and they worked their way through the scarves she had draped over one arm. Beth frowned, feeling her pulse racing. The young man seemed harmless enough — and yet alarmingly forward. *Perhaps that is just the way with Americans.* Beth tried to remember if she'd ever been introduced to one before. *Surely there have been occasions. Father has many American busi-*

ness contacts, though never a man quite so young as this.

He was shorter than most, yet athletic and muscular. His shirt was tight across his chest and arms. He reminded Beth of a coiled spring — all energy just waiting to be released. Beth blushed despite herself.

"Now, that one's perfect. She's gonna love it!" This Nick took Julie's hand and kissed it slowly. "How can I thank you, doll? I *do hope* I'll see you both again." Turning to wave at Beth, he went to pay for his purchase.

Julie moved closer, her eyes on the place where Nick had gone. "Bethie, did you see his eyes?"

Just then Mother arrived with Margret. "Are you nearly finished, girls? Margret and I would like a taxicab. We're just about spent. Where's our guide?"

Monsieur had two vehicles ready in moments. All the way back to the hotel, whenever Beth's eyes met Julie's, her sister would cover her mouth to stifle her giggles.

The docks were a glorious confusion of people and trolleys and preparations for departure. The travelers had boarded as early in the morning as they could, made their way through the narrow corridors to their suites, then gathered on the observation deck for a good view dockside as the ship cast off. Looking out toward the city as it began to slide away, Beth realized she easily could have enjoyed several more days in the Old World charm of Quebec City.

On the other hand, she was also anticipating relaxation in a deck chair with a book. A rather nice break from bustling from shop to shop, hoping for no further difficulties among their little group.

Beth leaned against the polished wood rail and let the bright sunshine and the cooling breeze flow over her face. It was perfect weather and the perfect time of year. Her fingers reached for the tucked-away handkerchief where she had placed another of Jarrick's rose petals as she dressed that morning. She was completely overwhelmed with joy and satisfaction, so grateful she had agreed to the cruise. *Jarrick was correct in encouraging me to come along with my family.*

She was soon enjoying the lovely shoreline — green forests, scattered farms, quaint little fishing villages, and once in a while a lovely mansion with lawns stretching down to the water's edge.

However, as they sailed farther east along the ever-widening St. Lawrence River, Beth began to feel a growing queasiness. She had not given further thought to seasickness, despite Victoria's earlier warnings. Soon she could no longer deny the fact and retreated to her cabin, pulled the drapes, and wilted onto the chaise longue, hoping for relief. Mother fussed and worried. Emma brought ginger tea, aspirin, and cold cloths. But Beth could hardly keep from giving in to her nausea.

Julie came and went frequently, at times flipping on the light switch or closing the door too loudly. A long respite of quiet came only after her mother and sister had dressed in gowns and gone off together. *What a shame to miss the first night's dinner on board. And how humiliating to seem to fulfill Mother's recent assessment of my frailty.*

Beth squeezed cool water from a rag into the basin balanced in her lap and draped it across her forehead again, trying to do so without shifting her head from its place against the upholstered chaise. If she were careful not to move quickly, she hoped the quiet and darkness of the room would soon relieve her dreadful headache.

Sometime in the evening, a muffled knock at the cabin door signaled her sister. "Bethie?" At least Julie was remembering to keep her voice soft this time. "Bethie, are you awake?"

Beth answered through gritted teeth, "Yes, come in." She could feel the penetrating light from the opening door even through the wet rag and closed eyes.

"Bethie? I have someone I'd like you to meet."

Incomprehensible, though certainly believable, that Julie would expect me to meet someone at just such a moment. Beth sighed and drew the cloth from her head, squinting at Julie's form and that of a second young woman just behind her.

"This is Jannis. We just met."

Beth closed her eyes again and whispered a greeting to the unwelcome stranger. She felt Julie's hand close round her own. "I told her how sick you've been. She wants to help."

Without waiting for further introduction, the girl interjected, "I have a pill for you. I know it'll help. It did wonders for my sister's seasickness." After a pause, she said, "Here, take it."

Beth felt a small tablet pressed into her hand and heard the sound of water being poured. "What is it?" she asked, struggling to raise herself onto an elbow.

The stranger giggled. "Oh, I don't know. Just something to settle your stomach and

102

stop your headache. But I bet you'll feel better in the blink of an eye. It worked that way for Penny. And how!" Then she added an afterthought. "That's my sister — Penny."

Without another word, the girls slipped through the door and into the hallway.

After what seemed a rather short time, Beth was indeed feeling much better. She cautiously raised her head. The pill certainly had seemed to work. Almost as if she were in a dream world, she rose and washed, changed from her clammy, crumpled clothing, and fixed her hair before the enormous gilt mirror. *It's such a relief to feel healthy again.* For a moment she wondered what had been in the medicine but soon brushed such thoughts aside. *Whatever it was, it did its job.* Beth slipped into the hall, intending to find Julie and her new friend to thank them. Then she saw the pair turn a corner toward her.

"Well, how about that!" the new acquaintance called up the hallway. "You look just ducky!"

"I feel just fine," Beth assured them both.

Julie asked, "Can you eat something?"

"Why, yes, I'm starving. Imagine that! I'm truly hungry."

"The dining room is closed," Julie said. "But that's no problem. There are a lot of other places to eat."

Beth reached out a hand to Jannis's arm. "I want to thank you. I really do feel so much better. It's almost a miracle."

The young woman simply smiled warmly in return. Beth had not really seen her previously in the dim light of the room. She was rather attractive, with fashionably bobbed blond hair and a boyishly pretty face — a relaxed and charming demeanor. Beth liked her immediately. "That's how it worked for Penny too," Jannis assured Beth. "Let me tell you, she was just as thrilled."

"I can't wait to meet her."

"Well then, let's get a wiggle on, gals. Penny is waiting for us in the lounge."

Beth paused. "Can we — oh, Julie, should we go to the *lounge*?"

"I've already been," Julie said with a laugh. "Mother checked it out — they don't serve anything wicked, what with prohibition and all. It's just a nice place to sit — kind of like the dining car on the train. But there are going to be shows in there later, comedies and music and such!" Julie stepped between, linking arms with both women. "We're going to have a marvelous time, ladies. This is the beginning of many happy cruise days, I'm very certain."

Beth was introduced to Penny at their table in the corner of the lounge, a piano playing softly in the background. The sisters made a lively pair, gushing with enthusiasm at taking their "first cruise together," they said. Compared to this younger sister, Penny looked a little drab — heavy eyes, broad face, and drooping mouth. They actually didn't look at all alike.

Jannis explained, "I don't mind telling you, Beth, our auntie had a hard time letting us go. As I was telling Julie earlier, she was gonna come on this cruise too, but she broke her leg, and the ol' doc said she should stay off it — not even walking around at home. So, needless to say, he didn't want her to go. She's quite old, you know. What is she, Pen, fifty or so?"

"Oh, maybe even older," Jannis's sister confirmed with a vigorous nod.

Beth couldn't remember hearing anybody chatter as incessantly as their new friends. Julie's questions inspired even longer streams of explanations. "Where did you say you were from again?" Beth asked.

"Buffalo — that's in New York. And it's our first time in Canada. Can you believe it, living so close and all? We've wanted to come up here for so long. Julie says you're from Toronto, Beth. But that you just came back from the West. How was that? Did you like it out there — a deb like you? I wouldn't have guessed it."

The rapid-fire conversation was all a little overwhelming to Beth, particularly since her head was still rather foggy and slow. "I *did* enjoy it there. It was wonderful. I hope to go back again soon."

"You do? And give up your swanky life-style. Say it ain't so!"

Julie seemed compelled to explain. "Penny and Jannis aren't in the staterooms. They've got a room on one of the lower decks — with only a porthole. But I told them not to worry about that. They can just come up and visit with us, borrow our balcony. We've got lots of room."

"Lots of *room* in your *room,*" Jannis laughed. "You're so clever, Julie."

Julie finally caught on and joined in the merriment over the play on words.

"Well, there's no sense sitting here beatin' our gums anymore," Penny cut in. "Golly, let's get up and *do* something."

"Yes, let's," Jannis agreed.

As they exited the lounge, Julie drew close to Beth. "They're flappers — honest-to-goodness *flappers,* Bethie! I know you can't tell by what they're wearing now, but you

106

should have seen them dressed for dinner. So modern, so chic." She sighed. "They don't get to share our dining room, but everything else on board is open to all. Aren't we just going to have the best time?"

CHAPTER 7

By morning, Beth's headache and queasy stomach had returned. It did not help that she had been out far later than she was accustomed. She had seen her first silent film accompanied by a pianist, watched part of a comedy routine that incorporated some silly magic tricks, and strolled along the deck in the moonlight with their new friends. It had been a "spectacular evening," as Jannis put it, but now it was morning, and she was sick again.

After Mother and Margret had gone off to breakfast, Julie slipped back in the room with another pill from Jannis. "Take it," she insisted. "You want to enjoy the trip, don't you? This is going to help."

There was certainly no question that the medicine had worked well yesterday. Having suffered through Mother's concoctions and cures over the years, it seemed reasonable for Beth to take this as well. As quickly as the previous day, she was on her feet again.

Beth was able to eat a satisfying breakfast. Afterward she and Julie went looking for Penny and Jannis. They were easy to find, with their bright laughter and outgoing antics drawing lots of attention. The four young women wandered the promenade deck, looking for some type of activity. During the night the ship had sailed into Saguenay Fjord, touting the best whale sightings. But beyond the railings an ethereal haze of fog shrouded the rugged landscape in mystery, while tall evergreens pierced through like sentinels along the rocky banks. The four assured one another that the warming sun would soon burn away the fog and agreed to try later for the whale sightings.

They passed the indoor pool which looked somewhat like a Roman bath in design, but decided against a dip, since so many others were already swimming. They happened upon tennis courts painted on the wood flooring in a far corner of the recreation deck, with tall nets pulled taut all around to confine wayward balls. At the moment there was no one else nearby.

"Have you ever played?" Penny asked Beth.

"No, I haven't even seen a game."

Julie stepped forward eagerly. "I'll try — who wants to join me?"

"In those shoes?" Beth was dubious Julie would be able to maneuver in her short heels and narrow-cut shift.

"Can't hurt to try." She tossed her felt cloche toward Beth and stepped out onto the court.

Jannis followed suit, picking up a second racket. "At least I've seen it done — while I was at a college visiting a friend." For several minutes they batted the ball across the net, making every effort to keep it slow and under control, but lobbing it as often as not into the net or out of bounds. Penny and Beth laughed at their feeble attempts and chased after the ball when it bounced their way.

Julie was huffing with the exertion. "I can do this. I know I can. Just give me a chance to get used to it." Jannis seemed far more suited to the activity, her blond hair whirling in circles around her head as she spun one way and then another.

"Keep your arm straight," she called to Julie. "That's how I've seen it done." She joked, "You look as if your arms are noodles. Stretch out. Toughen up."

"I'm trying!"

"Here, get this one," Jannis challenged. But with a turn of her foot, Jannis came down hard on the makeshift court, her legs sprawled out under her. Before Beth and Penny could hurry to her side, a young man had entered from the shadows and was helping her up.

"Miss, are you all right? Is your ankle hurt? I was just walking by — rats, and you were doing so well too."

"Thanks." Jannis laughed off the assistance. "I'm fine. Just embarrassed." He pulled her carefully to her feet.

"Nick?" Julie exclaimed, gaping in wonder from the other side of the net. "You're Nick, aren't you?"

The dark head swung around. "Hey, sure — it's my little fashion consultant! And here you are on board *my* ship. Lucky me!" He smiled around at each of them. "And here's your pretty sister too. Aren't you going to introduce me to your friends?"

"I'm Jannis, the damsel in distress." She shook Nick's hand heartily. "So glad to meet you. And this is my sister, Penny."

"Charmed," Nick answered with a mock bow. "Now, don't tell me your names. The two of you are . . . Beth? That right? And June, is it?"

"Julie!"

"Oh, sure — I remember now. Don't take it personally. I'm bad with names. Say, you ladies want some *real* competition?" He winked at Jannis. "I promise to go easy on you."

Jannis eyed Julie, and they had quickly cooked up a plan without a word being exchanged. "You can play us *both.*"

The match did not last long. The combined efforts of Julie and Jannis were no contest for the skill of the young man, who obviously had played often before. He clearly did all he could to send the ball where they could easily hit it back — but didn't. Beth's sides ached from cheering and laughing.

Other passengers were beginning to gather, and at last it must have been too much for Julie's pride. "I surrender!" she called, waving her racket. "That's enough — for this time. Maybe we can try again later when I can borrow Bethie's comfy 'old lady' shoes."

"Ah," Nick said, "you're going to blame your shoes, are you? I see."

Just then another man stepped forward. "Hey, buddy, how 'bout a game — you and me?"

Beth saw Nick's quick change of expression. "All right, *buddy.* Rally for serve."

Jannis ceremonially passed the ball to him, and he gathered a second from a nearby table. This time the ball was traveling much faster. The four women retreated to a table where they could watch the match. Soon a waiter dressed in white stopped at their table to ask if they'd like anything to drink.

"I'd like strawberry soda, please," Julie said. "What'll you have, ladies?"

He took their orders, and Julie gave him Mother's room number.

When he returned, Jannis lifted her glass in a toast. "Isn't this just living the high life!" she enthused. "I mean, can you believe it? Here we are, playing tennis, drinking soda pop, and looking out at all this beautiful scenery — and, girls, I *do not* mean the riverbanks." With her eyes she motioned toward the tennis court. "What else could a gal want?"

Beth blushed and thought of Jarrick. She felt for the hanky holding the tucked-away petal. She did not want to participate in even a hint of behavior or attitude that she might later regret. Rising suddenly, she said, "Julie, we should go find Mother and Margret. They must be wondering where we are."

"I doubt it," countered Julie, palms upward. "When we left this morning, she just told us to enjoy ourselves."

Jannis let out a hearty guffaw. "Well, you've surely done that, sis."

For some indefinable reason, Beth found the remark irritating. "Just the same, please excuse us. We should at least check in."

Julie rose slowly. "All right then, Bethie. Forgive us, ladies — the *wet blanket* wants to take me away from all this fun."

"Keep your chin up, honey," Penny called. "We'll catch you later." She smiled at Beth, then Julie. "You'll find us somewhere around. Why, of course you will! We ain't got nowhere else to go!" The hearty laughter followed them as they made their departure.

It took time to find Mother and Margret, seated with Mrs. Montclair, Victoria, and Monsieur Laurent in a lovely atrium. They had borrowed a pair of binoculars to watch for whales while JW played happily in a corner.

"Why, look who's here at last. Enjoying ourselves, are we?" Mother seemed remarkably pleased and content.

"Yes," Julie answered for them both. "We could have stayed longer, but Bethie wanted to check on the rest of you. You seem fine to me," she grumped.

"Well, thank you for your regard for our

well-being." Mother waved a languid hand at them. "We're having a lovely morning. We've seen several whales already — one had a calf, two of them were white. Come join us, my darlings. We're taking turns with the field glasses."

She waved Emma over. "Let's have a picture. Emma, would you take it, please, now that we're all together? Come, my dears, gather round — Monsieur Laurent standing behind. Bring the baby over, Miss Bernard. Edith, Victoria, we'd like you to join us. Emma, can you get the scenery in the background? Squeeze together, everyone." After some laughter and more instructions, several pictures of the group were captured.

Beth felt an odd relief to be safely back with her family. Perhaps she wasn't used to the almost brittle vibrancy, the casual easygoing nature of their new friends, or the novelty of the surroundings. But there seemed to be something about Penny and Jannis that made her uneasy. Whatever it was, she quickly put it aside, fascinated by the magnificent fjord and its whales.

"Watch for rings of bubbles," Monsieur instructed, "that could indicate whales about to breach. See there — on the surface to the left. Who has the glasses now? Can you see the bubbles?" His gestures became more energetic. "There — right there." Oohs and ahs followed as three whales surfaced together.

"Someday," announced Victoria, "I'd like to pilot a ship like this — no, a smaller one. And go looking for whales in the ocean. That's what I'd do, just follow them through the sea."

Her unusual remark was met with chuckles all around, but Victoria appeared to have been quite serious. Margret explained, "I'm sorry, dear. A woman could never be a ship's captain. It wouldn't be allowed."

"Nonsense," Mrs. Montclair put in firmly. "There's no reason she couldn't. There's nothing particularly *manly* about steering a ship."

Mother cast an eye around the group cautiously. "What do you say, Monsieur Laurent? Do you think a woman would ever make captain?"

His answer came slowly. "I have known women who were certainly capable. In fact, I've lived in places where it's not at all uncommon for a woman to work alongside her husband on a fishing dory or a small bateau."

"But not on a great ship like this!" Mother exclaimed. "Surely, Monsieur Laurent, you don't mean to suggest she might captain such a large vessel as this?"

"What might prevent her from doing so, Mrs. Thatcher?"

Mother seemed to grope for an answer. "Well, isn't there some type of permit needed? I hardly think a woman would be given a permit. But more than that, who would be her crew? I don't suppose for a minute that men — and certainly not rough sailors — would take orders from a lady."

The man shrugged and nodded. "Perhaps that is true for now. But in years to come — who knows?"

"Why, *Mr. Lorant,* I'm so pleased to find we agree at last!" Mrs. Montclair was exuberant. "I've always told my Victoria that she may do anything she sets her mind to. After all, we have the vote now — at long last. It only follows that many of the senseless ways in which women are excluded from positions of authority and leadership will eventually be resolved as well."

"That may well be, Mrs. Montclair," he responded, "but if I may add a thought. It is true that women have been granted the right to vote in federal elections and in most of the provinces too, yet they are not formally defined as 'persons' by the government of Canada. They cannot run for office or read the law or participate in any number of roles — at least," he added, "not throughout the country." He was clearly baiting her, and Beth wondered what his motivation might be. "What have you to say about that?"

"Stuff and nonsense!" Mrs. Montclair ranted, falling easily for his apparent scheme. "In England, from whence my family came and where our name still maintains considerable influence, that manner of thinking has long ago gone the way of the Dark Ages. And if we are to believe the newspapers, such will also be the case here before long — with or without the assent of *Canadian men.* Such paragons as Queen Victoria — after whom my daughter is named — and Queen Elizabeth the Great have set fine examples of British women in power. And with their historic influence, we shall soon see that the British will insist we keep pace with such obvious wisdom."

"Do you mean, Edith, that you support the intervention of Britain's power into Canadian matters?" Mother seemed genuinely shocked.

"Whatever it takes to see justice achieved," retorted Mrs. Montclair.

Beth was not sure she appreciated Monsieur Laurent's ability to stir the pot.

"Ah, Mrs. Montclair," Monsieur continued with a smile, "you take great pride in your English heritage, I see. How ironic, then, that your name comes from the French." He hurried on before she could bluster a response. "So you feel that the ends justify the means — I see. It is an interesting conundrum, though, that you would subjugate a country in order to grant additional freedoms to a subset within it. You do not see the paradox in such a political 'gain,' Mrs. Montclair?"

"Right is right, *Mr. Lorant*! There's no sense making the matter more complex than that."

Victoria cut in suddenly, as if she had heard nothing at all of the conversation. "Yes, I will be captain of my own ship. Just wait and see. I'll ask Father for one." The awkward comment worked to silence all others. Mrs. Montclair's eyes fell in embarrassment, but she refused to rebuff her daughter.

In the afternoon, Beth alternated between reading her seafaring novel from a deck chair and playing with JW. However, promptly at naptime JW was snatched away by Miss Bernard. Margret's face fell, but she said nothing.

Julie set up her tabletop easel and dashed off the first sketch for Beth, translating Saguenay Fjord masterfully, almost effortlessly. It was pleasant to simply rest nearby and enjoy the quiet moment of creation — in the scene before them and on the painting. The colors spread across the whitewashed canvas formed the background. Patches were left where the breaching whales would take shape or where the trees would be added later. Julie could certainly find shades and tones in the sky and water that Beth missed.

Mrs. Montclair presented a new pair of binoculars to Victoria, and she now blissfully stood scanning the waters around their ship. The others continued to share the borrowed pair. It was a lovely, leisurely activity.

All too soon, Julie chose to go off alone in search of Jannis and Penny. Beth wondered if they would also try to locate the young man, Nick. She made up her mind to occasionally search out the trio — to affirm that Julie was using good judgment in her choice of activity. For the time being, at least, it seemed wise to Beth not to bother Mother with her apprehension. In fact, she found herself too relaxed at the moment to even bring up some questions she wanted to pose in the hopes of conversing with

Mother.

"Hi, everyone!" Julie's voice called before anyone had noticed her approach.

Beth looked up and gasped. "What . . . what are you wearing?"

Jannis put in, "Ain't it nifty? Don't you just love her new duds?" She and Penny grinned as Julie spun in a circle, twirling the short pleated skirt, obviously delighted with herself.

Mother's eyes swept over Julie's outfit. "Julie Camille, what on earth?"

"It's for tennis, Mother. We've been playing loads of games today, and I've gotten quite good at it. This will help me win! What do you think?"

From the top of her head to the soles of her shoes, Julie was decked out in new clothes. White leather walking shoes, silk hose, knee-length skirt, a breezy top with no sleeves at all, and a drop-waist sweater vest in pale green buttoned up the front. Around her dark curls she had wrapped a silk scarf striped in all shades of green.

Mother was incredulous. "Where did you get it all?"

"Oh, there's a store on the ship. It has lots of clothing. Isn't it perfect?"

Margret had a puzzled expression on her

face. "How did you *pay* for it, darling?"

"I signed it to the room." Somehow Julie managed to say it as if her feelings were hurt, as if doing so were an established practice which should not be questioned.

Beth noticed that Jannis was wearing identical shoes. She decided not to mention it.

Julie almost whimpered, "Is something wrong?"

Beth had her own list of issues. Mother held her response in check. "We'll discuss it later, Julie. For the time being, I think it would be best if we all retired to the room to change for dinner."

Penny and Jannis excused themselves. Beth gathered her few possessions and fell in step with her mother and sisters on the slow parade through the halls. From time to time Julie would pose her question again, "What's wrong?" But Mother marched forward in tight-lipped silence. At the last moment, it occurred to Beth that she should retreat into Margret's room and wait until whatever discussion Mother chose to engage in with Julie had blown over. There was still plenty of time to dress for dinner, and JW should soon be waking from his nap.

Margret folded, then refolded a little blanket as Beth reclined on the sofa. "Beth,"

Margret said slowly, pensively, as if she were still forming it in her mind, "how well do you know your new friends? The ones with Julie today?"

"Not well. They're from Buffalo. Julie says they're flappers."

"Hmm." Margret seemed to be struggling with what to say. "Be careful. I don't have a reason. Just a feeling. I'm sometimes wrong — and of course I would very much like to be. Nevertheless, I feel I must advise you to please be careful where those two are concerned."

Beth frowned, shook her head. "Julie won't — it's not in her nature to use caution."

"Julie is . . . well, she's passionate. She goes at things with full speed. But I know in her heart she just wants to be a good friend. I don't doubt her motives at all. However, I can't believe the same of those new girls."

Beth encircled Margret in a tight hug and felt tears begin to swell, appreciating how strongly Margret guarded them, had always watched over them both. She was certain her emotions were silly, and yet what she felt most was a deep love and respect for her older sister. Only two years separated them in age, with six between Margret and Julie. Yet Margret had always played a motherly role to them both.

Beth stood back a moment, regarding the familiar face. "You're so beautiful, Margret."

A grim chuckle. "Don't try to flatter me, Beth."

"What do you mean? I'm very serious."

Margret pressed her lips together and pushed away. "Everyone knows that you two got the beauty in the family."

It would be laughable if it weren't for Margret's serious expression, Beth thought. "How can you say that, silly? Everyone says we all look so much alike."

Her sister had gone back to fussing over the blanket again. "Yes, in the sense that we all have thick, dark hair and similar-shaped faces. But you both have *curls* — I just have frizzle. You both have bright eyes and mine are so plain, hardly any lashes at all. You both have high cheekbones and strong jawlines. I have no nice features at all. It doesn't really matter — I'm used to it. But let's not pretend."

For a moment Beth stood dumbstruck, studying her in surprise. *There's some amount of truth here. Her hair is a thick mass, always worn piled on top of her head, a style much the same as Mother's. But it is soft and frames her face with gentleness somehow.*

She's the picture of modest propriety — of goodness, even. And, yes, Margret's chin is less pronounced, but it gives her a sweetness, a softness. Beth had never suspected any of the feelings Margret was expressing. "I truly don't see you that way. I don't even know how to reply."

"You're just used to me." Margret shrugged off the conversation. "It's fine. I've made my peace with how things are long ago. And John seems perfectly satisfied with how I look." Speaking his name brought a tremulous smile to Margret's lips. "But I could never be the life of the party the way you two are. Just look — two days at sea, and you're already the center of attention. Gracious, Julie has gone and decked herself out for tennis as if she's played it all her life. Moving in that modern crowd . . . I just feel, I don't know, Beth, I just feel so terribly plain. And I'm not as bright as you either. Compared to you, Beth, I'm just a dull, slow-witted —"

"Margret, you know that isn't true," Beth interrupted firmly. "Not in the least! Why, I've always believed you are easily the *best* of us all, head and shoulders above us two. We're the *troublemakers,* the ones who upset what is supposed to be. I insisted on heading off to college, then to the other end of the country. Julie . . . well, Julie's just —"

"Don't gossip, darling. Let her speak for herself."

"You see!" Beth almost ran across the room to where Margret had retreated. "What would we do without you? Who would we be?"

"You *have* a mother. And a very good one."

Frustration was nearly overcoming Beth. "Look, Margret," she said, grasping her by the arms, "I know you're beautiful — not just your spirit and your loving heart, but your face and everything you are. I said so a moment ago because I was overwhelmed by that very thought, how radiantly beautiful you are. I'm so sorry that's not what you believe, but you simply can't sway my opinion. I know the truth, that's all I can say."

Bashfully Margret whispered, "Now you sound like John."

"Well, I should hope so! And what's more, I *need* you in my life." This time tears filled her eyes. "Sister darling, I've been away for almost a year. Trust me when I say that I know what it is to miss you, and I've suffered because of it."

Margret was softening. Beth reached out

again and this time the embrace was returned.

"It's so silly," Margret said as she wiped
at her eyes. "I don't know why I've been
having such thoughts. I suppose being away
from home has made me terribly moody. I
haven't felt quite right for days. And all this
tension with the baby seems at times to be
more than I can bear." She dropped her eyes
again. "I'm afraid the truth is, I just want to
go home."

Beth laughed. "I surely know that feeling!
I felt it so often when I was away. But I
guarantee something to you, Margret. Trust
me, because this time *I'm* the experienced
one. The time is going to rush past, and
then we'll all wish we could do this trip over
again — though perhaps we'd bring John
along next time."

"Yes, that would change everything for
me. But, Beth, aren't you missing someone
too?" Margret had found her smile again at
last.

Beth flushed. "Of course."

"Come on then. Go dress for supper."
Margret straightened and drew her shoulders back. "We shall make the best of it —
you and I. We shall enjoy our blessings
rather than chafe against them."

"Yes, let's."

"And together we'll keep an eye on Julie, our darling little socialite."

"Well, we shall certainly try."

CHAPTER 8

The evening meal on board was a splendid experience. Though her appetite had greatly improved along with her health over the last day, Beth could not keep up with the rich dishes served course after course — shrimp cocktail in tall stemmed glasses, jellied tomato-cream bouillon on thin salty wafers, Waldorf salad, mushrooms stuffed with delicate crab filling alongside buttery steamed lobster tails, tender lamb medallions and roast potatoes au jus with a serving of asparagus tips au gratin, and a dessert of raspberry mousse dolloped with fresh whipped cream and drizzled with chocolate sauce.

"It's enough to feed a whole crew," Margret gasped as her lobster — almost untouched — was whisked away in exchange for the next course.

Monsieur Laurent smiled. "You can be certain, Mrs. Bryce, that it is nothing close to what will be served to the staff."

Julie, it turned out, was in a rather dour mood. As the main course was set before her, she complained, "I wish Jannis and Penny could dine with us. I can't imagine what they're eating in their drab little dining room — probably the same as the crew."

Mother's spoon rattled against her teacup as she stirred rapidly. "I assume they're eating precisely what they have paid to eat."

"Well, it isn't fair. Why should we have so much when others have so little?"

Beth blinked hard. *How can such a question be answered? Are Julie's friends who are also enjoying the pleasures of a cruise truly worthy of my sister's pity for not also experiencing the . . . the extravagances Father is able to provide for our family?*

First came a long sigh, and then Mother responded evenly, "I'm very pleased to hear you voice this concern, Julie dear. I'm certain we can put your benevolence to work once we return home. There is always room for one more at our ladies' charity meetings at church. I believe that the poor in our area will greatly benefit from your deep concern for them."

"You know what I mean, Mother."

"Yes, Julie. I'm afraid I do." She cast a warning glance at her daughter. Julie surrendered and started poking at her lamb.

"This is a lovely meal," Mrs. Montclair announced, "though not quite as nice as what we ate last night. I wish you had been well enough to enjoy it, Elizabeth. The striped bass was excellent, and I do love spring peas. I'm told that tomorrow we shall be served duck. I don't mind telling you that I'd just as soon miss that meal. Duck has never been my favorite —"

"Mother," Victoria interrupted, "are you going to eat the rest of your potatoes?" Already the girl's fork was hovering over her mother's plate. Mrs. Montclair seemed not to notice and continued talking as one by one the bite-sized pieces were whisked into her daughter's mouth.

"I had a discussion with some of the other passengers after lunch," Mrs. Montclair sailed on with her soliloquy. "Several of them have traveled on other lines as well, and they said that ours compares quite favorably with the CP ships — the Empresses. Ours is not as large, to be sure, but it is nicely appointed. What do you say, *Mr. Lorant*? Surely you have traveled on a Canadian Pacific ship."

"Why, yes, I have. I've gone both to the Orient and Europe aboard that line. I found them quite satisfactory."

131

"You know what they say," Mrs. Mont-clair added in a sing-song voice, " 'See this world before the next.' " She laughed as if she had come up with the slogan herself.

"Yes, I've seen that in the brochure," he responded. "I wonder, madame, how is it that you didn't select a CP cruise?"

"Of course that would have been my first choice. But, well, you know my husband, Charles — so dreadfully frugal. We were interested in a round-the-world cruise, but he put that idea aside very quickly, let me assure you. And yet I'm not dissuaded. I have every confidence that Victoria and I shall take a longer journey soon, and per-haps if we play our cards correctly, my son Edward and his new wife might be able to join us." The woman looked meaningfully at Beth.

"Won't that be lovely, Edith," Mother said. "Have they set a date for their wed-ding?"

"Oh, he isn't one to let the grass grow beneath him. I should think it would be very soon — perhaps even yet this fall."

Beth turned toward their guide. "What does tomorrow bring, monsieur?"

"We shall disembark at Tadoussac in the morning," he answered, no doubt just as pleased as Beth to change the subject.

"Tadoussac? I'm not sure I've heard of that before. Is that a town?"

"Yes, Miss Thatcher, one of the oldest ports on the St. Lawrence, mostly involved today with tourism. Many wealthy *Québécois* have built summer homes in the area, though the town has not grown much."

"But will there be shopping?" Mrs. Montclair asked, her head quickly coming around.

"Why, yes. There are many items to be purchased. But for those who come to explore this part of Canada, there are also delightful trails, a beautiful hotel, and a very old wooden chapel built in the seventeen hundreds — not to mention that one can often see whales even from land."

The thought of a hike, or even just a walk, on solid ground sounded wonderful to Beth. Then she had a sudden inspiration. "Could we bring Emma along, Mother? I'm sure she'd like to stretch her legs, and she could take photographs of us so that Father could appreciate this excursion too when we're home again."

"That's a very good idea, darling. Yes, I'll ask Emma to come along. And what shall we do about our sweet little boy, Margret? Shall we bring him too?"

Margret stiffened. "Of course. I'd like him

with us whenever it's suitable."

"Are you going to ask Miss Bernard if she feels it is apropos?"

This time it was Margret's turn to force a careful tone. "I will inform Miss Bernard of my intentions, yes."

Mrs. Montclair interjected, "Be careful, Margret dear. You don't want to lose your nanny for sheer stubbornness' sake. She would be painfully difficult to replace."

Margret's face turned ashen.

Beth smiled uncomfortably at Monsieur Laurent. However, he did not seem distressed by the turbulent undercurrents on display during the evening meal. *Perhaps his even temper is one reason he once was an ambassador,* she mused. How wise Father had been to select a diplomat. Their little group certainly seemed to need one.

"Julie, are you going to add some color to the sketch tonight?"

They were exchanging their gowns for more comfortable garb. "I don't think so right now. Maybe in the morning."

"But what if you forget how it looked, the colors and lighting and —"

"I won't forget." Julie brushed aside Beth's worries with a tap on her forehead. "It's all up here."

"Julie!"

"Don't worry. Somehow I do remember. Besides, I made arrangements to go to the lounge with Margret. She said she'd come along this time. But I'll be back soon enough." And without further explanation she was gone.

Beth pulled on a warm jacket, gathered up an afghan and her book, and headed out on deck to read. Only one or two passengers walked past. Beth was certain some solace away from the others was just what she needed — and a book provided an acceptable excuse. It was a perfect place to read, particularly Father's novel about the young sailor.

"What are you reading, Beth?" a male voice asked out of the quiet.

She had been so absorbed in the novel, the question caught her off guard. She peered into the darkness just beyond the circle of deck light where she had placed her chair. "*Redburn* — by Melville." She shielded her eyes and squinted to see who it was that knew her name.

Nick stepped into the light, hands in his pockets. He was still wearing a dinner jacket, though his bow tie dangled loosely. "Remember me?"

Beth cleared her throat. "Of course. We

watched you play tennis earlier."

"Can I sit down?" He was already drawing a second deck chair over and sat on the front edge of it, arms resting on his knees.

Beth closed her book and modestly drew her feet off her footrest. "I thought you claimed you were poor with names."

"Gosh, I am — but we *have* already met twice."

"Hmm," Beth murmured.

"I like reading too," he said quickly. "But I haven't had the guts to take on much Melville. He's a little preachy and wordy, in my opinion. I've read *Moby-Dick,* of course — at least some of it. And that was plenty for me."

Another reader, even if it's this strangely forward young man. "So whom do you prefer?"

He laughed. "Well, I guess my tastes run pretty straight, what you'd expect from a fellow like me — Jack London, Jules Verne, H. G. Wells. Nothing surprising. I *do* like adventure. I don't like much else. What's happening in your story?"

Beth looked down at the book in her lap. "*Redburn,* the main character and an American, has arrived in Liverpool. And though he has always viewed Europe as superior in every way, he discovers great poverty and suffering."

"And he's surprised at that?"

A smile. "Well, so far he's mostly taking it all in."

"Now, that sounds like ol' Herman. And of course that alone can go on for chapters — and in great detail."

"I don't mind." Beth shook her head. "I like a quieter, more thoughtful story. Some of the modern authors don't slow down long enough for the reader to contemplate what's happening — it's all action. And then it's over far too quickly for me."

"Then Melville's your man."

There was a long, awkward pause. He stood slowly, and Beth looked up at him. "I wanted to ask you a little more about yourself, Beth," he said, "but to be honest, I don't feel right asking while we're alone here. Can I share a soda with you tomorrow when we're all in town? You and your sister maybe?"

Beth felt a flutter inside. *How should I answer this young man, Lord?* "I'll be out and about in Tadoussac tomorrow with my family. It would be fine to share tea with you — or a soda if you prefer — but . . ."

"Yes?"

"I don't want to appear presumptuous, Nick. However I feel I should mention that

I'm already keeping company with some-one."

"Of course." He smiled but with a tinge of disappointment. "I should've guessed." He started to move away, then turned back. "Just the same, I'd like to get to know all of you anyway — if that's all right. We'll be traveling together for a while, and it would be nice to have some friends on board."

"Of course!" Beth offered a warm smile.

"Good night, Beth. See you tomorrow."

"Good night, Nick." *He seems a nice enough young man. Though a bit of a chame-leon — much less bold in his approach just now than he was earlier in the day or back in the scarf shop. Perhaps he would be a good prospect for Julie.* Hardly aware of it, Beth reached to uncover the day's rose petal from the folds of her hankie. It had already begun to crumble. She lifted it up so she could smell the faint fragrance. "Jarrick," she whispered, "I wish you were here." It would not be the last time she so longed for his presence.

"If she makes us late this morning, girls, we shall leave without her." Mother was put-ting her foot down where Mrs. Montclair was concerned. They were standing in a long line of passengers waiting to be ferried to the mainland. A small tender had drawn up to the side of their ship and a large door through the hull allowed transfer onto it. Beth and Julie nodded in support of her announcement.

"Monsieur Laurent has taken an earlier shuttle in order to secure a reservation for our lunch," Mother continued. "He intends to meet us at the dock, so if we miss this tender —"

"We'll make it onto this one, Mother," Margret assured her. "And the Montclairs can simply catch up to us at their leisure. All they want to do is shop anyway."

"Oh, not Victoria," Julie put in. "She's ready to hike all over those rocks. She was fairly pacing in anticipation after breakfast."

At the last moment, Mrs. Montclair bustled up and pushed her way in line to join the Thatchers. Victoria followed along, the new binoculars around her neck.

Miss Bernard had chosen not to join them for the outing. Beth wondered if it might be an attempt at showing her angst at Margret's decision to take JW along. *What does the nanny expect?* she thought as she took her place in the small craft. *After all, it's a vacation, and he's no longer truly a baby. An active little boy can benefit from the outdoors with his mother and the rest of us.*

Tendering to shore was windy and rough. Beth clutched at her hat with one hand and her stomach with the other. She sighed gratefully when the boat slid up next to the dock. Monsieur Laurent, true to his word, was waiting among the crowd. As soon as JW spotted his new friend, he clapped his hands together and reached out his arms.

The man scooped him up, tossing him in the air. "Bonjour, *mon petit ami.* Can you say 'monsieur' this morning, eh? Monsieur?"

"Mis-yur," JW giggled. "Mis-yur."

"Good boy!" He drew his straw skimmer hat from his head and swung the boy onto his shoulders. Far above the crowd, JW held on with large handfuls of gray hair, seeming thrilled to be up so high and with another grandfatherly figure. They set out toward the little town.

The gravel road held deep, muddy ruts. Beth chose her steps carefully, hanging tightly to Emma's arm. They laughed together at their awkward attempts to climb a small, slippery rise. Fortunately they soon had reached the wooden walkways of town.

Falling back into stride beside Beth, Monsieur Laurent eyed her mysteriously. "Miss Thatcher," he said in a low voice, "I have something for you. Something I believe you are waiting for. You see, your father instructed me to check for mail whenever we stop, and this was waiting for us this morning, addressed to you." He withdrew from his shirt pocket a white envelope with Beth's name and address carefully written across it, in a man's hand.

Beth's heart was already racing as she reached for it. She cast a wistful look around, then down at the letter — the very first. What she wanted most was to get away to enjoy whatever Jarrick might be saying.

"Miss Beth," the man continued softly, "we have planned to do some exploring this morning. There is a lovely promontory not far from here. We'll go there first and take some time to look around. I believe it would be the ideal location for you to slip away . . ."

"Thank you, monsieur! Thank you." She tucked the letter safely away in her handbag.

He strode to the front of their group, announcing, "If you please, ladies, we will let the others see the hotel and shops first. We can avoid most of the crowds if we begin with our walk. This way, everyone. Please."

He led them across the crowd of tourists, up a small rise, and toward a trail into the woods. Beth's thoughts were held captive by the envelope in her bag. She patiently endured the obligatory photographs taken at the rock outcropping. At last she saw her chance, with a nod from Monsieur Laurent confirming it. Beth slipped farther up the path and found a large rock on which to sit. Then she tore open the letter, her heart already full as she read the first line. In his handwriting, it seemed far more than a simple salutation.

My dear Beth,
 Hearing your voice tonight on the telephone was like music to my ears.

She couldn't help but smile, pleased that he had written immediately after they had spoken together on the telephone.

Although it's been just over a week since you left, I feel your absence every day in so many ways. I'm staying tonight with friends in Lethbridge. The same couple with whom you stayed when we brought little Willie into town. They didn't seem surprised when I told them that over the summer I'd be pursuing a relationship with you. In fact, various people here have mentioned to me what a fool I'd be if I lost touch with you. Most notably, Miss Molly. I find myself agreeing with them!

At any rate, I passed by our restaurant earlier today, and, well, I'll go ahead and admit to you that I will stop there as soon as it opens tomorrow to make a reservation for the fall. I don't really mind if they tell me I'm being ridiculous. I liked the sound of already planning our first true date when you mentioned it during our telephone call tonight.

Beth pressed a cool hand against her cheek. *Such a romantic gesture!* She tried to picture Jarrick, serious and a bit daunting in his uniform, insisting that the receptionist at least make a note of his intentions. Her eyes closed as she enjoyed the scene.

And then the nagging question, *What if a life with Jarrick isn't truly God's will?* Beth pushed the question away.

I saw Phillip, who sends his blessings . . . been very busy with a new congregation . . . planning a dinner soon with Edward . . . will pass along news of Kate . . . sad news from Coal Valley — Mrs. Grant attempted suicide . . . all are grieving for her situation . . . recovering in hospital but unlikely to return.

Beth was horrified at the words. Poor,

crotchety, old Mrs. Grant — wounded by the scandal her husband had created, surrounded by those who would befriend her, and yet living so utterly alone.

Beth turned the letter over, where Jarrick continued on the back.

. . . talk of what to do with the Grants' building . . . Miss Molly immediately suggested a school . . . no plans set . . . children well . . . happy news! . . . pensions extended . . . no families moving yet . . . empty lot has been plowed up and is ready to plant for a community garden . . . miners included in project . . . the men are commonly seen and accepted now in town.

Beth was thrilled at such a wonderful account of the good changes in her beloved little village and the many faces it called to mind.

Since I'm nearing the end of the page, I should probably close. I don't know where you'll be when you receive this letter. I suppose somewhere on the St. Lawrence still. I'm praying that you'll have a wonderful and very memorable time with your mother and sisters. I wish

I could be there to meet them all. I can only imagine that they're all beautiful and lovely women, just like you, Beth. Well, maybe almost as lovely.

With warmest affection,

Jarrick

Beth laid the letter on her lap and tilted her head so she could see through the cluster of tall evergreens to the clear sky far above. She took a slow breath and closed her eyes once more. She would prefer to remain alone here with Jarrick's letter. Or, better still, travel back to when he wrote the letter, sit beside him, and watch his face as he so carefully penned the words. Beth finally drew her handkerchief with its rose petal from her waistband, tipped the crumbled petal into the envelope, and raised the letter to read through slowly once more.

CHAPTER 9

"I'd like to take the next shuttle back to the ship," Mrs. Montclair announced as they finished their lunch. Monsieur had found a lovely spot with a round table shaded by a large umbrella. "I've seen as much as I'd like here in town, and the views of the countryside are just as nice from on board."

"I want to stay," countered Victoria.

Her mother peered over the rim of her glasses. "Then it would fall on you to ask the Thatchers if they're willing to let you remain with them."

Victoria stole a glance at Beth and then Margret.

"Is there anything left to be seen, monsieur?" Mother seemed ready to follow Mrs. Montclair back to the ship.

He was counting out the money for their meal. "*Mais oui* — there are several other trails and a very nice tea house," he responded. "The beach is also quite a comfortable location for watching the wildlife in the water."

Beth wasn't anxious to return to the ship just yet, and perhaps it would be a chance to build a relationship with the girl. "I'll stay with you, Victoria. I'm more than happy to walk the trails — wherever you'd like to go."

Margret sighed. "I must take JW back for his nap. No doubt Miss Bernard is waiting for him, and I feel a nap would suit me as well. JW, let's go back to the big boat —"

"Uh-uh. No, no!" He shook his head for emphasis and reached for their guide. "Mis-yur," he pleaded. "Mis-yur."

The man shot to his feet. "I shall be pleased to carry him to the shuttle for you, Mrs. Bryce, as I have no other pressing tasks."

"Why, thank you. That would be a great help."

"I will accompany you also, Margret. A nap sounds rather inviting," Mother said. "Emma, I believe we shall need your assistance. Please carry some of these extra bags. Julie, we'll bring what you've purchased back to the room, and you may stay with Beth and Victoria. Monsieur Laurent, would you provide the girls with a little money for a treat later?"

"Thank you, Mother." Julie pressed a kiss on Mother's cheek, and Beth was pleased they seemed to have made up after their difficulties the previous day. Their guide drew some coins from his pocket and placed them in Julie's hand.

Mrs. Montclair caught her young daughter's arm. "Now, Victoria, look at me, please. I want you to cooperate with Elizabeth and Julie. And I insist you wear your hat. We don't want your skin all dried out and brown by the time we return home." She shook the arm a little for emphasis. "I'm quite serious, my dear. You'll be grateful later that I've insisted you listen to me. You'll never find a husband if you look old before your time."

Victoria was already pointing along the shoreline. "I want to go back to where we saw the shorebirds. I think I could identify additional species if I had more time. I'm beginning to know their calls." Without waiting for a reply, she began marching away.

Beth and Julie spent the next few hours keeping up with Victoria. In this natural setting she seemed to have come alive — absorbing the splendor, sketching from time to time in a pocket notebook tucked into her waistband. Her shoes and stockings took the brunt of her explorations, growing damp and stained. Yet here was another passion besides the violin that Beth shared with this girl. She was, in fact, rather pleased to wander along behind the teenager, though Julie complained a little.

"My goodness, can't we stay a little longer at each site! I wish I could stop and sketch a while. Say, Bethie, why didn't you bring a canvas?"

"Would you have wanted that? Here?"

"Naturally it would be easier. But never mind, I'll just sketch instead. I have a notebook in my handbag."

"You should have told me. You know that I'd like to see you working on them."

"Well, how did I know we'd be toddling after Victoria all afternoon?" Julie's voice was rising. "I expected to be back on ship with my supplies. Didn't I?"

"It's fine, Julie. There's plenty of time. But we should try to keep current as we go in order to get the paintings done."

"That's fine for you to say, Bethie." A frustrated roll of her eyes, then, "Are you going to be pestering me about this the *whole* trip? I've other things I'd like to do as well, you know. If you want the paintings done, you'll have to take responsibility. And keep in mind that once we turn south to the East Coast, I may not even have time."

"You won't? But you promised. What would you be doing instead?"

"Sightseeing, shopping — *enjoying myself.*"

Beth paused, shocked at first by Julie's terse words. *It is a big favor I'm asking, after all. I didn't consult with Julie about painting for me before I bought the canvases.* Beth softened. "I should have talked with you before assuming you'd do the work, Julie, and I'm very sorry. Would you forgive me?" At Julie's nod, smile, and a little shrug, Beth continued, "What if we agree to this — that you paint only the Canadian parts of our trip. I don't really need the American ports to accomplish my teaching goals. Would you be willing to work on those few? It's such a gift to me, and I would be very grateful."

Julie laughed and shook her head. "I suppose I could commit to that much. But if I ever get famous, you'll have to promise not to sell them. Landscapes are not what I want to be known for — not my vision for a career at all."

They smiled at each other, relieved that things were back to normal between them. Beth said, "Of course. Anyway, I promise not to sell them *while you're still alive.*"

"What? What did you say?" Julie's eyes

150

had grown large, and Beth just grinned. At last she had managed to startle her sister, instead of the other way around.

By midafternoon, all three were ready for something to drink and a shady place to rest. Julie led them back down near the shore to find a vendor and some chairs.

"Hi, ya!" a voice called from across the crowded beach.

"It's Jannis!" Julie's sheer delight rang through her voice as she skipped away from Beth and Victoria. "Ahoy, Jannis! What're you doing, girls?"

"Ahoy-dee-hoo to you too!" The two giggled at their shared joke. "Well, we came down here where all these people are watching for whales, but instead we're watching people. Let me tell you, it's been loads of fun!"

Leaning against each other in order to whisper together, Julie and Jannis maneuvered through the crowd toward a table, where Penny waited under a wide umbrella. Victoria and Beth followed.

"Where've you been, doll? You look like something the cat dragged in." Penny looked Julie up and down. "Your hair's a mess. And, oh, Julie, your shoes!"

"I know, I know." She pushed a hand under her hat, attempting to straighten the windblown strands. "We've been tracking through the woods." Julie nodded toward Victoria, and Jannis and Penny nodded knowingly.

"Well, you're here now. So take a load off."

Ordering sodas and a plate of chouquettes, they settled in at the table. Victoria was more than willing to enjoy the snack. She took the binoculars from around her neck and set them carefully on the table, drew her feet up under her, and tucked her face into the notebook, periodically making new notations.

"Nice spyglasses," Jannis interrupted her brooding. "May I?"

"If you like," answered Victoria. "But the best birds are near the cliffs."

"Oh, honey, I'm not watching birds — just a flock of pigeons." This was met with laughter from Penny and Julie. Jannis lifted the lenses to her eyes and scanned across the crowd. "Golly, I can see everything with these. I can even read that man's book all the way from here. I gotta get me a pair of these."

Penny grabbed at the strap. "Let me see."

"Please be careful," Victoria objected. "That's a delicate instrument."

"Ain't hurting anything, honey. We're just giving things a look." Jannis raised the binoculars out of Penny's reach.

Victoria stood, her hand thrust over the table. "Give them back! Please!"

Penny dropped her hold on the strap, but Jannis merely moved the binoculars a little further away. "In a minute. I'm almost done."

Exchanging a glance with Julie, who merely watched idly, Beth sat forward and cleared her throat. "Jannis, the binoculars belong to Victoria. If she wants them back, please give them to her."

"Who died and put you in charge?" Jannis shot at Beth.

But Penny intervened. "Come on, Jan. If she wants them back, they're hers anyway."

The two eyed each other for a brief moment, some form of silent communication clearly taking place. Then Jannis shrugged and set the binoculars back on the table. "Suit yourself, little missy," she said crossly. "I'd be sharing if they were mine."

Victoria hung them around her neck and went back to her previous activity as if nothing had occurred. A heavy silence fell over the table.

"I'm sorry, Beth," Jannis admitted at last. "I know I should've gave them right back. It's just that I never even held a pair like that, and I wanted to get a better look at the ship from here. But I shouldn't have made such a fuss about it." The previous cross expression had been entirely replaced by a cajoling sweetness.

Beth was reminded of Julie's coaxing looks, honed to perfection since she was a little girl. She couldn't help but soften. "Well, Victoria doesn't seem upset, so there's certainly no need for me to be."

"Friends again?" Jannis asked with a perky grin.

"Why, of course."

When the girls finally returned to the ship, there was little time to change for dinner. Beth hurried along the corridors, Julie and Victoria in tow. It had been a rather nice afternoon after all. Beth briefly wondered why Nick had not appeared for their tea-time. She had decided not to say anything to Julie, but instead wait and see what might turn up. Now she was glad that she had said nothing.

Beth actually was tempted to make excuses and skip dinner altogether, have a quiet evening, and write back to Jarrick. Instead, she dutifully followed the rest to the dining hall and joined in with the conversation as best she could. When at last she was back in the room, she changed out of her more formal attire, gathered what she needed, including Jarrick's letter, and stole out through the long halls.

Being on deck would not work this evening. Beth needed a table and preferred not to be disturbed. She walked quickly past the noise coming out of the lounge, choosing a quiet corner in a little tea shop. She ordered a cup and sipped for a time, pulling together her thoughts. She picked up her pen and dipped the end of it into a small jar of ink, tapping it absent-mindedly against the rim for a while.

My dear Jarrick, she began, her hand trembling a little as she penned the words. They seemed so personal — so intimate. But Jarrick had already used the same greeting, so she pressed on.

We spent a lovely time today at Tadoussac, Quebec. Whales nearby in the fjord and wildlife abounding onshore were wonderful to see. In truth, it was a blessed thing for me to set my feet firmly back on land. I'll admit to you that I have experienced some seasickness on our journey, so I appreciated every single step I took today on terra firma.

The location is utterly breathtaking, right at the confluence of Saguenay

Fjord with the St. Lawrence River. And the town was delightful, so accommodating to us all. Yet it was the sense of history that I enjoyed most, the very age of the locale. Older than the fur trade, the voyageurs, and the earliest missionaries who built the little wooden chapel there. Older than the people who inhabited the forests long before the Europeans came. I amused myself by envisioning generation upon generation of whales gathering in the nearby waters in order to study how the strange land creatures, walking upright on two legs, were getting along through the many decades. As if the marine behemoths had come closer to observe mankind — the opposite of what we did today! I must say that I enjoyed it all very much.

Julie has agreed to paint some landscapes to share with the children as I teach Canadian geography. I also purchased a set of carved wooden whales, a mother and calf, which I hope to use when telling my schoolchildren about the majestic creatures. I do hope to be able to find words to describe the grace and elegance — despite its size — of a breaching whale.

So it was in this setting that I read your

letter while seated on a large rock in the forest. I'll admit that part of the reason for this was to find seclusion from my family, but it ended up as an ideal location. It was almost as if I were back in a corner of Coal Valley, minus the view of the Rocky Mountains. I could almost picture us there together.

Two elderly women looked in the door at her before continuing on their way. After smiling at them, Beth dipped the pen again.

I was so pleased to hear that none of the mothers will have to move away in the near future, that a community garden will be planted, and that there's already talk of a school in the fall. This has been a continuing matter of prayer for me. But I was utterly shocked by the sad story regarding Mrs. Grant. I certainly pray that she'll find peace of mind and an improved situation. Is there further news of Mr. Grant's trial? I do hope justice is served in his case, with our heavenly Father presiding as his true Judge. And yet, our Savior is willing to be his genuine Advocate still, should he only repent.

She paused, tapping on the edge of the jar

once again while sorting her thoughts.

It has been a joy traveling with my family and our friends, the Montclairs, and yet there are a myriad of minor complaints that occasionally surface. I suppose that's unavoidable when sharing tight quarters and many hours of "togetherness." The bright spot is that we've also made some new friends on board. A pair of sisters about our ages are traveling too. For Julie who, as you well know, enjoys a much livelier pace of activity than the rest of us, this has been great fun. My sister has become quite a tennis enthusiast already (there is a court for this on board), and she knows every other corner of the ship by now, I'm certain. There is a small group of other young people traveling too, though most of the passengers are of Mother's generation or older.

Beth hesitated, wondering if she should mention Nick at all, then decided it would never do to hold this back from Jarrick if she were contemplating a life with him. She added,

We met a young American named

Nick in Quebec City and were surprised to find him also on our ship. I discovered that he and I share an interest in reading, but I'm certain he isn't spending time in that pursuit while on board.

Already Beth was nearing the end of the second side of the page. Since she felt it was unnecessary to begin another, she would bring her letter to a close. She had saved what she thought was the best until last.

I have enjoyed the thought of you returning to our restaurant to make a reservation. I do hope that the idea was well received. The very image in my mind is a source of pleasure to me, to be sure. So much so that I've already begun to plan what I shall wear that evening. And, in the same sentiment, I decided to share with you that each day I carry along one of the petals from your roses which I saved in a handkerchief. They serve as a countdown of sorts until I shall see you again.

Again she debated with herself. *Jarrick closed his letter* "with warmest affection." *What would be a proper response to that?*

Once on the paper in ink, she would have no way of changing it.

Truly yours, Beth, she wrote. It was less than she wanted to offer — words she had written on most of her letters to friends. But propriety demanded restraint, for now, she determined as she waited for the ink to dry.

A man, perhaps, can risk being more forthcoming, but a young woman must guard her words carefully, she concluded, then gently folded the letter.

CHAPTER 10

Beth was on deck early enough to watch the sun climbing up over the river, the spreading glow giving way to a single bright ray, followed by a narrow band of brilliant yellow. She took a position near the prow and studied the ship slicing its way through each small wave, grateful that her body now had grown accustomed to the movement.

When she noticed other passengers appearing, she delivered her letter to the correct shipboard office and was told that it would go into the mailbag that morning for transport to shore. Pleased, she went to their usual deck space where her family had rented numbered deck chairs. While waiting, she leaned against the damp rail and breathed in the cool morning air.

This would be a day spent entirely on board as the ship made its slow course eastward. *Julie will surely have time to paint today.* Beth watched for things she would like to see included in the landscape — a fishing village and lumber mills, here and there a road appearing among the trees onshore, small boats and large ships gliding along in the distance. She hoped also to see more wildlife — perhaps with the help of Victoria's field glasses.

Father had said his ship would pass theirs at some point during the day. Beth scanned around carefully, wishing she knew what time that was likely.

"Hello, little miss early-riser." Beth turned to discover Mrs. Montclair joining her at the rail.

"Good morning. I hope you slept well," she answered cordially.

"Well, yes — or I would have but for Victoria and her everlasting violin. She's up early, like you, I see. I tell you, Elizabeth, be grateful that the walls aren't thin, that the hum of the engines drowns out her racket somewhat."

Beth nodded agreeably and smiled. There seemed to be no point in protesting her ill-advised description. She was reminded of how lovely it would be to play Victoria's violin soon.

"Is there time for a lap or two around the top deck before breakfast?" Margret asked as she walked out into the sunshine with

JW. Beth held out her arms for the grinning boy, and he snuggled his head into her neck.

"Oh, Margret, that feels so good," she whispered, and they exchanged appreciative smiles.

When Mother joined them, they climbed the nearby stairs, emerging in procession onto the uppermost deck. The rising sun already promised a day both splendid and warm.

Mother cast a glance over her shoulder. "What shall we do with such a marvelous morning?"

Julie's suggestion came quickly. "There are games on deck later — near the tennis courts."

"I don't play tennis," Victoria asserted.

"Oh, that's just *where* they're playing. I've heard that the games will be designed to give everyone a pleasurable activity. I'm certain we'd all find something to enjoy, or even just watch."

"Of course, dear," Mother said. "But this is a *family* vacation. Can't we find something we can all enjoy together?"

"We haven't had a swim yet. I'm sure JW would enjoy the water," Margret proposed.

Beth agreed. "That sounds fun."

But Mother hedged. "I don't know about swimming here on ship. It's a different situation at the beach. . . . But I'm afraid I'd feel quite uncomfortable with it today — all those deck chairs pointed inward toward the pool, passengers watching."

"But we were just *at* a beach, Mother!" Julie's face said more than her words. "We should have gone swimming *then.*"

Mrs. Montclair offered, "I read there's to be a sing-along in the theater this morning. We all enjoy music. The tunes will be old favorites we're sure to know. That sounds delightful, doesn't it, Victoria?"

"Oh, yes, Mother."

Julie muttered, "Well, that's the end of it then. A dowdy sing-along with dowdy old songs."

Beth tried to encourage her quietly. "We don't have to do *everything* together. After all, we are adults. We're fine to make our own decisions where our personal interests are concerned. But let's go along with the music first. We want Mother to fully enjoy the trip, of course. But afterward she'll probably want to just sit on deck for a time — and then we can putter about on our own. Julie, you can go join the games, and Margret, you and I can take JW for a quick swim before his nap. He probably won't want to stay long anyway."

"Yes, that does sound fine," Margret

agreed. "And once he's down for his nap, we can go watch the games — cheer for our Julie."

Even Julie seemed to find it a satisfactory solution. True to Beth's supposition, after the concert, Mother and Mrs. Montclair were content to find a sunny location in which to recline and read for a while under umbrellas.

"Are all these Julie's friends?" Margret stared wide-eyed at the array of young people. The noise and laughter had reached them long before they arrived at the recreation deck. And there was their sister in the center of it all, laughing in obvious delight at the attention and throwing a ball to a young man who was trying to catch it beneath his chin, his hands apparently tied behind his back.

"At any rate, Margret, it certainly doesn't look like she minds," Beth said, not knowing whether to be alarmed or pleased that Julie had found the fun she was looking for. "And she does know the man with whom she's teamed."

"Turn around, Nick!" the crowd shouted. "Catch it on your back!"

It seemed that so long as he did not use his hands, and no words would pass between

165

the two teammates, winning was achieved by catching and holding the ball by any means possible. A second two-person team had already switched tactics and were trying to get their ball to land between the receiver's shoulder blades without rolling off. The spectators pressed forward at each attempt. Beth laughed and clutched at Margret's arm, also caught up in the competition.

And then Julie made a dramatic motion. Nick must have understood her sign language, and he dropped to a sitting position on the deck, an awkward maneuver with his hands still tied. But with a single toss Julie dropped the ball squarely into his lap, his knees quickly rising to trap and keep it there.

All around them applause erupted, and voices began to chant Julie's name in unison. It seemed their sister had devised the winning strategy. Beth and Margret joined in the ovation while Julie's face fairly glowed, obviously pleased. Nick struggled to rise, which brought more laughter. After he was untied, he stood next to Julie and accepted a small plastic trophy. With a flourish he passed it to Julie, who held it high after a theatrical curtsy. Beth watched in awe at the grace and charisma that Julie displayed as she carried the prize toward a red cloth spread across a table and set it with the collection. The blue cloth next to theirs carried only three trophies. So it appeared Julie's team was winning the competition.

Over the noise Beth said into Margret's ear, "I think maybe they're *all* friends of Julie's." Margret shook her head in wonder.

They waved for Julie's attention. At last she saw them and hurried over. "We won!"

"We saw you. That was brilliant. Good for you."

Julie was still out of breath. "I told you they were silly games. But we're having such a good time. Come join us. You can be on our team."

"Oh, we'll just find a seat and watch. But you go on — win some more trophies!"

In a moment Nick appeared by Julie's side, his hand patting her shoulder good-naturedly, letting it rest there. "Hello, Beth. Isn't your sister just the berries? Hey — I'm sorry I stood you up at that last little town. Something came up that I had to take care of." Before Beth could respond, he grinned at Margret and said, "And who's this, may I ask?"

Beth stepped back. "This is our older sister, Margret."

"Pleased to meet you. You gals sure look alike — beauties, all three of you." Margret blushed and looked down, Beth noticed. "You two gonna join us?"

"Oh, no." Margret blushed more deeply. "Julie's the outgoing one. We'll just watch."

"Suit yourselves," he said, then smiled broadly again and squeezed Julie's shoulder. "Come on, doll. Let's see what's next." As they walked away, Beth noticed Nick place his hand against Julie's back, guiding her through the crowd. She frowned, uncomfortable with the casual familiarity.

Margret whispered, "He seems nice."

"Um-hmm," Beth murmured, still uncertain.

A wheelbarrow race was next. Two men from each team waddled across the deck to much laughter, one walking on his hands with his feet tucked into the crook of the other's arms. There were several falls, to the further amusement of the spectators. The first team — Julie's — crossed the finish line first to even wilder cheers. The new trophy was awarded, and the director called for everyone's attention to explain the next event.

Margret leaned close to Beth. "I'm sorry, but I just can't seem to keep my eyes open. Do you mind terribly if we head back to the room? I think I'd like to take a quick nap while JW is still down for his. That is, if he hasn't already awakened." Seeing Beth hesitate, she added, "You don't need to come back with me, darling. You can stay if you'd like. Yes, why don't you stay?"

"No, I'll come along. I don't want to stay here alone."

Beth somewhat reluctantly followed Margret through the corridors, her mind still troubled by what she had seen of Julie and Nick. She wondered if perhaps they had been spending more time together than Beth realized — if they were becoming a little too familiar.

Oh, Julie, don't be reckless, she begged silently, and then turned it into a prayer.

Julie was joy personified at dinner, sitting in her chair like a celebrity with her royal blue gown turning her all the more regal. Her sparkling wit and effervescent personality were now on display for all — teasing and complimenting everyone around her, including several of the younger crowd who stopped by the table to help celebrate her team's victory.

"I must say, Julie, it seems you've had quite an enjoyable afternoon," Mrs. Montclair said with a knowing look. "Aren't you just the center of attention?"

Monsieur Laurent nodded. "I believe that is precisely where our young friend is most comfortable."

"Indeed, *Mr. Lorant.* She does enjoy the spotlight." Mrs. Montclair cast a disappointed look toward Victoria. "You could take some cues from her, my dear. See how she engages those around her, the way she smiles and interacts. If only you were more like Julie —"

"By the way, Julie, have you had a chance to work on the paintings today?" Beth was desperate to distract Victoria's mother.

A withering look shot back at Beth from across the table. "Pardon me?"

Everyone seemed puzzled at the unexpected interruption from the usually serene Beth. "It's just," she continued, softening her voice, "we're out to sea now. And — well, I was hoping we'd have time to get more done."

"You mean *I'd* get more done, don't you?"

"I'll help in any way I can, Julie."

"You? How would *you* help?"

Beth hesitated, dismayed at the public squabble she had inadvertently begun. "Isn't there some way? Maybe I could sketch a little —"

"It's not as easy as it looks, Bethie." Julie

170

rolled her eyes. "I'll help you when I'm able, darling, but I won't let your silly project ruin my vacation. I intend to enjoy myself — despite your seeming inability to do the same."

Mother shook her head. "Girls, please. This is neither the time nor the place."

"I'm sorry." Beth's face flushed at having caused a scene. She cast a quick glance toward Victoria. The girl seemed oblivious to it all, reaching for another roll from the basket in the center of the table, her eyes focused downward on her little notebook. *She must have heard nothing of her mother's comments. It was a senseless, ill-conceived diversion.* Beth sighed deeply.

CHAPTER 11

"Margret is not feeling well this morning," Mother said as Beth and Julie emerged from their bedroom.

"Oh, dear. What's wrong?"

"Her stomach is rather upset . . . perhaps something she ate last night. At any rate, Emma came just a moment ago to inform us that Margret won't be joining us for breakfast."

Beth frowned. "Does she need any help with JW?"

"No, Miss Bernard will care for him until we return from breakfast. We'll check in on Margret again before we go ashore to attend church, but I don't think we shall take JW along with us. Miss Bernard will watch him during services. I doubt Margret will be feeling up to joining us."

Beth had forgotten that it was already Sunday. "What time is the service?"

"The English service for the tourists

doesn't begin until one, so there's plenty of time before then. Monsieur Laurent will be on his own today. He has left us money to cover our needs for the day."

Sunday — a nice quiet day mostly on board. The little French town on the Gaspé Peninsula and a church service. Beth was certain Mother would not condone much activity, even if the ship would be providing games and concerts and silent movies. Julie would not be pleased. Beth quickly determined she would *not* ask about the paintings again.

"May I go see Margret?" Julie asked.

"No, dear. Let's leave her alone till after breakfast. We'll see how she's doing then."

Julie hurried off alone after the meal while Beth and Mother chatted for some time with the Montclairs. Returning to their suites, Margret answered the door to their knock. She was in a soft, pink knitted dressing gown. She had not put up her hair yet, so it was spilling around her shoulders in thick waves. Her face looked rather pale, and her eyes quite red. Mother brushed a hand over Margret's cheek. "At least you're not feverish," she said.

"You poor dear." Beth sighed aloud.

"I do feel a little better. I think it's going away. My goodness, though. I was quite nauseated. I might want to stay close to the room today."

Beth grasped her hand tenderly. "Do you think it was seasickness?"

But Mother brushed aside the question, lifting JW, who was on the floor playing with blocks. "Not after this many days. It's probably just something she ate." She snuggled the small boy against her and kissed the top of his head. "Good morning, darling."

"Bah-zhur, Ga'mama," he giggled. "Bah-zhur."

"What's he saying?" Mother asked.

Beth chuckled. "I'm quite certain he's trying to say '*Bonjour,* Grandmama' — thanks to Monsieur Laurent, of course."

Mother smiled broadly at the wriggling toddler in her arms. "Bonjour, my sweet little boy."

"Can we bring you anything, Margret?"

"No, thank you, Beth. Emma brought me some tea already. And I think I'd better not overdo it. I'm sure I'll feel better soon." She hesitated for a moment. "Mother, would you be willing to take JW for a little walk? Miss Bernard is taking her turn at breakfast, and it would be good for him to stretch his legs."

Beth opened her mouth to volunteer, but a quick shake of the head from Margret cut her short. Beth waited until Mother had left with her grandson.

Margret closed the door softly. "I want to speak with you, Beth."

"Oh?"

"Julie already stopped by — before the rest of you." Margret drew closer with a concerned expression, her voice lowering. "She offered me a pill. She said she got it from Jannis."

Beth shrugged off her apparent worry. "Yes, it's probably the same thing she offered to me when I was feeling ill."

"And did you *take* it?" Margret's eyes grew large.

"I didn't see the harm."

"Oh, Beth, what were you thinking?" Margret paced away and then came back, biting her lip. "Do you even know what was in it?"

"No, not really. But it certainly worked for me — both times."

"You took it twice? A pill from a stranger?"

"Oh, Margret, you make it sound so dark and wicked. It was just medicine for seasickness, they said. And they're not really strangers, just two girls from Buffalo traveling for vacation. I'm sure they'd never do anything to harm me — or anyone else, for that matter."

"My darling sister, you don't know *what* their intentions might be, whether harmful

175

or merely foolish. You should never have trusted them — not without knowing much more!"

Beth stepped away. "You're overreacting, Margret. It's not so monumental as all that. And the proof is that I *benefitted* from taking it. Anyway, I'll ask them what it was. I'm sure they'll tell me." She dropped down onto a nearby chair. "What do you think they would stand to gain anyway — from making me *well*? How could that be anything but helpful?"

Margret lowered herself to the adjoining seat. "I don't know. I really can't say. But I've already told you that I don't trust them, and now you've fallen for it."

"To be fair, Margret, this happened before you warned me."

"And do you think I'm wrong?"

Beth hesitated, remembering recent exchanges with the girls. "No, I don't think you are — not really. I've had some concerns about them at times too. And Julie's judgment regarding them. I'm afraid she pays for food and other items for them."

"Then you must be the one to use wisdom, and don't take anything else they have to offer. If I'm wrong, no harm is done by undue caution. But if I'm right . . . who knows?"

Beth smiled and rubbed at her forehead. "You're right, of course, Margret. You're so good to me — to all of us. I know it comes from genuine concern. You're such a wonderful mother that you can't help mothering even me."

A look of shock registered on the gentle face.

"Margret?" Beth questioned. "What is it?"

Instantly a mask descended, and she insisted it was nothing. With deliberately careless affectation, she rose quickly and moved to the nearby mirror, picking up her brush. "Nothing. I'm just pleased you agree." Without looking back at Beth, Margret began pinning up her hair. "I'm actually feeling much better. I'll be ready soon. I'm sure I'll be all right going with the rest of you into town."

The tender skimmed across the waves toward the little town, passing near two expansive, natural stone arches that hung above the swirling waters. A striped lighthouse stood as straight as a sentry on a neighboring cliff, watching as the waves dashed against the ragged shore.

After their noon meal of the freshest of seafood in a quaint local restaurant, followed by a lovely church service, the

Thatchers and the Montclairs walked around the town. But all the shops were closed for Sunday, and Mrs. Montclair soon announced that they might as well return to the ship, for there wasn't anything else to do.

They gathered at their favorite spot on deck, reading and chatting while the ship lay at anchor. Just as Beth had expected, Julie was restless. However, she must have resigned herself to setting up her easel with its beginnings of her work from Saguenay Fjord. Julie began slowly mixing several colors on her palette. Beth breathed a sigh of relief and settled in the chair next to Victoria. *At least Julie is staying here within sight, and maybe I'll get a painting or two from her to take to my students.*

Victoria responded, binoculars in hand, to every nearby passenger's enthusiasm over the distant passing of whales or a flock of shorebirds. A lone, leggy moose among the thick rushes brought the young girl to the railing to watch it wade into a broad marsh emptying into the St. Lawrence.

Beth chose to ignore all the exclamations, tackling the remainder of her book. She expected to soon finish *Redburn*. However, it was becoming excessively dark and dismal — the young sailor encountering ever more poverty and inhumanity in England. It reminded her of Coal Valley, though what was described was far beyond what any of her friends out west had endured. At last, unable to read any longer, she set the book aside.

A conversation with Mother was interrupted when Jannis and Penny wandered past. Julie begged with her eyes to join her friends, but Mother calmly dismissed the silent plea. "You're welcome to sit with us for a while, girls," Mother offered. "We'd also like a chance to get to know our Julie's new friends."

"Oh, applesauce! That would certainly be nice, Mrs. Thatcher. But we already told the gang we'd meet them at the pool. Golly, we'll have to chat another time."

Julie insisted they stay for at least a moment, pressing them to sit in Victoria's vacant seat and on its footrest. She peppered them with questions about how they had spent their day, what else they had planned. But after hardly any time, they seemed determined to scurry away, leaving Julie with a glum expression. She settled back in her own chair and resumed painting, though she now seemed rather distracted.

Monsieur Laurent appeared on deck,

whistling a happy little song. "Bonjour, *mes amies.* I do hope you've had a pleasant day," he offered cheerily. It looked to Beth like they all were as glad as she was for the diversion. JW lifted his hands to the old gentleman and was tossed into the air while all smiled at his delighted giggles. "Bonjour, mon petit ami. *Comment vas-tu?*"

"What were you whistling, monsieur," Mother inquired, "when you arrived just now?"

"Ah, it's a little French song about a silly old bailiff. I should teach it to our little one." Taking a nearby seat and placing JW on his knee, he began to sing softly. Although he paid no attention to the rest of those assembled, all eyes were fixed upon him.

"Cadet Rousselle a trois maisons, Cadet Rousselle a trois maisons. Qui n'ont ni poutres, ni chevrons, Qui n'ont ni poutres, ni chevrons. . . ."

Beth knew very little French, and Monsieur Laurent was singing far too quickly for her to catch any of the words. JW, however, was transfixed. This didn't surprise Beth at all, since Monsieur Laurent's weathered face animated every phrase. Soon he had JW singing his best imitation of the easiest words. *"Ah! Ah! Ah! Oui, vraiment, Ah!*

180

Ah! Ah! Oui, vraiment!"

Beth thought to herself, *They make an unexpectedly lovely pair.*

When they rose to prepare for the evening meal, Mrs. Montclair fell in step beside Mother. Beth overheard her caution sternly, "Priscilla, he's going to ruin that little boy. Don't let him teach French while your baby's still so young. It'll only confuse him, and he'll never learn English."

"Oh, Edith," Mother answered, "I hardly think it will do any more than strengthen his growing mind."

"Suit yourself. But you can't say later that I didn't warn you."

Great or small, it seemed to Beth that each day brought further turmoil among them. *Can't we all simply enjoy these days of leisure and companionship?*

Victoria was sliding her key into the lock of their stateroom door next to Beth's when she let out a gasp. "My binoculars! I left them by my chair."

"Then you'd best hurry back before someone takes them," scolded her mother.

Beth offered to go along. Not even bothering to reply, Victoria hurried back through the narrow corridors. They searched carefully all around the chairs. "I know they were here. I had them when I was by the railing. I only put them down to sketch in my book. I can't understand where they might have gone." She gasped again. "Do you suppose someone has taken them?"

"I don't know," Beth answered honestly. "Perhaps one of the crew turned them in to the lost and found. I've seen the staff straightening chairs and picking up after the passengers. When the office opens in the morning, I'll show you where we can check."

"Oh, thank you, Elizabeth, ever so much," Victoria said, grasping Beth's arm with a worried expression on her face.

Well, thought Beth, *that's as much appreciation as I've ever seen from our Victoria. I wish I could help her be as interested in the rest of us. Maybe if I can help her find the glasses. . . .*

But the girl's disappointment at her loss was even more pronounced when the next morning they learned the binoculars had not been turned in.

CHAPTER 12

Sometime during the night, the ship had weighed anchor and was en route to Anticosti Island. Margret opted out of breakfast again, citing a recurrence of her stomach complaints, though she joined the family soon afterward for their morning walk on deck. Julie had disappeared, and Beth spent time attempting to transfer onto a blank canvas her own sketch of the lighthouse perched above the arches. *After all, it isn't merely Julie's project. Why not at least begin one painting for her?*

The next social cataclysm occurred not long afterward. Julie appeared in the suite, fresh from three hours on the recreational deck. Her cheeks were rosy from whatever her recent exertions had been, and she had an obvious spring in each step. She was dressed in her white tennis outfit, this time with a yellow sweater, complete with a bright yellow fringed scarf around her head.

Beth eyed her suspiciously. "You look like the cat that just swallowed the canary."

"Thanks, Bethie," Julie responded with a giggle.

Beth answered dryly, "My dear, that is *not* a compliment. What have you been up to?"

Julie whisked past, slipping out of the sweater and tossing it over the back of the settee. "Why, Bethie, whatever do you mean?"

"Julie Camille," Mother called from the open door of her bedroom, "please ready yourself for lunch."

"Yes, Mother." But there was still a tone of frivolity and amusement in Julie's voice.

Beth followed her into their shared room to wash up and tidy her own hair. *There's clearly a secret Julie is playing up for all it's worth.* "What aren't you telling?" Beth said sternly.

Her eyes twinkling, Julie closed the door. Then she drew the scarf slowly from her head and spun in a circle.

"What have you *done*?" Beth demanded.

"Don't you love it? Jannis did it for me."

Julie's long, dark tresses had disappeared. There was now only a row of blunt curls hanging around her head. "It's a 'bob,' " Julie enthused. "It's all the latest rage. Don't you love it, Bethie darling?"

184

"Oh, it'll *cause* a rage, you can be sure of that." Swallowing hard, Beth tried to gather her composure. "Julie, you know full well that Mother would not have allowed it. How could you do such a thing behind her back?"

"You said it yourself — we're adults. We should be free to make our own decisions where our personal interests are concerned. How could my hair be anything other than my own *personal interest*?"

"When did I ever say such a thing?" Beth demanded.

"When we were deciding what to do the other day. You said we'd go with Mother to the sing-along to keep her happy — and then we would do what we wanted afterward. You and Margret went swimming, and I played deck games since we were free to make our own choices as adults. That's what you said, Bethie! I heard it clear as day."

Beth was still staring at the shockingly short hair. "Whatever I said, I certainly didn't mean *this.*"

Tears began to form in Julie's eyes. "But it's *my hair.* Why shouldn't I wear it the way I like?"

Beth turned away, adding water to the basin and dunking a washcloth into it. "I don't know what to say, Julie." Her head was spinning. "Mother is going to be very upset."

"Do you think she'll be cross with us?"

"Oh, no, sister dear. This is not about *us*." Wringing out the washcloth more forcefully than necessary, Beth muttered, "This is only about *you* and your foolish decision. It has nothing to do with me."

Julie huffed from behind in a flash of anger. "I meant Jannis and me. There isn't an 'us' anymore with you, because you haven't spent any time with me for days!"

"What? I . . . but we . . ." Beth tossed the washcloth over its hook and stalked toward the door. "I won't be with you when you tell Mother. You can just do that with Jannis — if you think it will help."

When Mother discovered Julie's haircut, she sent the others on to lunch. With all her heart, Beth felt sorry for the woman who had such a difficult burden — a daughter who would blissfully allow herself to be sweet-talked into doing what a casual acquaintance suggested. And then she remembered the pills that she had accepted from the same source. Her heart softened. *Julie probably was not thinking clearly either when she trusted her new friends. But Margret's concerns certainly are proving to be correct.*

And then she was struck once more. *What*

186

will Father say? He's always complimented Julie's long curls — so much like Mother's hair. The mental image of his disappointment tugged sorrowfully at Beth's heart.

Julie and Mother did not appear for lunch. When Beth and Margret returned to their suite, Emma, her eyes wide, informed them that they had made a hurried appointment in the on-board beauty salon in order to "fix" Julie's hair.

"Her hair will grow back," Margret said with a sigh, "but broken trust might take longer to restore."

Mother must be greatly dismayed right now. Father too, soon enough. It seemed as if Julie had chosen to move beyond her family, allying herself with her new friends. Beth wished for a long walk through a woods to sort out all the emotions twisting themselves together in her mind. Then she remembered a previous suggestion.

She hurried back into the hallway and knocked on the neighboring door. "Victoria, may I please accept your gracious offer to borrow your violin? I believe that would be particularly pleasant just now."

"Of course," the girl agreed at once. "I'll get it from my room."

Out in the warm sunshine on her stateroom's balcony, Beth brought the strings into tune. She deliberately ignored the fact of nearby passengers, though she could not see them. The soulful timbre of the instrument expressed her turbulent thoughts perfectly. The strains of the familiar hymn, *It Is Well With My Soul,* lifted on the breeze, and Beth wondered if it were truly so with her soul. There was so much beauty in the idea of *family,* and yet an undercurrent of sorrow or even angst seemed always woven into the word as well. Their closeness had only heightened the impact of each word and deed. Tears formed in Beth's eyes as she squeezed them shut and willed the world away.

"Heavenly Father," she whispered, "help us to love one another adequately, no matter what. They're each so precious to me, and yet I don't always demonstrate that well. Why does it seem to grow harder just when we should be the closest? I've missed them for so long. It seems as if it should be easy now to be together again."

The sweet tunes drifted from one song to another. Soon Beth recalled another favorite hymn, the words flowing through her mind as she played. *"Blest be the tie that binds our hearts in Christian love; the fellowship of kindred minds is like to that above."* She

188

prayed for grace to live up to such an exalted vision of unity.

Watching through the large porthole-shaped window for Julie's return with Mother, Beth went inside as soon as she saw them enter the suite, hoping to convey her improved attitude to Julie somehow, even if she were not able to do so in words. They stood awkwardly for a moment, uncertain what to say to each other.

The haircut had been improved. It was no longer quite as chopped off — softer now, releasing more of the natural curl around Julie's face.

"I wanted it to be like Jan's," she said, her face crumpled, after Mother had moved on to her bedroom. "But her hair is straight, so they told me it wouldn't work for me." She frowned, but added stubbornly, "I'm going to sleep with a silk stocking on my head. If I go to bed with wet hair, maybe it will be straighter by morning."

Beth reached out to tousle one of the curls. "It's elegant the way it is, dearest Julie. Your pretty face would make any hairstyle look lovely. However, maybe the stocking trick will make you happy. You'll have to try it and see."

"It's funny," Julie lamented. "Penny said she loved my curls, but I like how straight

189

Jan's hair is. She can't get hers to take a curl at all — not for all the pin curlers she's tried. Wish we could trade, at least for a while."

"You have no reason to covet anyone else's hair," Mother chided from her doorway, though her tone had no sting. "One must be grateful for the way God has created each of us. Or one will never be satisfied at all."

"There." Beth smiled at her sister, their eyes fully meeting at last. "Be grateful, darling. I've always known you were special, and now I guess we can say that you're . . . well, even *specialer*!"

Julie rolled her eyes in response, but Beth was pleased to see a glimmer of humor there. She reached out for a strong embrace and was grateful to find it returned.

"Well, look who's here!"

Startled, Beth turned toward the sound. Julie and Jannis giggled in immediate recognition. The four young ladies were waiting in line for transport to their sightseeing event.

Penny spoke for all of them. "Nick, we didn't know you were taking this shuttle."

"Of course." He grinned confidently. "I wanted to see this fishery — or cannery —

whatever it is we're headed to. But where's the rest of your clan? Are they too high-hat for this place?"

Julie motioned for him to cut in line with them for the next tender to Anticosti Island. He did not need to be invited twice.

"Golly, Jules." He stared at her hair. "What happened to you?"

"Jannis did it. Don't you like it?"

Reaching to pull one of the curls out straight, he let it spring back into position. "And how!" he answered with a wink. "You look positively scrumptious."

"Thanks." She blushed. "Mother and Mrs. Montclair weren't at all interested in going today. Too rough for their taste, they said. And Victoria wouldn't go if she couldn't get out into the woods. A group of men is going fishing, and Victoria was desperate to travel along and see the wildlife, but her mother put her foot down on *that* idea." Penny and Jannis joined Julie in giggling at the thought. "And Margret — well, I think she would have come, but she wasn't feeling very well this morning."

"Say, you're dressed awful nice for gals who are headed out to see where fish are gutted and filleted. Just look at all of you," he continued in a flattering tone. "You're all dolled up as if you're going to a cotillion

191

instead of a smelly factory."

"What did you expect," Jannis bantered, "overalls and rubber boots?"

Beth glanced down at her light-blue skirt and white frilled blouse. She hoped he wasn't right, that they had been foolish in their choice of attire for the day.

The tender entered the broad harbor and approached the little town of Port-Menier. Beth was not surprised that the more elegant passengers hadn't bothered with this excursion. But it was reminiscent of Coal Valley — a small industrial town surrounded by the most wonderful scenery. *Can the similarities be captured in a painting, with fishing boats instead of the Rockies? Will Julie even bother to finish it if I somehow manage an adequate sketch?* Beth climbed out of the tender with the aid of Nick's hand.

In long overcoats made of white cotton duck to cover their clothing, Beth found the fish odors in the cannery very strong, but all the clattering machinery was fascinating. She purchased several cans of seafood fresh off the canning line and tucked them away in her bag. *Won't my students be excited to taste lobster?*

"Let's hit the town," Nick called out. "Gotta be something here besides fish, even if it's just a café where we can get ourselves a good cup of joe."

Beth hesitated. She wasn't certain of the tender schedule and didn't want to miss the last ride back to the ship. And she still was unsure of Nick's intentions. "When are you planning to head back?" she asked.

"Oh, I don't have a *plan*. Let's just have some fun — make it up as we go. What say, girls?"

The others wasted no time falling in line behind Nick. "Drop us off at your best watering hole," Jannis instructed the driver of the dusty bus. "We wanna see the other sights here."

Beth cast a glance at Julie, whose eyes were pleading that she concede. The two made their way back to their seats. *Julie is very hard to deny, especially after her recent statement about feeling neglected. Perhaps the driver knows how many more shuttles there are. . . .*

As it turned out, they were not the only passengers who had decided to remain a little longer in town. Beth breathed a sigh of relief when several other couples from the cruise also found their way to the small diner.

Nick ordered five cups of coffee and a platter of fish and chips to share, struggling with the few French words he knew. The waitress nodded abruptly and hurried away.

Penny rolled her eyes. "Golly, she's a little touchy. You'd think they'd be grateful for the tourists, even if we're not French enough."

Julie laughed. "They probably get tired of all the pantomimed orders, as if we couldn't be bothered to learn a little French. You'd think we've never been anywhere."

"We haven't been," Jannis said with a shrug. "This is the most foreign place I've ever seen. Can you imagine that?"

"How about you, Nick? You traveled much?" Julie wondered.

"Nah. I went south to New Orleans with friends one summer while I was still in college. I picked up some French there, but it doesn't look like it works very well here."

Beth asked, "Where did you attend school?"

He seemed genuinely surprised at the question. "Uh, University of Pennsylvania. I studied economics for a couple of years . . . didn't graduate."

"That's right, he didn't," Jannis blurted. "He got kicked out before his senior year, the dumb cluck."

"Oh, dear. I'm sorry." Beth wasn't sure if she should pursue the topic.

194

Julie, however, didn't waver. "What for, Nick?"

He sighed. "It wasn't my fault. A little disagreement between me and another guy that got outta hand. They wouldn't listen to my explanation — just booted us both. It's a shame too. I was doing real well. Thought I'd get a job in the stock market or something highbrow like that. Instead, I went right back to driving a jitney for five cents a ride. Some cushy job, huh?" He told the story with a careless tone, but Beth was certain it concealed his true feelings.

"How come you're on a *cruise* then?" Julie pressed further.

A slow grin spread across his face, and his words were evasive. "I'm working some angles — getting a foot in the door, I guess you can say, till I figure it out better. I'd hate to give away any secrets, if you know what I mean. But there's no way I'll be stuck at a dead end forever. Not me."

Beth stared wordlessly. *What does he mean? Is he trying to find a job on the cruise ship? A young man with an incomplete economics degree? And what of his family? Had they forsaken him?* It made no sense to Beth.

When the plate of food had been consumed and the coffee drained, the waitress dropped the bill on the table. Julie reached for it and fumbled in her purse for some coins.

Penny pushed away from the table, sighing contentedly. "Thanks, Darb," she said with a little smirk at Julie, who was laying out the money.

"You're welcome." Julie smiled back sweetly.

Beth cast a sideways glance at her sister, but Julie merely shrugged. As they rose to leave, Julie explained under her breath, "She calls me that sometimes. I think it's some kind of compliment, but I don't really know what it means. Then again, I often don't know what their words mean. Isn't it fun?"

"Hmm. I don't like the way she said it."

"Oh, Bethie. You're so overprotective! Just like Mother."

The words stung. *Is that how she sees me? Is that what I am?* Beth immediately made up her mind not to reproach Julie as much — to be more open to the new people and new experiences.

CHAPTER 13

"Come roller-skating with us," Julie coaxed as Beth began to gather her broad-brimmed hat from its hook beside her bedroom door and her book to read on deck. "I've rented four pairs of skates, hoping you'd join us."

It took a moment to register. "What did you say? You're going to *skate* on board the ship?"

"Yes! On the rec deck. Won't that be fun?"

"But we've never roller-skated before. And the ship is *already* rolling, so to speak."

"We've been ice-skating, though. That's close enough. Come on, Bethie. Have an adventure."

"Well, I'll give it a try at least. It does sound fun. But I can't promise I'll be any good at it. I don't even ice-skate very well, you know."

"Now, what should you wear?" Julie hurried to find something from Beth's closet, returning with a thick wool skirt and a light top in hand. "Trust me," she said, "you want your skirt to be a little longer, and nothing that the wind might catch." Her explanation did not calm Beth's fears.

The deck was already crowded by the time they arrived. All the chairs and tables had been drawn to the center so the track could be as large as possible. Several participants were already skating laps. To Beth it seemed an awfully small space for roller-skating. Yet she was here to spend time with her sister and so would do her best. She seated herself and slipped the base of the skate under her own shoes, adjusted their fit, and buckled the straps tightly.

"Julie, I'm going to need your help to stand."

"I'm here. Grab hold."

Using the back of a chair and clutching Julie's shoulder, Beth lifted herself up and felt the wheels begin to roll beneath her. "Not so fast!"

Julie's laughter was her answer.

Together they glided away from the chairs and moved into the stream of other skaters. Jannis and Penny flew by them with a wave. "Oh, don't let go, Julie! Let me get used to the feeling." Soon Beth was comfortable enough to release her sister's arm and giggle along with the other three girls. Once she felt more sure of her own movements and was able to relax somewhat, Beth found she was enjoying it immensely.

Julie could spin in slow circles and also skate backward. She and Jannis would grasp hands and spin together, drawing closer and spinning faster until they lost their grip and spun away with a rush of laughter.

"I need a rest," Beth admitted at last. She made her way to the nearest table, caught hold of one of its chairs, and let herself down, still puffing.

Julie whisked past. "Order us sodas," she called. "Then we'll sit with you."

Beth placed the order, giving Mother's room number, certain that Julie would be treating her two friends. Then she watched the energetic group doing laps around her. She noticed quickly that Julie fit well among them all with her outgoing nature and modern clothing. In fact, her short hair seemed to have been the last piece of the puzzle.

Indeed, it was now Beth who was the odd one out. Scanning the area, she realized she was the only one of the young women to still have her hair pinned up. Her hairstyle fit only with the few older ladies who were observing the activity. Some of the other girls had long locks, but their hair was flowing freely down their backs, blowing in the breeze — which seemed in this setting to look alive and vibrant. Beth began to understand and sympathize with Julie's determination to adapt. She could feel the allure of being so carefree and trendy.

"Is this seat taken?"

Beth recognized the voice immediately. "Good afternoon, Nick. Please, make yourself comfortable." She motioned to the empty chair.

"It's good to see you joining in the fun today. I was beginning to think you might be a bit of a flat tire." He winked at Beth.

Beth stiffened, remembering his hand on Julie's back. She refused to allow this kind of familiarity from the young man. "I suppose that *is* what I am sometimes. But I'm not opposed to fun — really."

"Have you finished your book yet?"

"No, I've taken a break from it. The scenes became a little too sad for me, too realistic in a way that was . . . well, rather appalling."

He leaned forward across the table. "How so?"

"The poverty, for one."

"Gimme a 'for instance.' " He was smiling playfully, still seeming to be teasing her.

"Very well. There is a section where a

woman and two little girls are starving. Redburn discovers them in an alley. But when he tries to call a policeman or beg for food on their behalf, no one will help."

"Yeah, that's pretty balled up, all right." Nick shrugged.

"But it gets worse." The memory caused Beth's brow to furrow. "Redburn returned with a little bread and water which he had stolen. But later he laments that he even bothered . . . he realizes that all he'd done was to *prolong* their deaths. He even considers that it would be more of a mercy to have just killed them outright." Beth gripped her hands tightly together at the grim memory.

"Are you serious? The guy was considering bumping them off?"

"And then Redburn realizes that if he did kill them, society — the very ones who refused to help as he rushed through the streets begging for food — this same society would spend any amount necessary to prosecute him for that crime, money they hadn't bothered to spend in order to *rescue* these poor souls in the first place."

"Gosh! I guess there may be some truth in it, but I agree that's a pretty appalling idea."

Beth shook her head and sighed. "I understand the vignette is fictional — but I suppose there's some amount of reality there. It makes me sick to my stomach just to contemplate it."

A shadow crossed Nick's face. He confessed, "I've seen things that are just about as twisted as that — when you know something ain't right, but you don't know how to make it work out any more fair."

"You have?"

"Sure, I bet everybody has. Guess all you can do is roll with whatever life gives you, and get yours before somebody else gets there first."

"Oh no, Nick." Beth sat forward and searched his face. "We can do so much better than that. We can right at least some of the wrongs. We can work toward changing things for the poor and cast-out. We have to."

"What, *you*?" But the shadow lifted as quickly as it had come. *He must be teasing me again.* "You in your ivory tower — you think there's something you can do about all that? When would you have ever even *seen* poor people?"

"Oh, but I have," she answered quietly. "I worked in a coal-mining town out in western Canada as a teacher last year. I can't say that I really changed things much . . . but we have to try. We're answerable before God at least to do our best."

He pushed himself back, his expression slightly dour. "Even if you did — even if you could get some other folks to help too — you can't stop all the evil. People will still suffer. How could God ever make that *our* fault?"

Beth hesitated. "I'm not saying that suffering is our fault. I believe we suffer because sin has taken hold of the world. And with sin comes selfishness and heartlessness and wickedness. But I also think there will be a day of reckoning, Nick, when God lays out all we've done and judges our actions. That's not as popular to talk about anymore, I suppose. We all like to hear about a God who loves and forgives and rewards. But He isn't holy and just if He doesn't deal with all those wrongs. I would never want to stand before God without having done everything in my power to extend His mercy to the people around me whenever I could."

He shook his head, as if to whisk away her weighty words. "I don't see it. If there even *is* a God, He's the one with all the power. Let *him* fix it."

Just then the waiter set four glasses of soda before them and hurried away. Beth tried to return to their discussion, but Julie and her

203

friends descended on them just as quickly.

"Nick, you old piker! You better not be pinching our drinks." Jannis slapped him on the back and slipped into the seat next to him.

"You gals can have them. I've got places to go." He stood rather abruptly, pasting on a broad smile. "See you around, ladies."

"Yeah, scram," Penny demanded with a wink.

He nodded at Beth and hastened away. She wished they had not been interrupted and hoped for another chance to talk with him. He had seemed rather troubled. Beth realized she knew almost nothing about the man. In her concern about his influence on Julie, she had overlooked the fact that he too might be someone needing a friend.

The girls sipped on their sodas, chatting about upcoming activities and the remaining cruise stops. Glasses emptied, the others went back to skating again, but Beth decided she was finished for the day and unbuckled the skates.

As she lifted her eyes, she noticed Margret making her way through the stream of skaters, a laughing, wriggling JW in her arms.

"Whew . . ." Margret shook her head and sank into a chair. "I wasn't sure we'd make it safely — dodging the crowds and wrestling with this one."

Beth reached for her nephew and seated him on the table in front of her. The boy struggled against her hold on him, until she offered him one of her skates. It immediately became a car, clattering and rolling across the tabletop. He sputtered out boy noises, his best attempt at an engine sound.

Margret leaned forward on the table and watched the skaters whizzing by. "Julie's doing very well with skating, isn't she?"

"Yes," Beth agreed. "She and the other girls have taken to this like — like horses to the races."

"And you?" Margret teased.

"More like a turtle on ice!" They laughed together, watching the frolicking skaters around them.

Julie spotted the new arrivals and, to JW's delight, rolled toward them. "Hello, little buddy boy. What'cha doing?"

JW crashed the makeshift car onto the table and reached up for Julie. "Annie Doolie — I go? I go?"

"Margret, may I take him?"

Margret hedged. "Do you think it's safe? Do you ever fall?"

"I haven't fallen all day! But I'll be extra careful — I'll skate slowly."

"Well, I suppose. I know he'd love to go along for a ride."

Julie scooped JW up into her arms and rolled slowly away from the table, out of the path of the fastest skaters. Beth could hear his laughter ringing across the deck.

"I wasn't expecting to see you out here. I'm glad you joined us, Margret."

"Oh, well, I couldn't sit with Mother anymore. If I hear one more word about Miss Lucille Bernard, I'll just scream."

"Is it that bad, darling?"

"Oh, Beth, it's worse. I'm afraid we're in constant tension — the three of us — about nap times and feeding schedules. And, truly, it's two against one — three, even, if you count Mrs. Montclair. So how much does my opinion count? I'm only his mother, after all. And all I want is to enjoy him while he's little. He's growing up so fast." Margret cast a longing look toward the cluster of girls around JW. "He's turning into a little boy right before my eyes. Where did my baby go?"

Beth couldn't help but laugh. "Your baby! When I left last summer we were still rocking him to sleep — talk about growing up too fast!"

"And yet that's how it feels to me too."

Julie, Penny, and Jannis reclaimed the

seats around them. By then JW was riding on Julie's back, kicking with his heels and clutching around her throat.

"Sorry you took him?" Margret asked with a grin.

"Oh, no, he was loads of fun."

"Sure, and he draws a crowd," Jannis put in. "All the fellas were offering to take him, but Julie wouldn't give him up. She kept him all for herself."

"I'm glad. I wouldn't have wanted him in the arms of strangers."

"Not even for a break?" Penny seemed incredulous. "Babies are so much work! My cousin lets anybody who'll take him hold her baby."

Shaking her head, Margret received JW back from Julie.

He was still wriggling and clapping. "Annie Doolie — mo' — mo'."

"Yes, they're a great deal of work — but they're also an important trust. And he's always *my* responsibility."

Jannis laughed. "I don't know. I'd trade a baby for attention from one of those fellas over there any day."

"Then you can surely understand why he'll never be put in your charge." Margret's words sounded unusually terse. Beth eyed her quizzically. Her sister seemed suddenly to be quite out of sorts. *Perhaps the conflict regarding JW's care?*

Margret gathered her bag and tucked JW against her hip. Forcing a pleasant smile, she said her good-byes and hurried away.

"Golly, your sister's quite a peach, ain't she?" Penny muttered.

Julie glowered back defensively. "She's all right. Just leave her alone. And, like Margret said, you won't be holding him — not ever."

"Ah, horse feathers! Who wants to bother anyway? He's like any other — just a drooling, stinky mess. Babies are a dime a dozen." With a flip of her hair, Jannis stalked away, leaving her skates on the table for Julie to return. Penny shrugged and followed after her sister.

Beth and Julie gathered up the skates and returned them in relative silence. Beth wondered if such outbursts were usual among the trio. She knew Julie could be stubborn, but she was rarely argumentative. Although it was no surprise at all that Julie's hackles would be raised when she was defending her precious nephew. And her sister.

Prince Edward Island appeared on the horizon in a long stretch of coastline. Beth,

Julie, Penny, and Jannis leaned out over the rail and watched it take shape before them, the recent spat already forgiven and forgotten. As the ship drew nearer, the rugged rust-colored shoreline gradually showed more detail.

"How perfectly copacetic!" Jannis pronounced the view before them. "I heard it was real pretty here, and now I see why. The red cliffs, the bright green grass. And to top it all off, those lovely white houses perched like dainty little birds above it all."

Beth smiled at the girl's poetic wording and asked, "Have you read *Anne of Green Gables*?"

"Yeah, I read it. It was real cute, but I didn't enjoy it that much since 'Anne with an *e*' was an orphan and all. Guess it turned out okay for her in the end, but then again, that's just a story. In real life, losing your parents doesn't end up quite so swell."

Beth cringed. She had forgotten that Jannis had mentioned an aunt, but not a mother or father. She wondered what had happened to them. "How long have you lived with your aunt?"

"Our who?"

"Your aunt — the one who broke her leg and couldn't come?"

"Oh, Aunt Mary." Jannis exchanged looks

with her sister. "For a couple years, I guess. She's all right. A funny old bird, but she takes care of us well enough."

"Yup, Aunt Mary," repeated Penny. "She's a good egg, overall."

Beth let the topic go.

"I know what let's do," Julie suggested. "Let's go get ice creams and sit where we can watch the sailors hitching our ship to the docks."

Beth shook her head. "Oh, we've got a long way to go yet before we're in port."

"Fine!" Julie laughed. "Then let's just go get ice creams!"

They sauntered away toward the atrium. Then, after an hour of relaxing and waiting, Beth suggested it would be good if she and Julie checked in with their family.

"Aren't they the greatest?" Julie exclaimed as they walked back to their stateroom. "I just love those girls."

"They're lots of fun, to be sure." Beth was amazed at how quickly Julie could overlook the recent exchange regarding JW.

"I still wish we could eat meals together. We spend so much time in different parts of the ship, and I doubt their food is nearly as good as ours. Jannis asks me about our dinners sometimes. I try not to make it sound very good."

"Oh, Julie, those things are all extras — just trimmings around a lovely vacation. You don't need to pity them for not sharing in everything. My goodness, I think you're already paying for most of their treats on board — or rather, Father is."

"I know, and that helps me feel a little bit better. But Jannis has told me more about their family, and I just feel so sorry for them both."

"What do you mean?"

"Oh, they haven't had it easy. Their parents died when they were quite young. So they went to live with an uncle. But he was rather a crotchety old man — didn't treat them very well, so finally they were sent to live with a cousin instead."

"I thought it was an aunt who couldn't come along on the trip."

Julie shrugged. "I suppose. I guess I'd forgotten that."

"But you said a cousin."

"Yes, something like that. I could have heard her wrong. Maybe they live with both an aunt *and* a cousin. We were playing mahjong when she told me about it," Julie added absently. "I just missed the details."

"I'm truly sorry to hear it. That must have been very difficult for them."

"And Penny told me a little about their

mother. She was not at all nice either."

Beth frowned. "How so?"

"Well, I didn't hear the whole story, only bits and pieces, and then Penny was too embarrassed to finish it, I suppose. But for some strange reason their mother actually named her 'Penance' — that's her official name on her birth certificate. It had something to do with an old church lady who told her that God was punishing her mother by giving her a baby when she wasn't married. I guess she chose the name to spite the church or something, kind of a way of getting her revenge. But they can both remember their mother saying quite often that Penny was God's punishment for things their mother had done before she was even born."

"Oh, Julie, I can't imagine! To think of any mother saying such a dreadful thing! How old was Penny when she lost her parents?"

"I'm not sure. I haven't asked. She was certainly old enough to remember her well. But I try not to ask too many questions, since I know it makes them uncomfortable to talk about it." They had reached the last hallway. Julie sighed deeply. "I tried to tell her that God isn't like that, that children are *never* a punishment. They're always

God's blessing and dearly loved by Him. But I don't think I said it very well — at least, it didn't seem like Penny understood. Anyway, I guess that's part of the reason I want to be friends with them both. I'd like to find some way to show them that God really does love them."

The story pierced Beth's heart. "I'm glad you've befriended them, Julie. I'll pray you find the right words." Her sister's simple compassion actually stung a little. Beth had chosen to keep the girls at arm's length — distrustful and unsympathetic. She determined then to try harder to include them in her goodwill. Perhaps she would even set aside her questions about the pills. There had been no negative results, after all.

Despite their plans to watch the ship dock, Beth and Julie were far too busy in preparations for debarking once again to catch up with their friends. Father had reserved rooms in a fine hotel for the two days they'd be touring the island province. Beth anticipated sleeping in a bed that didn't rock with the motion of the waves. Still, the change of residence required that bags be packed for their two days and two nights ashore, and Mother insisted they lock away anything valuable in the closet safe.

One by one, their suitcases were loaded onto a wheeled cart, until Mother released the porter with a nod, placing a generous tip into his gloved hand. He bowed and pushed the cart into the hallway. "Now, if only Edith and Victoria are finished packing as well."

At last the ladies were tucked away in a corner of the cozy hotel restaurant for a light evening meal while Monsieur Laurent saw to it that their hotel rooms were properly prepared and the bags delivered.

"Travel is exhausting," Mrs. Montclair remarked over her steaming tea. "I declare, if it weren't for all the folks who said Prince Edward Island was remarkably beautiful, I would have been tempted to stay on board and just relax instead. I suppose the ship is nearly empty now."

Mother clucked patiently, "You don't mean that, Edith."

"Now, Priscilla, I do. You wait and see. One of these times I'll just surprise you all and do exactly that. I'll leave the hustle and bustle to the rest of you and have myself a nice quiet rest — all alone."

"You don't really like to be alone, Mother," Victoria countered. "You're always saying that."

Julie grinned. "Well, you wouldn't want to

miss New York anyway."

"Why ever not? I'm not as young as you four girls. So I don't feel the need to endure all the unpleasantness of every one of the cities on our route. If I take a notion at that time, I assure you, I shall even be willing to miss out on New York City too. Besides, I've seen photographs of the skyline. That's the only view I truly wish to see for myself."

"Mrs. Montclair," Julie said playfully, "I don't believe you've remembered about the *shopping*."

For a moment the woman froze, her cup lifted halfway to her lips. Then she set it down again, smiled widely and joined in Julie's laughter. Pointing her glasses good-naturedly in Julie's direction, she announced, "Ah, my dear, you *do* know me well. I confess, *that alone* would surely induce me ashore."

"Are your friends staying in a hotel here in Charlottetown?" Margret asked Julie.

"No, they can't afford it. So they'll board the ship again tonight."

Mother noted, "I believe many of our fellow passengers are doing the same. And with the island trains, it's not so very difficult to see what one wishes and still sleep on board. In fact, with all the fuss of packing and moving, it hardly seems an added convenience."

"I suppose," Julie sighed. Beth, however, thought sleeping ashore once again sounded just fine.

CHAPTER 14

Monsieur Laurent appeared in the hotel's small bistro where they were waiting and hurried toward their table. "There is an evening carriage tour of the city in one hour. That will give you time to settle into your rooms beforehand if you wish." Dropping napkins onto the table, they began to rise. "Miss Thatcher," he said, leaning over to address Beth, "perhaps you would prefer to stay here in the dining room for a moment." He then slid a thin packet across the table toward her.

Letters! "Oh, yes. Mother, I believe I'll wait for you right here. There's nothing I need from the room."

Mother eyed the envelopes and nodded knowingly. "I see. Well, of course, darling. We'll be back before the tour begins."

Beth waited until they had all filed out before she opened the packet. There were two letters bound together by a string — a welcome surprise. Using the stamp cancellation dates, she arranged the envelopes in the order in which Jarrick had sent them. A waiter stopped at the table to refill her tea, and Beth drew out the anticipation, choosing to order dessert before slicing the envelopes open with her butter knife.

It was quickly evident that Jarrick had not yet received her letter. But he had mailed another without waiting for her reply. Beth was so grateful he had done so.

My dear Beth,

This morning your journey begins. I'm so excited for you and your mother and sisters. I trust that this will be a time you'll remember always. A time filled with intimate conversations and beautiful memories to treasure for a lifetime. I pray that God will grant you safety and freedom from unforeseen obstacles.

Over the last few days I've given much thought to our telephone conversation and its implications. I want to assure you that I'm praying daily that I would have the wisdom to use these long weeks of waiting as a time of preparation. God willing, I would like to be the best man that I can be before your return. That I would carefully measure my heart and my actions against God's desire for me in order to be aware of the ways in which I fall short. Toward this end, yesterday in church here in Blairmore I approached an older man whom I've long respected. I've made arrangements to meet him for coffee once a week in order to glean from him what I can about what makes a good man and a good husband.

Beth blushed, despite the fact that she was alone. She reached for her handkerchief and squeezed the drying rose petal to bring up a little of its fragrance. The words washed over her with such a thrill of joy that she could hardly continue reading. *Perhaps Mother could be a source of similar influence for me.* She decided she would look for opportunities to ask leading questions for personal advice, though she would honestly have found it easier to seek advice from Miss Molly instead.

Lester Carothers is a church elder there . . . wife of forty-some years . . . four sons and a daughter . . . hospitable and generous . . . above reproach . . . Mrs. Carothers was a schoolteacher once . . . seems a happy and contented wife . . . certain the relationship will be of great benefit.

No news yet of the teaching position . . . had a fine meal with Molly and Frank . . . the two have become quite a pair. . . .

Beth sighed contentedly at the thought. She liked to think of Frank and Molly spending time together. She felt that although they were very different from each other — an elderly Italian miner and a hospitable, aging widow — they were so completely compatible.

The mine is producing well again . . . perfect start to summer . . . mountains are so beautiful, dressed in a haze of fresh green leaves here and there among the evergreens . . . engagement announcement . . . Esther Blane and Bardo Mussante, one of the miners . . . a good friend of Philip's . . . perhaps a marriage of convenience, but they seem quite comfortable together.

"I hope he's good to the children," Beth whispered aloud. She tried to remember Bardo, but found she could not draw up an image. However, it was easy to recall the little face of Anna Kate and her two only slightly older brothers . . . and their shabby clothing. She hoped they would be better provided for soon, with their new papa.

The waiter set a wedge of cheesecake on the table, and Beth returned to her reading.

Not much other news . . . can't wait to hear about your trip . . . finding solace in the fact that we share the same sky overhead and the same moon at night. When I see it hanging above all, I am picturing you not so far away. (But don't tell Philip I said anything so woefully starry-eyed, as he would never let me hear the end of it.)

> With fondest affection,
> Jarrick

Beth folded the letter again and placed it back inside its envelope. She considered saving the other until the next day, but found it far too difficult to wait. This one was shorter, written on only one side of the paper.

My dear Beth,

It's Wednesday here. One week since we chatted on the telephone. And this time I do have news for which I hope you are sitting comfortably. Good news — the very best, in fact!

Molly and Frank have eloped!

Beth sat bolt upright in shock, staring down at the words. Reading them over again to be certain her eyes weren't deceiving her. Could it be true?

Jarrick continued,

Perhaps due to the announcement of Esther and Bardo's engagement, perhaps even in order to promote the goodwill of the townsfolk to such an idea, they have slipped away to Lethbridge and come back in wedded bliss. I'm quite certain they have been contemplating such a decision for quite some time. Of course, they didn't want anyone to fuss over them. So they opted to "run away together."

Beth's hand trembled as she lifted it to her cheek. *How lovely and romantic!* Yet in the same breath she lamented the fact that she had missed their wedding. It would have been so nice to be there to congratulate the happy couple. *What a joyful thing to imagine!* Beth made up her mind to write a letter as soon as the others had settled in for the night — addressed to Mrs. Molly Russo.

"Oh, Molly! I'm so happy for you," she

whispered.

Frank has moved into Molly's place. Teddy Boy and Marnie will have a father. Or rather, a grandfatherly figure, since Molly is not actually their mother and more like a grandmother to them. But what should that matter? They'll all be the better off for each being part of a family. And I'm grateful to see those children secure and loved.

I believe they've offered Frank's cabin to Heidi Coolidge and her children. That should help her to be out from under the expense of renting from the company. And there's talk now of Abigail Stanton buying the Grants' place to open a small restaurant and teahouse. She's already promised a job to Heidi if she can get the place up and running soon enough.

Oh my, Beth thought, *what a lot to happen so quickly.*

Well, my Beth, I had been determined not to write to you more often than once a week, but the news was simply too important not to tell. And I knew you'd want to hear of it as soon as possible.

223

I believe you said that your ship was to depart today. So, without further fanfare, I shall bid you adieu and hope to receive a return letter from you any day now.

Affectionately yours,

Jarrick

P.S. I'm ashamed to say I almost forgot my second intention in writing. I spoke to your father again. He tells me that you'll spend the day in Charlottetown on Tuesday of next week. I plan to be in Lethbridge. I'm not certain if it will be possible, but I would like to try to reach you by telephone at that time. I plan to place a call to your hotel desk on Tuesday at noon (your time), assuming I can accurately figure out the time difference. Please don't worry if it won't be possible for you to be there at that time. I just couldn't think of any other way to try to get in touch with you. JT

Beth could hardly contain herself. So much good news all packed into one short letter — and a call from Jarrick to top it off — and Tuesday was tomorrow! *How wise of him to leave so many days between sending the letter and our telephone appointment.* Beth wasn't certain what the plan was for the morrow, but she immediately decided she would be waiting in the hotel lobby, beginning at eleven o'clock, just in case he was off an hour. "Thank you, heavenly Father," she whispered. "His letter came just in time."

Beth heard very little of the discourse from the Charlottetown tour guide. Squeezed between Victoria and Julie on the narrow seat of an open-air coach, Beth could think of little else than Jarrick's upcoming telephone call. She had mentioned nothing yet to the others, preferring to think through how she would address the issue.

"And here we have Province House." The young guide gestured at the impressive stone structure. "Most of you will already know that this site is most famous for hosting the Confederation Conference in 1864, where the Maritime Provinces joined with what was then known as the Province of Canada to discuss the formation of a confederation of the remaining British provinces in North America. What you might not have heard is that there was also a *circus* in town that attracted far more attention by the public at large." He winked. "Some might even say that makes for *two* circuses hosted by our city at the same time."

His amiable banter continued as Beth

thought about how to convey the news of Jarrick's call to her family. She sighed, wishing she were able to be more attentive. She hated to miss out on any of the history or the charming old street sights.

"Annie Bet?" JW tugged at her sleeve and pointed toward the front of the coach. "Horsies! See?"

"Yes, darling." She smiled at the boy, but he slid back onto Mother's lap before she could chat with him for even a moment.

As they later descended from the coach and entered the broad mezzanine of their hotel, Julie drew near her and muttered, "Where have *you* been, Bethie?"

"I'm sorry?"

"Well, sister dear, you're clearly lost in thought. It's so unlike you not to absorb every bit of historical significance and to ask a thousand questions begging for more. Tonight you've hardly spoken at all."

Beth smiled feebly. "I guess my mind is preoccupied today." *Here was a wonderful chance to be with my family, but I let myself get caught up in daydreaming.* Beth remembered Margret's request that she be *present* with them, along with Father's encouragement to use the summer wisely.

"I sensed 'preoccupation,' as you call it," Julie said. "But you haven't said what it is that's so much more interesting to you."

"I'll tell you later," Beth whispered.

Julie caught hold of Beth's elbow and drew herself closer in mock intimacy. "Oh, goody! That can only mean it's something well worth hearing."

Beth shook her head. "Don't be so melodramatic, Julie."

Monsieur Laurent wanted everyone to meet in the hotel dining room following their tour. He was waiting to greet them in the lobby and directed them to the proper table. Mrs. Montclair, who had skipped the tour, was already seated and reading a newspaper.

"How was the carriage ride?" she asked as they joined her.

"Good," declared Victoria. "The horses were very bright, but not as clever as my pony." Just mentioning the beloved animal brought a frown. "I miss Clover. I haven't been riding for ever so long."

"Now, Victoria, don't start with that again. You know that David is exercising her while you're gone. She'll be just fine — and so will you."

Beth was amazed at the sudden mood swing. The girl had been fine only moments before and now was slumped in the chair beside her mother.

"Eat something," Mrs. Montclair commanded. "You'll feel better."

"Let us begin," Monsieur Laurent inserted into the exchange. "We have several decisions to make regarding tomorrow's agenda. . . ."

Beth held her breath, praying silently that God would work out the details for her conversation with Jarrick. In the end, it was decided that the morning would be spent shopping in the city, with an afternoon train ride to other parts of the island. Beth had tried not to influence the decision toward her own wishes, but she sighed with relief at the outcome. All she would miss would be the shopping.

"The operator is trying to connect you now. Please hold." It was the third attempt to set up the call with Lethbridge.

"Hello? Jarrick? Are you there?" Beth pressed the handset against her ear but heard only crackling over the line. "Jarrick?" No response. "Operator?"

A singsong voice answered, "I'm sorry, ma'am. I'm afraid we keep losing your connection. We'll try again in a few minutes."

"May I send a message to the party on the other end?"

"I'm sorry, ma'am. There's no way for us

to send a message if they can't get a line through. I can only advise you to wait for a few minutes while the operator reconnects the call from the other end."

"Thank you," Beth said, looking across the lobby to where Margret waited with JW. Beth placed the receiver in its cradle and smiled weakly at the hotel receptionist. "I'm afraid they couldn't get through again."

"That's too bad, honey," she said. "But don't go far. I'm sure they'll try again in a bit. Those telephones can be finicky things. I'll bet they fix the problem soon."

"Yes, thank you. I'll wait right here."

"No need, miss. I'll send a page to find you if they call back. I'm sure it'll work eventually. Don't give up."

"Thank you. That would be very kind."

Margret rose and hurried over, JW at her heels. She had opted out of shopping during the morning, complaining once more of nausea. So the two sisters had stayed behind and entertained JW, lingering around the lobby as the appointed time drew near. Margret had purchased a little toy ship with wheels for the boy, and he had spent the time on his tummy, pushing it across the tiled floor, making noises that no doubt sounded to him like the ones their own ship made. Miss Bernard would surely have

229

shushed him because of it being a public space, but Beth had been rather delighted to observe his playing.

Margret touched Beth's arm. "I guess your telephone call didn't work again. I'm so sorry, darling. I know you're disappointed."

"You could try to call John," Beth offered dejectedly. "At least one of us should be able to speak to our . . . should get to talk with . . ." Beth couldn't find a single word with which to finish the sentence. She wasn't sure how to refer to Jarrick.

Margret moved nearer, searching Beth's face. "It's sweet of you to think of me. But John and I have arranged to speak tonight after dinner. I do empathize with how you feel. I'm so anxious to hear John's voice I can hardly think of anything else." Margret's eyes misted as she spoke the words. "I feel as if it's been years since we've been able to talk together, and I was able to call him at Tadoussac."

JW had followed Margret across the wide checkerboard tiles. He watched their conversation, Beth's face drawn tight with sadness, tears rimming her eyes. He lifted his arms. Beth pulled him up. "Annie Bet cwyin'?" The little hands patted her face with rough affection.

Beth pressed a kiss against his cheek. "Yes, Auntie Beth is crying. And Mommy too, a little. But it's all right."

"Hug?" He circled her neck with his pudgy arms. "Luf you."

"Oh, darling, I love you too."

"Let's get a table in the dining room," Margret suggested. "I'll let the woman at the desk know where we'll be so the page boy can find you easily. We'll get a cup of tea."

"I suppose." Beth was fighting for composure, painfully aware of the many others moving around the room. When Margret returned, they crossed together through the lobby to the hotel's quaint bistro.

Soon they were settled in a corner table, a wooden high chair pulled close so that JW could pick up the oyster crackers Margret scattered on the tray.

"I'm sure he's just as anxious as you — probably more so. Men want to fix things, to be in control. He's probably pacing around, trying to get something to work out."

Beth pictured Jarrick in the station, surrounded by all the other officers. She hoped he wasn't being pestered. "I don't feel there's any privacy at all. There are always people watching, and it's such a complicated endeavor. I feel as if the whole world knows we're trying to speak with each other. Surely someone could come up with a better way."

"Yes, that would be nice, darling. But remember, he's clear across Canada."

"Oh, I know," Beth sighed. "I'm just being unreasonable."

Margret settled her teacup back in its saucer. "I'd certainly like to meet him. When do you suppose that will be possible?"

Beth shook her head. "I don't know. I can't even tell you when *I'll* see him again. Everything's so uncertain right now — so many unanswered questions." Beth dabbed her napkin at the corners of her eyes and breathed in slowly. "You would like him, Margret," she said with a wobbly smile.

"Of course I would. You're a fine judge of character."

"I wish I had a picture I could show you. There just wasn't time."

Margret placed a few more crackers on the baby's tray. JW scooped them up greedily and shoveled them into his mouth. "Perhaps you could ask him to send one to you in one of his letters. He might have a photograph he can give you."

"Maybe. I'll ask." A movement nearby caught her eye. Beth steeled herself. But it was only the waiter, approaching with their tea. After the cups were on the table, she composed herself once more. *Perhaps I should simply change the subject.* "How are you feeling now, Margret? Any better?"

A brooding expression fell over her sister's face. "I feel much better. I'm fine, but . . ."

Beth studied her. Margret was choosing not to lift her eyes, instead fussing with the silverware on the table in front of her.

"What is it? What are you thinking?"

She cleared her throat. "I'm almost afraid to say."

Beth reached a hand across the table. "You're not coming down with something, are you?"

"No." A tentative smile. "Well, maybe. But not what you think."

"What?"

Margret's eyes rose just enough to meet Beth's. Her face was flushed. "I think I might be . . . with child."

Beth's mouth dropped open.

Margret laughed. "It's not such a surprise, is it? It's not as if John and I weren't planning on another child sometime soon." She looked at JW tenderly. "And my J-bird needs a little sister — or a brother. He's ready. Don't you think?"

"Oh, Margret! That's wonderful!"

233

"Now, you must know I'm not certain of this," she hedged, giving Beth's hand a squeeze. "And that's precisely the problem. How do I see a doctor here — so far from home?"

"If that's what you want," Beth declared, "I'm sure we could find someone. And we've got two days here in Charlottetown. You could probably get an appointment for this afternoon or tomorrow."

Margret raised a finger in warning. "I plan to talk to John about it tonight — that is, assuming *I* can get a line through. There's no reason to act rashly. I'll see what he wants me to do. But, yes, it should be possible to see a doctor here. It's just that . . . oh, just what you said earlier — such a complicated endeavor, drawing so many people into our personal business. I have half a mind to just wait and see."

"Oh, Margret — another baby!" Beth slipped from her chair and drew her sister into an awkward hug. "What a blessing!"

"Yes," she whispered back, leaning her head against Beth's side. "I'm so happy."

It was a great boost for Beth to be chosen as Margret's confidante, to share the wondrous possibility together.

CHAPTER 15

By the time the others returned from their afternoon shopping trip, no page boy had appeared to call Beth's name for the telephone. She had gradually accepted the fact that there would not be a conversation with Jarrick that day. Margret, a most beneficial distraction along with her little son, suggested that there was no need to tell the family about Beth's great disappointment. With a nod and a sigh, Beth agreed.

"We found the best millinery shop," Julie called as she rushed over. "I bought a lovely wool cloche to go with my brown suit. Mother bought a delightful white beaded number with the fluffiest feathers! And I think Mrs. Montclair must have bought at least half a dozen new hats. Wait till you see them. You'll just die."

"Julie," Mother scolded mildly, "please temper your words."

"Yes, Mother." Julie shrugged. "Girls,

you'll be just *green* with envy. Is that any better?"

Mother just shook her head.

Beth surveyed the group. "Where did you put everything?"

"Oh, Monsieur Laurent arranged for them to be delivered to the ship. Except for this one." Julie held up a hatbox. "I thought I might wear it to the show tonight."

"There's a show?" Margret asked.

"Why, yes. We found a dinner theater out in Cavendish. The play is *The Enchanted Cottage*. It sounds like it's quite good. So we're going out in the early afternoon to spend a little time at the beach first."

"How are you feeling, Margret darling? Any better?" Mother went to her daughter, arms out.

"Yes, much better."

"Well, we have to hurry so we can catch the train."

Margret's eyebrows drew together. "I'm sorry, Mother, but I made arrangements to speak with John tonight by telephone. I'm afraid I'll have to miss again."

"Oh, no. Must you?"

Margret nodded. "Yes, and actually I'm rather set on it."

Mother paused and eyed Margret, but Julie caught her attention, and they both

236

turned toward the elevator.

As the others followed, Margret drew close to Beth. "Perhaps you should stay with me," she whispered. "What if Jarrick tries to call again?"

Beth shook her head mournfully. "Then I suppose you'll get to speak with him instead. I can't stay back this time just in case he calls. I know that's what he'd say if he were here."

"I understand. But I can also understand your frustration and sadness."

"Thank you, Margret." Beth touched her sister's arm. "And I'm glad that you do."

A short time later, they were settled on the train and headed to the other side of the small province. Beth enjoyed the farm scenes whisking past and especially the surprising ocean views. She thought through a description of what she would ask Julie to paint, if only her request would be well received. The dramatic colors, the tidy farmyards, the peekaboo ocean bays . . . Soon the missed telephone conversation and even Margret's news had drifted to the back of her mind.

Past clusters of other sunbathers, they carried their bags and borrowed folding chairs to the water's edge. Beth looked around a bit uneasily. She still felt uncomfortable in her new bathing suit. The flounce at her knees was whipped in one direction, then another in the gusty wind, at every moment her fabric hat threatening to take to the skies. She reached down to pull her stockings higher and winced as the sand began to accumulate inside her beach slippers. *If this is necessary in order to enjoy an ocean swim, it seems like a lot of fuss.* Beth shaded her eyes to look out over the horizon. *And yet the vast ocean, the salty wind, the beach — it's all so picturesque and inviting.*

Julie was already leading the charge. "Look at the waves! I had no idea they'd be so big. Come on, Victoria. I'll race you!"

Victoria skipped along close behind. Halfway to the water she stopped to roll her stockings down to her ankles, seemed to consider for a moment discarding them entirely, then hastened in after Julie. With a whoop the teenager tossed her hat onto the sand behind her.

"That girl," muttered Mrs. Montclair. "She'll be the death of me yet."

Beth watched the two for a while, then settled into a chair, marveling at how Julie's short hair danced in the breeze, appreciating the energy with which her sister attacked the tumbling surf, and anxious whenever the two swimmers disappeared for any length of time among the waves.

"All right, ladies," she finally said playfully to her mother and Mrs. Montclair, "let's join them in the water. We might not have another chance, and this will be a great anecdote when we return home." She motioned them to their feet, and the three, laughing and arm in arm, made their way to the water. They called out in unison as the cold, foaming ripples swept against their feet and ankles.

Julie and Victoria soon noticed them, shouting and coaxing them to venture farther. Mrs. Montclair firmly motioned them off. "No, no, this is quite enough," she called back. But the woman was smiling, obviously enjoying the new experience. Beth and Mother advanced a few steps, and Julie came rushing up to cheer them on.

"Oh, Mother, isn't this so much fun?" she enthused, grabbing her by the arm.

But Mother laughingly pulled back. "You, my dear, look like Jonah on the shore," she said, taking in her youngest's dripping hair and soaked bathing outfit.

The swells felt chilly, contrasting perfectly with the warm sunshine on Beth's arms. Soon she was knee-deep in the water, the sand beneath her feet washing away from around them, a totally new experience. The panoramic view beyond the rows of incoming waves seemed to go on forever.

This is glorious, she thought as she listened to Julie and Victoria shouting as another wave pushed them toward shore. But by the time Beth had gotten up her courage to face one of the waves herself, Mother was calling and motioning them in.

They slipped one at a time into the dressing tents provided. Donning her regular clothing again was a struggle — there seemed to be grains of sand trapped between every layer of clothing. Beth wished for a good soak in a tub.

As she pushed back the stiff canvas and emerged from the tent, Beth cautioned, "Don't step off the mat, Victoria darling. If you get sand on your feet, it's bound and determined to spread itself through everything else you own."

Victoria only laughed and stepped into the tent, her clothing bundled in her arms.

Just then Beth heard Julie call out, "Nick! Hello, Nick!" They all turned to look where her finger pointed.

"I'm sure I saw him — over there by the ice-cream stand. Did you see him too, Bethie?" She shook her head. "No? I guess he's gone," Julie said. "Or maybe it was someone else. But I thought I saw him." Julie was clearly disappointed.

"You're just imagining things," Beth teased. "We aren't nearly as exciting as the crew you're used to running with these days."

"To be certain," Julie laughed.

Mother cleared her throat. "May I ask, dear, who is Nick?"

Beth and Julie exchanged glances. "Just a young fellow, someone Beth and I met. But it wasn't even him."

"Hmm. You haven't mentioned him. Perhaps you can point him out. I'd like to meet this young friend of yours."

"Oh, Mother . . ."

"I'm going to make a request, Mother, but I don't want you to be alarmed." Margret kept her voice low enough that the others who were eating breakfast at the table could not hear. Beth, who was seated at Margret's elbow, leaned forward to hear and see both Mother and Margret.

Mother put her roll back on her plate. "What is it, darling?"

Margret whispered, "I would like to visit a doctor." She hurried on, "I hate to be any trouble, but I spoke with John last night, and he'd prefer that I see someone today, if

241

possible."

"You're still feeling nauseated?" Mother placed her hand on Margret's, studying her face. Beth watched her skillfully reading for signs with practiced eyes.

Margret smiled faintly. "Actually, not as much today. But it would be wise to confirm or disprove . . . a notion I have."

A meaningful pause, and Mother sat back in her chair with a little smile. "I couldn't help but wonder, my darling. I have experienced certain — well, indications myself, four times over, you know."

Margret returned a shy smile. "So you wondered . . . ?"

"Yes, it did cross my mind, Margret darling. And we must get you to a doctor as soon as possible. I'll see to it immediately." She stood, excused herself with a smile at the group, then hurried out of the bistro toward the front desk.

Mrs. Montclair looked around in bewilderment. "What's gotten into Priscilla? Are you ill again, Margret? Can I be of any help?"

"No, thank you. I'm fine — truly I am." Her modest sister shrank away from the unwelcome attention and pretended to wipe JW's mouth.

"Gracious. I've not seen your mother

move so quickly." Mrs. Montclair shook her head but mercifully let the matter drop.

In the end, secrecy was rather pointless. Julie certainly was not one to "let the matter drop," and by the time they returned to the room, the fact that Margret was hoping for a doctor's visit had made the rounds in excited whispers. Margret was duly fussed over, advice raining down upon her from all sides as they crowded into the Thatcher suite.

"Put your feet up, dear," directed Mrs. Montclair. "You'll want to keep your legs from swelling."

Mother added, "I hope there wasn't a great deal of salt in your eggs and ham this morning. I'm still convinced that salt was the culprit last time. You'll know to watch that now."

Even Julie had her tidbit to add. "I can get you a cold compress. That helps whenever my ankles feel puffy."

"I'm fine," Margret insisted. "No part of me is puffy. Honestly."

But the morning excursion for the day was canceled. Through the concierge, Mother had discovered a doctor's office nearby, and soon Margret and Mother were in a taxicab on their way there. Monsieur Laurent made no comment, but his eyes held a knowing glint. Beth, Julie, and Victoria decided on taking a stroll past the little shops adjoining the hotel, not remembering they had no money with which to make purchases. But it felt good just to window-shop and stretch their legs in the fresh air. They had whisked JW away before the nanny could remind them of his nap time. When he saw a little puppy in a pet-shop window, they could hardly cajole him into returning to the hotel.

They found that Mother and Margret had not yet appeared. Beth tried to read but found it difficult to keep her mind on the story. Victoria was sketching again in her notebook, and Julie had merely collapsed into a padded armchair, her feet resting on the bed in rather unladylike fashion. *I don't suppose I could get Julie to paint for me right now any more than I can focus on reading,* Beth thought wryly.

At last there was a sound at the door, and Mother entered first, followed by Margret, her cheeks pink.

Beth was at her sister's side in a flash, her silent question between them as she looked deeply into Margret's eyes.

Margret nodded quietly. "Yes, he's quite certain I am."

The room erupted into a frenzy of hugs and laughter. "And I predict a *girl* this

244

time," Julie shouted. More laughter and opposing predictions filled the air.

"The doctor warned me, though," Margret admitted when finally things had quieted down, "I do need to stay off my feet in reasonable measure, get enough rest."

"Oh, we'll take care of you." Julie leaned down to pat Margret's still-flat abdomen affectionately. "We'll take care of both of you. Don't you worry one little bit, little *girl.*" And the merriment started up again.

With rather halfhearted interest, the remainder of the afternoon included one last jaunt into the countryside. Beth watched the bright colors of the picturesque island sweep past the train windows. She made a point of moving from seat to seat to chat with each of the family by turn — nothing particularly profound but pleasant conversations.

"I'd like to come back here again," announced Victoria, her arm hanging out the open window, the hand opening and closing in the stream of passing air. "I want more time at the ocean."

"Yes, let's," her mother agreed contentedly. "I believe your father would find it most pleasurable. I think he would even enjoy the beach."

Beth borrowed the camera from Julie,

snapping several scenes in hopes of retaining the images of the island. *Perhaps Julie will be willing to refer to them once we're home.*

Back in the hotel lobby, they found their suitcases packed up again by their maids and ready for their return to the ship. Monsieur Laurent was looking at his pocket watch. "I can't hold the taxis much longer." As usual, Mrs. Montclair was not yet in sight.

Suddenly Beth heard her name called. "Page for Miss Elizabeth Thatcher. Page for Miss Elizabeth Thatcher."

"I'm Elizabeth Thatcher." She raised her hand to a uniformed young man now making his way toward her with a smile.

"Miss Thatcher." He bowed slightly. "There is a telephone call holding for you at the receptionist's desk."

Beth's eyes grew large. She shot a glance at Margret and hurried across the wide floor.

"I'm Elizabeth Thatcher," she repeated to the clerk. "Is there a call for me?"

"Why, yes, Miss Thatcher" — he motioned — "the last telephone at the very end of the desk."

Beth raised the receiver with a trembling hand. *It could be anyone. There's no reason to assume . . .* "Hello?"

"Beth! I can't believe I caught you. It's Jarrick. I'm so glad —"

"Oh, Jarrick, I thought I'd missed your call entirely." Her heart fluttered at the sound of his voice.

He laughed. "Actually, you did. I tried to call earlier today too. But I guess you were out and about. How are you? How has your trip gone so far? Are you enjoying yourselves?"

"It's been . . . wonderful." The one-word description was far from adequate, but she rushed on. "We're on Prince Edward Island just now." The comment brought a laugh. "But then you already knew that."

"Yes, I presumed you were," he joked. "I've always wanted to visit there. Philip has an aunt in Nova Scotia, and the two of us have often talked of traveling east together. We've just never found a good time to go."

"Oh, I wish you were here now," Beth heard herself saying and felt her cheeks grow warm. "It's well worth it. I hope you can sometime." Beth paused, scrambling through her mind for a topic of more importance. "Did you get any of my letters? I've written more than one."

"No, I haven't. And I've been watching the mail every day, as you might imagine."

She could hear the warmth in his voice.

"Oh, they should start to come soon. I'm surprised since I've gotten three from you already."

"Maybe tomorrow," he said hopefully.

"We went to the beach yesterday, and I even went into the water! We did some sightseeing by train. There's plenty more to do here — we haven't seen any of the shipbuilding yards, which I would have enjoyed. We were supposed to do that this morning, and then something came up." For a moment Beth considered sharing Margret's news, but decided against it. "We're heading out now to our ship again. It departs this evening."

"And where are you off to next?" His words sounded almost wistful.

"Nova Scotia. We'll make a stop in Cape Breton, travel northeast around the island, then head back south toward Halifax. Oh, Jarrick, I just wrote to you last night. I posted the letter this morning."

He cleared his throat. "Don't tell me what it says, Beth. I want it to be a surprise."

She smiled. "I'm afraid it's quite nostalgic. It was a somewhat disappointing day — an emotion-filled one."

"I'm sorry to hear that."

Beth's eyes lifted toward the ceiling. She

248

knew her expression was anything but guarded, but she could not seem to constrain her feelings, the strange mixture of pleasure and discontent that speaking with Jarrick — so far away — generated. "It was mostly good things, I suppose, but for the missed telephone connection. I'll admit it cast a pretty long shadow over my mood all day."

"I understand that, believe me, I do." The tone of his voice was almost more than she could bear, and she quickly blinked back tears.

Mrs. Montclair was emerging from the elevator. Beth turned toward where the others were waiting, now assembled and ready to leave. Monsieur Laurent was watching her intently.

"I'm afraid I can't talk further, Jarrick. Everyone is waiting, and we're overdue catching a taxi. I'm sorry. I wish —"

"It's all right, Elizabeth. I'll do a better job of arranging things next time. I'm sorry I botched it yesterday."

"Oh, it's not your fault, I'm sure. The connection just didn't come through."

"Well, I shouldn't have given you a set time. I should have . . . I don't know. But I'll figure out something better for next time. Where and when is the next good time to call?"

Beth could see Monsieur checking his pocket watch again. "I'm not sure. Halifax, I suppose. But I don't know which day —"

"Your father gave me the first two main stops. Will you mail me a schedule, Beth? I know that'll take a week to arrive, but I'd sure like to know where you are along the way."

Beth flushed. "Of course. I should have thought of it sooner."

Mother waved, and Beth said, "I'm so very sorry, Jarrick. I'm afraid I truly do have to go."

"Beth?" he hurried. "Please — I wanted to tell you something first. Two men from the provincial school board were in Coal Valley on Monday. They were taking stock of your little town to see about opening a school there."

"What? Why, that's wonderful!"

"I knew you'd want to know. Your name came up in almost every conversation they had with folks in town. Miss Molly was laughing about it when she told me all who were boasting that they were the person who had suggested you be contacted for the position."

Beth drew in a slow breath. "I'm so grateful. That's just the best news!"

"Yes, I think so too. Well, I just wanted you to know." A pause. "I miss you, Beth." Her breath caught in her throat. "It's not at all the same here without you."

"I miss you too," she whispered. Her heart was aching and exulting all in the same moment. "It won't last long. We'll see each other again soon."

"I know that . . . but not nearly soon enough."

Beth could feel her pulse still racing as she squeezed into the taxicab beside Julie. A conversation was so much better than a letter. Over and over she replayed Jarrick's words in her mind, reveling in the warm emotion she had heard in his voice. Her hand found her waistband where she had tucked another dried petal inside a hanky that very morning.

CHAPTER 16

"Mother, I'd like to send a telegram," Beth said quietly on their way to the shipboard breakfast the next morning. "I don't mind paying for it myself, but I'd like to send it this afternoon — that is, if I can figure out how to do so."

"In regards to what, Beth?"

She didn't let herself hesitate and said forthrightly, "I promised Jarrick I'd send him our port schedule, so we can find another time to speak by telephone."

"Oh, darling, don't you think that might seem a little forward — too presumptuous, even a bit needy?"

Beth paused a moment. "No, I truly don't believe so. He and I discussed it and agreed it would be most helpful. Honestly, I don't know why I didn't think of it sooner. And I've already given my word to Jarrick."

Her mother still looked uncertain, but finally she said, "You'll no doubt be able to find out information on sending telegrams from Monsieur Laurent."

After breakfast, Mrs. Montclair asked in her sprightly manner, "To where are we off today, *Mr. Lorant?*"

He cleared his throat. "We'll see a perfectly lovely landscape — Cape Breton Island. It truly has some of the nicest scenery in all the Maritimes. We're to visit an offshore lighthouse there and, Victoria," he added, turning to the girl, "we can expect to cross paths with any number of wildlife today. I'm sure you'll be very pleased."

The teenager sat upright, looking determined. "Mother, I simply *must* have a set of binoculars. I won't see a *thing* if I don't." The extra bit of dramatics had Beth hiding a smile behind her napkin.

"Yes, dear. I suppose it's time to give up on the others as a lost cause." Mrs. Montclair shook her head and reached down under the table to rub at her knee. "I suppose then, *Mr. Lorant,* that there will be a great deal of walking? My bursitis is acting up again. I'm afraid I must keep off my feet for a day or two."

"Oh, Edith, won't you even see the lighthouse? I'm sure you'd enjoy that."

These table discussions had become rather similar from one day to the next, and Beth found her mind wandering. *When will Jarrick and I be able to talk again?* She couldn't help but mull over yesterday's conversation once again. *Hopefully in Halifax . . .*

Cape Breton Island came into view, its long coast like folds of a deep green blanket trimmed in brown where it touched the water's edge. Beth stood in the sunshine on the stateroom balcony, the wind tugging at her dress. They were still far from the point of the tender's departure when Mother took Beth and Julie aside. "Now, my dears, I said yesterday that I'd like to meet this young man — Nick, was it? I would like to get to know all these friends of yours. We've hardly even spoken to those girls. What would you say to inviting the three to lunch with us today? Monsieur says the lodge on the island serves a decent enough luncheon."

"Oh, yes, Mother — that's a wonderful idea!" Julie was enthralled. "I'm sure they'd like to meet you too."

"Fine, then. Would you please find them before we debark and make the invitation, Julie?"

"Of course. They're probably up by the pool. I'll go right now." She nearly skipped her way out the door of the suite, her mother shaking her head with a long sigh.

Beth turned to follow Julie out into the hallway. The copy of the port schedule had been delivered by Monsieur Laurent, and the office would probably be open by now so she could send the telegram. *Won't he be surprised . . . and pleased!*

"One moment, Beth," her mother said, interrupting her thoughts. "I'd like to speak with you alone, please."

"What is it, Mother?"

Mother motioned to a nearby chair and took the other beside it. She paused. "I feel that perhaps I should know more about the status of your relationship with this man, this officer. I had no idea you had become so familiar with one another in a very short amount of time. You had said he first spoke to you about keeping in touch just before you left your little mining town."

"Yes. But, you see, by that time we already knew each other quite well."

"I see. When we spoke while we were still at home, you knew little about his background and his family."

"Yes, I suppose that's true."

"There are any number of questions I wonder if you've considered."

Beth could feel her face growing warm. *If only Mother could meet him.* She was certain that would put an end to her worries.

"Please understand, darling," Mother continued, "I'm speaking only from my deep concern for your well-being. Marriage lasts a long, long time. To be yoked together with someone . . . well, unsuitable would have tragic effects for the whole of one's lifetime, and for every facet of it. It is something to be contemplated soberly, with great care and much prayer."

"Of course, Mother. I do understand that — and believe it sincerely." She watched as Mother unconsciously spun her own wedding ring around her finger. "For instance, Beth dear, do you know if he's been engaged before — if he has courted someone previously?"

"I don't believe he . . . no, to be truthful, we never discussed that." Beth's face grew even warmer at her inability to answer.

"And what of his own parents? Do they have a good marriage, a good family life?"

"His father is a pastor." Beth was so glad she could provide that piece of positive information.

"My dear," Mother said softly, "that is no guarantee."

Beth stiffened. "But if you'd already met him, Mother, I'm certain you wouldn't —"

"You know better than that, Beth. You know that if we *had* already met him, your father and I would have asked all the same questions — had all the same concerns. People can so easily deceive us by their charming demeanor. I am certainly not assuming he's been deceptive, but I would not regard him with such trusting eyes as you seem to be doing. Not yet."

Beth's heart sank, and she wanted to ask if Mother had trusted Edward Montclair, if she had felt she knew *him* well enough to accept him as an appropriate match for her daughter. Edward, who had a nice enough family, but who was so full of himself and his own importance . . .

Beth stared at her hands twisted together on her lap and remained silent.

"It's not that I want to steal your joy, Beth. I want to see you well-matched in the happiest and most enriching marriage possible, though I know that for every couple there will always be difficulties and hardships to overcome. But that ability to overcome requires a certain compatibility, a bond 'till death do us part,' and an unshakable faith. These are determined through significant time, through questions being asked before the heart is entirely committed. Do you understand?"

Beth wrestled with the loyalty and respect her mother deserved and the embarrassment she felt at being questioned like this — and, most of all, for not being able to answer well. She recalled those overheard remarks from Mother to Mrs. Montclair on the train at the beginning of their journey, articulating doubts about Jarrick, Beth's health, and her chosen profession.

Mother pressed further. "You've said he grew up on the prairie, but has he always lived there? Or did he spend any time on his own elsewhere as an adult?"

"I don't know," Beth whispered. "I shall make a point of asking him."

"And you've said that you think he's thirty or so."

"Yes."

"So is it possible he served overseas?"

Beth froze. She had never even contemplated the question. Edward and the other boys she had grown up with had been just young enough to have missed serving in the Great War. They had all helped with the war effort within their community. *Had Jarrick been a part of any actual fighting? What might he have seen?*

She finally said, "It's possible that he served. He's never mentioned it, though." Beth hated to admit even to herself that she did not know this.

"We want you to be well informed, Beth

— and to know him well ourselves."

Beth lifted her gaze to her mother's face. "I understand, Mother. I truly do. I see the importance of . . . of going forward with eyes wide open." She nodded slowly. "I'm sure Jarrick will be more than willing to answer any questions you have of him, or that I have. I'm sure he'll be an open book." Beth hesitated. "But he's not an employee, Mother. It's a relationship, not an interview."

"Of course, darling." Mother rose. "It's far more important than that. This is for a lifetime."

Grasping at the rail, once again Beth eased herself down into the shuttle. She was able to smile at her traveling companions, but she found it difficult to meet Mother's eyes. She harbored a strange sense of confusion, and she resented the unanswered questions now rattling around in her mind about Jarrick. If only she could speak with him again soon. She was certain he would cooperate fully with any questions she asked, but it was most uncomfortable to realize how little she actually knew about him. *Has he indeed courted a woman in the past? He is, after all, older than I am . . . but I don't even know his age for certain!*

Beth smoothed her dress and tried to keep her face turned toward the railing and the water beyond, lest her sisters — or anyone else — should read her conflict. The prow bounded up, then down in the waves, aiming toward the white obelisk lighthouse looming larger with every splash. The island on which it stood was merely a tiny, barren patch of rocky ground.

Could it be that Jarrick was able to make her feel so special because he had learned about romance before? She felt her heart squeeze in pain. Then again, he'd said he would be meeting with a gentleman from church to learn to be a good husband. Didn't that count strongly in his favor? Unless it indicated some hidden secret that might put obstacles in their path.

Beth's thoughts fluttered back to her mother's question about service in the army. *If he indeed served overseas, what scars and memories might he retain? Do they cast a shadow over his life still?* Beth took a deep breath, tried to slow her racing thoughts.

Mrs. Montclair, Miss Bernard, and JW had stayed behind and fortunately missed the laborious climb up the pinnacle of the lighthouse. The view was breathtaking so long as Beth resisted the urge to look directly down from the dizzying height. The mainland was an emerald jewel set against the clear sky, and several ships were visible in the distance.

The sight reminded Beth of Father. How she wished that he could have joined them here, just for the day. It would have been such a blessing to talk through her dark broodings with him. Beth sighed and moved further around the cupola, shading her eyes to focus her attention on one more out- standing cruise experience. She would make sure Emma took several photographs of the lighthouse to pass around to her students in case Julie didn't complete the task.

They waited longer than expected for Penny, Jannis, and Nick to join them for lunch at the rustic lodge. Beth spent the time doodling an image of the lighthouse on the back of a brochure. Julie smiled quite graciously as she looked over the drawing, yet she made no comment.

When at last the others arrived, Beth noted that Nick was well groomed and wearing a dress jacket and tie. She wasn't certain if this was simply for Mother's sake, but she acknowledged it was the right deci- sion if he wished to make a good impres- sion.

"Most pleased to meet you, Mrs.

Thatcher. I'm Nickolas Petrakis." He reached out to shake Mother's hand. "Thank you so much for the invitation. I always appreciate a good meal, particularly with such excellent company." His smile was broad and charismatic.

"I'm pleased to meet you too. We're glad you were able to come." Mother motioned to the chairs near her own, and the trio filed into the places she designated. Nick was next to her on the left. "I hope you've been enjoying your travels so far."

"Oh, yes. It's been very exciting. And I've met some of the nicest people." He smiled at Julie, who gave a little giggle in response.

"I've been told that you young ladies are from New York state." Mother turned to the sisters just beyond Nick.

"Yes, ma'am," Jannis answered politely, much more subdued than was usual. "We're from Buffalo. In New York."

Mother nodded. "How is it you've come to be traveling on your own?"

Penny drew herself up just a little. "We were supposed to have our aunt along — Aunt Mary — but then . . . then she wasn't able. So we came anyway, since we didn't want to miss out on all this fun . . . on account of our poor auntie," she finished in a rush.

Julie inserted, "She broke her leg. The doctor wouldn't let her come."

"Nor should he," Mother agreed. "There's been much walking. Even with crutches it would have set her back weeks in her recovery, I'm sure."

"Have you heard from your aunt?" Mother continued, to Beth's dismay. *Why is Mother pressing them like this?*

"Yes, ma'am. She's on the mend now, just fine."

"I'm glad to hear it. I suppose you received a letter from her at one of our stops?"

The two girls quickly answered in unison, but they named two different ports. They looked at each other and giggled nervously. "Actually, it was Halifax," Penny affirmed. "Jannis is just confused. She's so busy with everything that . . ."

But Mother had already turned back to Nick. "From where do you hail, Mr. Petrakis?"

"Oh, I'm from a little town near Philadelphia. And I haven't been too far from home before this. So it's been great to get out and see the sights a little."

"Julie tells me that you attended university."

"Yes, ma'am." He laid his napkin over his lap as the waiter set stemmed glasses of cold water and linen-lined baskets of rolls around the table. He smiled with ease. It appeared he wasn't bothered by Mother's questions in the least. Beth felt empathy for him, remembering her own session earlier. *I wish it were Jarrick facing off with Mother right now.*

"I studied economics for a while," he said, repeating what he'd told Beth, "but I'm afraid I didn't graduate. I do plan to get some good use out of my years there, though. I'm planning to break into the business world. With a friend."

Julie inserted herself again. "I told him, Mother, that he should talk to Father, who could be very helpful, I'm sure, in getting Nick started in business."

Mother smiled politely.

Overall, it appeared Nick passed the luncheon test with Mother. Even Beth was impressed by his manners and straight-forward answers. She wasn't so sure about Mother's view of the sisters. But Julie grinned like a Cheshire cat throughout, maintaining a good amount of discretion despite an interruption or two. As they rose to leave the restaurant, Monsieur Laurent invited the three guests to share the walking trails.

"Oh, I'm sorry," Nick said, shaking his head regretfully. "I have to catch up to some of the guys. We planned on going as a group."

"Us too." Jannis nodded quickly. "We've already made other plans. But it's so kind of you to invite us along."

Julie made no effort to hide her disappointment, but she followed Beth to the waiting car. "Wasn't he just as charming as any man we've ever met?" Julie said in a loud whisper as they climbed in.

"He was very polite — almost too much so."

"Whatever do you mean, Bethie?"

Beth found it difficult to put her feelings into words, ones that Julie might receive. "He didn't seem *real,* darling. It seemed like it was all for show."

She watched Julie's face darken into a scowl. "We all do that! We're always putting on our best manners at important times. You can't hold that against him. You just don't understand." Julie folded her arms and stared stiffly ahead.

Beth couldn't help but regret her comments. *It's probably just my own disappointment about the talk with Mother that made me react negatively to Nick. It's unfair and unkind to burden Julie with my own doubts and concerns.* She determined to make things right with her sister as quickly as possible.

The scenery in Cape Breton was everything Monsieur Laurent had promised. Their touring car skimmed along through the hills toward Bras d'Or Lake, and he told them about some well-known inventors from the region. Beth was fascinated to learn that Guglielmo Marconi had sent the first radio signal from the rocky shores of Maritime Canada all the way to England — drawing the Old World almost miraculously closer to the New. Also, Alexander Graham Bell, the inventor of the telephone and much more, had chosen to build his estate on the shores of this lake. Monsieur claimed the beautiful region reminded Mr. Bell of his ancestral home in Scotland.

And seeing it in person, Beth felt she could fully understand Bell's choice. The hike down toward the shore was just the therapy she needed. The rich smell of earth and evergreens, the sun on her shoulders, and the sound of the wind across the broad span of glittering water — all of it served as a balm for her troubled spirit.

She had been mentally writing and rewriting a letter to Jarrick, asking all the questions Mother had posed. Then she had imagined his responses — first one way, then another — which she knew was fruitless and silly. But the most troubling thought of all, how would she feel if some of his answers were not what she wanted to hear? Would her feelings about him change?

At last, resting on a cushion of moss stretched across a fallen log, she gazed out across the pebbled beach and prayed to release all the worrying questions. "Father God, I think I *can* trust Jarrick. I think I *do* know him well enough for that. But even if he proves to be someone other than the one I have come to . . . to appreciate and value, You are my strong defense, and I know You will set a hedge around my emotions, my desires. Please help me adjust my vision of my life, my future, to match Yours — Your will always coming first, not my own. Thank You, Father." It was almost as if she could see her troubled thoughts sweeping away from her in the wind, carried across the lake into the hills beyond.

Footsteps crunched behind her, and she turned quickly, shocked to see Mother picking her way carefully over the uneven stones. Beth stood and hurried to her, hand held out to take her arm. "Mother! I thought you were walking with the others along the beach."

"I was, darling. But you seemed so alone. I wondered if there was something troubling you. Is there, Beth?"

267

Yes, your questions about Jarrick have been troubling me — your doubts about him. "I've just been praying about . . . about everything. What we talked about this morning concerning Jarrick." But before Mother could respond, Beth added, "Tell me about your courtship, Mother. Please. I know you and Father met at church, but I'm sure there's much more to the story than I've heard before."

Brushing at a spot on the log and spreading out a handkerchief, Mother lowered herself gently, sitting rather stiffly on the unfamiliar bench. Beth joined her. "You don't want to hear about that," Mother said with a dismissive wave of her hand. "It seems a different lifetime now, it was so long ago."

"Oh, but I do. I truly do."

For a moment she wondered if Mother would answer. She was shaking her head and trying to push stray strands of hair back into place under her hat. But at last she said quietly, "We were very young — or rather, from my perspective now, we seem to have been awfully young. In truth, I was almost an old maid by then, all of twenty-four."

"Did you know immediately that he was *the one*?" Beth asked.

"The one? Such a notion!" her mother

268

said with a chuckle. "He was a sensible choice, or so I felt then. My parents, however, were not entirely convinced. He hadn't proven himself yet, had not risen much above his rather meager beginnings. But he was clever, and such a good listener. And he remembered things — like your grandmama's favorite candy, and the kind of fishing lures your grandpapa liked best. He was a true gentleman by nature, and in his own quiet way he won them over."

"What sorts of things did you do together . . . before you were married?"

"Oh, my darling, we weren't *ever* allowed to be alone! It wasn't at all proper in our social order. We could sit in the parlor together so long as the doors remained wide open" — she swatted away a fly — "and my father was near at hand. And we might walk together along the main road of town with at least one of my brothers trailing behind, though never too many steps away."

Beth shook her head and laughed aloud. "They didn't trust *him*? We're talking about *Father*!"

Mother joined in the laughter. But she had turned serious again when she said, "Trust must be earned, and that's still true today, darling. Expecting anything less was considered poor parenting, like letting a fox in among the chickens, so to speak. So, you see, I'm not as strict as your grandparents were. That's something, isn't it?"

Beth only nodded, and they sat in silence as the wind whispered around them. At last her mother spoke again. "I haven't thought of that time for so many years. About the way we were then — your father and me. Margret came along in our second year of marriage, and then all my attention seemed to be focused on her. Father was gone much of the time, in the earliest days when he was working hard to build the business. I had no one with whom to share my days and my nights. I was happy, of course, but I was rather lonely too — setting up a household, without any experience hiring a staff, raising a child, expecting a second . . . who turned out to be you."

She reached for Beth's hand. "You might not think so now, but I do understand what it is to be married to an adventurer, to in effect manage a home alone. I wouldn't choose that for you if it were up to me. But you must make up your own mind. I can only guide you with advice in the way I see things."

"I appreciate that, Mother. I do understand that you want what's best for me. I do."

Your will, Father God, Beth prayed silently as they sat together. *Neither Mother's nor my own. Your will alone.*

CHAPTER 17

With no further prompting from Beth, Julie produced three finished paintings during a quiet day at sea. The fjord with whales breaching, a small fishing village tucked among the trees with a row of bobbing boats tied to the pier, and the intricate ocean-carved shoreline that Beth had sketched out herself. She was thrilled with each, amazed that her sister had captured not just the correct shapes and colors but the *feel* of each locale. And even with the lovely details, Beth found that she most appreciated the water — the many shades of blues and greens in the waves, the sense of movement — as though she could hear the roar and smell the salty spray. She was mesmerized.

"They're magnificent!" Margret complimented their sister. "How did you ever . . . ? That's just how it looked!"

Julie smiled and accepted their laudatory comments before dashing off to be with her friends, obviously enjoying the seagoing portions of their travels over the ports of call. Beth tried not to wonder if her sister preferred the new friends to her family, and hoped it was simply the appealing pace of activities on board.

They were set up in the familiar deck area, where JW spread out his favorite toys, now tiny boats and a tub of water. He splashed happily next to Mother's chair, sometimes bringing a dripping toy to share with "Annie Bet." Margret left to rest below. They lapsed once more into the comfortable rhythm of life at sea.

"Mother, I believe I'll go for a short walk."

"Of course, darling. Be sure to take your hat. Do you know when you'll be back?"

"I won't be long," Beth promised.

The seed of an idea had been forming. She had tried to set it aside as absurd, but it had remained. *Why not send another telegram to Jarrick? I could suggest a time for us to speak again.*

Beth walked to the ship's office once more, the click of her heels echoing in the corridor as she neared her destination. As she reached for the door handle, she hesitated, then moved on past toward the deck beyond. She leaned against the rail and gathered her thoughts. *What would I say —*

exactly? Who might also read it? Should I send it to the RCMP post in Lethbridge, or could it be sent to Jarrick personally?

A strong ocean breeze pulled at her hair, with more strands coming loose by the minute. Beth knew if she stayed much longer, she would look even more outlandish than she felt.

Resolutely, she stepped inside and ran her hands over the unruly locks. Drawing back her shoulders, she moved toward the office. "I'd like a form to send a telegram, please."

The young man seated on the other side of the desk slid a sheet of paper across to her. "Fill this out exactly as you intend it to be read. We charge per letter, so you'll want to be as brief as possible."

"Yes, thank you." Beth assured him, "I've sent one before."

Stepping to the other end of the counter, Beth hunched forward around her project. *What would Mother say if she knew? And worse, Mrs. Montclair would scold her being so forward!* Beth steeled herself against the mental lectures. *It's Jarrick. He won't mind. He will understand; he will want to know.*

Carefully she wrote the words in pencil, erasing only once or twice to edit it all.

Questions from Mother — STOP — need

to talk — STOP — best time for call Halifax Sunday PM — STOP — Barthum House — STOP.

Beth set the pencil on the counter beside the form. She could think of no other way to indicate what she wanted him to know. She fervently hoped that anyone other than Jarrick who might see the telegram would have so little information, they would make no assumptions from it.

She slid the form back to the man behind the desk. He scanned it and smiled. "Spell the name again for me, miss."

"J-A-C-K T-H-O-R-N-T-O-N," she answered, remembering in time that no one else referred to him as Jarrick.

"And you want it sent to the RCMP post in Blairmore, Alberta?"

"Yes," she murmured.

"Uh-huh." He smiled again but made no further comment.

Beth counted out the money. It was more than she had expected, since Monsieur Laurent had instructed her to charge the previous telegram to her room.

Hurrying back through the narrow corridor, Beth hoped she had done the proper thing. The expression on the young man's face had etched itself in her mind. It seemed as if he had seen right through what she had hoped was the unspecified nature of her message.

CHAPTER 18

When Beth awoke the next morning to a cloudy, dripping sky, the ship was already docked in Halifax Harbor. If Jarrick had received the telegram yesterday, this could well be the day he would call. The thought sent a shiver of excitement, as well as apprehension, through her. How would he react?

"Bethie, are you awake?" Julie's sleepy voice mumbled from the other side of the small room.

Beth turned from the window and shot a questioning glance at her sister. Julie had not yet emerged from under her jumble of covers. "Yes, darling. I'm up. And you should be too. Or Mother will be knocking at the door."

The blankets shifted, but Julie did not appear.

"We're in Halifax. We must have docked during the night."

"Are we doing another tour? I hope not."

Beth smiled. "No, sister dear, it's Sunday. We're going to church instead."

Julie groaned.

"Don't be like that. I know you want to be with your friends. But why don't you invite them along?"

One hand reached out and drew the covers away from her face. "Do you think Monsieur Laurent would let them ride with us?"

"Well, Mother probably would. I'm sure she'd be in favor of them attending with us."

Bare feet slid out from beneath the blankets to the floor, and Julie rose slowly. "That's a good idea. I'll ask them after we eat."

For the first time in several days, Margret made an appearance at breakfast. She had dressed for church and seemed determined not to allow any further nausea to keep her in. "I lined the inside of my bag," she whispered to Beth. "Just in case."

"Oh, my goodness, I certainly hope you don't need to use it!" Beth clutched at Margret's hand.

"Mercifully, by the time we reach church I should be feeling better. I don't want to miss the service from fear of embarrassment."

Then a dejected Julie returned. Her invitation had been declined. The travelers made their way to the taxis.

"It's strange," Beth remarked as she looked at the passing scene. "The trees are all so small here. Monsieur, don't trees grow well in this part of Nova Scotia?"

He turned to answer, a serious expression on his face. "Oh, no, miss, that is not the case. But I applaud your attentiveness. What you've noticed is due to the massive explosion in Halifax Harbor during the war."

"It knocked down all the trees?" Beth had been in her teen years when she'd heard of the calamity. She couldn't imagine such an event.

Monsieur Laurent nodded. "It leveled almost everything in this part of the city, blowing out windows for miles in every direction. The shock wave from the blast was felt as far away as Cape Breton and Prince Edward Island. Much of what you saw near the harbor is new construction. And though the city is working hard to rebuild itself, the sad truth is that the vacant lots we're passing now once held thriving businesses."

All of this area laid waste! Those poor

people! Beth silently mourned.

Mother said, "Oh, gracious, I can't even imagine. It was caused by a collision of ships, was it not, Monsieur Laurent?"

"Yes. One was loaded heavily with explosives, destined for the war. When the two collided, a fire resulted on board which spread very quickly, detonating its cargo all at once."

"I remember reading about it in the newspaper," Mother said.

"Yes, madame. Sadly there were thousands of dead and wounded. My son Henri passed through the harbor not long afterward. He could scarcely put words to the devastation he saw. But much progress has been made since — a great deal more than when I was last here." He turned his face away, his voice trailing off a little. "But God is good. He can restore. It's what He does so masterfully. The new green growth for now . . . and one day, even loved ones who have been taken from this world."

"Amen," Beth whispered softly.

The small church the families visited had clear glass windows, though the photograph displayed in the foyer showed the lovely stained glass which had once been. There was a box set beneath the photo for donations to replace what had been destroyed.

The faithful devotion of these people was more compelling to Beth's heart than the message from the pulpit. As Beth filed out behind her family, she dropped what money she had into the collection box. She noticed that Mother and Mrs. Montclair had done the same. Even Monsieur Laurent had made a point of contributing something.

"Bethie, sit down." Julie had already complained several times, although Beth had no idea why her movement seemed to matter so much. "You're making me dizzy."

There was little for Beth to do but pace around the hotel room. Reading had become impossible as she waited. Victoria's violin was heard from the bedroom next door. Though she played beautifully, Beth wondered if perhaps the sound was what was taxing her sister's patience.

"Want to play mahjong, Julie?"

"No."

"How about chess? I saw a set in the parlor."

"No — you know I can never beat you."

"You might if you didn't give up halfway through." Beth shook her head. "Checkers then? What about that?"

Julie lifted her head from the small canvas in front of her. "If I could just get some peace and quiet, please. I'd like to finish this lighthouse. Isn't that what you've been pestering me to do? How can you nag me now while I'm working?" She shook her head, but looked only mildly annoyed. She clearly did enjoy painting.

Beth dropped onto the bed. It was already well past two. She had visited the front desk enough times that she knew they were starting to be perturbed. She stretched out across the bedspread and stared up at the ceiling.

Giving up at last on remaining in their room, she descended again to the lobby alone, taking a seat near the window. Shortly after four o'clock she heard the page's voice. "Miss Elizabeth Thatcher, there is a call holding for you at the front desk."

Beth bolted from her seat, almost knocking into the young man approaching her. He pointed at the small room off to the side of the lobby in which a telephone waited on a small desk with a wooden chair drawn up beside it. Beth closed the narrow door and lowered herself onto the seat, grateful for the unexpected privacy.

Lifting the receiver, she spoke breathlessly, "Jarrick?"

"Yes, Beth, it's Jarrick. I got your telegram. Is something wrong?"

"No, there's nothing wrong. It's just —
I've been — that is, we have been discussing things, and . . ." The carefully planned
speech had already evaporated from her
mind. "It's been so hard to reach you. We
weren't really able to talk back in Charlottetown. And then Mother . . . well, she began
asking questions that I couldn't answer. I so
badly wanted to speak with you." Beth's
faith in her own judgment was wavering.

"I see."

"I hope you don't mind. I knew a letter
would take so long."

"But, Beth, it's just that . . . I was worried
when I read your telegram. I thought maybe
there was a problem."

Beth coiled the telephone cord around her
finger. "Oh, I'm sorry. I didn't mean to
worry you. I just thought I'd speed up the
process a little — for Mother's sake. And
mine too."

"I was away from our post here. They told
me about your telegram when I radioed in.
So I drove back out to Lethbridge this
morning to speak with you."

Beth felt herself go weak. "Oh, Jarrick,
I'm so sorry. I had no idea it would cause
problems for you. I'm very, very sorry! I
don't even know what to say." The words
were choked by her regret and humiliation.

So Mother was right after all! This is a mistake.

The sound of Jarrick clearing his throat crossed the hundreds of miles of telephone line until it resounded in Beth's ear. His words came gently. "It's all right, Beth. I'm just relieved there's nothing wrong — and, well, it's worth the trip just to hear your voice again. I was disappointed too about our last conversation being over all too soon. I had so much more I wanted to say."

"Can you ever forgive me?"

"Really, there's nothing to forgive." An awful pause lingered between them before he took charge. "How is Halifax?"

Beth tried to laugh but it sounded rather hollow. "It's fine. It's nice. We saw a great deal of evidence of the explosion, but the city seems to be recovering quickly . . ." Then she stopped, repeating once again, "Jarrick, I truly am sorry."

"Please don't mention it at all. I know you'd be the last person on earth to deliberately put someone out. You're considerate to a fault, Beth. Please, let's just forget all about that now and enjoy the time we have to talk. Who knows when we'll get the chance again?"

"Thank you. You're very kind."

They chatted awkwardly for a few moments about the places the vacationers had seen most recently, and Jarrick explained some of the work that had been keeping him so busy. Beth felt herself grimace as he described how frequently he was required to travel through his large posting.

At last he seemed to remember the urgency in her message. "You said your Mother had questions. I can only assume they were about me. What is it that she would like to know?"

"It's really not that important now," Beth said.

"If not now, then when?"

Taking a deep breath, Beth steeled herself. She had made such a mess of it, and this was very different from the way she had envisioned the conversation. "Well, for starters, I suppose I should know how old you are."

He laughed. "Yes, I guess you should. I'm twenty-nine. My birthday is in December."

"I was in Coal Valley last December," Beth argued. "I don't remember anyone mentioning that."

"I wasn't around on the third. And I wasn't looking for a lot of attention given it anyway."

"December third." Beth made a mental note. "And if you're almost thirty —"

"Thanks a lot!" he interrupted in a wry tone. "There's no need for you to take a shot at me in the process."

Beth giggled. "All right then, if you're as young as twenty-nine, Mother wondered if you had served in the war."

There was a pause. When he spoke again, his voice had turned serious. "Well, I wanted to enlist. It was a pretty big issue between my dad and me. He put a great deal of pressure on me not to go unless I was drafted — told me to pray that God would make the decision for us both. I watched one of my brothers and many of my friends get called up and, I assure you, I felt like a washout not joining them. My notice didn't come until near the very end. I only completed a little basic training, and then the armistice was reached. My mother was overjoyed. But I've always felt it wasn't fair somehow. Like I hadn't done my duty."

Beth realized that Mother had been right. The information added a whole new layer to the image she had formed of Jarrick in her mind. She was grateful too that he had been spared, yet proud of him for wanting to help protect his country.

"You don't need to feel that way," she reassured him softly. "You honored your father's wishes — that was the right thing to do. And besides," she added, "you're serving your country now."

"I certainly hope so."

A question occurred to Beth. "Then what did your father think when you chose to become a Mountie?"

"He wasn't very pleased at first, especially when he realized I'd likely be sent to the West. He'd been working to get the farm going while pastoring too. He really wanted his grown sons to stay close, to share in the work and the benefits."

"Oh, dear. I know how that feels — parents who have their own plan in mind. Believe me, I do."

For some time they shared questions back and forth about their lives before Coal Valley. Jarrick was very surprised to hear of Beth's childhood health issues, and she was pleased to add further to information that might help put Mother at ease — particularly that he had not courted a woman previously, having been too single-minded about his career.

"It sounds as if you have a very close-knit family," Beth marveled. "Your stories remind me of the gatherings at my grandpapa's, though we were able to get together far less frequently than your family. Those times are such special memories to me."

"I don't want to give the impression that my family is perfect, Beth. Or that we always got along well. I think we focus on what we choose, and we minimize what we purposely decide to overlook. For instance, I could have told you some of the not-so-pleasant things that some of my family members would likely have started with. My cousin who just says aloud whatever she's feeling, no matter who might be listening. My uncle who's pretty harsh with his sons and sometimes his nephews too. My very competitive older brother. I could go on. I think we all have something in our characters that can make us difficult to endure at times. And our families always have a front-row seat for all of our quirks and foibles."

"What about you?" she tried to tease him. "What makes you difficult to endure?"

"Well, that's direct." Beth could hear the sound of a cringe in his voice. "Goodness, I'd hate for you to lay it all out for your mother in so many words, but, yes, of course I have my faults."

"Oh, Jarrick, I'm not asking for Mother's sake. I have no intention of reporting anything like that back to her — and, honestly, you don't even have to answer at all if you'd rather not. Maybe it's just too difficult a question."

A pause. "No, I think it's fair. And you can be sure that Lester Carothers — that's the older gentleman I've been meeting with from church — he doesn't hold back from asking. For one thing, I tend to focus all my energy on just one thing. And maybe that sounds like it might not be so bad. But just ask Philip what happens to everything else when I get too wrapped up in work. He'll tell you that I'm liable to let other things fall by the wayside. And sometimes I'm too hard on people close to me — I probably get that from my father. I tend to expect others to be as uncompromising as I am."

"Yes, I can see how that might be difficult." She smiled to herself. While she was missing him so much, those things hardly seemed to be obstacles at all.

He sighed. "Not only that, but there's a rather unhappy incident in my past that kind of hangs a shadow over my hometown for me. It's entirely possible that when you come visit, someone will think they're clever in bringing it up again."

Beth's heart leaped at the words *when you come* rather than *if you come.* She waited while he gathered his thoughts.

"When I was younger — around thirteen — my friend and I were hired by a neighbor to do some work around his farm. He had a brand-new tractor, one of the first ones in our area. It was a heavy, enormous thing, and he'd paid a small fortune for it. He was going to let one of us drive it while the other one worked alongside him. The truth is, to this day I'm not even really sure what happened. I don't know if somebody was playing a prank on him or what. But the engine ground to a stop right when we fired it up again after lunch, and we found a large chunk of metal jammed into the open gears of that just-bought beast of a machine. It couldn't have gotten there by any natural event. Someone had to have wedged it in on purpose. At any rate, it did a great deal of damage. And then it seemed like the whole community got involved — everybody trying to judge whether it was my friend or me who had done it.

"I was crushed. I expected my mom and dad to stand up for me, because they knew me well enough. I suppose they'd seen me fail enough times too, and that no doubt factored into their reaction. But in the end, I guess they weren't sure they could trust my version of the truth. Of course, the other boy was adamant that he hadn't done it, and the farmer's son backed up his story that he was never out of sight. Whereas I had used the outhouse with no one else around. So my dad ended up paying the bulk of what it cost to make the repairs. Money that, I assure you, as a pastor's family, we did not have to spend like that. Every once in a while somebody at home will bring up that story again — like it's a joke. But it's never funny to me. It's still pretty crushing, even to this day. I hated to see how quickly my reputation could be destroyed. And there are plenty of people in town who have never let me forget it either."

"People can be so thoughtless — even cruel." Beth felt sorry for him.

"To this day I keep wondering if I should repay my dad for the repair costs. I want to. It wasn't fair that he had to bear the consequences. And then the other side of the argument kicks in. He said he believed me, but he must have doubted — or at least wasn't sure I was telling the truth since he went ahead and paid the damages. If I paid him back now, it could seem like a guilty conscious was finally getting my attention. I just can't bring myself to forfeit his last shred of faith in me. It may sound like . . . like I'm still a kid, but my parents' trust in me is still important.

"So I guess that's part of the reason I went into law enforcement," he continued. "I want to be a person who makes sure the truly guilty party is found as quickly as possible — and that the judgment is fair. No scapegoats, no cutting corners on justice. I know I can't be right all the time, but I take it very seriously. And I never want to see the innocent punished."

Beth shook her head, though she knew he couldn't see it. "That's terrible. I'm so sorry that happened to you."

"Well, like I said, nobody's history is perfect. None of us goes through life without picking up some scars. But that's a big one for me, and I think God has used it to teach me a lot. So, I suppose this side of heaven, that's the most one can ask for."

"No," Beth said gently, "that's not *all*. Because He also brings people into your life who want to share those painful memories, and hopefully will help with the healing. You're not alone, Jarrick." She closed her eyes and pictured his face before her. "I believe in the man you are."

A long sigh. "I wish you were here, Beth. I'm afraid that you've become that *one thing* in my life that makes it hard to think of anything else. And I want some evidence of a future together for us — an expectation. I'm doing everything I can to pursue you, and you're not even here." He hurried to add, "I'm not trying to rush you, Beth. Just being honest. Is that okay?"

He had never been quite so candid before. Now it was Beth's opportunity to respond. She knew he was waiting, silent until she dared be as bold with her words. Very slowly, she phrased her careful answer. "Jarrick, I'm still accountable to my father. I don't mean that in a dreadful, old-fashioned way, but because he's my guardian and he loves me. I want to honor him as best I can."

"Of course, Beth. I want that too."

"I'm well aware of how difficult it would be for my family if I should move away from them — for good." Her pulse was racing. "But I am confident of God working in my life, directing me. And I know He brought me to Coal Valley for a reason — lots of reasons, in fact. I'm a different person now than I was when I left home last year. More confident in God. More willing to let Him be the leader, the guide in my life. I do trust that He has a plan in this too. And I'm praying that He will reveal it." Tears flooded her eyes. "But if I speak from my heart, then yes — yes, I'm completely certain I want to share your life. God willing, to be your wife." Her last words were barely audible through the crackles of the telephone line.

A long pause. She could hear the smile in

his voice when he said, "Your answer is so well-structured, so different from the way I think. I've never met anyone at all like you. Somehow just in this conversation you've managed to make me want you even more. I wouldn't have thought that was possible."

Beth laughed through happy tears. "What a terrible thing to do to one another, with weeks of absence still standing in between us — maybe even longer."

"You're right. But I'm determined to be patient, though it won't be easy. Every day I miss you more. I keep reminding myself I must have confidence that you'll be back before too long. Or else maybe I'll just put in an application to come east."

"No, no, Jarrick — there's no need to force things. God will make His will happen if He's in this. And I do think He probably is. But waiting is still the only true option." She could feel her cheeks glowing, her heart overflowing with emotion. "I feel as if we're very well-suited to each other, that there's much we can accomplish together since we share a similar mission in life. You need someone who can care for all the untended details while you're out taking up the gauntlet and pursuing your dragons. I would be so honored if I might be your helpmate."

He exhaled slowly. "It's going to be a *terribly* long summer."

"Yes," she echoed, "it is."

The last words Beth heard before the click of the disconnecting receiver sent her pulse to racing again. "I love you, Beth. Goodbye."

She set the telephone back in its cradle slowly. *Was there still any hesitation? How could God* not *be guiding this?* And then she sobered. She wondered how she would respond if God were to lead elsewhere. Could she truly walk away from Jarrick now? She pushed the question aside.

Beth hurried back up to the hotel room she shared with Julie. Her sister was still in the same position, placing the finishing touches on the brightly striped lighthouse she had been painting. *Has she even noticed my absence?*

"Julie," Beth said, breaking the silence at last, "I was finally able to speak with Jarrick."

"That's nice." She dabbed her brush in the smear of red on her wooden palette and added more to the stripe.

Beth tried again. "Darling, I said I spoke with Jarrick by telephone just now. Did you hear me, Julie?"

Her sister laid the paint brush down, smiled at her work, and looked up.

"I just spent time with Jarrick by telephone. I was finally able to talk with him."

"Oh, how nice. Did it go well?"

"Very well."

One glance at the glow on Beth's cheeks and Julie sprang closer. She was giving Beth her full attention now. "How well? How well did it go?"

"Very, very well."

Julie reached for Beth's hands and giggled her joy. "I knew it! I knew it!" They threw arms around each other and laughed. "Tell me more," Julie commanded.

Beth blushed, looked down at her clasped hands. "It seems we're of the same mind."

"Oh, Bethie, don't be so cryptic. Does he love you or not?"

Beth nodded mutely, and Julie exploded into joyful squeals. "I'm so very happy for you, my dear sister."

Julie caught sight of their reflection in the hotel room mirror. She turned Beth's attention toward it and whispered, "Look at you! You'll be such a beautiful bride." Julie's head came to rest against Beth's, their arms still wrapped around each other. Short, tight curls framed Julie's animated face. Beth's own, much more serene, still flushed with joy. For a moment they gazed together at the image of themselves, so very close, so very different.

Then the delight on Julie's reflection waned. "But, Bethie, how can I let you go? I'll miss you too much." She seemed to ponder for a moment and then smiled again. "I suppose I'll just have to follow you."

Chapter 19

"Madame, I strongly insist that we remain together."

Mrs. Montclair stood her ground. *"Mr. Lorant,* if the girls' own mothers are comfortable allowing them a short excursion on their own, then I don't see what grounds you have to resist. We are, after all, their *mothers* and *guardians."*

With equal obstinacy, though more controlled, he replied, "And I, madame, am the guide hired by their *fathers* to keep all of you safe. I was chosen for this position because I have an extensive knowledge of travel in these areas. A knowledge which, I reluctantly must point out, you lack despite your status of motherhood. This trust I have not taken upon myself lightly. I have no intention of shirking that responsibility now."

"It makes no difference to me how you resolve the issue in your own mind. Regardless of your convictions, I am giving my consent to Victoria that she may go with a group of her peers to this concert in the park. I see nothing wrong with my decision, and thus I shall not be swayed. For heaven's sake, it's just a concert! Victoria has attended any number of them. She'll hear bagpipes, along with Celtic fiddling, of all things. I'm not going to deny her that experience. It's precisely the kind of thing I had hoped she would encounter on this vacation."

Beth had not observed Mrs. Montclair quite so ruffled for some time. She kept her face aimed downward toward her plate.

"Priscilla," Mrs. Montclair said, turning to Mother for support, "what do you say?"

From where she sat next to Mother, Beth could see her gripping her hands together tightly on her lap. "I'm not sure, Edith. Who did you say would be supervising?"

"Three of the ship's employees are attending. They will be with the children every minute — it couldn't be safer."

"I'm not a child," Victoria muttered.

Beth glimpsed Julie's face in time to catch her eyes rolling and tried not to smile. It was an entirely inappropriate time for either of them to be amused.

"You may do as you like, Priscilla. As for

me, I am allowing Victoria to go along, and that's my final word on the matter."

Beth could easily feel Mother's tension. The seconds ticked away. Beth had expressed her keen interest in going, while Julie had practically stamped a foot and insisted on the concert. Mrs. Montclair and Mother were expected to attend a business-related luncheon on behalf of their husbands. Beth remembered Father's expression of gratitude that Mother had been willing to step in. Monsieur Laurent had his own appointment, meaning it would be the three youngest at the concert on their own since Margret had bowed out.

Finally Mother asked calmly, "What do you think, Beth? You've traveled on your own."

Beth stopped eating and looked around the table. She swallowed hard. *Is this a test? Is Mother truly seeking out my opinion?*

"I'm not sure, Mother." She knew without looking that Julie was desperate for a positive answer. "Father did choose Monsieur Laurent to be our guide," she began slowly. "On the other hand, we'd be riding on a bus that the ship provides, and we'd only be staying in the park long enough for the concert. I can't imagine what harm we'd face. It couldn't be *very* dangerous." She

300

nodded slightly. "If it were entirely up to me, I'd say yes. And I would step in as chaperone. I suppose that means chaperoning myself," she added with a little smile, hoping to lighten the moment.

"I see," conceded their guide without a return smile. "Very well." He wiped his mouth, folded his napkin and laid it beside his plate, which still held most of his breakfast. "Then I shall release you to be accountable for yourselves." He rose and strode away.

"Aha!" Mrs. Montclair exclaimed. "We have bested him at last."

"Oh, Edith! That was not the intention." Mother's eyes followed the man from the room. "And I'm somewhat concerned about the consequences —"

"That we get to go to the concert, of course," Julie interrupted brightly. She dropped her napkin over what remained on her own plate. "I'm going to tell Penny and Jan."

The broad, grassy knoll in the city park was filled with concert-goers sprawled out on blankets, sitting on folding chairs, or walking and chatting in small groups. Beth and Victoria threaded their way through the crowd to find a spot large enough to spread a blanket, Julie following some distance behind with her friends.

At the first distinct sound of the bagpipes, Beth was mesmerized. She had seen any number of instruments in concert, but nothing had prepared her for this unique device — like some sort of creature tucked under an arm and squeezed mercilessly until it produced its mournful call. She closed her eyes and lost herself in the astonishing, magnificent sounds.

When the piece came to an end and applause erupted, Beth looked around. Victoria was seated beside her, but Julie was not in sight.

Beth motioned with her hand. "Where is Julie, Victoria?"

"She never sat down here — went off with her friends," she said loudly above the sound of the applause.

"Where?"

"Don't know. I heard Jannis say they should move closer to the platform."

"What?" Beth strained to understand the girl's reply.

"They're sitting closer!"

People were settling back into their places, and Beth quickly scanned around. She stood to look more carefully, reminding herself that Julie was an adult and would never venture beyond the crowd at the concert.

The music began again, and a soloist took his place at the center of the bandstand for a lovely ballad that Beth had heard before. She was able to join with the audience in singing the chorus. " 'Oh, ye'll take the high road, and I'll take the low road, and I'll get to Scotland a'fore ye. But me and my true love will never meet again on the bonnie, bonnie banks o' Loch Lomond.' " Beth had not realized that it was a sorrowful song — of love spoiled by discord. She listened more closely to the words of each verse before joining again in the chorus.

Once the last notes of the song died away, hearty applause rolled again across the park. The soloist waved and bowed to the appreciative audience as he left the stage, and the man with his bagpipes reentered from the other side with a quartet of violins. Beth decided she would wait to find Julie until after the next piece. She cast a glance toward Victoria, round-eyed with delight at a new violin style. Beth was certain she would be attempting to emulate it in her room come evening.

It was a shock to Beth when the last performance was announced. It was well past time for her to find her sister. "Victoria, I'm going to look for Julie."

"It's almost over. She'll come back then."

"Once the crowd all gets up at the same time, we'll never find each other."

"I suppose," the girl grumbled. "I'll go with you."

They began searching for a path among the spectators, unable to call out Julie's name but often enduring irritated demands to "Sit down!" "Out the way!" "Move!"

At last Victoria waved for Beth's attention. Julie was standing beside her, a few yards away. Beth's relief filled her whole being. The three picked their way back to the blanket. "I don't know why you're so worried," Julie grumbled. "It's not as if I didn't know where to meet the bus, or that the girls and Nick weren't going to the very same place."

"Nick was with you?"

"Sure, he's kind of sweet on me, I think." Julie chuckled to herself. "He's my little shipboard romance."

Beth grabbed hold of her sister's shoulder. "That is not funny, Julie. You're not encouraging him, are you?"

"Of course not, Bethie. Well, maybe a little. But it's all in fun, I promise."

"Julie, no. It's not something to joke about. If Father were here, you wouldn't be

304

so cavalier about it. You know he wouldn't approve."

Julie nodded slowly. "You're right — as always." She gave one of her eloquent shrugs. "But good gracious, I never really mean anything by it anyway. And neither does Nick. He's just a big tease."

During their bus trip back to the hotel, Beth felt subdued and regretful in a whirl of *what-ifs*. Julie indeed was safe, but Beth couldn't help remembering her "chaperone" promise and how distinctly she had failed. It was such a difficult line to walk, keeping her sister close without seeming to smother her.

At dinner, Monsieur Laurent appeared as willing as ever to participate in the conversation, yet Beth sensed a new reserve in his demeanor. She felt rather shy under the gaze of his clear blue eyes, as if they were both aware that trust had been broken. Yet Beth couldn't find herself sorry they had attended the concert — a truly marvelous experience with delightful music. *And without any negative results,* she thought, but had to add, *though there could have been.*

"Monsieur Laurent, what can we expect for tomorrow?" Mother asked.

He returned an easy smile. "We'll need to

board early. Our ship departs at ten o'clock, and we should be at the docks by half past eight. I've arranged for breakfast in your rooms tomorrow morning in order to save time."

"That's very considerate, monsieur. Thank you."

"You're quite welcome, Mrs. Thatcher."

After the meal, Monsieur Laurent approached Beth with a smile. She hesitated about what to say, still feeling a sense of having disappointed him, of being lax in her avowed responsibilities. His hand reached inside his jacket and withdrew an envelope. "You've received another letter, Miss Thatcher."

"Oh. Thank you, monsieur," she said, feeling like she could now turn the page on her negligence. As she took delivery, he winked and turned away, whistling a familiar tune. Her mind added the accompanying words, *"Ye'll take the high road, and I'll take the low road . . ."*

Beth stopped with a little gasp. *The Scottish ballad sung in the park — was Monsieur Laurent at the concert after all? Did he cancel his appointment to be there for his assigned duties? And is it possible he observed Julie's long absence?*

CHAPTER 20

Beth determined to finish reading *Redburn*, even if the voyage home was as dark and depressing as Melville's portrayal of England during that period. She raised her hand against the bright sun to shield the page from the sun's strong glare. *If I had chosen the wider brimmed hat . . .*

"Where's JW?" she finally asked, looking around for a nice distraction with her beloved nephew.

Mother sounded a bit defensive. "He's with his nanny. Margret, of course, is still not feeling well in the mornings."

"I was just wondering," Beth said. "I like to watch him playing with his toys."

"Well, it's too much sun for him anyway. We need to be careful of his delicate skin. Both Miss Bernard and I agree, as does his mother."

"Victoria," Mrs. Montclair fussed at her daughter from two chairs over, "cover your arms or you'll burn. I'm not going to warn you again. Do as I say — please."

Beth gave her head a little shake and sighed. *The woman will continue to pester Victoria about her skin as long as the sun is in the sky. Her "I'm not going to warn you again" declaration indeed will be happening again. Maybe she believes fair skin is the most important qualification for securing a husband.*

Victoria only sighed. "Mother, isn't there another beach soon? I'd like to swim in the ocean again. It's not nearly as refreshing in the ship's pool. That water is — why, it's actually *warm.*"

Beth set her mind to tune out the patter of conversation, but she couldn't focus. *The book is unpleasant, the days tick away in perpetual leisure . . . such a waste of precious time.* She set the book aside and turned to the woman seated beside her, the one for whom her emotions ran the gamut of deep, abiding love to occasional exasperation. "Mother, I'd rather talk with you. Is that all right? Is this a good time? Could we talk a little?"

Mother's mouth drew down at the corners in surprise, and her eyebrows lifted with unspoken questions, but she answered,

"Yes, of course." She laid aside her magazine.

They rose together and moved along beside the rail. Beth tried to put into words the idea that had been lingering in her mind during the trip, though she wasn't sure she wanted to hear her mother's response. "I've been thinking a great deal about the future, about the potential of marriage. This is not just about Jarrick, but about the concept as a whole." The eyes affixed themselves more carefully on Beth's face. "You know me so well, Mother. I wondered if there might be some points you'd like to share." *There. The question is asked and can't be rescinded now.*

Mother straightened, looking puzzled. "I haven't been certain you *wanted* my unsolicited advice."

"I'm soliciting it now." Beth managed a smile.

"Well then . . ." She seemed to gather her thoughts.

Beth felt the seconds tick by slowly.

"As I've said before, marriage is never easy," Mother began, looking directly at Beth. "A woman, in some ways, lacks the advantages afforded to men. She's never fully in control, will always be dependent upon whomever she marries to care for her and to provide. I must confess to being more conscious of this in regard to my daughters than I ever was for myself. It's a heavy burden for a mother to have these worries."

Beth had not been aware of such a weight on her mother.

"And I realize, darling, that I have hovered — perhaps too much. But the three of you have been my world, carrying my greatest devotion and care since the moment you were first placed in my arms, and all the years after. Every decision, every choice made only with your benefit in mind. I can only say that I've done my very best. Believe me, Beth, not perfectly, but my very, very best."

"You're a wonderful mother. Truthfully. You know we love you dearly, all three of us." Beth reached for Mother's hand, and she squeezed back in response.

"And then the time comes when one must step aside — slowly at first but always feeling it's too soon, to allow a child to proceed forward alone. I can't tell you how much sleep I lost after Margret's coming-out party, when the young men began to call. I have never prayed so much in my life. It seemed that all my days spent with her had led up to that one decision — and that forever after all her life would rest upon it.

Thank God for John. He's been such a blessing to us all."

She dabbed at her eyes before continuing quietly, "And then you chose an education instead of courtship. None of the women in our family — none of the women I had ever known — had considered such a thing. I had no idea . . . no way of judging the wisdom in such a modification of my expectations. No way of knowing what it might imply. The world has changed so quickly. One can hardly imagine. For generations mothers and daughters have dressed the same, thought much the same, and expected the same familiar patterns in life. But your generation, Beth! Your generation has turned its back on all of it. I can't express how unnerving it's been to watch. No, how absolutely frightening."

"I suppose I *don't* really understand, Mother. It's all I've ever known."

"And it's not that I want to stifle you, hinder you. I have tried to predict what might happen, where danger may lie, if your life takes such a different path than my own. You're walking where I've never gone, could never even have dreamed of going. How can I trust my own judgment about what might follow? I can only give you over to God again and again, and do my best to guide you. Solicited or not." She shook her head and smiled.

"You've been blessed with so much giftedness, darling. Your intelligence and musical abilities. Your courage and convictions. I've never wanted to nurture my pride in you, but I've had to restrain myself at times. It's been positively heaven to watch you mature into such a fine young lady."

"Oh, dearest Mother . . ." Now Beth was wiping tears.

They descended a set of stairs together before Mother continued. "The only hindrance is your health, darling. And I've never truly forgiven myself for that failure. When baby William fell ill, I should have sent you away to Grandmama's immediately. But I gave way to fear and kept you close at home instead. Had I trusted that God was your Keeper rather than me, it might never have happened. That's such a dreadful thought."

Her words were shocking. Beth had never imagined Mother felt responsible for her childhood bout with whooping cough.

"I know how precious each of my daughters is. And I've learned over the years that one's offspring are a borrowed trust . . . for such a short time. I've prayed to be faithful and wise in how I influence you still, though perhaps I've not been very popular nor appreciated. But I have determined to continue on doing my best for your sakes. In walking faithfully before my God. I hope you understand, darling."

"I do, Mother. Better now than ever before."

"Then you'll be cautious and prayerful, Beth? And patient too?"

"Yes, Mother, I will. I promise I will." She stepped closer once more to grasp her mother's hand and lowered her voice. "Mother, just one more thing . . . thank you for your questions about Jarrick. At first I was put off by them — probably feeling like you didn't trust my judgment, maybe also that you were judging Jarrick without even having met him. But I gradually realized you had raised some important 'facts' of his life that needed to be addressed, not only for your sake but for mine too. I was able to talk with him about them during our last conversation, which was rather lengthy, I might add — I hope not too costly for him. Besides the items you raised, we were able to cover many more matters also, and I'd like to share them with you . . . at least some of them." She smiled at her mother, and it was slowly matched as they looked into each other's faces.

Their deck mates were gathering up their things to leave for lunch by the time Beth and Mother returned, having shared a precious and intimate conversation.

By midafternoon, Beth slipped away for a shipboard walk alone. The promenade deck had been mostly abandoned in the heat of the day. Beth breathed in deeply and began a hurried first circuit. *Father certainly has been far more perceptive about Mother than I. She has so much more wisdom than I credited her with.* As Beth continued to pace around the deck, beads of sweat rising at her neck and trickling down her back, she felt energized rather than tired.

"Does your mother know you're out here?" The close proximity of the voice startled Beth. Her reaction was met with laughter. "You should see your face!"

"Oh, it's you, Nick." Beth wiped at the perspiration on her forehead.

"You jumped a mile." His eyes were dancing. "Who're you running from?"

"What do you mean?"

"You're moving so fast. Everybody else is lounging around down below in the shade. How come you're up here, racing around like the ship is on fire?"

Beth stepped into a small patch of shade.

"I just wanted to stretch my legs. I'm used to much more walking."

He seemed ready to toss out a retort, but hesitated instead. "Why don't we go down below — there's a soda fountain and much cooler air. You look as if you could use a rest."

Beth smiled. "I think you're right. I'm ready to cool off."

He followed her down the nearest flight of stairs to a broad patio area covered with billows of thin white canvas like a ceiling of sails floating on the breeze. Walking to a table near the railing, he drew back a chair for Beth and pushed it carefully under her.

"Thank you, Nick."

"Don't mention it." Beth thought his smile was a bit mischievous.

Fans blowing from all directions created a lovely coolness. Beth lifted a napkin and dabbed at her neck. "I *am* rather warm," she admitted. "It's a good thing my mother hasn't seen me in such a state."

"Yes, proper young ladies in your league should never perspire, right? I wouldn't have thought it possible until seeing it for myself." He seemed to find great pleasure in needling her.

She chose to ignore his slightly too-forward remark. She asked, "And what league is that, Nick?"

Her question seemed to catch him off guard, and he looked a bit sheepish that she had turned the tables. "The very wealthy, I suppose," he answered, glancing away.

"What makes you think we're wealthy?"

He forced a chuckle. "Well, your clothes for one, and your fancy staterooms — even the airs you put on. Well, not you maybe, but your sister for sure. Golly, Julie isn't shy at all about saying how rich your father is."

Beth winced. "I'm not sure that Julie hasn't overstated things. At any rate, Father has worked very hard to build his business. He actually spent years as a sailor at first — long before he managed to open his own shipping company. He certainly wasn't born into money. Though we are now comfortably well off, I rather doubt we're in any special 'league.' "

Nick was studying her face, the façade of humor he normally wore slipping away. "I didn't know a fellow could still do that — work his way up and build an empire, even a modest one. He must be a tough old . . . well, you know, the real McCoy."

"He's a wonderful man." Beth shook off his rather coarse assessment. "We expect to meet up with him once the ship reaches Florida."

"Where is he now?"

"In South America." Beth chuckled. "Didn't Julie already tell you that, along with everything else?"

"Say, Beth, I don't want you to think when we're hanging around I'm grilling her about your family."

Beth paused and eyed him carefully. "What *are* you doing when you're hanging around her?"

"What do you mean?"

"It's not about . . ." Beth cleared her throat and reminded herself that she had every right to ask the question — that her young sister was, indeed, her concern. "It's not about *romance,* is it?"

Nick laughed, then looked at Beth crossways, then laughed again. "You think I'm carrying a torch for your sister? You think I'm some kind of masher?"

"No, but you're a single man traveling alone. And I suppose that gives me reason enough to ask, don't you think?"

He sat back in his chair and crossed his arms, grinning slowly. "I'm not out to woo Julie, if that's what you mean. That's not what comes next for me — a rush to the middle aisle and wedded bliss. I'm just biding my time, putting together some business contacts in a place where it seems like

I might find some hefty investors."

"So you're saying you'd actually be spending time with my father — if he were here instead of Julie."

Nick looked away, the same crooked smile that seemed to spell mischief playing across his face. "Is that how you see me? A guy with some kind of underhanded intent? I'm just someone working things out to get ahead. We're all doing that — one way or another, right?"

Beth watched his face. He met her gaze in return, smirking back confidently. She hated to admit that almost against her own will, she found him charming.

"Look," he continued, nodding his head as if to concede, "I like your sister. She's a great gal. But I know there's no possible future for the two of us. So it's purely hands off, so to speak. And I don't think she takes it any more seriously than me. We're just friends. I would never do anything to hurt Julie —"

"So this is where you were off to, Bethie!" Julie's voice came from behind them. "You should have invited me along." She pulled out a chair and sat down, looking rather put out.

"I went for a walk . . . and happened to see Nick," Beth explained. "He suggested something cold to drink out of the sun."

Julie eyed the empty table.

Nick bolted upright. "Say, you're right! Where's that waiter, anyway? A fellow's gotta get his own drinks around here?" He stood. "What're you gals drinking?"

"Cherry soda for me." Julie smiled up at him.

"I'd just like water — with ice, please. Thank you."

The young man hurried away, and Julie immediately leaned forward. "I'm quite surprised to find you here alone with Nick. That can either mean you're getting to know him — which would be good — or it means you came to question him. And that would be rather disappointing."

"Neither," Beth promised. "I was just out walking, we crossed paths. It would have been rude not to accept his offer to get in some shade, have something cold to drink."

"Hmm." Julie eyed her thoughtfully, not looking convinced.

"Where have *you* been?"

Julie's expression turned grim. "Doing another of your silly paintings. And then I went looking for Jannis and Penny."

"You didn't find them?"

"Yes, but . . ."

Beth leaned in too. "But what?"

"Well, they were on the rec deck, talking with some of our friends. Now, Bethie, don't be angry when I tell you this, promise me?"

Beth could feel herself already bristling. "Tell me what?"

Julie sighed heavily and blurted, "I think I saw Jannis with Victoria's binoculars."

"What?"

"They could have belonged to someone else. But they looked just like the ones she was using."

Beth allowed the possibility to sink in slowly. *They stopped to visit us the day the glasses went missing. In fact, they even sat for a few moments on Victoria's deck chair. Of course, it's also true they could have bought a pair at the small shop on board. There are bound to be identical ones belonging to any number of other passengers. . . .*

"It would be easy to tell," Beth finally remembered. "Victoria wrote her name on the strap."

"I'm not sure I'd be able to get close enough. Jannis certainly hasn't brought them out any time *I've* been around."

"Could she just be borrowing them?"

"From whom?"

"I don't know, one of your other friends?"

Julie shook her head. "It's doubtful. Not many of them have any interest in something the 'old folks' do."

Nick returned with the three drinks and set them on the table with no small effort. Julie and Beth waited in silence. "What's up?" he asked, looking from one to the other. "Cat got your tongue?"

Julie stared up wordlessly at Nick, then back across at Beth. There was a question on her face, which Beth instantly understood. She nodded, and Julie began to explain, "I can't be sure, but I think it may have been Jannis who took Victoria's binoculars. You know, I told you about it the day after it happened. I just saw her holding some that looked just like Victoria's."

Nick looked oddly perturbed. "You saw her — with them in her hands?"

Julie nodded glumly.

He lowered himself into his chair and took a long, slow sip of his lemonade. "All right," he said at last, "here's what I'll do. Let me look into it."

"You? No, Nick. It's not your problem. I can speak with Jannis about it —"

"Nah, you know how girls are," he put in quickly. "If *you* bring it up, they'll both be mad at you — and it'll be days before you're talking to one another again. That'll put a damper on anything we were gonna do next. And we're almost back in the U.S. That's *my* playground. I was gonna show you four women around Boston in a couple of days. I don't want it all balled up by some stupid spat. No, I'll talk to Jannis and find out for sure. If they're Vickie's, maybe it'll all go away if she just up and gives 'em back. What d'ya think?"

Beth frowned, but Julie burst out in relief. "Sure, that's fine. If Victoria gets her field glasses back, it'll all be okay again."

Beth wasn't certain. *Nothing can be decided right now without knowing if one of the girls took them. And if so, such a thing should not be swept under the rug.*

"No need to tell your mama about it then, is there?" Nick was watching for Beth's reaction rather than Julie's. *Why is he protecting them? Why should he care about people he just met on a cruise?*

Julie pressed on, "Come, Bethie. There's no sense making a mountain out of a molehill. It's enough just to right the wrong."

"But Mrs. Montclair already purchased another pair. They're out the extra money either way."

"No, didn't you hear? Victoria lost those too — they fell into the water while we were in Halifax. So you see, it really would be setting things right again."

Beth lowered her head for a moment to

think. "Are you going to ask her how she got them, Nick — so we know the truth?"

"Of course. I'll get to the bottom of it for you. And I'll tell you everything she says. You can trust me. Honest."

There was great anxiety and commotion about the attire necessary for the clamming excursion in the Bay of Fundy. Beth and Julie were searching their closets for their most humble garments, over which they were to don a pair of rubberized fishing overalls, as well as heavy galoshes. They would be walking out onto a muddy landscape that half the time was covered with ocean water, depending on the tides.

Mother was not convinced. "It's not that I don't understand the functionality, girls. I'm just trying to decide what your father would say."

"But we can't back out now, Mother. We've already told everyone that we're going!"

"I'm sorry, Julie darling. But I must decide based on my best judgment — not on promises you've made to others."

Julie stormed out of the bedroom, and Mother allowed her to leave without reprimanding her for such disrespectful behavior. It was so uncharacteristic of her to tolerate insolence. Beth's surprise must have shown on her face.

Mother confided, "She's become increasingly temperamental lately. I'm quite beside myself about what to do. I wish your father were here. He'd bring it all to a hasty end. He has a way when dealing with her that seems much more effective than mine."

Beth rested a hand on Mother's arm affectionately. She seemed dreadfully wrung out for a woman on a vacation cruise. Her eyes held a brooding disappointment. "Perhaps it's just too long a trip to make in one stretch. I think all of us are feeling rather weary of one another by now."

Beth gathered the garments Julie had abandoned on her bed. "She'll be herself again soon, Mother. Just give her a little time."

"And the hideous clothing *made for men* you're to wear? What should I say about that?"

Beth laughed with a funny expression. "Well, we'll certainly be *covered.* And even though it's pants, I hardly think it will be considered immodest. No one will be able to tell the men from the women, since we will all be looking equally shapeless and foolish."

Mother allowed herself to smile at Beth's

description. "It'll be the first time I've consented to any of my daughters wearing pants. And I hate to do this without your father's agreement." She hesitated a moment longer. "But I suppose you're right. He would agree if he were here."

"Has Margret decided if she'll come along?"

"I doubt she will. It might be too risky in her condition."

Beth had hoped all three sisters would be able to share the experience. She said over her disappointment, "Well, I don't think I want Emma to take any pictures of us!"

They chuckled again, then her mother added, "Now, Victoria, on the other hand, will be in her element. I hope you'll keep your eye on her. She's quite impulsive at times."

For all the matter-of-fact discussion about their clamming attire, Beth couldn't help but groan at her first sight of the bright yellow overalls being held up by the attendant. "I'm sorry," she said, "but might you have something smaller?"

The young man stepped back and looked her over. "You're right, lady. Can't roll 'em up *that* far. Hey, Joe!" he called over his shoulder. "Do ya have any more fer kids?"

Beth was embarrassed, but she managed to gracefully accept the smaller garment, and soon the yellow-clad tourists were making their way down the steep stairs and out onto the mucky floor of the cove. With each step the oversized boots threatened to slip from Beth's small feet, and she couldn't help but laugh as she struggled to avoid a misstep and maybe end up flat on her back.

Special digging forks were distributed to pull the clams from their holes. The guide demonstrated how it was to be done and sent them off in all directions, searching for proper-sized holes indicating a clam lurked below. Mother was correct — Victoria lost no time in plunging her tool deep underground, though at first it seemed almost a futile endeavor. None were able to drag one of the hard-shelled creatures from its burrowed hiding place.

Julie had joined her friends in a small group, though Jannis and Penny were not among them. Nick, however, was serving as leader, and there seemed to be more conversation and laughter than digging going on. Beth sighed away her concerns and dutifully followed along after Victoria.

At last the girl let out a happy, "I've got one!" Soon there were several in the bottom of their shared bucket, and Victoria was coaching Beth on the proper technique. "You have to get under it, like this. And then you kind of scoop it up."

After many failed attempts, Beth also managed to extract a clam. She laughed at her thrill with so humble a feat.

The young man who received her overalls when they were done said, "Heard ya did okay, lady. You an' that other gal did better'n some of the men."

"Thank you," Beth chuckled. *It's a delightful story to tell my schoolchildren. Maybe I should have let Emma take a picture of me in my getup after all.*

CHAPTER 21

Long, low blasts of the ship's horn signaled another departure as Beth pulled her silky evening gown over her head and let the folds tumble out around her. The pale mauve was her favorite, soft and beaded and draped attractively at the shoulders. She had already worn it twice and knew Julie would disapprove of her bringing it out again. But Beth liked how she felt in this particular dress — certainly a contrast to overalls and knee-high boots.

She was still smiling at the mental image when she heard "Elizabeth! Elizabeth!" from the hallway. She quickly went out to the parlor and opened the door.

"I got them back — see!" Victoria held up her lost binoculars, lifting the strap to show where he name was written in smudged letters. "One of the bellboys just dropped them off. He said they were found somewhere on deck, and somebody turned them in to the lost and found. Can you imagine? When you took me to the ship's office and they weren't there, they wrote down my room number. But I never imagined they would turn up again!"

"That's wonderful, Victoria. I'm sure you're glad to have them back." Beth looked at the girl's simple frock. "Aren't you dressing for dinner?"

"No, Mother said I didn't have to go tonight. I'm going to watch from our balcony while the ship heads out of port. I'd rather do that than sit in the dining room waiting for everyone else to finish — especially now that I've got these again. You can borrow them when you'd like."

Beth agreed with a nod. "Thank you, Victoria, for telling me. I'm so glad for you."

"Well, Elizabeth, I just thought you'd want to know." Victoria disappeared. *How nice that she's so happy to share her good news. Perhaps a friendship is developing after all.*

"Who was that?" Julie asked as she emerged from the bedroom, casting a frown at Beth's dress. "It sounded like Victoria."

"It was. Her binoculars have been found and returned."

"Really?" Julie glanced at Mother, who turned from the correspondence she was writing.

"Did they say where the glasses have been all this time?" she asked. "Surely they must have been taken by someone to have been gone this long, then returned."

Beth wanted to say she didn't know, but it would not be true. "Victoria didn't say," she managed.

"I see. Well, then, did they tell Victoria who turned them in?"

"I don't think so." Beth could feel the color warming her cheeks. She knew she was teetering on the brink of lying. The sensation was painfully unpleasant.

"I see." Mother rose from her place at the desk, folding her note and slipping it into an envelope. "Then perhaps we shall never know." She cupped a hand under Julie's chin and smiled toward Beth. Beth felt certain Mother would see her anxiety. "It's a wonder, really, that they should be returned intact."

As Mother moved into her own bedroom, Julie's eyes met Beth's.

"Well, that's just fine," Beth muttered. "Now we're deceiving Mother!"

Julie grasped her hand and led her back into their room. "We're not — not really. Because Jannis didn't take the silly things."

"What?" Beth shook her head.

"Nick told me all about it. She said she

found them beside the pool. Who knows how they got there. And by then Victoria's name was almost worn off, so she didn't realize they were hers. Loads of people have binoculars just like that — they all bought them on board. Nick says she was so embarrassed to have had them all this time that she couldn't stop crying. He says it's probably best if I just don't mention it — so I won't make her feel bad all over again."

"And you *believed* him?"

Julie's eyes were wide with innocence. "Nick's got no reason to lie to me, Bethie. And why would he care about Jannis? He never even met her before this. He hardly even talks to her. He said if it were him, he'd probably just find a new friend, but I told him how much those girls have come to mean to me. And that it really didn't matter to me. Victoria got them back. So it's settled."

"All right then, Julie, so go explain all of that to Mother."

Julie stepped back quickly. "You know she wouldn't understand. I don't think she's ever given my friends a fair chance — the way they look, the way they talk. Keep the secret with me, won't you, Bethie? It doesn't hurt anyone, now that Victoria's happy."

Beth frowned. *Nick seems a lot more*

familiar with the girls than a new acquaintance should be. Then again, he's become rather familiar with Julie too. But why did he take it upon himself to talk with Jannis, make this attempt to find the truth and fix things?

Beth sighed her consent against her better judgment. Julie's plaintive pleadings had won her over once more.

"Come on, sleepyhead. We've already docked, and it's almost time for breakfast."

Beth rolled over and stared into the shadowy room, attempting to focus on Julie. "What time is it?" she mumbled. "Why are we getting up so early?"

"We're at Bar Harbor today, remember? And I want to be onshore as soon as possible . . . you know, so we can get a good look around." Julie held out a robe for Beth. "Come on, darling."

Beth pushed herself to a sitting position, reached for the wrap, and pulled it around her shoulders. "Is Mother up yet?"

"Of course. She's up every day before everyone else."

Beth stared. "How on earth would you even *know* that, silly? You're usually the *last* one —"

"Well, she is when we're at home. Anyway, it's *Bar Harbor,* our first American city! And if we're lucky we'll see someone famous — maybe even a millionaire. Imagine that!"

Beth made her way slowly to the bathroom. "Julie, how would you know a millionaire if one happened to pass on the street?"

Julie giggled. "Oh, Bethie, how could you *miss* one?" Beth wondered fleetingly what had given her sister such a cheerful outlook this early in the day.

It seemed that Mother was of the same frame of mind as Julie. Whatever their plan, it did not include the Montclairs, who had opted out of the day's morning excursion. Hurrying through breakfast and leaving Margret on board with her son and nanny meant they were on the dock before most of the shops were open. Monsieur Laurent went to hire a cab as Julie paced impatiently.

"They sell these maps," she told them. "Soooo," she added dramatically, "we can find where most of the really important people vacation — like Coco Chanel, and John Astor and his new wife, and movie stars like Mary Pickford. Wouldn't that *just be the berries!*"

Beth glanced at Mother, wondering how she felt about Julie's latest jargon. She sighed. *Is this truly how we'll be spending the morning? The cause of all the fuss and hurry?*

"She's been excited about it for days," Mother murmured to Beth's unspoken query. "I don't suppose it will hurt to have a look around."

Beth blinked and sighed again. The die was cast.

"Besides, Penny and Jannis had invited her to ride along with *them* today. When I saw how disappointed Julie was that I wanted us to stay together, I couldn't say no. You don't really mind, do you, Beth?"

She lifted a shoulder. "No, I suppose it might be interesting."

The map Julie had purchased was turned over to the driver. Beth supposed he would have been able to find all the celebrity homes if they had simply asked. He struck out into early morning traffic, Monsieur Laurent beside him and already deep into his newspaper, leaving all commentary to the cabbie.

"That there's the Rockefeller estate. They call it 'The Eyrie,' " the man explained, pointing through the trees at some distance. "The best way to see it is from the water, if you ask me — hard to get a good look from here. You can buy a picture postcard in town. They sell 'em all over. I know a guy who can get you a good watercolor painting, if you want."

Suddenly Julie was telling him to pull over. "Please!" she insisted.

Everyone stared at her as the driver moved to the side of the road. Julie swung the door open, camera in hand. She gave it to Beth as she slid out. "Take a picture of me, Bethie. Be sure to get the mansion in the background," she instructed.

"Oh, Julie, you'll hardly see a thing. It's so far away —"

"Please try. That's right."

Beth sat on the edge of the seat at the open door, adjusting the lens so Julie was in the foreground, the distant Rockefeller mansion hovering behind. "I don't know if this will do any good. It's not as if I can focus on you and the house too."

"Then take another shot of the house by itself. Perhaps I can cut them apart and paste the pictures together. Or," she said with some excitement, "I can just paint it — something for *myself* this time!"

Julie was right — she certainly should be able to capture her own memories from their trip. But Beth couldn't help wondering how many of the paintings already started for her students would actually be completed.

Back in the taxi, they were off to the next

location — all a blur to Beth, since she was hardly aware of any of these famous people who had so captivated Julie.

"Oh," she exclaimed at the sight of the John Jacob Astor mansion, "it's *so romantic!* Did you know that he was the '*Titanic* baby'? His mother survived, but his father went down with the ship."

They all stared out the windows at the beautiful dwelling with its sorrowful past as they slowly drove by.

"If only Jan and I were seeing the homes together," Julie muttered.

By noon they were back on board. Mother insisted they have lunch with Margret and the Montclairs. As they rose from their chairs, she suggested, "And we can all go shopping now, if you'd like."

Julie shivered with excitement. "Maybe I can finally get a Chanel bag."

"You'll pay more for it here than you would elsewhere," Margret warned.

But Julie would not be deterred. "I don't care. It's worth it at any price."

"Well, Father might not think so," Margret answered dryly, lifting JW into her arms and gathering up the bag laden with items she carried along for him. She looked tired. Beth was rather surprised that Margret was insisting he come along. *She's already not quite up to things, and there's nothing of particular interest to JW. Is it simply to let Miss Bernard — and Mother — know who's in charge?* Holding out her arms for the boy, Beth smiled at her sister. Taking a cue from Beth, Julie reached for the heavy bag.

"Annie Bet." JW smiled happily. "I's comin'," the boy said, and Margret sighed gratefully.

Beth would just as soon have remained on board herself, but she really didn't want to miss out on these times with her family. She had realized at lunch that the trip was almost half done, and she wanted every minute possible with them. *Who knows when we'll be together like this again, especially with Margret's new little one on the way and the uncertainties with my future?*

Shopping completed, Beth lingered on the dock until the rest were headed up the gangway, followed by two porters loaded down with even more packages and bags.

"Any letter today?" she asked Monsieur Laurent a bit timidly as he waited with her.

"I'm sorry, miss. There was a letter for your mother and one for your sister, Mrs. Bryce, but nothing for you today. Perhaps it will arrive tomorrow when we dock in Portland."

"Thank you." She tried not to allow her disappointment to show.

Julie and Margret each had purchased a new dress for dinner. They'd wanted Beth to buy one too, but she still had not worn two that she had brought along.

Mother had been convinced by an eager salesman to purchase an elegant pearl necklace. She now sat at the dressing table, gazing into the mirror at its beautiful luster with the diamond accents and looking like she regretted its purchase. "So extravagant," she fussed, shaking her head. "I don't know *what* your father would say."

Julie leaned in close behind, hands resting on Mother's shoulders, and smiled at their reflections. "He would have bought it for you himself, Mother. You know he would have. And he would love to see it on you right now." She pressed a kiss on the soft cheek.

Mother shook her head and let her fingers slide over the gems in the pendant. "That would have been so much better. I don't feel that I should have bought it for myself."

"It's the first expensive purchase you've made on the trip," Beth assured her as she drew on her gloves. "As long as you don't do it often, I'm sure Father will be most happy with you. And what Julie said is true

— he does seem to enjoy spoiling us, at least occasionally."

"I suppose you're right," Mother said. "It's too bad, though, to have overspent so early on, only days away from New York City. I shall have to be very prudent there." She ran her fingers once more over the pearl strand. "Yet I do believe it's the nicest thing I've ever owned."

Julie twirled across the room in her new gown so its fringes flared around her. "I wish Father were here. He would enjoy seeing us all so happy."

Julie burst into their suite, wiping away tears.

"What is it?" Beth grabbed her sister's hands and led her to the sofa. Julie had gone off with her friends after dinner. "What's happened? What's wrong?"

"It's Jannis. She's so . . . so angry with me," she gasped out between sobs.

"Whatever for?"

Julie leaned against Beth, her shoulders shaking. "Because of . . . Bar Harbor. Because I . . . I didn't go with *them*."

"*What?*" It was too strange to be believed. Surely Julie had misunderstood. "How could she be upset about that? Doesn't she know Mother wanted us to be together, that she insisted on it?"

Julie blew her nose into her handkerchief, shrinking away from Beth into a pitiful-looking waif. "I don't know, Bethie. They just . . . just wanted me to come with them."

"Regardless of what Mother said?"

Something about the comment made Julie stiffen, and her tone turned bitter. "That's just it. They don't think I should *have* to do as she says. After all, I'm not a child. They think I'm shockingly dependent — I need to learn to stand on my own two feet!"

"Well, that's ridiculous!" Beth immediately wished she hadn't sounded so scornful. She tried again. "Julie, a person doesn't demonstrate independence by rebelling. You do it by shouldering responsibilities, making wise, thoughtful decisions. You know that."

Immediately Julie was on her feet. "What do *you* know about it? All you do is bow to Mother's every wish. And that's fine — if I wanted all the same things that *you* do, that she wants. *But I don't!*"

Beth recoiled, a gasp caught in her throat. "Please, Julie, Mother is sleeping," she cautioned, hands clasped in distress.

Julie pushed her fingers through her short curls. "I don't care! I don't care if she hears me. She might as well know."

340

"Darling, this is so uncharacteristic of you. I don't understand this. I've never seen you so upset."

Julie's face twisted, more tears streaming down. "I don't want them to call me a mama's girl. I want my independence too. I can't live in a world with so many rules. It's not fair." She slumped down onto the footstool, hands covering her face. "She's always been this way, Bethie."

She suddenly sat up straight, strident once more. "She watches me every moment, judges my every move. I can't *endure* it any longer. It looks like the only way to break free is to marry — and then I'll just be exchanging Mother's rules for those of some man. Why can't a woman just make her own way?" Her harsh tone was totally unlike anything Beth had ever heard from her sister.

Is Julie parroting phrases she's heard from her friends? Beth studied her sister's furious-looking expression, willing her own reeling thoughts into something she could say and praying earnestly that God would provide wisdom that Julie would receive.

Beth drew a chair closer to the footstool and seated herself, one hand sliding across Julie's back. "It's not exactly the way you are picturing things, darling. We weren't meant to fly away like birds — free and on our own. We each were put into families, every one of us integral to the whole. Like a gear from the center of a clock. If it were to demand to be free, what would happen to the rest? And the gear itself would no longer have a purpose."

"That's a fine thing for *you* to say! You're on your way out the door as soon as we get home."

"All right," Beth began again. "Then it's not merely a clock. Our Creator makes things grow and change — like a living cell. Have you read about those?"

"No," Julie muttered, though Beth was grateful she was at least responding.

"Cells are marvelous things. We're just starting to understand them better. We read about them when I was in college. They're so complex — so many parts, each doing its own task. And if one small part fails, the whole cell dies."

"What does that have to do with me?" Julie obviously had lost patience with the metaphor.

"Just listen — I'm almost done. Our family is like one of those cells. Someday we'll split off into new families, like how a cell grows and divides, like Margret and John did. But until then, we need each other. And no single part survives on its own. It wasn't meant to."

Beth prayed that Julie would hear what she was so desperately trying to put into words. "And further, we're still a part of the body as a whole, inextricably linked together. And that doesn't change when we each begin our own families." She squeezed Julie's shoulders. "I know it's not a perfect picture, but I hope it at least speaks against the lie that we could be happy if only we could just break free. We wouldn't be happy. We were made to love and support and protect one another." Beth could feel her own tears welling up. "Don't you see? I love you. And so do Mother, Father, and all the rest of the family. None of us wants you to wish yourself away."

Julie turned toward Beth and whispered, "Sometimes they make me feel so . . . so childish, the girls. I don't know what to say to them, how to defend myself and our family."

"I'm sorry for them, that they weren't raised in a family. They don't know there are wonderful things about families, about mothers and fathers, who help us with our decisions, with their experience and wisdom. They probably only see what they perceive as restrictions to 'freedom' —

343

which might not turn out to be freedom at all."

Long into the night, the sisters whispered together. They agreed to listen more intently to each other's sorrows, to be more open. And also to find wise distinctions between submitting to their parents' authority and bearing responsibility for themselves as women.

When morning came, Beth was hopeful the emotional storm had passed — that what had been troubling Julie had been brought to light.

CHAPTER 22

Monsieur Laurent slid a small packet across the table toward Beth. "You see," he said with a little grin, "the young man has not forgotten you."

Beth drew it out from under his hand and thanked their escort. *If only the mail could be delivered directly to the room,* she thought. It was getting a bit tiresome to see the same knowing expression on his face each time he played deliveryman. *But then I'd probably have those same looks from Mother or Julie,* she reminded herself.

Hurrying away to a favorite corner in the ship's atrium, Beth had quickly put aside her annoyance by the time she tore open the first envelope and withdrew its contents. She read slowly, savoring the strong connection she felt. But even in this, his fifth letter, Jarrick had not yet received any letters from Beth. She was so glad they at least had been able to converse by telephone. She shifted her thinking back to when the letter was written so many days before.

It appeared that all were faring well. Jarrick had shared a meal with Edward and Kate. He seemed to like her well enough but gave few details. *Just like a man,* she thought with a wry smile. Molly and Frank had settled into life together. Abigail was well on her way to setting up her own business in the Grants' old tavern. There was promise of a new group of miners, and the company was breaking ground for a series of additional homes across the rough little road from the current ones. The first three would soon house new families. *"New children likely will be in school in the fall, God willing,"* Jarrick wrote.

She folded the letter and tucked it away, looking at her watch pin before reaching for the next one. The tour of the Portland docks would not begin until after lunch. For now there was still time to savor the second letter.

My dearest Beth,

I'm certain you feel as I do, that though it was a boon to my spirit to speak with you today, it was a disappointment as well. I'm sorry I wasn't better able to coordinate our telephone call — that we had so little time. The men with whom I work suggested that yesterday's difficulties might simply have been a problem with the lines. They may be right. There are certainly many, many miles of wire stretching across Canada from east to west. However, the truth of that doesn't make my frustration any easier.

Jarrick went on to write that little had changed in the few days since his last letter, except for the visit from the school board he had already mentioned by telephone, and also he now had finally received a letter from her. He expressed again his hope that Beth would soon be able to teach her young students about the places she had traveled and what she had seen. He was certain her descriptions would open unimagined horizons to the children of her town.

Beth sighed, the familiar ache of missing him filling her heart, and looked again at her watch pin. She covered a yawn, reminded that her night had been awfully short. Julie was still sleeping, groaning her objection to anything else. With Margret absent at the beginning of the day, and Victoria occasionally choosing to breakfast alone in her room, their table felt rather empty in the mornings — though Mrs.

Montclair certainly kept up her end of things.

Beth gathered the letters and slipped them inside her handbag. There was still plenty of time before their party would assemble, but she thought she'd check to see if Julie was awake yet. As she walked toward the door to the deck, she heard angry voices outside. She dared not proceed.

Rising to her tiptoes, she peered through the porthole-shaped window. In shock she saw Penny and Jannis, their hair blowing wildly around them, standing at the ship's rail, clearly having an unrestrained scrap. She hesitated, feeling it was rude to eavesdrop, and yet she also felt she must know if their argument had anything to do with Julie. Beth cracked open the door.

"You never *listen,* Jan!" Penny spat out. "You weren't s'posed to *use* them — and we sure could've used the money."

"I *told* you not to bring it up again!" Jannis started to turn away, only to be swung back by a pinching grip on her arm. She jerked it away and shouted, "She's got 'em back now! Why do you keep throwing it in my face?"

Jannis recoiled, but Penny grabbed her arm again and shook it roughly. "I don't care if you think you weren't wrong. The

348

fact is, you blew it! And as to the other thing, I told you how it was s'posed to go, and you didn't pay attention. So now you've *got to listen* to me."

"Can't blame me, Penny! You're the one who said we may as well be hanged for stealing a sheep as for a lamb. Well, I thought so too, in my own way." Once more Jannis wrenched her arm out of Penny's grasp and cocked her head defiantly. "Anyway, it wasn't my fault. You couldn't have done any better."

Their voices drifted away as Penny stalked behind Jannis out of sight. Beth allowed the door to close softly and hurried away. *They must be talking about Victoria's field glasses . . . but I can't be sure. And what was the other thing?* Beth's heart was racing.

"Julie, how about staying with me tonight? We haven't played a game in ages."

The expression on Julie's face was genuine bewilderment. "A *game*? You can't mean that, Bethie! I promised the girls I'd go with them to the show. There's a barbershop quartet tonight with an ice-cream social besides." She paused, looking thoughtfully at Beth. "Maybe you'd like to come too?"

Beth sighed. She had gotten very little sleep the night before because of Julie, and she had planned to turn in early. But after what she'd overheard, she was unwilling to let her sister out of her sight. "Thanks, Julie — that sounds like fun."

But Julie was exclaiming, "Oh, darling, would you? That would be just keen! But you can't wear that old mauve number again. You'll have to borrow something from me. We won't be running with Mother's crowd tonight, you know."

Julie drew one of her short fringed dresses from the closet and held it up to Beth. It was shiny gray satin with a white band of trim high across the bodice, and swirls of white beading that sparkled as the garment moved. "This is perfect. I haven't worn it yet. You can use my long pearls with it. Oh! I have a red feather that would be stunning if you just tucked it at the back of your hair."

"No, thank you." Beth was firm. "No feather."

Julie shrugged. "Suit yourself. I just thought a good accessory would draw attention away from that old-fashioned hairstyle. But you do whatever you'd like." The teasing expression on Julie's face softened her words. "Oh, I have an idea — you can wear your hair down, you know, pulled back on the sides . . ." Her voice trailed off as she looked at Beth's expression. "All right, you can wear my ruby earrings. It will give you that dramatic bit of color."

By the time they left the stateroom, Beth felt she had been preened over and primped beyond all recognition. Julie seemed to be fully energized by her efforts on Beth's attire and makeup. She herself was striking in deep purple satin with a wide sash at her hips and a matching band around her forehead.

"Jan is forever lamenting that she has only three or four good dresses. But I tell her, 'Darling, it's not *what* you're wearing; it's how you wear it.' "

"Oh, Julie, looking in your closet, one would be hard pressed to believe *that.*"

Her sister laughed lightly. "It still rings true." She linked her arm with Beth's. "I can't tell you how pleased I am you're coming. You might find yourself actually enjoying the evening. And of course Mother will be happy you're there to chaperone."

So that's all I'm good for. But then Beth remembered that was indeed why she was tagging along. And it turned out she did fully appreciate the barbershop quartet. The men stood together in a corner of the rec deck, wearing red-striped dinner jackets, voices blending in remarkable harmony. The bright full moon low in the sky behind them and dozens of paper lanterns hung all round created a magical setting.

Sharing a table with a group of young women, Beth was able to observe more closely other friends Julie had made besides Jannis and Penny — mostly debutante types, comfortable in their perceived roles and willingly enjoying the social activities that accompanied their station. They spoke of places they'd been and famous people they had met, exuding confidence and charm. Only Penny and Jannis seemed atypical. They were the edgy ones — speaking a little louder and using terms that would not surface in the company of parents. But here the two were considered cutting edge and chic by these society girls.

Jannis seemed to have recovered her usual sparkling demeanor, but Beth detected a simmering resentment from Penny. Beth made an effort to engage her in conversation.

"Did you enjoy Portland today, Penny? I particularly liked the sailboats. I was glad we took the time to walk along the docks. Were you and Jannis able to see any of the port?"

"We stayed on the ship. It was just as easy to see the sails from here." It seemed Penny was at least making an effort to be sociable.

"I much prefer quiet settings to crowds myself."

"No, that doesn't bother me at all. But we've seen boats every day since we started this cruise. I just didn't see the need to see any more."

"I suppose." Beth smiled. "That's a lovely dress you're wearing. The shade of teal goes very nicely with your eyes."

"Thank you," Penny replied and turned away.

"Well, look here!" Beth recognized Nick's voice and turned with the others. "What a fine brood of hens!"

"Hi, Nicky," a chorus of voices greeted him.

"Hi ya right back!" His eyes swept the table and came to a stop on Beth. "Well say, somebody's crashing our party. I never thought I'd see *you* out past eleven."

Beth cocked her head. "Oh my, is it that late already? Julie must have hidden my watch tonight."

"Glad to have you aboard, Miss Thatcher. Like I said before, you and your sister make a nice matched pair — a swell set of book-ends. At least you did before they turned Julie here into just another flapper — all that pretty dark hair gone. Such a waste."

He reached out to catch and kiss Julie's hand.

"Say, Nicky, why don'tcha bring us some ice cream" came from Jannis. "It's supposed to be an ice-cream social, ain't it?"

He gave a crooked smile and said, "Do I look like a waiter to you?" Then he laughed. "All right, but I'm not taking orders. Whatever I bring, that's what you're gonna have."

"Sure, and thanks, Nicky." He disappeared on his way to the serving area.

One of the young ladies leaned in toward the center of the table. "He's stuck on you, Julie. You know that, don't you?"

"Ah, Sophie, he acts like that with everybody."

"Sure thing, but you're the proud owner of the only hand he *kissed.*"

Someone else blurted, "*Tonight!* The only hand he kissed tonight!" Laughter exploded around the table, but Beth noticed Jannis didn't join in.

The moon cut a slow path higher into the night sky while the laughter swirled around Beth. She heard very little of the banter. She gazed at the sprinkling of stars above, thinking about Coal Valley and the multitude of diamond lights visible above the darkness. She hid a yawn, wondering if Jarrick was seeing the moon along with her.

"What'cha thinking?"

As before, Nick's question caught Beth by surprise. She sat straighter. "Just trying to stay awake. I'm not as used to this late-night life."

"It takes a while, I guess. When I was in college, I learned to do without much sleep."

"Perhaps that contributed to your not finishing." She tried to laugh lightly as she said the words — like Julie did — but it seemed she had not mastered the technique. Nick's face twisted a little.

"I'm sure you're right. I should have buckled down more."

Beth drew herself away, wishing he had seen the remark as jest, or that she hadn't spoken at all. "I didn't mean to criticize, Nick. I'm sorry. I was just teasing."

"It's okay. You're dead right, of course. There was so much going on — I hated to miss out."

I can't help myself, Beth thought, feeling the teacher rise up. She leaned her elbows on the table to speak in a quieter tone. "You could go back."

"Nah. That ship has sailed, so to speak." He tried to shrug it off. "It was tough enough getting in the first time. My family's not as set up as most of the others. No connections. No old money. But it's fine. I'll land on my feet anyways."

"Where are you from, Nick?"

He looked mildly alarmed. "Oh, didn't I tell you that before? I'm from . . . uh, New England. Yup, getting pretty close to home now."

"And what does your father do?"

For a moment his eyes locked on Beth's uncertainly. Then his expression softened, as if surrendering his bold pretense. "Don't have a father. Never did. It's just my mama and me — and a whole bunch of aunts and uncles and cousins and all. It was pretty tough that way. I never felt as good as all the rest. But soon I'll be able to take care of her myself, and we won't need to live with family. She means the world to me." His brow furrowed, and he dropped his gaze. "I don't know why I told you that. Guess for a minute I thought somebody maybe cared."

Beth was overwhelmed by the amount of vulnerability he had exposed. "I *do* care, Nick. I truly do. And if there is a way I could help, I'd be happy to do so. Our father *does* have connections, like Julie said. I'm not sure if any of them would fall in line with the business endeavors you have in mind, but I'm sure he'd be happy to have a discussion with you once we get to Florida." She knew as she said the words that they were likely weak and empty, ungrounded in the real world.

"Thanks," he answered slowly. "It's kind of you — that you'd even say it."

The sorrowful look in Nick's eyes broke Beth's heart. It haunted her as she laid her head on her pillow at last, and she breathed a prayer of blessing over the young man and his mother.

CHAPTER 23

"Boston," Beth whispered as she descended the gangway behind Monsieur Laurent. She gazed above the dock area for glimpses of the famous city whose rich history she had always enjoyed. Seeds of independence had germinated and grown here. Those infamous crates of tea had been dumped into Boston Harbor by rebels disguised as natives. Lanterns swinging in the historic church tower signaled that the British were coming.

Beth smiled. Her own ancestors were British — Mother's family descended from good Welsh stock, and Father's from northern England. Indeed, there was a line of the family tree living in the American colonies at that time. But the story went that when the rebellion had broken out, their homes were seized, the men tarred and feathered. They had all escaped to British holdings farther north.

"We'll begin in the Old City Historic District," Monsieur Laurent directed. "I have two taxicabs waiting just beyond these buildings. Your luggage will be sent on to the hotel while you have your tour."

He had hired a local guide, and Beth was delighted that he included many colorful anecdotes related to the old buildings they passed. They stopped at Old North Church for a look inside and also Faneuil Hall, the site of many great speeches from the time of the revolution. When their cab was headed through the traffic on the way to their hotel and a very late lunch, Beth was both satisfied and exhausted.

"There's a classical music concert tonight at Symphony Hall," Monsieur Laurent told them as they climbed from their taxis. "If you'd like to attend, I could still secure tickets through the hotel concierge. However, I would need to know as quickly as possible."

"Oh, yes," Mrs. Montclair exclaimed. "Victoria and I would be most interested. Please do procure seats for at least the two of us."

"I don't think I'll go," said Margret. "I'd prefer to stay here with my little J-bird. But thank you, Monsieur Laurent."

"And the young ladies?" Monsieur Laurent asked with a smile directed at the Thatcher sisters.

Julie quickly answered for them both. "I believe we'd rather not. We'll find some other way to fill our time. But you go along with the Montclairs, Mother. There's no reason to be concerned about us. We'll find something for our amusement, I'm sure."

Beth watched Julie's face as she confidently spoke as if they had made other plans. Julie gave her a knowing smile and an almost imperceptible wink, indicating she would explain later.

"What on earth have you got in mind?" Beth asked. She and Julie waited while Margret purchased Epsom salts at the tiny hotel store to soak her aching feet. Mother and the Montclairs were finishing their lunch in the lovely dining room. Already the various elegant hotels in which they had stayed were becoming a blur to Beth. "I know you've got something cooking, Julie. I wouldn't believe you simply want to stay in tonight if the announcement were signed by King George himself."

Julie tittered and drew Beth aside, checking to be certain Margret couldn't overhear. "The truth is," she confessed, "there *is* something for us this evening. Something

I've been hoping to do for quite some time."

"For heaven's sake, just tell me."

Julie grasped Beth's hand in both of hers. "There's an exhibit of Georgia O'Keeffe's work here in Boston. I've seen a few of her pieces over the years in Toronto, and I would very much like to see more. The museum isn't far from our hotel. We could catch a taxicab and be there within minutes. What do you think?"

"But why not tell Mother? She likely would approve of this kind of cultural outing, and she might very well want to go too —"

"Mother doesn't — she doesn't *linger*. When she sees an art piece, she looks it over once and immediately feels she's seen it. I want to *study* the work. I want to notice O'Keeffe's brush strokes and technique, her choice of colors. Surely you understand that, Bethie."

Beth grinned. "What makes you feel as if I might be a more willing companion, Julie dear? When have you ever seen me 'linger,' as you say, over a piece of art?"

"You would in this case. You should just *see* some of her paintings — the absolute *scale* of them. They're breathtaking."

Margret joined them, and they said nothing further on the subject. Throughout the afternoon, Beth wrestled with the minor dilemma. *Should I support Julie's subterfuge and share the art exhibit?* Maybe it could be postponed until tomorrow. There was plenty of time.

As Mother donned her gown and draped the new pearl jewelry around her neck, Beth moved closer to fasten the clip. She hoped she would not be asked a direct question about their evening plans, then wondered if that might be the very reason she was staying nearby — so Mother might discover and put an end to the venture without any help from her. However, there appeared to be not the faintest suspicion.

"Try not to stay up too late, my dears," Mother said as she paused in the door. "You've been keeping some late nights recently. It would be good for you both to get a good night of rest. I love you. Good night."

As soon as she was gone, Julie leaped off the bed where she had been carelessly reclining. "Let's get dressed, Bethie. You can wear my green pinstripe. I'm going to wear the pink jacket over my paisley print."

"I do have my own clothes, Julie. I don't need to always borrow from you, thank you very much."

"Suit yourself." Julie's eyes sparkled,

delighted at her own pun. "I could help you choose —" Beth already was shaking her head.

In short order her sister was ready for their evening plans, but Beth was still hedging, asking questions that she hoped would trip up Julie and put an end to the scheme. "How will you pay the driver?"

"I've gathered a little back from paying for other things. Monsieur Laurent doesn't always ask for the change. I have enough for a grand time tonight — at least for what we intend to do with our time," she said airily. "I don't mind using it up so soon. I can always manage a little more for later in New York City. And what does that matter? Father would have given us the money anyway."

"Oh, Julie. Can't you see how one poor decision leads to another? We shouldn't be doing this. We should have explained our plans to Mother, or at least Margret. I can go across and tell her —"

Julie stopped her with a firm shake of her head.

"Honestly, I can't imagine why you feel the need for so much secrecy."

"Don't you think it's fun?" Julie asked, wide-eyed delight on her face. "Not to ask permission for a change? Just to make our

363

own decisions — like the adults we are?"

"No," Beth answered flatly. "I do not. I would prefer not to go skulking about."

"I don't know, darling." Her sister's face was lit up in wily anticipation. " 'Skulking' sounds rather exciting to me."

"Julie!"

They walked together into the elevator, and the attendant drew the gates closed. Beth was still arguing under her breath. "We'll have to call for a cab."

"Already taken care of, Bethie dear," Julie told her. "You need to trust me. I've thought of everything."

As the gates opened into the lobby, Julie turned with a stern expression. "Now listen, Bethie, that's the last disparaging remark I want to hear from you about our evening. We're going. That's decided. So I want you to *enjoy* yourself. If not for your sake, then for mine. I'm positively ecstatic to be out on the town, and I'm glad to be going with you — that is, if you will improve your attitude. There's no one I'd rather be out with, believe me, if you'll just stop being such a ninny about it."

Beth sighed and gazed into the charming eyes. "I said I would go. But it's against my better judgment."

"You've made that perfectly clear. So let's

not keep harping on that point, shall we?"

Beth simply nodded and stepped outside into the evening crowds in front of the hotel, moving out from under the canopied entranceway. A mass of pedestrians hurried past in competing directions, and cars were honking and rushing along only steps from them. She drew in a breath and scanned around for a waiting taxi. "I don't see our taxi, Julie." She turned to the empty space beside her, stunned to see that she was alone.

"Hi! Over here!" Julie's voice called from some distance. When Beth finally spotted Julie's bobbing head, she realized the greeting was not intended for her. Her sister was skipping quickly across the sidewalk, waving a hand to someone else. And then Beth saw a man in a black suit moving purposefully toward her. Panic exploded inside Beth, and she shoved her way forward in pursuit.

Relief flooded through her when she realized it was only Nick. *But what's he doing at our hotel? And why does it look like Julie's expecting him?*

"Julie, stop! Wait for me." Beth weaved her way doggedly through the crowds until she had caught up with her sister. Breathlessly she demanded, "Was this your plan all along? To meet up with Nick?"

Julie laughed and reached out to grasp Beth's arm. "Isn't it a nice surprise? We'll have the very best of company — you'll see."

"No, I won't see." Beth glared into Julie's face, this time immune to her charm.

Nick looked surprised, but he was already reaching for the door of a waiting taxicab and opened it with exaggerated gentility.

"Julie, I said *no.*"

Her sister stepped closer to the open door, blissfully defiant. "Oh, Bethie," she said with a wave of her hand, "Nick's the one who told me about the O'Keeffe exhibit. I wouldn't even have known about it without him. So it's only fitting that he escort us. Besides, isn't this more appropriate than being out *unattended*? Surely you'd agree —"

"No," Beth repeated, the word steeped in anger. "I'm not going to allow you to do this!"

Julie was already lowering herself onto the seat of the cab.

Nick stepped between them. "Come on, Beth. Be a sport. We're just out for a nice evening at an art show. And what could be safer than a *museum*? They don't even let you *talk* too loud." He tried a grin as he kept Beth away from the door with his broad body. She fought against him, pushing back with all her might, but he was much too strong to make any headway. The stab of fear at such a display of power made her even more angry.

"We'll be back before your mother is home," he assured her, holding her back with one arm. "Please, Beth. You know you can trust me with your sister." He flashed that charismatic smile.

Julie called merrily from inside, "Oh, but Nick, she's coming with us! Come on, Bethie. Don't make me go alone. What would Mother say?" Julie slid further across the back seat to make room for her sister.

"No! Julie, get out of that cab *now*. I insist." Beth reached out toward her sister's beckoning arm, but Nick quickly slipped into the seat, slamming the door.

Beth launched herself at the open window. "Julie Camille, that's enough!"

Julie's laughter was the last sound Beth heard before the taxicab shot away from the curb and lost itself in the rush of traffic. Beth stood for several moments staring after it, seething with anger and hurt, the accompanying fear making her knees weak. She could not comprehend what had just occurred as she turned around in horror on the sidewalk, streams of people flowing around her.

At last she ran back to the hotel, then stood like stone in the lobby. *What should I do? I ought to tell someone. Monsieur Laurent is at the symphony. Perhaps Margret, the only one around . . .* She rushed toward the elevator.

Margret was asleep on the bed beside JW. Beth's pulse raced. And yet it seemed there was nothing to be done. She closed her eyes and prayed while silently pacing the room.

CHAPTER 24

"I'd like you to call a cab for me, please."
Back in the hotel lobby, Beth waited impatiently at the front desk. She hadn't entirely formulated a plan, and random ideas tumbled around inside her aching head. She would follow Julie and Nick to the museum, and then — well, she wasn't certain. Perhaps she would make a scene until Julie surrendered to her bidding. She might even summon a police officer if need be. At any rate, she had soon decided she would not be able to merely wait until Julie returned again at her leisure. She must go and retrieve her sister.

"The taxi will meet you at the curb, miss."

"Thank you."

Beth hurried out of the hotel, and the doorman directed her toward a waiting vehicle and opened the door. She was inside and directing the cabbie to the Museum of Fine Arts before the door was shut behind her. Were it not for the flashes of fury shooting through her, she knew she would have long before surrendered to tears.

It was only minutes before Beth was placing her coins in the cabbie's hand, though the whole way she had willed him forward from the edge of her seat. She hoped she could locate Julie before her sister had spent the rest of the money pilfered from Monsieur Laurent. They would need some for their return fare.

Beth ran up the few front steps and into the mezzanine beyond.

"Excuse me, sir, is it possible to have someone paged?"

The man at the reception desk answered pleasantly, "Yes, miss. Do you know where in the museum they might be located?"

Beth breathed a small sigh of relief. "Yes. Her name is Julie Thatcher. She'll be in the O'Keeffe exhibit."

He hesitated. "I'm sorry, but we closed down that exhibit last month. It has moved on to Washington, I believe."

Another shock of alarm ran through Beth's body. She stammered, "Is it . . . is it possibly in another museum, here in Boston perhaps? I may have gotten the location wrong."

"No, miss. I'm quite certain it moved on

to Washington. But I'll look it up to be sure."

Beth could feel her hands clenching at her sides, her heart pounding furiously.

"Never mind, sir. I'm certain she said they were coming here. Maybe they were mistaken about the exhibit. Could I just run through and see if I can find her? Do you have a map?"

"Of course, miss. But you'll have to pay the entrance fee."

It could not be helped. She searched in her handbag for enough coins.

"Thank you." Beth clutched the printed diagram and began a methodical search of the building. With every room she checked off the sheet, her tension heightened. *Where have they gone? What will Mother say?* The anger returned again. *There certainly will be choice words for Julie . . . and possibly for me.*

But soon the anger dissipated into a dread she had never felt before. *I will not find Julie here. Dear Father, help me . . . help Julie . . .*

"Excuse me, sir." She was back at the receptionist's desk, trembling. "Is it possible to call a cab — to take me to the Century Hotel? But I don't have enough money for the fare." Hot tears threatened, and she knew she sounded pathetic, but that was no longer important.

"And you have a room there?"

"Yes, sir."

"What's the name and room number, please? I'll see what I can do."

Once more, Beth waited at the desk, watching those walking past — just in case.

"Miss, I've contacted the front desk for you. They know you're coming, and they'll take care of the fare for you. The charge will go to your room. The taxicab will be here momentarily."

"Oh, thank you!" Beth gasped out. "I . . . I was afraid I'd have to walk."

"Now, we wouldn't want you to do that, miss. Not alone in the city and at night."

The words he meant to be reassuring twisted like a knife in Beth's heart. *Julie is out there. She's as good as alone . . . in the darkness.* Beth tried to formulate the speech she would like to give to Nick when next she saw him, but anxiety so filled her, she was unable to complete a sentence. She tried to thank the clerk again, but found her mouth had gone dry.

At last she was back at the hotel's front entrance and hurrying through the lobby toward the elevator. She was certain that by now the lift operator had caught on to her distress. She lowered her eyes to the floor, fervently praying again. This time she was begging that Julie might already be in the room, or that Mother and Monsieur Laurent had returned.

"Margret," Beth whispered, patting her shoulder. "Margret, please. I need to talk to you."

Finally her older sister stirred. "What is it? Is it morning? Why is it so dark?"

"Mother and Mrs. Montclair aren't back yet," she said. "But I must talk to you. It's about Julie. She's gone."

"Gone? Gone where?" Margret lifted herself up on an elbow.

Tears were streaming down Beth's cheeks. "In a taxi. Nick was going to take her to an art exhibit." Her voice caught in a sob. "But I went to the museum and couldn't find her. I think they might have . . . maybe gotten lost."

"*Who* was she with?" Margret's feet were already on the floor, and she drew Beth away from the sleeping baby. Turning on the light in the small bathroom, they huddled inside. "You're crying. Oh, Beth, don't cry. Tell me again where she is." Margret's arms reached out for her, but Beth pushed her away impatiently.

"Listen," she said, wiping her eyes. "We were supposed to go together. Julie talked me into it. But when we got to the taxi, Nick was there. I kept telling Julie not to go with him — but she wouldn't listen. And now I can't find them." She dissolved into sobs.

Margret caught her hands. "When were they supposed to be back? Before Mother?"

"Yes. What's Mother going to say?"

"Probably things she should have said long before this." Margret directed Beth out of the bathroom and opened the door into the hallway. "I'll put the baby in his crib. Then I'll speak to Miss Bernard so she knows I'm gone and can sit with him. It'll take me a few minutes. You go down to the front desk and wait for me there. At the very least, we'll see Julie as soon as she gets back . . . or Mother, whoever comes first."

Beth nodded and hurried down the hall that seemed to have lengthened on its own. This time she determined she would take the stairs, bypassing the elevator man altogether. She paced back and forth across the lobby, looking out each window in turn. The darkness seemed even deeper beyond the city lights. Margret finally made an appearance, and the sisters set themselves up in a corner of the foyer where two sofas faced each other, able to see all who entered and exited the building. They fixed their eyes on the door and began to confer quietly.

"Tell me again, Beth. What was the plan for the evening?"

Beth's shoulders sagged in defeat. It was already painful to recount the story. "She wanted to see the O'Keeffe exhibit at the Museum of Fine Arts. I thought we were going together — just the two of us."

Margret moved closer, asking in hushed tones, "The two of you were going out without telling Mother?" She was clearly puzzled.

Beth dropped her face into her hands. "It was Julie's idea. She wanted me to go along with her . . . to a painting exhibit. She sounded so enthralled with the artist, and . . . well, I shouldn't have agreed, Margret. But I didn't know anything about Nick being there. That was a complete surprise."

"I see." In two simple words, Margret had managed to sound exactly like Mother. Beth's spirits sank further.

She rushed on. "I went there myself to try and find Julie. And I walked through every room, but didn't see them. I have no idea *where* they went instead."

"You went alone?"

"What else could I do?" Beth's voice was rising, pleading with Margret to understand.

375

"I watched her ride away, Margret. She was *laughing* — thought it all was a big joke. I *had* to go after her."

Margret gasped. "Oh my . . . oh, Julie." Tears were forming in Margret's eyes too.

Time dragged on until Mother and Mrs. Montclair at last materialized through the door, looking pleased with their evening as they made their way into the lobby, Victoria dawdling at her own pace. Following behind them all, Monsieur Laurent was the first to notice Beth and Margret off to the side, rising to their feet.

"What's this? It's quite late for you to still be awake, isn't it? Mrs. Bryce, is something wrong?"

Mother turned toward them as Beth and Margret moved slowly across the floor, dreading what they knew was to come.

"What is it, girls?"

Beth swallowed hard. "Julie is missing."

"What!"

Beth's words, once they began to tumble out, could not come quickly enough as she recounted the frightening events. Mother's face turned pale, then gray. "How long ago?"

Margret reached for Mother's arm to steady her, and Beth said, "At least three hours. She said she was going to be back before you were." Beth clutched at her own neck. "I went looking for her, but they weren't at the museum where they said they would be." Her words caught in her dry throat. "I'm so sorry, Mother," she choked out.

"I shall call the police immediately," Monsieur Laurent announced solemnly, turning toward the front desk.

Beth stared at the front doors, desperate for Julie to come bounding through them at any moment, pleased with her own emancipation, putting an end to this terrible uncertainty. But Julie did not come. Instead, after what seemed an eternity discussing the situation, Monsieur Laurent returned.

"They cannot send an officer until morning, though I certainly tried to convince them of the urgency. We shall have to wait. Miss Thatcher, will you please explain once more what happened as thoroughly as you're able?"

Beth repeated her story in agonizing detail, wedged against the end of the sofa, Margret's arm draped around her for support. Mother was now pacing between the windows, listening to Beth's more detailed description of what happened, scrutinizing the dark streets outside. Beth was asked for more specifics — the time as exactly as possible, a description of the taxicab, of the driver, the direction in which it left, what had been said by each as Monsieur Laurent took what seemed to be meticulous notes. With every answer, the gravity of the situation heightened. Beth was vaguely aware of a general stir around the lobby, those working at the desk and still in the offices at this late hour, buzzing about their dilemma. It all seemed unreal and impossible. *Oh, Julie, where are you?* But each time Beth lifted her gaze toward the door, her heart seemed to fall even further.

Out of the corner of her eye, Beth saw Mother's figure crumple to the floor. She had fainted. With the shock — the tight corset — the restricted breathing, it was no wonder.

All descended upon her immediately. She was lifted to a second sofa and revived with smelling salts. Beth and Margret crouched next to her, clasping each other's hands and their mother's. Again Beth raised a futile gaze to the door, pleading for Julie, for them all.

CHAPTER 25

Beth roused herself enough to realize she had fallen asleep with her head resting on Margret's shoulder. Rays of morning light filtered through the lace curtains over the large windows. Several employees and hotel guests were walking back and forth, heels clicking far too cheerfully on the marble floor. The corner of the lobby with the sofas had been given over to family — and to three policemen whose arrival, it seemed, had stirred Beth awake. She shivered in the realization that it was not yet over. That Julie had not returned. Tears once more trickled from her swollen eyes and down her face.

In the middle of the night they had been asked to vacate the lobby and had been offered an office on the main floor of the hotel. But Mother had refused to leave the place where she hoped to be the first to see a chastened Julie, back and fully repentant after a night of imprudence. The women were still hoping, praying that this would be true. They dared not consider any alternative answer. But with every tick of the minute hand around the face of the hotel clock, it became increasingly evident that something darker was likely transpiring.

From his seat at a round table set into the large bay window, Monsieur Laurent seemed to notice Beth had awakened. "Miss Thatcher," he called softly. "Would you join us, please?"

She extracted herself from her place beside Margret and stepped gingerly past her mother. "Yes, Monsieur Laurent?"

"We'd like you to tell us what you know of this young man. Anything at all."

He and the officer with him drew up a chair for Beth, and she strained her memory to recall and relate what she could. There seemed to be very little. "He had claimed to be from Pennsylvania . . . in the vaguest of terms. I think he mentioned it was a small town outside of Philadelphia, but I'm not certain about that detail. He said he attended the University of Pennsylvania but didn't complete his studies. He played tennis, seemed to dress well as one of the upper class. But eventually he said he was the child of an unwed mother, living with a large extended family. And then he said he was from New England. Is Pennsylvania in New England? I don't really know."

But the officer was busy jotting in his notebook and gave no reaction.

"It's so difficult to believe he might be part of . . . part of something . . ." She couldn't go on. After they waited a moment, she said, "He seemed such an ordinary young man. Rather a nice person." Then another thought. "Penny and Jannis — they might know more about him," she suggested hopefully. "They spent more time with Nick and Julie than I did."

"Yes, well, you see," Monsieur Laurent said quietly, "I already tried to contact them. I went to the ship during the night and spoke with the security officer on board. It seems their room is empty — all their possessions gone. As are the young man's."

"What?"

"They've disappeared, Miss Thatcher."

Beth groped for the significance of his statement. *Do all three have something to do with Julie's disappearance? Are they working together? But the girls claimed not to know Nick well. It makes no sense. . . .*

"I want you to think carefully, miss," said the policeman. "Had they ever tried to draw your sister away from your family before?"

Remembrance lit a beacon in Beth's foggy mind. She took a deep breath. "Yes, I do believe so — at Bar Harbor. They were very angry when Julie spent the day with us instead of going with them. We couldn't understand why. Maybe they were trying to . . ." But Beth could not put into words such evil intent.

"It seems likely this may have been planned for some time — with some fore-thought." The notion was inconceivable to Beth, and she sank back against the chair as the officer stood with a nod of thanks toward her, retreating to where his partners were conferring together.

Beth lifted her eyes to meet Monsieur Laurent's. "I'm grateful the policemen came quickly."

He nodded solemnly. "Yes, with enough money you can even energize the services of the local police these days."

Beth was startled for a moment, then sighed. She had never been more grateful for Father's money.

"We must get Mrs. Bryce up to her room," Monsieur Laurent announced as Margret and Mother began to stir. "In fact, it's time for all of you to withdraw from the public eye."

"But Julie . . . ?" Margret moaned. "What if she comes?"

"She won't . . ." Monsieur Laurent stopped and began again. "If she comes now, she'll be greeted by the officers and hotel staff, who will notify us immediately. But we must remove ourselves from the lobby. The staff can only keep reporters out for so long. And they do need their business space returned to normal."

Beth was sure that each of them felt as she did — that to retire was to concede, to admit there was no hope for Julie to return on her own. They hesitated and lingered, wistfully casting glances toward the door. At last they entered the elevator together. Beth closed her eyes and once more let the tears slide freely. *It's my fault. I failed to protect my sister. I'm as guilty as Julie of rebellion against Mother's guardianship . . . and the costs are more than I could have ever imagined.* Her own accusations were carved at the point of a knife into her wounded conscience.

Beth lay on the bed beside Margret, but even in her exhaustion her mind refused to stop. *Where is Julie? Where did he take her? How could he do something so horrific? He had promised in his last words to me that he could be trusted.* Hard sobs began to shake her as she wondered, *Is Julie terribly frightened? Is she fighting him? Is he treating her cruelly?* And the most frightening of all, the words she could not form, *Is she still alive?* The torment of fears came in unrelenting waves. Beth knew she would not sleep. She rose to draw a bath. Lowering herself into the water, she wept again until a stupefied silence descended.

The water had grown cold before a loud knock sounded at the bedroom door. Beth scrambled out of the tub and threw a thick robe around her shivering body. She opened the door enough to hear but not be seen.

Monsieur Laurent's voice was saying, ". . . the note said a ransom is demanded. We'll inform you as soon as we know more. But this is very good news," he insisted firmly. "She is alive. He won't harm her so long as it's money he seeks. We're sending another telegram to your father right now. I'm certain he'll arrive as quickly as is humanly possible." The door closed behind him.

Money? Father's money is the cause of Julie's . . . abduction? She could barely acknowledge the word. Beth lingered on the cruel irony. The coveting of his money had stolen her sister away. The use of it had brought the police so quickly. And that same money would bring Julie back again. She sat on the edge of the tub, face in her hands. *How could Nick do such a thing? Was this "the business" to which he so calmly referred? What kind of man* is *he?*

But for now it was enough to grasp at one thought among Monsieur Laurent's report. *He won't harm her. He won't harm her. He won't harm her.* Beth hurried to dress.

A tray of food rested on the corner table. The platters appeared not to have been touched. Her sister stood at the window. "Margret, you must eat."

"You also."

"But you're with child."

Margret turned a tortured face. "I'll eat if you do."

Beth lifted a piece of toast from one of the platters. It felt like sawdust in her mouth. "Where's Mother?"

"In the next room. Emma is with her."

"Is she sleeping?"

"I can't imagine she would be."

"And Monsieur Laurent?"

"I believe he's below with the policemen."

He won't harm her. He won't harm her.

Beth drew a hanky from the dresser drawer and blew her nose. "Did he say how much they wanted?"

"I didn't hear." Margret's voice grew cold

and harsh. She spat out, "I don't want to know."

As they forced themselves to eat, Beth asked, "Where's JW?"

"With Miss Bernard." Margret's face twisted. "Said I was scaring him — with my crying."

"Oh, darling!" Beth reached for Margret, and they clung together on the edge of the bed.

At a soft knock at the door, a voice asked if they were awake. Beth hurried to open it, and Mother entered — dressed well, her hair as neat as normal. Only her reddened eyes betrayed the deep emotional turmoil through which she was treading.

"I'm glad to see you've eaten. I've been worried about you girls."

Beth led her across the room, where Mother took a seat on the bed, and Margret asked, "What else have they said, Mother?" Beth drew a tender hand across their mother's back and lowered herself to sit between the two.

"Not much," she replied. "I believe that most of what is currently being discussed is the source of the document we received this morning. It came by courier, so they've gone to speak with the company that performed the service."

Beth asked, "Have they heard anything more about Penny and Jannis?"

Mother shook her head. "We shall continue to pray that they might be located soon in order to discover what part, if any, they played, what they might know. . . ."

"He won't harm Julie," Beth repeated aloud, trying to sound confident, "if it's money he wants."

"So it would seem. However, the young man may not be in charge at all. He seems to be working with others — more than just the girls."

Beth's lip began to tremble. "I'm so sorry, Mother. I . . ."

Immediately she felt arms drawing her close. "You mustn't blame yourself, Beth. We each make a hundred decisions a day that might bring danger. No one believes that you would ever allow harm to your sister if there were anything you could do to stop it. This is an evil plot perpetrated against us. You instigated nothing."

"But I made such poor decisions," Beth wept, her head on Mother's shoulder.

Beth felt a gentle hand stroke her rumpled hair. "Yes, dear. You did choose poorly. And at another time I might have reprimanded you for it. But you are *not* responsible for the consequences brought on by someone else's choice. Remember, Father and I allowed Julie to travel west alone when she visited you. This . . . this event could have happened as easily at that time — more easily, in fact."

Beth wanted with all her heart to cling to the merciful words. However, it was much more difficult to imagine being able to forgive herself. *Perhaps it will be possible once Julie is back safely again. Yes, she will be back, won't she, Lord?*

Mother continued, "In the same way, we can't be angry with Julie. She is young and impulsive — but she *did not* bring this upon herself. And I'll not allow a word to be spoken against her in my presence."

"Of course not, Mother," Margret and Beth said in unison.

"What happens next?" Beth managed to ask.

"I truly don't know, my darlings." She released Beth and began straightening the spread carefully as Beth and Margret watched. "We have sent a telegram to Father. I'm told it will take him several days to travel to us here in Boston."

"Several?" Margret gasped.

"Unless he can secure a seat on an aeroplane — I have no idea how long it would take if he's able to do so. But we can't know anything until we hear back from him. I am hoping that will happen today." Mother cleared her throat and began to scrape and stack plates on the tray. "Also, Mrs. Montclair has sent word to Edward. She's asked him to use whatever connections he is able to see that we receive all possible help."

Beth said quickly, "Jarrick told me that he's an excellent investigator. Do you think Edward might actually come?" The thought was both comforting and terrifying to Beth. The idea that he might be needed was further proof of the dire nature of the situation.

"I'm told he would have no jurisdiction," said Mother, "but that he might be able to investigate privately. We shall see. For now, we will get ourselves through one more day — praying always that this trial will end as abruptly as it began."

"Oh, yes, Mother. That's what we're praying."

"Now, please, you must pull yourselves together. I'd like to see you neatly dressed. I'll send Emma to help with your hair. Whatever is to come next, we shall be ready to meet this challenge with dignity, with our faith strong."

"Yes, Mother."

"Oh, yes, and there's just one more thing," she added with a somewhat forced smile. From the inside of her jacket she produced an envelope. "This is for you, Beth."

The letter was not from Jarrick. "What is it?" she asked, though it was already in her hand and she was staring down at it.

"It looks like it's from the school board. It may be the offer for you to teach."

"Yes . . . thank you." Beth set it aside on the top of the dresser for later . . . sometime.

During the long day they took turns distracting JW, keeping him away from Mother's room, where updates were being relayed. Beth cuddled him as often as he would tolerate, until he would push away and complain, "Down, Annie Bet — down." She knew that the expressions of tenderness were more for her sake than for the baby's.

Father had received the telegram and had sent an answer in return. Edward also replied. Beth chose not to hear either of their telegrams read aloud. She could not bear to know how her father had reacted.

By late afternoon, the officers in the designated room below believed they had discovered a clue, only to dismiss it as erroneous after an hour. Everyone was watching the clock. The money was to be handed over at noon the next day. The instructions claimed that Julie would be returned once the money was safely retrieved by her kidnappers. Monsieur Laurent was busy making the arrangements, though Beth overheard him say he was working to have the deadline extended. Her heart sunk once more. *Extended? But that only makes the wait longer.*

Their cruise ship, scheduled to depart during the early evening, had been instructed by the police to remain. Beth could only imagine what the other passengers were discussing and surmising about the situation. She gazed out the window of her room and breathed her never-ending prayer, "Oh, God — my dear sister, keep her, please. Father, she's yours even more than she's ours. Give her courage. Keep her safe . . ."

A storm moved over the city, and the evening was punctuated with flashes of lightning and rumbles of thunder, seeming to match Beth's jumble of thoughts and feelings. *Is she hidden somewhere near enough to hear the storm rage? Or has she been taken farther away by now? Is she sheltered, warm? Oh, where* are *you, Julie?*

Mother was rummaging through her luggage, drawing out items and laying them out on the bed. Beth noticed that many were accessories. "What are you doing, Mother?"

"Oh, just sorting," she murmured.

Beth moved toward the bed and lifted the box containing the new pearl necklace. Under it was Mother's fur stole and several other pieces of jewelry. "What are you doing?" Beth repeated.

Mother sighed, then said, attempting to sound matter-of-fact, "I'm going to give these to Monsieur Laurent. Maybe selling these things could bring in some of the money."

"Oh, Mother, no."

"It's all I can think to do," she said, her voice constricted. "And they're only *things*. They don't matter a single bit."

"I understand." Beth resolved to do the same, though her possessions were worth nothing compared to Mother's. She would contribute whatever might have value.

"When will you take them to Monsieur Laurent?"

"In the morning, I suppose."

"I'm going back to my room," Beth said. "I'm going to read my Bible for a while. I might try to lie down if I can endure it."

"That's a good idea, darling. We'll of course call you as soon as we hear anything."

"Thank you."

Alone, Beth set aside items she felt might be worth something. She placed them together on the nightstand, but they amounted to very little. Ultimately she lacked the heart to carry them in to Mother and instead drew the Bible out of her bag. She had not read it this morning, as was her habit — nor could she think of simply proceeding where she had left off. Pulling the chain on the light beside her bed, she curled herself under the coverlet and opened to the first pages of the Psalms, knowing that the poetic truths always offered encouragement in difficult moments. It seemed that almost every Psalm contained a comforting thought. Beth breathed them in, moving from one to another rather quickly.

"For the LORD knoweth the way of the righteous: but the way of the ungodly shall perish . . . I cried unto the Lord with my voice, and he heard me out of his holy hill. I laid me down and slept; I awaked; for the LORD sustained me . . . For thou art not a God that hath pleasure in wickedness: neither shall evil dwell with thee. The foolish shall not stand in thy sight: thou hatest all workers of iniquity . . . God judgeth the righteous, and God is angry with the wicked every day. If he turn not, he will whet his sword; he hath bent his bow, and

made it ready."

Beth was appreciative to know that God at that moment was angry too — but His fury was not ignorant and impotent as was her own. Every detail of what was happening lay uncovered before Him. She clung to the promise that there would come a day of certain judgment, that there would be no place to hide. As she contemplated the words, she wished them rather vehemently upon Nick, upon Penny and Jannis and whoever else might have been involved in the horrendous deed.

She forced the tears away and read on in Psalm 10. *"Why standest thou afar off, O LORD? Why hidest thou thyself in times of trouble? The wicked in his pride doth persecute the poor: let them be taken in the devices that they have imagined."* Never before had these words meant as much to Beth. *"The wicked, through the pride of his countenance, will not seek after God: God is not in all his thoughts. . . . His mouth is full of cursing and deceit and fraud: under his tongue is mischief and vanity."*

"That's Nick, Father God," she whispered aloud. "So much deceit and pride. I doubt a word he ever spoke to us was true." She wondered how she had been taken in so easily. How had she ever empathized with such a liar?

"Break thou the arm of the wicked and the evil man: seek out his wickedness till thou find none."

"Yes, Father. Break his arm — even while he plots against my sister and my family. Make his evil scheme come down on his own head." But she knew that would not be enough. Beth preferred the sentiment of Psalm 11. *"Upon the wicked he shall rain snares, fire and brimstone, and a horrible tempest: this shall be the portion of their cup."*

"Oh, yes, Lord. That's what I want. I want him to pay for what he's doing."

Closing her eyes tightly and squeezing out angry tears, she listened to the sound of the downpour drumming against the windows. "Rain Your wrath on him, Lord — with fire and brimstone." She shuddered at the passion of her words, and yet the knowledge that there was a great and terrifying God who could exact such justice on everyone involved in Julie's disappearance came as an overwhelming comfort — the only thought in which she could at this moment take refuge.

CHAPTER 26

Beth slept fitfully, harassed by nightmares, until she awoke to Mother at her bedside. "We've heard back from them. I knew you'd want to know," she whispered.

"What did they say?" Beth's stomach flipped sickeningly.

"They won't delay the payment. They want it today." Mother paused, watching for Beth's response. "We're going to meet together to pray."

Beth pushed the coverlet aside. "I'm glad you woke me. Give me a minute to tidy up."

"Of course, Beth." But instead of hurrying away, Mother reached out for another consoling hug.

She waited as Beth straightened her hair, pinning it again in several places, and smoothed some of the wrinkles from her dress. But instead of turning up the hall toward her room, Mother headed for the elevator.

"Where are we going?" Beth blinked against the bright lights of the hallway.

"There's a small chapel on the second floor. We're meeting there. A local chaplain is going to lead us. It's Sunday today."

"What time is it?"

"It's almost morning."

Beth found herself wishing they would be alone together — and even more so when she arrived in the dimly lit room to find strangers already seated, all eyes upon them as they entered. She hesitated. "Who are all these people?" she whispered.

"They've come to pray," Mother told her. "A few came with the chaplain, and some are from the hotel staff."

Beth followed Mother to the pew beside Emma and Mrs. Montclair. Beth heard very few of the prayers offered from around the room. She chewed hard on her lip and phrased once more her silent calls for God's wrath. She knew she dared not speak these thoughts aloud. And since she could not honestly declare what was in her heart, she did not participate in the corporate prayer.

Beth stole a glance at Mother, then reached over and took her hand. The words of a verse in Romans came suddenly to her mind. "Be not overcome of evil, but overcome evil with good." *Heavenly Father, don't let evil win. Help me to trust in Your Great Good instead.*

Beth paced from the window of Mother's room to the half-open hallway door and back again. It seemed forever since Monsieur Laurent had promised to return with any new information.

"Do you think they'll give us another day — that they may have reconsidered?" Beth asked the question for the umpteenth time, understanding now the need for additional time to collect the money.

"We'll see." Mother's answer was patient and composed. "Monsieur Laurent has explained in his note that they must understand — we're in a foreign country, and it all takes time."

"If only Father were here," Beth said, repeating aloud the recurring thought. *Why hasn't something happened yet? Have her kidnappers disappeared with Julie? Have they broken their word already?* She took a chair next to Mother's and lifted her eyes. "I don't know how you can stay so calm, Mother. I'm ready to jump out of my skin. She's been gone a day and a half already!"

Mother set her teacup on the table next to her chair and sighed, leaning forward to grasp Beth's hand. "I'm not calm, darling. I could very well surrender to my frantic feelings if I allowed myself. But I learned long ago to actively rest my faith in God. It's all I can cling to at times like these. I would be lost without that."

When has there been another time like this?
"That's so hard, though, Mother."

"I know, Beth. And it may not help for me to say this to you just now. It's something so personal that perhaps only God's Spirit can speak it to your heart in His own way. But I try to remember there is no moment in life when we are as able to show our Father how much we *trust* Him as when life throws us the worst. With all I've come to understand about His faithfulness through the years, I'm determined not to falter."

"When do you mean, Mother?" Beth was incredulous. It seemed that their family had always been happy, well cared for by Father with all the things they needed and wanted.

Tears glistened in Mother's eyes, but she continued with unguarded honesty. "I suppose I began the journey toward learning to trust God long ago . . . when we lost baby William to whooping cough. I thought my broken heart would never heal. And then you were very sick so long after your own bout with the disease. Then also whenever

Father was delayed returning home from his travels, and I was tempted each time to give in to the worry that he wouldn't return at all — that my vain imaginings of what would become of us all would become reality. I chose to believe that God is entirely trustworthy despite my fears." She added emphatically, "However, I assure you that none of this means I won't do everything in my power to *act* on Julie's behalf."

Beth lowered her head. "I'm afraid I'm losing hope, Mother."

Mother's forehead came close enough to rest against Beth's, one hand clasping at the back of her neck to hold them closer still. "You are never without hope, my dear. You have a God who is your hope in an actual Person. So when you are His child, it's one thing you can *never* lack. You may not feel it just now, but don't allow yourself to believe what you *feel.* To lose hope is to move away from God."

A quick knock at the open door interrupted the moment. Monsieur Laurent strode into the room and wasted no time. "They won't budge on the deadline, but we've gotten the money together. And I did not have to sell any of your possessions, Mrs. Thatcher." His eyes swept from one to the other. "Now the police still disagree about how it should be handled — if they should allow the bag to be taken from where it is to be delivered, or if they should charge at whoever receives it."

Mother gasped and scrambled to her feet. "Let them *have* the money! If it gets my daughter back, let them have it all and get away besides. I won't allow an attempt to ambush the thieves to put Julie's life in jeopardy. You tell them that, Monsieur Laurent. You tell them that's my final word."

"Yes, madame. I will."

Beth knew she would never be allowed, but she nursed a secret desire to stand nearby when the money was collected from its designated receptacle down by the docks. To see these thugs who had snatched her sister, an image of their faces as she called for God's holy judgment on them. But she remained in the room and tried to eat a little soup instead. Her mind worked hard to focus, as Mother had described, on the trustworthiness of God, on His great power. *And,* she reminded herself, *Father is on his way. The money is ready.* "Oh, God," she recited over and over, "bring Julie back today — this very hour."

At last footsteps sounded in the hallway. Beth, Margret, and Mother flew toward the door. Monsieur Laurent appeared, uncharacteristically breathless.

"They took the money. But they weren't seen! It seems they cut a false bottom from the crate into which the ransom was to be placed. Somehow they managed to access it from a cellar beneath and get away through the basement — so they were not seen at all!"

Beth was aghast. "They got away?"

He stopped to catch his breath. For a moment Beth could see his age revealed. "Let's not forget it was our expressed agreement to *let* them get away. Our officers had hoped to be able to follow them unseen. However, it appears they have been outwitted."

"And Julie?" Margret begged.

"There's still no sign. But she was to be released within the hour. There are policemen all around the docks — everyone is looking for your sister. She'll be spotted immediately if and when she is handed back."

Beth could feel a scream of anguish bubbling up in her throat. She turned away and clutched at the dresser. "Help me trust You," she begged. "Oh, Father, help us all!"

CHAPTER 27

"I want to go down there," Beth insisted. "I want to look for her myself. What if *I* can find her, Mother? What if they're not looking as carefully as we would — or they don't recognize her?" She knew even as she said the words that she was being foolish, but she felt so *helpless,* so *frustrated* with the waiting.

"I'm sure they're looking very hard, dear. That's what they're trained to do."

Mother wiped a tear from her cheek. "And please, Beth, you must stop asking. There are reporters. There are . . . there are . . . *spectators.* I will not allow you to be seen, to be accosted, to be *photographed.*"

Beth's face contorted. She draped an arm over the top of her head and held it in place with the other, as if she could still her pounding headache with enough pressure.

"The doctor has offered us a sedative . . . if we should want it."

"No — no, I can't. No."

"Perhaps tonight."

"*Tonight,* Mother?" Margret's expression filled with horror. "You think she'll still be gone *tonight*?"

"I simply don't know, darling." Mother rose and walked across the room. She stopped at the window and gazed in the direction of the harbor, though it could not be seen from their vantage point. Beth watched silently as Mother turned back, set eyes on her suitcase, and lifted it onto the bed. Stoically, she began to repack the belongings she had removed earlier. Then she set the case aside and turned in place as if looking for something else to do. Beth could fully empathize with what she was feeling.

Mother's eyes fell on the unopened letter. "Beth, why don't you read to us what the school board has to say? I'd like to hear it. I'm thinking it would be a breath of fresh air."

"Oh, let's not bother just now."

"I think we all could do with a little good news. Something else to think about," she added with a tired smile.

Beth moved obediently to the dresser and lifted the envelope. After opening it, she scanned the letter, then read aloud, " 'The

404

board is pleased to offer the position of head teacher for the new provincial school of Coal Valley, Alberta, to you . . .' " It was the only phrase that registered in Beth's foggy brain. *I will return to Coal Valley — if ever we find our Julie.* It was strange how insignificant the news seemed just at that moment.

Another knock on the door generated gasps from all three. But it was merely the bellboy, bringing their afternoon tea.

"Thank you," Beth murmured as he hurried away. The second day was dragging even more slowly than the first. Beth shuddered. *Is it possible that we might still be waiting tomorrow . . . and the next day?* "Oh, Heavenly Father, give us strength. Give Julie strength," she whispered again.

From where Beth stood across the bedroom, the flicker of an expression on her sister's face caught her eye. "Are you all right?"

Margret shook her head, her eyes wide with sudden fear. She pressed a hand against her stomach. "I'm not sure. I don't think so."

Mother was at her side in an instant. "What is it, darling?"

"A pain," she said. "It's not the first. But this was much stronger." Her face went white.

Mother quickly ushered her to the bed, drew her shoes from her feet, and pulled the covers over her. "Beth, go find Monsieur Laurent. Have him send for a doctor right away."

Oh, God, no! Not this! Beth rushed into the hallway and headed toward the elevator. Beth wasn't even certain where to find Monsieur Laurent's room. The elevator gate clattered open, and Beth rushed toward it, almost running headlong into Monsieur Laurent as he stepped out. She grasped his arm. "Margret needs a doctor!" she choked out.

He awaited no further explanation. "I'll have them send for one immediately." He retreated again into the elevator, and the iron gate rattled shut. Beth stood for a moment watching after him, then roused herself to hurry back to their room.

"You found Monsieur Laurent?" Mother asked, looking as frantic as Beth felt.

"I did, Mother. He was in the hallway and left immediately to call."

The room lights had already been dimmed, the curtains drawn. Beth could hear Margret sniffing softly. Mother applied a cool cloth against her forehead, dabbing her neck and cheeks.

Beth crawled across the bed and lay down

close to Margret's side, a hand resting on Margret's shoulder. Silence hung over the room. Beth was certain they were all lost in their own prayers.

The doctor arrived shortly, and Beth retreated to the hall as Margret was examined. "Oh, Father, my two sisters . . . Please show us Your great mercy. We need You so much." She walked from one end of the hall to the other. It occurred to Beth that she might knock on Mrs. Montclair's door, but decided against it. The mother and daughter had been keeping their distance. Beth wasn't sure why, if it were due to their own preference or Mother's. But she wanted to respect the boundary. She also was fearful she would regret whatever Mrs. Montclair might decide to say.

When Beth returned to the hotel room after the doctor strode away, Margret was resting comfortably. Mother lifted a finger to her lips, and Beth slipped quietly into the chair by the window. She tipped her head back, and eventually weariness of body and soul overtook her and she drifted off to sleep.

CHAPTER 28

"How are you feeling today, Margret?" Mother asked the question with careful cheerfulness. Beth held her breath for Margret's answer.

"Much better. I believe I'll stay in bed as much as possible, though."

"That's very wise, darling."

"What day is it, Mother?"

"I believe it's Monday."

"Only Monday? That's so difficult to believe."

Miss Bernard brought JW to visit Margret once they had finished their breakfast. The little boy played quietly beside his mother on the bed, seeming to sense that she needed peace. When Monsieur Laurent arrived to speak with them, JW leapt from the bed and into his arms, glad for the possibility of some rough-and-tumble play.

"Ça va, mon petit ami?" their guide said with a grin, tossing JW up into the air.

"Ça va," JW giggled from the man's arms. "Ça va, mis-yur."

Mother's voice sounded strained. "What was it you came to tell us, Monsieur Laurent?"

He set the boy back on the floor, straightened his jacket and tie, and explained quietly, "There was a meeting this morning of which I wanted you to be aware. The local police have been in contact with other districts. They are widening their search. There may be information gained about similar crimes — perhaps enacted by the same ones who have Miss Thatcher. They might interview some suspects from regions farther away."

"Oh? And are you saying they have interviewed suspects from this region already?"

"Yes, madame. Several have been taken in for questioning."

"I see. We had not known of any such activity. In the future, Monsieur Laurent, we would appreciate having this kind of detail immediately."

"Yes, madame. Of course." Monsieur looked down at JW playing with the laces on his shoes. "May I take the little one for a walk in the hall?"

"That would be very kind," Margret answered quickly. "I know he's been feeling very confined. He'd be so happy to spend a little time with you."

The man scooped him up. "And I with him, I assure you."

"Thank you."

"It's my pleasure, Mrs. Bryce." He and JW left the room.

Margret spoke again gently, "Mother, you were rather cross with him."

At first, Mother's face turned in surprise toward Margret, no doubt startled at the unexpected rebuke, but she softened almost instantly. "I know, darling. You're right. I shall have to apologize later. It's just that I want so badly to hear any news — and I don't feel he's telling us all there is to know."

"He's probably filtering it for our own good."

"Yes, dear, but *what is it* he's leaving out? Wouldn't it be better just to know everything?"

Beth agreed. "I want to hear all of it. I don't want to be kept in the dark, even if . . ." But she couldn't finish the thought.

Another long, slow hour crawled past, followed by a scurry of movement outside the door. Mother's hand went to her mouth, and she stood frozen in place.

A quick knock and the door opened to

frame a tall young man in the doorway, his gaze sweeping around the room with an expression that indicated deep concern. It took several moments to register the face — seeming out of place here in their nightmare.

"Edward!"

Mother rushed forward to embrace him. "We're so grateful you've come." Her voice quivered. "That you've come so far to help us . . ."

"Mrs. Thatcher, I can't even begin to say how very sorry I am." He looked at Margret on the bed, Beth standing beside her. "Margret, Elizabeth. I'm so sorry."

Beth drew closer, and he held out his arms. Despite more recent events that could have made the meeting awkward, she could not hold back and entered the circle of his embrace. Her shoulders shook, and she felt his arms tighten comfortingly.

"We'll find her, Elizabeth," he said, though Beth knew the promise was only a hope. "We'll find her soon. You must trust us."

If only it could have been Jarrick who was sent. Yet she knew it was unreasonable of her even to wish.

"Why haven't they *released* her? They *have* their money." Beth's frustration reflected

411

that of her mother and sister, but she already knew no one was helped by her expression of it, least of all herself.

Edward sat in a chair next to Mother, Margret on the edge of the bed, while Beth stood apart, one hand braced against the dresser for support. He explained, "It isn't uncommon, actually. The whole nasty business is a lot more difficult to control than what one might think. Sometimes best-laid plans unravel for the perpetrators in unexpected ways. Sometimes they haven't thought very far in advance. But," he added firmly, "the positive truth is that they want very much what we want at this point — to have the whole thing over with, to get away from here with their money. They won't want to bother with a hostage for that."

Hostage. The word filled Beth with new dread.

"They won't . . . they won't harm her?" All eyes turned to Margret, who dared to give voice to the unimaginable.

Edward's calm answer was meant to assure them. "If they were to harm her, they know it would only serve to increase our efforts to find them and punish them to the full extent of the law. If they release her safely, they can escape more quickly. And they'd figure there would be less determination to pursue. You see?"

His words sounded comforting, but Beth knew the truth also must include the very worst possibility — that they would simply get rid of Julie. She shook her head and gripped the edge of the dresser. For Mother's sake — and for Margret's — she pretended to believe him. "What happens next?" she managed through stiff lips.

"I of course can't interfere with their investigation. That's why I am not in my Mountie uniform. But they've told me I can have a look around myself."

"What are *they* doing? It doesn't seem like much."

"Oh yes, they're watching every ship that leaves port, an enormous task, and looking at each manifest to see that its history is respectable. They're boarding and searching many of the smaller, independent vessels. And they've surrounded the area of the docks. I've never seen so much attention given to one investigation. They're being very methodical and comprehensive. It's most likely that the kidnappers never imagined so much coverage — it's likely hindering their movements and therefore Julie's return. They may have released her by now if they could find a clear path to escape. And from what I heard, they may have planned to take her earlier — so they were forced to change their plans, to improvise, which also could make delays afterward."

Mother suggested quietly, "Maybe the policemen should get out of their way —"

But Edward was shaking his head. "No, that's not an option. They have to keep the pressure on. Trust me, that's best. It sends just the right message. And you have to keep in mind that the guilty are watching all this too — determining their actions based on what the officers are doing. It's a contest of wills, and we have to be the ones with the upper hand in order to win."

Beth asked, "How did you get here so quickly, Edward?"

"I hired an aeroplane — actually, more than one — each taking me a portion of the distance."

Mother reached over to squeeze his hand. "That was very kind of you."

His gaze fixed on Beth. "I could do nothing less. I only wish there was more I could contribute."

"You'll help as they search the docks too?" Mother's question seemed to prompt his exit, because Edward rose.

"Yes," he said, "I'll work with one of the local officers to see if they've missed something. I will stop briefly to greet my mother and Victoria — I came directly to see you since I knew you'd want to know I'm here." He took several steps, then paused. "Have you heard further from Mr. Thatcher?"

Mother shook her head. "I'm told he's on his way. No doubt facing the same transportation obstacles that you did."

Edward smiled encouragingly. "He shall certainly be here soon too."

Mother walked with him to the door. "Thank you, Edward. Thank you ever so much."

Once he was gone, the room seemed to crowd in on itself again. Beth slipped away to the bathroom for another bath. It wasn't necessary, but it seemed the simplest way to spend time alone. She couldn't bear the solemnity any longer. As quietly as she could, she wept alone. *How can we stand this any longer? We're* all *hostages!*

But Beth repented of the thought almost as quickly as it had come. *Julie is among wicked strangers. She's surely terrified . . . maybe even hurt.* "Oh, God," she whispered as the tub filled, "I'm so sorry. This is all my fault. I never should have let her leave in the taxi. I should have gone with her. I should have clung to the door until I was dragged along. If I ever see my sister again, Father, I shall never let her go!"

Mother insisted they gather together and share the meal delivered on a cloth-covered rolling table to her room in the late afternoon. Beth knew she was hungry, but still it was unexpectedly difficult to swallow down the food.

Mrs. Montclair now joined them, while Victoria had preferred to remain in her own room. For a change, Mother's friend seemed to be having a great deal of difficulty in finding topics of conversation. With a sigh that seemed to release her tongue, she finally offered, "It's been such a boon to my spirit to have Edward near. I feel as if he might make the difference in the investigation — and this will all be over soon."

Mother smiled weakly. "That would be very nice, Edith."

"I've heard he is very good at his job. He'll think of things others have overlooked, I'm quite certain."

"Perhaps he will."

"You do know that the cruise ship has moved on today."

Mother's face clearly indicated that she had not heard. Beth exchanged glances with Margret.

"Of course, that would be necessary for them," Mrs. Montclair hurried to explain. "All those passengers aboard have nothing to do with this terrible business. They've paid for their vacations, and it would serve no purpose for them to remain. And at any rate, it's unlikely that we shall be joining them again."

It hadn't occurred to Beth to wonder what would happen if Julie were suddenly returned. As far as she was concerned, it would be very easy to forgo the remainder of the trip for some peaceful days at home, and she was certain her mother and sisters would feel the same.

Just give her back to us, Father — and nothing so inconsequential will ever matter again. By the look on Margret's face, Beth wondered if her thoughts were taking a similar path.

Mrs. Montclair babbled on as if that would help allay the fears of them all. "*Mr. Lorant* has retrieved our baggage from the ship. I sent my Lise along to help pack up, and two or three of the maids on ship assisted her too. We didn't want to bother you with such things, Priscilla. Our things have been placed in storage for now." She drew in a long breath, no doubt reloading for another soliloquy. "I should have enjoyed seeing Florida. I've seen plenty of cities all along the way, but I should have enjoyed the palm trees." And on and on she went.

Beth could see the tension written across Mother's face, the weariness in the slope of her shoulders. Beth wished Mrs. Montclair had remained in her own room.

But Mrs. Montclair was taking her time over the meal, speaking around her bites of food, removing and replacing her glasses by turn. "Perhaps we can join up again next summer, for a longer journey. I'd like to see South America. If we were to travel there, it might be that our husbands would travel along with us — for business *and* for pleasure — killing two birds with one stone, so to speak."

Mother nodded and forced a smile. Beth almost groaned aloud at her inappropriate phrase.

"I've heard that the flora and fauna in South America are fascinating, so very different than our own. I should like to have a look at the Nile and the Andes —"

"The Nile is in Egypt. It's the Amazon in South America." Beth's automatic correction had slipped through before she considered the consequences.

"Oh? What did I say?"

"You said the Nile."

"No," Mrs. Montclair argued. "I believe I did say the Amazon. I *do know* my geography, Elizabeth."

"Perhaps I heard wrong." Beth could feel Margret nudge her leg under the table and quickly took a bite to hide her smile.

"At any rate, we shall soon see an end to our troubles, I assure you. With Edward here, and our husbands on their way, I'm convinced we shall have Julie back among us within another day." She patted Mother's hand. "And then you'll want to keep your daughters home with you for quite some time to come, I imagine."

Mother glanced at the dresser where the school board's invitation still lay. Beth inwardly begged, *Don't bring up the letter. Please don't bring up the letter.*

But it was Mrs. Montclair who spoke again, her voice trembling a little. "I'm so sorry, Priscilla. I'm afraid I've monopolized the conversation. And I intended to try to devote myself to listening instead." There was genuine remorse in her eyes.

"No, Edith, don't apologize. It's just this situation . . . this terrible waiting."

Mrs. Montclair dabbed at her eyes with her handkerchief. Beth was astonished at the heartfelt compassion she saw in the woman's face. "I haven't known what to say to you all . . . but I've prayed." She raised troubled eyes, looking at each one. "We're so worried for her, for our dear Julie. If there's anything — anything at all I can do . . ."

Mother reached for her friend's hand. "We know, Edith. But you sent for Edward. And you've given up your plans and stayed here with us through this nightmare. We surely know." The glistening in Mother's eyes said more than her words. "How is Victoria?" she asked.

"She's rather bored, of course. But she's given herself over to her violin. I'm afraid the noise upset some of the other patrons — however, their rooms were promptly changed and a crisis was averted. She's taken now to practicing on the rooftop. There's a small patio up there, and she tells me the sound is quite lovely when it isn't too windy. I haven't scolded her — as you advised, Priscilla. I've tried to allow for this means of expressing herself."

"I'm sorry this all is so difficult, Edith, for you also," Mother said. "We're grateful for your encouragement."

"It's nothing," her answer came back emphatically. "You're as dear to us as family. Whatever you walk through, we shall walk through together."

"Thank you, my friend. That means the world to me just now."

CHAPTER 29

Once Mrs. Montclair returned to her own room, the dismal specter of doubt and fear seemed to descend upon them once more. Margret tucked herself back into bed, and Mother returned to her meaningless fussing over this and that. Beth tried to read but found it possible only to pretend.

Light through the windows began to dim, marking off the passing of another long, painful day. Edward had stopped twice but had very little news to offer. Even Monsieur Laurent seemed to have made himself scarce, no doubt feeling the awkwardness of having nothing substantial to tell them.

Beth was overwhelmed with how well Mother was managing, all things considered. There was a strength in her that Beth had missed previously. She was well aware of the truth that Mother had handled her emotions much more honorably.

Then the sound of a key in the door. *Who*

on earth has a key? Mother froze in place, and Beth rose.

It was Father who burst into the room.

"Oh, William! At last!" Mother fell into his arms, openly weeping now.

Beth and Margret hurried to join in the embrace. Moments passed before any of them could speak.

"I came as quickly as I could, dear ones. All I wanted was to see your faces." He looked from one to the other, then back again.

Margret leaned her head against his shoulder. "You too, Father. We just wanted you with us."

"Have you spoken with the police, Father?"

"No, my dearest Beth. I came straight to you. Emile — Monsieur Laurent — met me at the airfield and gave me all the information to which he was privy. Poor man, he feels this is his fault. He's beside himself with worry."

Beth lowered her head. "No, Father, it's *my* fault. I should never have even considered going off with Julie like that. I should have —"

"Nothing of the sort." Father looked directly into Beth's eyes and held her shoulders. "The scoundrels would have created an opportunity at some point, regardless." He waved her troubled thoughts aside. "We'll have no more talk of blame. That can rightly be placed only on those who perpetrated this crime — precisely what I told Emile. Let's focus instead on securing Julie's release."

Beth whispered, "Yes, Father. Thank you."

"Now, I believe I shall go speak to the police. And I would very much like to see you rest. You three do look exhausted. Have they offered you something to help you sleep, Priscilla dear?"

Mother nodded.

"Then it seems to me this is a good night to take that help. I'll stand on watch. You don't need to worry about that."

"But Margret can't — she's . . ." Beth's eye grew wide. She had almost blurted out Margret's news.

"With child? Yes, I know. Mother informed me by telephone a while ago." He slipped an arm around Margret's shoulders. "I'm so happy for you, my sweet Margret. You're a wonderful mother. I'm sure John is very pleased."

"He wishes I were at home with him," Margret said.

"Yes, I'm certain he's beside himself with concern."

"I told him not to come, but I never thought we'd still be . . ."

Father leaned closer with a smile. "He's on his way now, my dear. He couldn't be stopped. But we're not surprised by that, are we?"

Margret's face filled with joy and relief.

Father left to talk with the authorities, yet everything had changed. There was no longer a need for constant vigil. He would be standing guard, as he had always done. Beth slipped into her nightgown for the first time in three days and crawled between the soft sheets. There was no need for a sedative. Sleep came easily at last.

Beth woke early, her mind scrambling to figure things out. *Yes, Julie is still gone. So why are we sleeping soundly in bed? Oh, yes, Father has arrived. He is in charge now — that role he does so well.*

Rising slowly so as not to awaken Margret, Beth was surprised to discover her sister already absent. She hurried into the bathroom to wash and dress for the day, brushing out her hair carefully and pinning it neatly in place. She had been neglecting her appearance, and it was nice to feel fresh and presentable again. Having ignored her little ritual since Julie had disappeared, she chose a rose petal from the shrinking packet in her suitcase and folded the corner of her hanky around it.

Just as she exited the bathroom, she heard a knock at the door and opened it to find Father, looking rather flushed and somber. "You're awake?"

"Yes, Father."

"Come with me."

Beth hurried after him, struggling to match his long strides. "Where's Margret?"

He answered without pausing, "John arrived late in the night. They've taken a room further up the hall."

"Oh, I'm so glad." But Father, leading her forward quickly, wasn't paying attention.

He rapped on Mother's door, and it was immediately opened. Mother was already dressed, looking fresh as well. Beth followed him inside. Father drew Mother close. Beth held her breath. *What . . . ? Oh no, please, God, no!*

"I want you to remain calm, Priscilla. Can you do that?"

Mother swallowed hard. "I'll do my best, William." Her hands clutched at his lapels. Beth's own trembling hands rose to cover her mouth as she fought tears.

"Edward has discovered where those two girls went after leaving the ship."

"But that's good," Beth whispered, "isn't it, Father?"

"Perhaps. But it's disappointing as well." Father bent his face closer to Mother's, his voice growing softer. "They've headed west — far west. They purchased train tickets for the coast. If they aren't apprehended before they get to California, it's likely they won't be seen again."

"Oh no! And Julie? Is she . . . is she with them?" Beth watched Mother's hand clench tighter around Father's lapel.

"That's unlikely, but we simply do not know. It *is* possible, of course. Just unlikely. And there's more." He stooped to study Mother's face. "They have criminal records — both young women. They've been arrested before, several times, for petty theft mostly. It appears they often prey on vacationers, taking advantage of people at times when they're less guarded. It's uncertain when they became involved with the young man, but it was undoubtedly rather recently. They were operating much farther south only a couple of months ago."

Our family was deceived! Beth wanted to scream aloud — to drop the feeble grip she had on self-control and shriek until her lungs could produce no more sound.

Mother was clinging to Father, and he was

holding her up in a strong embrace. Beth tried to piece together what he was telling them.

". . . two tickets purchased . . . train departed Saturday . . . local officers communicating with police stations ahead of the scheduled stops . . . could possibly be intercepted in Missouri late this morning . . . the girls, if arrested, may be able to give us more information."

"Edward discovered this?" Beth managed to choke out.

"Yes, dear. He's been working tirelessly. He had Emma's photographs developed, the ones she's been taking along the way. And from them Emile identified those two girls . . ." His voice cracked. "And also one of Julie. He took the photographs around with him when he asked questions — to see if anyone recognized their faces, and someone at the train station did, at least the pictures of those other two. It was rather brilliant of him to think of it."

"I want to thank him," Beth said.

"That would be very fitting. There's my brave girl." One of Father's arms reached around Beth's shoulders to pull her close.

Beth did not feel brave at all, merely overwhelmed to the point of incomprehension. It was slowly dawning on her, truly sinking in, that Julie could easily be long gone and lost forever.

CHAPTER 30

Beth merely picked at her lunch, moving the pasta salad around her plate in hopes it would appear she had eaten. In truth, she had already decided that dining would be impossible.

"Why isn't there any news?" Margret fretted. "When did Father say Jannis and Penny were to arrive at the next station? We've been waiting for hours."

"I don't remember —"

"And where are they all now?"

"Down in that little office."

"We should be there, Beth. Let's go down and hear what's being said."

"Remember, Margret? They told us to stay up here. The room is crowded, and it's less stressful . . ." Beth bit back the words *for you, Margret. They don't want you upset. John, in particular, wants you protected from —*

"Can't we open another window?" Margret waved a handkerchief in front of her face. "It's so hot today. Even the breeze off the ocean seems to feel steamy."

"I don't know. I'll look."

Beth rose from her seat, grateful to forsake any further pretense of eating. She pulled back the drapes and checked to see if additional glass panes were moveable. At last she found that the smallest window would open, and it allowed for a slight cross breeze. "Is that better, Margret?"

"I suppose — I'll sit right in front of it." Margret moved over to the stuffed chair and collapsed, working the handkerchief for all it was worth. "Thank you, Beth," she managed.

Beth wanted to empathize with her sister, out of sorts as Margret was, but she had lost all interest in conversation. She moved toward the bathroom.

"You're not going to bathe again, are you?"

Beth stopped. *It would be a ridiculous waste of water.* Returning, she scraped their plates onto one and gathered the utensils onto the tray. "I wish they had brought tea."

"On a hot day like this? I can't imagine."

Beth took a deep breath, waited as long as she could before trying a new subject. "Where's JW?"

431

"With Miss Bernard."

"Could we play with him?"

"He's sleeping."

"Oh, that's too bad." It occurred to Beth how grateful they should all be to have Miss Bernard to care for the baby, but she chose not to express the thought aloud. Instead she spun in a slow circle. There was really nothing with which she could distract herself. The beds were made up, the dishes stacked, their bags packed and resting on the stands. She could read, but it would be only meaningless words.

"Where is John?" Margret wondered fitfully.

"Oh, goodness — I just told you. He's down in the office with the policemen and everyone else."

"Yes, you're right. I forgot. I'm sorry."

"I'm sorry too. I should be more patient. Do you need anything, Margret?"

"No . . . not right now."

"How are you feeling?"

"Fine. Just tired. I wish I could sleep."

Beth lowered herself to the edge of the bed and stretched her arms. "So do I."

"Why don't you try to sleep for a while?"

Beth groaned. "I'll try. But I doubt it will do any good."

She had a fleeting thought of transferring

one of her sketches to a canvas . . . and then remembered this was Julie's . . .

Before she could give in to tears, she lay down on the bed, praying that sleep would fall over her. She felt the mattress move as Margret quietly lay down beside her.

The door opened slowly and Mother appeared. "My darlings, are you here?"

Where else? "Yes, Mother. We're both here, trying to rest."

"Beth," she said, entering cautiously, "there's someone here to see you. Is it a good time?"

Her feet slid quickly to the floor, and she straightened her dress. "Who is it, Mother?" She forced herself to move forward.

Jarrick stepped inside the door, his blue eyes searching her face as if there were no one else in the room, his forehead knitted together with deep concern. "Beth?"

How is it possible?

Casting a puzzled look at Beth, who stood as if paralyzed, Margret rose and extended a hand toward Jarrick. "My name is Margret. I'm Beth's sister."

He smiled politely. "It's nice to meet you. I'm Jack Thornton. Beth calls me Jarrick."

"It's nice to meet you." Without further comment, Margret slipped past Mother,

433

and they both retreated, leaving the door open.

"Beth?"

She felt the room begin to spin and sank down on the edge of the nearest chair. Her hands lifted to her face. *Jarrick? He's here?* She could feel herself trembling.

He crossed the room noiselessly, dropping to one knee on the carpet in front of her. "Beth," he whispered softly.

For several moments she could only take little glimpses of him through her fingers, unable to articulate what was most urgent in her heart. He waited in silence. At last she lowered her hands just a little. "Julie . . ."

"I know." His words stumbled out. "I . . . I was very reluctant to intrude like this. I didn't want to be a distraction or get in the way, but I just couldn't keep myself from seeing you — seeing for myself how you are."

Tears streamed down her cheeks. "Did they tell you — ?"

"Yes, I believe they told me everything they know."

She swallowed hard. "But did they tell you it's all my fault?"

"No, Beth." She could hear sorrow choking his voice. His hand touched her arm gently. "No, they didn't. Because it's *not.*"

"That's what they all say, but it isn't true. I know it. I should have stopped her —"

"I know your sister, Beth." He leaned closer, whispering yet speaking with firm conviction. "Once Julie made up her mind, she wouldn't likely listen to anyone else. And of course she had no inkling of what was going to happen."

Beth finally raised her wet eyes to his, pleading, "Do you *believe* that? Don't tell me what you think I want to hear. Tell me the *truth.*"

"Yes, Beth, I believe that. I certainly do."

She let her head drop against his shoulder. His arms reached around her, one hand resting on the back of her head, holding her close. "Jarrick," she sobbed, "I don't know what to do. We've been stuck in here for days. I want to *do* something."

"You've been doing all you can. In fact, the thing no one else can do as well as Julie's family is the most important thing. You're praying."

Beth's sobs shook her body.

"Don't give up, Beth. God is watching — He knows where she is."

"Oh, Father," she whispered, "please let Jarrick be right."

There was not enough seating in one of their hotel rooms for all the family and friends to gather. Father had arranged to use the hotel's chapel. Jarrick followed Beth through the creaky elevator gates, down to the second floor, and into the simple room. Margret and John were already seated, his arm around his wife with her head resting against his shoulder.

She and Jarrick slipped into the row behind, and Beth laid a hand on Margret's shoulder as they settled into their places. She wished Jarrick was able to draw her close against him in such a comforting manner, but it was enough for now just to have him beside her. Mr. and Mrs. Montclair and Victoria had joined them, as well as Lise and Emma and Monsieur Laurent.

Father rose at the front of the room and cleared his throat. "Well, most of you have already heard the latest information. But I want to know if you have any questions — and we also want to pray together. Does anyone have a question before we do that?"

"When is the train scheduled to arrive?" John's voice came first.

"We believe it should be at the station

within half an hour. We expect a call to tell us what happens, one way or another. Of course, we're praying that the girls will be detained and information gathered from them quickly."

Beth let out a shallow breath and turned her face to Jarrick's. "They should separate them," she whispered. "I think Penny might talk if Jannis isn't around."

Jarrick nodded. "You should tell him that."

"Father?" She forced herself to speak out. "Father, is it possible to tell them — the authorities — that maybe Penny and Jannis should be separated immediately? I think if they're kept together, they'll gain strength from one another, be less cooperative."

"The officers should be told that. Thank you, Beth." He looked around the room. "Emile, would you please pass that along?" Monsieur Laurent stood immediately and departed.

Beth's hands trembled in her lap. Her eyes closed, and she tried not to picture the scene, yet the faces were flitting back and forth behind her eyelids. First Penny and Jannis, then Julie. *Please, God, let the two feel some compassion for Julie. Make them willing to disclose what they know.* She felt a hand cover her own. The fingers tightened slightly, loosened, but continued to hold hers.

Mrs. Montclair spoke from the opposite side of the room. "Has anyone found evidence of the young man? We haven't heard about him for quite a while."

Father shook his head. "Not at this time. He seems to have slipped away."

"My son — Edward, you know — wasn't able to find a picture of him. He was clever enough not to allow himself to be photographed."

"Yes, Edith, that appears to be true. So we do not have any news of his whereabouts at this point."

"Were Jannis and Penny their real names?" Margret's voice was almost too quiet to hear.

"We don't know. The tickets were not purchased under those same names, but there's no way to know which ones are correct — or how long they've been concealing their true identities."

Is the story of Penny's disgraceful given name a fabrication? Yet why would anyone make up such a lie? So that Julie would be empathetic, see the girls as victims? Then she remembered the fight she had overheard. "Father," she spoke aloud, "when they thought they were alone, I overheard them call each other by those names."

"That's helpful, Beth. Thank you."

Father waited another moment, his eyes scanning the small room. "If there are no further questions, I think we should pray now."

A general stirring followed as they shifted positions together. From beside Beth, Jarrick leaned forward and bowed his head. She was grateful he did not release her hand. They earnestly cried out for mercy, for truth to prevail. Beth's focus was on Nick. *You know where he is, Lord. He can't hide from You. Speak to his heart. Let him repent even now. Let the enormous weight of what he's done overwhelm him —*

Then the sound of a man clearing his throat at the back of the room brought their prayer time to a close. A hushed silence overtook them as a policeman strode to the front. He leaned forward to whisper in Father's ear.

"It's all right, Officer. We're prepared to hear whatever you've discovered."

The man cleared his throat again. "The women weren't on the train," he announced. "They probably never got aboard. It's possible — and I think more 'an likely — they got off somewheres along the way, switched trains. Or met up with somebody else, somebody they planned to meet. But, anyways, they weren't aboard."

Beth closed her eyes and let her breath escape slowly. She felt Jarrick's hand tighten again around her own. There were no tears. *Perhaps the reservoir is too depleted,* she thought.

"I would give almost anything for a walk."

Jarrick sighed with her. "I'm sure you would. I suppose you've been cooped up here this whole time." He added, "We can't go outdoors, but surely there's a balcony or a rooftop deck or something."

Beth remembered that Victoria had been playing her violin on some type of patio. She cast a glance around the crowded hotel room and whispered, "We'll be back soon."

Mother lifted her eyebrows, but Father merely nodded his assent. Jarrick followed Beth out into the hall.

"I think there might be a patio on the roof," she explained. "I hadn't thought of it before. But surely we can find it." Beth chose the stairs and began their upward journey, feeling relief already at being away from the stifling and somber atmosphere. The strain on her legs as they climbed was very welcome after so much inactivity. When they had passed three landings, Jarrick asked, "How are you, Beth? Really?"

She paused and turned toward him, hoping he was prepared for honesty. "I'm everything at once, I suppose. I'm angry and sad and frightened, and in far greater measure than I've ever felt before. But I'm *trying* to be strong — for my family. For Julie. I just feel so . . . so lost. So helpless."

Jarrick motioned to the steps, and she sank down onto them. He took a seat beside her, stretching out his legs and leaning an elbow against the rail, the other on a step behind them. "I can't even imagine. I wish there was something I could say, but —"

"There's not," she mouthed, shaking her head and hoping he understood.

"I can listen, Beth." It was said with such gentleness she knew he was sincere.

"I don't want to talk about it just now. It's too, too much," she managed. They sat in silence as several moments slipped away. At last she asked him, "How is it you could come, Jarrick? Your work? And the long distance . . . ?"

He smiled. "That's kind of an amusing story, Beth. I spoke with Lester Carothers, the older man I meet with from the church. I told him what was happening. And I'll never forget his response."

Beth turned to watch Jarrick's face as he

441

continued, a twinkle of playfulness in his eyes. "Lester said, 'I know ya think yer work's important, son — and it is. But there's plenty a' men who can fill in for you. Leavin' a job behind is like drawin' a fist from a bucket a' water. You don't leave much of a hole. But a family — well, that's altogether dif'rent. When you're absent from the ones who need ya most, ya leave a hollow no one else can plug.' " Beth couldn't help but smile at his portrayal of his friend's accent.

"So I told my superiors that it was a family emergency, and I caught the first express train I could find heading in this direction." He laughed. "I would've flown out with Edward, but the plane he managed to locate was only a two-seater — we figured it was best if one seat were left for the pilot."

Her throat constricting with both laughter and tears, Beth leaned into his side. *He's including me in his family. He came to fill the crater-sized hollow of his absence.* "Thank you," she whispered. "He's right. Mr. Carothers was right. I'm so glad you're here, Jarrick."

His arms encircled her. They sat in comfortable silence. At that moment, there was nowhere else she would have preferred to be than in a hot, dusty stairwell . . . with Jarrick.

CHAPTER 31

"Edward delivered the remainder of the photographs," Mother said. "They're in that box on the table if you would like to look at them."

"No, thank you, Mother. Perhaps later." Beth was all too aware that there would be pictures of Julie — of all of them together. Seeing their smiles, remembering their happy, shared experiences was simply too painful.

JW burst through the door, dragging his father by the hand, with Margret following closely behind. "Ga'mamah!" the boy called, "Papa comin'."

"I see that, darling. I'm so glad."

"We p'ayin' wif cars."

Beth understood John's conflicted feelings as he somewhat sheepishly followed his bouncing son into the room — the joyous demeanor, totally unperturbed by the emotion hanging heavy over the room.

She ran a hand over the boy's head. "It's awfully good to see you so happy. You're our little ray of sunshine."

He looked up at her, puzzled. He tried, "Bah-juhr, Annie Bet. Papa here."

"May I see your cars?" Jarrick slid off his chair to the floor. "Will you show them to me?"

The pudgy hands held up the pair of tiny vehicles. "See. Lellow and g'een."

"You got it backwards, son." John crouched down. "This is the yellow one. And this one is green."

" 'Kay," he agreed easily, holding the cars up again to show them exactly as before. "Lellow — and g'een."

Jarrick laughed. "Aren't they nice? So new and bright. Can you show me how they work?"

Needing no more encouragement, the boy dropped to his belly on the floor and began pushing them over the carpet. "Brrrrr," he sputtered.

Margret stopped at the box of photos for a moment, drawing one or two from the top of the stack. However, she soon abandoned them. Beth was certain she was feeling the same way about such reminiscing just yet. The only sound was JW playing with his father and Jarrick in the center of the room.

At last Beth surrendered to the thought of attempting another night's fitful sleep. She gathered up her few belongings and moved toward the doorway. Jarrick hurried to fall in step beside her down the hall, hesitating as she unlocked the door to the room she now shared with Emma and Miss Bernard. She had moved out of her previous room so that Margret, John, and JW could have it. Jarrick had been assigned the extra bed in Monsieur Laurent's room. She wondered how much longer they could all maintain harmony in such crowded conditions.

"I would have liked to have looked at the photographs," he admitted slowly. "I understand you aren't up to it yet, but maybe once Julie returns . . . maybe we can find some time for you to show them to me — to tell me all about your trip."

"You still think she's going to be found?"

"Of course I do." His voice sounded confident, more confident than Beth could manage.

She slumped against the doorframe. "I can't help imagining what's happening to her. And even while I'm wishing the best, it seems unlikely that she won't be . . . won't be harmed by now." Her lips trembled.

"You don't know that, Beth. We need to hope for the best." He reached toward her, but Beth turned away.

"It's been four long days, Jarrick, and it *feels* even longer. It must be an eternity to poor Julie." Her voice was strained, agony seeping around the edges of her words. "And they already have their money. If they were going to give her up, it would have happened already. I can figure out that much without anyone saying it aloud." She dropped her gaze to the floor, letting more questions tumble out. "Tell me the truth, Jarrick. Why would they be keeping her? Is she already *dead*? What do they *want* with her?" She knew her voice had risen sharply by the end of her outburst.

She watched him tense with the gravity of her ragged emotion, his jaw contracting as he gathered his thoughts. *What will he say? Will he address my questions honestly? Can I trust his answer?*

"Beth . . ." He looked into her eyes. "I doubt they would have killed her. She's more valuable to them alive." Clearing his throat, he added, "They might keep her prisoner for their own purposes . . . or possibly sell her for further profit."

"Sell her?" The words came without any breath behind them. "Sell her — a woman, a *human being*? Who would — *could* — do such a thing?"

"It's slavery, Beth. It's as old as civilization, I suppose."

Beth felt her face contort at the thought. "It's unspeakable."

"Yes, it is." He stepped closer, lowering his head. "What can I do, Beth? Just tell me what to do. I want to make it easier, and I'm afraid I've just added to your pain."

She straightened and raised a hand, palm out. "No, it's nothing you said. It's not as if I haven't been wondering — imagining — already." She shifted away from Jarrick and felt the cold doorjamb against her back. "I need to be alone, Jarrick." A gasp caught in her throat. "At the same time, I'm so afraid to be. Nothing seems right. Nothing helps."

"You're never alone," he whispered. "*I* can't be what you need right now, but God can. I'm praying for you, Beth. Almost every moment. For Julie too. But I'm thinking about you almost constantly. I know the shadow you're walking through is taking you where I can't follow. Only God is enough for you now."

Nodding dumbly, Beth retreated inside. His eyes were clenched tightly as she closed the door, shut him out. The sorrow on his face burned itself into her memory. It was what she deserved — alone, comfortless —

the accusing words whirling through her mind.

"Oh, God," she whispered. "Please punish me." The familiar litany was all she could think to say. "Please spare Julie and let the consequences fall on me instead. I should have stopped her. Why didn't I stop her? Do whatever You want to me, but please bring my sister home." The world was truly evil. She understood that now. As evil as the tales in Melville's story.

Beth burrowed under the covers without undressing and wept — utterly broken. At some point she became aware that Emma and Miss Bernard had entered the room. But she lay quiet, no acknowledgment of their presence.

Beth awoke to sounds in the hallway — footsteps and whispering as they passed by the door. She lay still, barely breathing in the darkness, tears trailing down her cheeks.

A glimmer of hope had begun to stir in her heart. She found herself reciting the familiar Psalm over and over again. *"The Lord is my shepherd . . . the Lord is my shepherd . . ."*

Jarrick is right. She had never quite understood it before, that no man, no *person,* could ever be enough. Only God could lead her through such pain, even the ultimate pain she dare not put into words.

"I shall not want . . . though I walk through the valley of the shadow of death, I will fear no evil."

"Oh, God, I'm so afraid. *Make* me trust You if You must. Help me know with all my heart that I don't have to live in dread. I don't have to give in to my worst fears."

"For thou art with me; thy rod and thy staff they comfort me. Thou preparest a table before me in the presence of mine enemies."

"Father God, please do that for Julie. She's the one in the enemies' presence. Care for her there — as long as she's forced to stay."

"Thou anointest my head with oil; my cup runneth over. Surely goodness and mercy will follow me all the days of my life, and I will dwell in the house of the Lord forever."

"This is not the end, Father," she whispered into her pillow. "Sustain us through all of it. We cannot possibly manage so great a burden without You. I know I cannot endure this alone. But please, please bring me to a place where I can praise You again. I know — I'm certain — that's where this will lead, if I can only be faithful, trust You, not give up. You promised. Help me trust You through *anything*."

Her darker prayers of recent days dogged at the edges of her mind. "You don't hate Nick, do You, Lord? Or the girls. Their sin is not who You made them to be. I just don't know how to feel about such hurtful people." The face of Coal Valley's Davie Grant returned. She remembered that she had prayed for him when she had read in Jarrick's letter about his trial — had been relieved to remember that justice would ultimately be done . . . but that Jesus would be his Advocate, if only he would surrender to God's mercy. *Could this be true of Nick — of Penny and Jannis?*

"You understand my anger, Father. But You're not a God of hatred. Please forgive me. No matter what, I want to follow You with all my actions and all my heart. But I can't do it without Your help. Please put Your love in my heart, Your desire for mercy over retribution." Jarrick's distraught face filled her mind. Her struggle with all the confusing emotions had caused her to turn from him as well — someone so important to her, someone so anxious to demonstrate grace.

"I'll talk to him. I'll tell him how very sorry I am. I'm sure he's feeling pretty miserable too. But he was willing to be honest with me, Father. Painfully honest —

451

even at such a difficult time, and that's so very important to me. I'm grateful for that."

Before the sun was up, a sharp knock at the door brought Beth upright on the bed. She listened as Emma opened it, spilling hallway light across the floor. Beth squinted and raised a hand to shield her eyes.

"Beth?" Father called past Emma. "You're needed. Please come now."

Already dressed in yesterday's clothing, she hurried after Father. He was knocking on Margret's door and urging them to come.

Gathering in Mother's room, Beth waited impatiently for Margret and John to arrive, dressing gowns thrown around their shoulders. Father entered and took a position in the center, drawing Mother close against his side.

"There was a telephone call received early this morning," he explained, "at the front desk of the hotel. An officer was on hand, monitoring for just such calls."

Beth and Margret gasped in unison, "What did they say?"

Father drew a slow breath. "It was apparently from the young man, the one who befriended Julie, though he did not identify himself by name."

Beth was afraid to breathe. She could feel herself begin to shiver. *Nick.*

"He admitted that he had been part of the kidnapping — had conspired with the two girls from the beginning to deliver Julie over to men from the Philadelphia area."

"Why, Father? Why *Julie?*"

"They were looking for an easy target, I would presume — a young woman of means who seemed . . . unprotected." The look in his eye pierced Beth's heart. *Father is blaming himself, sorrowful that he wasn't present.*

Beth thought about Julie's behavior, and even her own. How easily she had become a target. The first day in the marketplace was merely Nick's effort to identify prospects. Maybe the pills given early on had been simply a test for blind trust and naïveté, or some kind of medication that didn't work like they had planned. And Julie's lavish generosity no doubt increased their desire for more . . . the stolen binoculars merely another attempt to profit from their friendship.

Beth would probably never know, never have an opportunity to ask the many questions. But in her heart she acknowledged that her own gullibility, along with Julie's, had left them both terribly vulnerable. It was a crushing realization.

Father's voice broke into Beth's thoughts. "He said it was his understanding that Julie would have been returned as soon as the money was received. That before they even left New England to go their separate ways, he had been told she would be safely home again. He also implicated the other girls, to whom he admitted he had been introduced specifically for this 'job.' " Beth could hear Mother's gasp.

"He did give us some good information too," Father pressed on resolutely. "He claimed that she has been moved — farther away — by the others involved. That she has been taken in a milk truck to another state."

"Oh!" Mother's moan was echoed around the room. Father took her arm and led her to a chair.

"But the young man said he could provide a description of where they likely were taking our Julie," Father continued. "He said he couldn't be certain, but expected he was correct."

Beth begged, "He told the police where she is?"

"It's possible that he did. They've sent cars and telephoned the area police force. They should all be converging on the farmhouse shortly."

454

"She's at a farm?"

"We're hopeful. It's the best lead they've had to date."

What prompted Nick to make the call? Could he have regretted his previous actions? Might he have remembered the conversation we had? Beth's mind hummed with questions as she waited for Father to continue. Instead of any further report, he closed his eyes and began to pray aloud for God's intervention at this moment. Beth surrendered to the tears, now of some hope, streaming down her cheeks.

Knowing that the police would soon be in place at this farmhouse, knowing that they would either discover and regain Julie or that she would not be found at all made time grind nearly to a halt. Beth stared at the telephone, willing it to ring. One hour passed, then two. It was unusual, but moving, to see Mother on Father's lap, her head against his shoulder. Beth was next to them in the second chair. Jarrick and Monsieur Laurent had also been summoned from sleep. They waited together on the far side of the room. Beth determined she would talk to Jarrick soon — but at this moment she could only join the prayers for Julie. Margret and John were huddled together in the corner.

As each hour passed it seemed less and less likely there might be a positive outcome. *Was Julie gone forever? . . . a standoff surrounding the house . . . a gun battle raging? . . . Edward with them, pistol at the ready . . . But if her captors were killed, who would be left to tell where Julie was?* Beth's mind was a lurid spiral of haunting, clashing images. There seemed to be so little possibility that a peaceful end would ensue.

Father had prayed, "Thy will be done." Beth repeated the words over and over again. "Your will, God. Your will. I choose to trust Your will. Help me trust You even in this — most especially in this."

The telephone's ring sounded through the room. Father reached for it and lifted it to his ear. "Yes, this is William Thatcher." A pause. "I see." Another pause. Beth clenched her hands in agitation, fingernails digging into her palms. Father managed a quick nod toward Mother. "Yes, sir. Thank you, sir."

He set the receiver back into its cradle, calling out, "They've found her. She's alive. Safe. Praise God!"

CHAPTER 32

A great deal of commotion surrounded the family as they gathered belongings and loaded them into taxis for the train station. As swiftly as they had organized things after the telephone call, it did not feel nearly fast enough to Beth. Julie had been taken to a hospital in a small town in New York State near the farmhouse where she had been discovered. Beth and her family had been instructed to come right away, resulting in a joyful, frantic scurry of activity. Underneath it all, Beth could not shake the dread of what they might find. "I will fear no evil," she prayed. "I will fear no evil. Oh, God, I just want to hold my sister again."

Monsieur Laurent was sending the family ahead, taking care of any remaining details himself. Jarrick chose to remain behind to offer any assistance he could in the process. Beth wondered if he might be also extricating himself so that the family could have

457

this time without his presence — a stranger still to most of them. The Montclairs were planning to return to Toronto, along with Emma and Lise.

Beth could not board the train quickly enough. She hastened into her seat, making room for Margret and John on the bench. Only the baby seemed unaffected by all the fuss and anticipation.

Julie is alive, but will she be well? And what about the emotional healing? That could take many months. . . .

JW pounded on the glass window, waving bye-bye to the strangers standing on the platform below. He tried his new greeting, "bah-zhur," on whoever would listen.

Turning her eyes to the window as they pulled out, Beth watched the station disappear and eventually the telephone posts flashing past, lulling her eyes shut. She was only next aware when the conductor called out a stop and Mother patted her arm.

"Beth, we're arriving. You've slept the whole way."

Beth sat upright and scanned the little compartment, grateful to see all the familiar faces together. Only Julie was absent from among them — *Julie and Jarrick both,* she thought.

"I know you needed the rest, darling, but

you managed to miss lunch," her mother told her.

"That's fine. I'm not hungry."

"No, dear, but you'll waste away to nothing if you don't begin to eat more."

Beth smiled at Mother's familiar little lecture. It was such a relief to feel things already beginning to return to normal. Father had been right. Mother's fussing was just her way to give love.

Edward was waiting on the platform as they descended the steps. "She's feeling much better already!" he announced. "Of course, she's very anxious to see all of you."

Two waiting taxicabs whisked them to the hospital, taking only moments to cross the small town. Beth fell in step with the family following a white-clad nurse, heels squeaking with every step through a series of hallways to Julie's room.

Mother disappeared through the door first. Beth could hear Julie cry out, "Oh, Mother! You're here!"

There were lots of tears and a tangle of arms around their daughter and sister. No one asked questions or remarked about recent events. There would be plenty of time later for discussion. It was sufficient for now just to surround Julie's bed together and fervently thank God.

The next morning, while their parents spoke with the doctor, Beth helped Julie dress in the clothes they had brought. Beth struggled, her fingers clumsy and inept as she lifted the slip over Julie's head to draw her bandaged arm through the straps, pretending not to notice the cruel bruises on Julie's other wrist. *What happened to our precious sister?* Beth was too frightened of the answer to pose a question — any question.

"I'm fine, really," Julie murmured at last, her voice tightening as she whispered, "There's nothing wrong with me, Bethie — not anything I won't recover from."

Beth's face crumpled a little, though she tried to speak calmly. "Did they *hurt* you?"

Before answering, she could tell Julie was also working to compose herself. "I'm not nearly as bad off as I expected to be." She paused again, a sorrowful expression in her eyes. "The men . . . well, they were rather rough. I think the big bald one probably had no difficulty being cruel. But the smaller one kept reminding him that I was their 'bread and butter' — and if they ever wanted to pay off their debts, they'd have to deliver me undamaged."

The words were grisly and contemptible. Beth lifted her handkerchief to dab at the tears on Julie's face. *What can I say — is there any comfort to offer?* "You're safe now, darling. We'll never let you go again." But the words rang hollow.

"I should have listened to you, Bethie." Her words were barely audible.

"You're not to blame. It was those criminals . . . and Nick. Where was he while all this was going on?"

Julie lowered herself onto the bed, reaching down gingerly to pull on her stockings as she spoke. The action seemed to help her words come more easily. "He was responsible — that's certain — even if the whole thing wasn't his idea." She cleared her throat. It looked to Beth that there were things she needed to speak aloud . . . to someone. "From what I've figured out, he was the one who orchestrated the details of my abduction, and it seems by doing so in the way he did, he somewhat double-crossed Penny and Jannis. The whole thing was supposed to have happened in Bar Harbor, but he came up with the second plan in Boston to deliver me over without them. So they didn't receive any of the money they'd been expecting."

Beth shuddered, glad the girls had not profited from their part in the scheme.

Julie sniffled, keeping her hands busy with dressing, her eyes avoiding Beth's. "The cab driver was one of the men involved. I knew almost immediately when, of course, we never went to the museum. Nick took me directly to a warehouse."

"Oh, Julie! Weren't you frightened?"

"Terrified — at almost every moment. But then I managed to pray. I've never prayed so much in my life! It helped a lot. Even though I haven't paid all that much attention to God, He seems to have been paying attention to me," she said, her smile a bit crooked.

"Did they feed you — care for you at all?"

"A little." She smiled sheepishly. "Nothing much. But I refused most of what they offered anyway. I was terribly frightened that they might give me drugs of some kind, slip something into my food. I'd have never thought of it except I kept wondering about those pills Jannis gave to you."

Beth shook her head. "I can't imagine that Nick could be so pitiless — that he could have known you as he did, then been such a brute."

Julie paused and studied her hands pensively. "You're not going to want to hear

462

this, Bethie, but he's not as bad as you think."

"Oh, Julie!"

"He was very sorry for his actions . . . by the end." Her face lifted, the words sounding like the rasping of sandpaper. "From what I heard, he'd dug himself into a very deep hole, had worked for these men before, stealing things that he passed along to other criminals to sell. Somehow he justified it all because of being expelled from college." She shook her head slowly. "He's never gotten over that perceived slight against his character. I suppose growing up in a family that felt his mother had shamed them all didn't help." She wiped at her eyes in frustration. "I don't know — he clearly has no moral compass. He has a very different sense of right and wrong. He spoke to me on a couple of occasions and actually tried to justify what he had done."

"Oh, no, he couldn't!"

"I suppose in a way, his twisted sense of justice led him to rationalize most of his actions, as if it were fair for him to take what he should have had anyway, that life should recompense him for the future he had been cheated out of. And then sometimes he would stop talking and just stare at me — tied there to a wooden pallet — and I could read on his face his inner turmoil. There were tears in his eyes. He was a very broken man . . . at the end." She paused, venturing a glance up at Beth, her tears beginning again. At last she whispered, "I told him I forgave him, Bethie."

Beth gasped and covered her mouth. *How did Julie do it? How had she said such words to the one who had endangered her . . . and while she was still in peril?* Beth lifted Julie's blouse from the bed and shook out the wrinkles, giving herself a moment to regain her composure. Then Beth slid the sleeve carefully over her sister's injured wrist and pulled the blouse into position so Julie could slip the unwrapped arm through the other side. Finally she said, "I'm . . . I'm so proud of you, darling. And I think God is too."

Julie began the slow process of buttoning the blouse. "I'm glad I said it just then. Later, it seems Nick was sorry enough to turn his partners in — and I can't imagine they'll forgive him for that. But," Julie forced herself to choke out, "I'm not the same person anymore, Bethie. I feel so much older . . . kind of used up. It's almost worse now that it's over. I don't know if I will ever *trust* anyone again like I did Nick — and Jannis and Penny. I don't know that

I'll ever be able."

Beth's arms encircled her sister, clung to her. "You weren't wrong to care about them, Julie. You don't know what God might be doing, might still be doing because of your friendship with them. It might be some time before you can be so open and free, but I do believe He'll help you to trust again. And as for Nick, I can only imagine he'll be forever changed by this — by knowing you and hearing your forgiveness."

At last Julie was fully dressed. Beth tried to produce a smile for her sister's benefit. "You look very nice."

Julie leaned forward against Beth's shoulder, her mouth close to Beth's ear before she whispered, "I was very nearly gone forever — I can barely speak of it, and don't tell Mother. They were going to send me south somewhere, and I doubt you would have heard of me again."

Beth tightened her hold. "No, Julie, no. If I've learned anything at all, it's that their evil plans could never have prevailed against a God who loves and keeps you."

"Amen," Julie whispered, but she was trembling in Beth's arms.

Beth rubbed at her aching head. With all that had occurred, she hadn't noticed the familiar dull throbbing. She was seated in a corner of the train station, watching her family assembled around her. For a moment she considered asking Mother for an aspirin, but decided against initiating the usual series of questions about how she was feeling. They would likely all sleep on the train anyway.

Father had secured sleeping compartments. What was even better, the train was an express, meaning they would arrive in Toronto by morning and be safely at home soon enough.

Beth raised her eyes to scan the small waiting room. There was little evidence of what had so recently transpired. It was almost as if the past few days were being deliberately set aside — for the moment at least. Mother and Margret were seated, sipping hot tea. Father and John were speaking quietly together.

She thought briefly about Victoria, already home with her mother, and wondered if she had been able to encourage the girl at all. Beth did know her own sisters much better now. She was certain that goal had been achieved — though not as she had intended. And Mother . . . Beth would never feel about her quite the same way again. She had seen such reserves of strength, such dogged faith. She smiled as she realized how fully she wanted to carry on those characteristics and values.

Silhouetted against the large station windows, JW was chattering and giggling, leaping from his papa's arms into those of Monsieur Laurent, delighted with all the attention. Even Jarrick had joined the small cluster of men around him, laughing at the toddler's attempts at speaking French. JW and Monsieur Laurent were fast friends now. Beth hoped the man would be able to keep in touch with the family in the years to come, that her nephew might be a kind of grandson whom Monsieur Laurent hadn't previously known.

Margret rested an arm around Julie's shoulders as they went through the box of photographs, reminding each other of the happier memories of their travels. Father crossed the room and laid a hand on Beth's shoulder. "You aren't looking at the photographs with your sisters. You might enjoy sharing them together."

"Soon," she answered him quietly. "Soon enough, Father."

"Did you finish my book?" he asked, lowering himself onto the bench beside her.

"I did. I almost gave up though, it was such a dismal story. But at a certain point I wanted to see where Melville was going with it — where he would end it."

"You're correct that it is rather bleak. I was reluctant to recommend it — so much sadness. But now, watching your sisters there, it makes me think of the last chapter, the words I felt were worth the trouble of reading the novel in the first place. I memorized them long ago and have thought of them often when I've been far from all of you."

He sat back and began, " 'For the scene of suffering is a scene of joy when the suffering is past; and the silent reminiscence of hardships departed is sweeter than the presence of delight.' My dear, perhaps we're not so far along the road to recovery as all that, but this is a considerable start." He gestured toward their family — all near at hand and all accounted for.

Beth nodded, a pain that she had tried to ignore rising in her heart. *Will it be possible to leave them all? To travel west in time for school to begin in the fall? It seems unthinkable at present.*

But the letter had come at last. She had felt it might be the piece of the puzzle that would reveal God's will, and she would leave for good — travel back to Coal Valley and Jarrick.

Father patted her knee and rose, leaving her to her own thoughts.

Cautiously, Jarrick approached, standing and studying her face without speaking. Beth tried a feeble smile. *What is there to say? What does he think of me? I haven't yet apologized for my coldness toward him. He watched me fall apart while the entire time he remained strong.*

"Would you like to take a walk?" He offered her his hand.

Beth reached up to receive it. His fingers wove themselves around her own as he pulled her gently to her feet. "We can't go far," she murmured. "My mother — well, she worries."

"I understand." He nodded and led her away. They walked hand in hand through the nearest set of doors and out onto the station platform, where they found themselves suddenly alone.

He chuckled. "Something feels strangely familiar. This is a similar situation to when I said good-bye to you — a little over one month ago. Is that possible?"

"But I was leaving without you then. This time you're coming with me."

He stopped walking and turned toward her. "Am I, Beth? Am I *with* you?"

She glanced down at their hands. Her

small fingers were almost lost between his. "I don't deserve you, Jarrick. I'm embarrassed and ashamed."

"Because of what? Do you still believe this was somehow your fault?"

"No . . . well, I don't really know. But I haven't borne up well under it all. I'm so sorry for how I treated you. For how anxious and . . . and . . ."

"Who could have done better?" His head bent low as he took a step closer. "You're not expected to handle life alone. Don't you see that? Especially when life takes a twist like this." He reached for her other hand. "All we can do is to keep turning each other toward the truth — to a God who loves and cares for us. Maybe that's what I've tried to do for you this time, but next time I might be needing you to do the same for me. If we had to earn God's favor by always performing perfectly, we'd all suffer as failures alone."

She leaned her head against his chest, breathing in the scent of his shaving lotion while she processed his words. She wanted to believe it. *It would be such a comfort to trust his love despite it all.*

"You have an amazing family, Beth. I can understand that you wouldn't want to leave them, at least very soon. So I don't think you should feel pressured by the job offer for this fall. You should take all the time you need with your loved ones — a time to heal together. That's most important just now. Everyone will understand. Your Father even offered that I might stay in Toronto with your family for a little while. But . . ."

Sniffling, she urged him quietly, "But what?"

"But I don't know where *we* stand."

On impulse she reached for the rose petal she had tucked in her handkerchief that morning. Slowly she unfolded it so he could see what it held. "Jarrick," she whispered, lifting it up, "do you remember this?"

"It's a flower petal?"

"It's from you."

"You kept it, Beth?"

"I kept all of them." *It's such a small thing. Yet perhaps it expresses best how dear he has become to me.* "I carried one with me every day — well, almost. It made me feel as if you were with me . . . a little. Actually, I'm afraid I just couldn't bear to be without you."

"I'm so glad to hear it." He cleared his throat. Taking the dried, crackling petal from her hand, he tucked it gently into his shirt pocket. His voice tightened. "A poor substitute for not being here in person when you needed me."

Beth loosened one hand to wipe at the tears trickling down her cheeks. She grasped at his shirt with the other, drawing herself closer. "You're so gracious to me, Jarrick. I really don't deserve —"

But he had touched a finger to her lips. "I love you, Beth," he whispered hoarsely. "Don't I get to decide who I'm going to love?"

For several moments she was unable to speak. At last she choked out, "But if I say yes, what then? How can I be sure? Is this God's will, after all?"

He cleared his voice again, quietly answering, "Only God knows. But we can't let the search for His will paralyze us. I believe that He brought us together. So I know that I can trust Him. I'm willing to set aside my fear of the unknowns in our future and take each day as it comes. The Bible says, 'In all thy ways acknowledge him, and he shall direct thy paths.' It's God's promise. Can you do that with me? Let God direct our paths — even if we don't see where all it leads? Because I believe that whatever He's already walked us through together is just getting us ready for whatever He's got in store for us next. And I do know I need you beside me for that."

Beth leaned back and peered up into his eyes. The reality of what he was saying rushed over her, filled her heart. *He still loves me — loves me deeply. He wants a future with me, even if we don't know what it will entail . . . or when. And he's right. It certainly seems we can trust that God's hand has brought us to this moment.*

She knew without a doubt, with all of her heart, that she wanted him beside her too. Could she communicate to him that all she really wanted at that moment was to be held tightly in his arms? And to be kissed for the first time — for always? She would never be able to bring herself to say the words aloud. Was there any way she could express such a request with her eyes? He was looking back so intently. Reading her face. *Please, Jarrick, if you move toward me now . . . it's what I want too.*

He leaned forward, silently asking her permission with his hesitancy. She tipped her face back and closed her eyes. He kissed her slowly, gently, their lips lingering. At last he whispered against her cheek, "I love you, Beth. I don't ever want you to leave me again."

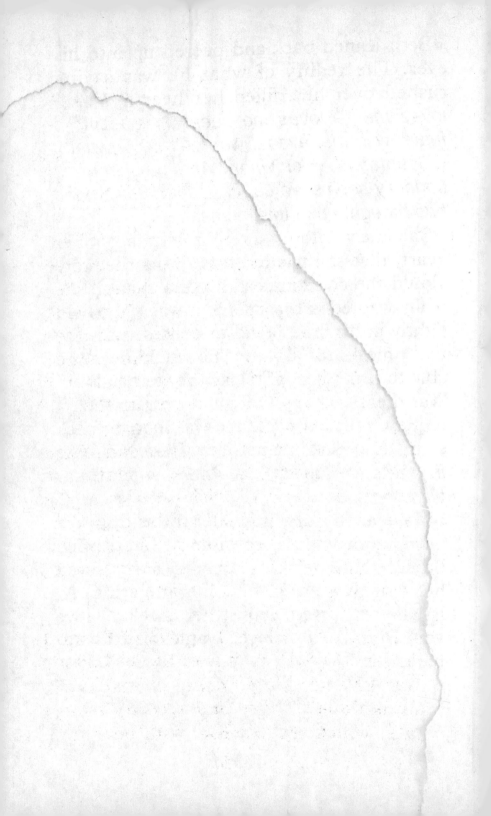

ABOUT THE AUTHORS

Bestselling author **Janette Oke** is celebrated for her significant contribution to the Christian book industry. Her novels have sold more than thirty million copies, and she's the recipient of the ECPA President's Award, the CBA Life Impact Award, the Gold Medallion, and the Christy Award. Her novel *When Calls the Heart,* which introduces Elizabeth Thatcher and Wynn Delaney, was the basis for a Hallmark Channel film and television series of the same name. The Return to the Canadian West series tells even more of the Thatcher family's story. Janette and her husband, Edward, live in Alberta, Canada.

Laurel Oke Logan, daughter of Edward and Janette Oke, is the author of *Janette Oke: A Heart for the Prairie,* as well as the novels *Dana's Valley* and *Where Courage Calls,* which she cowrote with her mom.

Laurel and her husband have six children and two sons-in-law and live near Indianapolis, Indiana.